Demonsouled

Jonathan Moeller

ISBN: 1481298763
ISBN-13: 978-1481298766

EPIGRAPH

It is a fact, then, that in the heart of every man there lies a beast which only waits for an opportunity to storm and rage, in its desire to inflict pain on others, or, if they stand in his way, to kill them...

-Arthur Schopenhauer.

JONATHAN MOELLER

CHAPTER 1
THE JONGLEUR AT THE INN

Mazael Cravenlock saw the apple trees and smiled.

He put spurs to his horse, a sturdy old gray palfrey named Mantle, and rode for the trees, ignoring Gerald's cry of protest. The setting sun painted the grass a deep crimson and the hot, dry wind of the Marches tugged at Mazael's cloak and whipped at his face, but he was used to it. He had grown up here, after all.

The apple trees rose at the shore of a clear pond, encircled by a low stone wall. Nearby stood a crumbling brick chimney and some foundation stones, all that remained of a small peasant house. The inhabitants of that house had likely been killed fifteen years past during Lord Richard Mandragon's uprising against Lord Adalon Cravenlock. No one had claimed the land since then, to judge from the tall grass covering the old foundation.

Mazael steered Mantle through the low wall's fallen gate and reined up beneath a tree. The apples hung heavy and red from their blossoms, and he plucked one with a gloved hand and took a bite.

"Sir Mazael!"

Mazael turned his saddle, chewing, and watched Sir Gerald Roland and his squire Wesson ride through the ruined gate. Gerald had inherited the aquiline features, blue eyes, and muscular body of his father. His shoulder-length hair shone like gold, and he had recently grown a mustache that he attended with the fanaticism of an Cirstarcian monk. Gerald was not wearing any armor - Mazael could have thrown his dagger and killed Gerald before the younger man could react.

Instead, Mazael reached up and took another apple. "Hungry?"

"Certainly." Mazael tossed the apple. Gerald cut it in half with his dagger, taking half for himself, and feeding the other to his horse. "Wesson, would you care for an apple?"

"No, Sir Gerald," said Wesson, a pimpled youth of eleven. "I am not hungry."

"Pity," said Mazael. A single sure sword stroke would kill Wesson. "Never pass up a chance for an apple, my boy."

Gerald snorted. "Never pass up a chance for fresh food, you mean. An opinion I wholly favor after all these travel rations, but I could never understand why you were so mad for apples. I prefer pears, myself."

Mazael flicked the core aside, and picked another apple for Mantle. "I might tell you someday." The sun's setting rays caught in the pond, and for a moment the water resembled blood. Mazael shook off the thought.

"Shall we stop here for the night?" said Gerald.

"No," said Mazael. "There's an inn two miles east of here, just before the Northwater bridge. We can get there before dark."

Gerald laughed. "Are you in such a hurry to reach your brother's castle? You told me that you'd rather be elsewhere."

"No, I'm in a hurry to have a bed and a hot meal. Fresh food is fine, but hot food is far better." Mantle finished the apple, and Mazael turned the palfrey around and rode back to the road and their other animals. Mazael and Gerald's war horses stood grazing alongside a pair of pack mules laden with their supplies and armor. Wesson took the animals in hand and followed the two knights as they rode eastward.

"I would rather be elsewhere," said Mazael, "but since I am here, I would prefer to be within castle walls. I have no great eagerness to see my brother, but should war come, I'd rather be inside Castle Cravenlock than out in the open."

"We should have brought more men, as Father wished," said Gerald. "With two or three hundred armsmen as escorts, attack would not trouble us."

Mazael snorted. "Yes, three hundred men with the banner of the Rolands flapping overhead? That would have drawn the eyes of every man from Knightcastle to Swordgrim. And how do you suppose Lord Richard Mandragon would react if he knew that Lord Malden Roland's youngest son had brought an army to the Lord of Castle Cravenlock?"

Gerald fell silent for a moment. "Do you really think it will come to war?"

"I doubt it," said Mazael. "Mitor's a fool, but a slug as well. He's too much a coward to rouse himself against the likes of Richard Mandragon the Dragonslayer."

"I hope you are right. I have seen enough of war," said Gerald.

Mazael nodded. He had fought alongside Gerald when Lord Malden had invaded Mastaria. They had survived the bloody battles of Deep Creek, Castle Cateron, and the Siege of Tumblestone. The slaughter had sickened Mazael, yet some part of him had found it beautiful. He had relished the fighting, reveled in it. No enemy, common soldier or Knight Dominiar, could stand against him, and he had danced through their bloody blades.

"I wouldn't worry," said Mazael. "Mitor might hate Lord Richard, but Lord Richard terrifies Mitor. And all anyone has heard are rumors of mercenaries and bandits. Most likely Mitor is simply hiring whores." Mazael laughed.

Gerald frowned. Lord Malden Roland's youngest son had a pious streak that Mazael often found wearisome. Yet the young knight was the best friend Mazael had made since leaving Castle Cravenlock, and Gerald was one of only four people to whom Mazael would entrust his life.

"I see lights up ahead," said Gerald.

Mazael saw the lights, and heard the rush of water. "The inn, most likely. At least, there was an inn here fifteen years ago. Just past that is the Northwater bridge and then it's only another three days to Castle Cravenlock."

"Finally," said Gerald.

Full dark fell by the time they reached the inn. It had changed little from what Mazael remembered. A high wall of sharpened wooden logs surrounded the rambling stone building, and torches burned in sconces atop the wooden palisade, casting a circle of light around the wall. A pair of crossbow-armed mercenaries stood guard before the crude gate.

Mazael could have killed them both before they reacted.

He reined up instead. "Ho, the inn!"

The mercenaries trained their crossbows in Mazael's direction. "Who're you, and what's your business?" said a mercenary with a broken nose and a shading of beard stubble.

"A traveler," said Mazael, "and my business is with a bed, hot food, ale, and a whore." Gerald frowned, while Wesson looked intrigued.

"You've the look of knights," said the mercenary. "Pardon the questions, sirs, but in these dangerous times the innkeeper's hired us to keep peace."

"That so?" said Mazael. "Danger from what?"

"People have been disappearing near Lord Mitor's castle. It's the wood elves, I say," said the mercenary, making the sign to ward off evil.

"Lord Richard has stirred them up to make war on Lord Mitor. I've even heard tell that Lord Richard treats with dark powers, and has the Old Demon himself as an adviser."

"No," said the second mercenary. "It's the barbarians, come down out of the mountains. They're the ones behind this. Lord Richard will raise his vassals and that black-hearted son of his, and smash them the way he smashes everyone who crosses him."

"Such fine tales," said Mazael. He flipped them a copper coin. "Tell them in the common room and you might get a few more coins."

The mercenaries laughed, but Mazael heard the unease in their voices. "Aye, so we might, but everyone in these parts speak the same tales. People have been disappearing, and it's the work of those wood devils, taking them off for their dark rituals."

"No, it's the barbarians," said the other mercenary. "They eat babies. My grandfather told me so when I was a lad."

"I don't care if it's the Old Demon and a troop of barbarians sacrificing people to the god of serpents," said Mazael. "I want my ale, my bed, and my food."

"Very well, milord," said the first mercenary. "Make no trouble, and we'll make no trouble for you."

Mazael nodded. He rode through the gate, Gerald and Wesson behind him.

"Do you think it's true?" said Gerald. "Peasants have been disappearing?"

Mazael shrugged. "Perhaps, or perhaps not. Most likely Mitor has ordered virgins kidnapped for his bed."

The two knights dismounted, and Wesson received the task of stabling the mounts and carrying the armor and weapons into their room. Mazael did not remember his own years as a squire with any fondness. He pushed open the inn's door and stepped inside.

The common room was crowded with mercenaries and landless knights. Many looked drunk, and specks of fresh blood marked the floor. A bartender and a half-dozen serving girls hurried back and forth to the kitchen. Mazael marked some of the prettier ones.

A man playing a harp stood atop a stage against the far wall. The jongleur wore simple clothes for one of his craft, plain boots and trousers and a tunic. Gray shot through his black hair and beard, and a hooked nose rested above his smiling lips. Mazael frowned, thought he recognized the man for a moment, then brushed away the odd feeling.

The bartender came over. "What'll it be, my lords?"

"A room, and food for three," said Mazael.

The bartender licked his lips. He squirmed beneath Mazael's gaze, something people often did. "First room at the top of the stairs. As for food, I've got a few joints of beef left, and some fresh bread..."

"That will be fine," said Mazael. He left some copper coins on the bar and went to find Gerald. Wesson lurched through the door, bearing an armful of armor. Mazael directed him to their room, and the boy clambered up the steps, huffing.

Gerald had claimed a table near the jongleur's stage, and Mazael joined him.

"Look at this place," said Gerald. "It's packed full of mercenaries and ruffians of every stripe, and they are all making for Castle Cravenlock. It seems the rumors of your brother hiring men are true after all."

"I wonder why," said Mazael. "Castle Cravenlock can only raise four thousand knights and armsmen. Swordgrim can raise eight thousand, and Lord Richard can call ten thousand more. If Mitor thinks to use this rabble to stand against the likes of Lord Richard, then he's a bigger fool than I thought."

"Perhaps he's hired them for use against the wood elves," suggested Gerald with a laugh.

Mazael snorted. "What, the Elderborn? Hardly. They wouldn't venture out unless Mitor devoted himself to burning down the Great Southern Forest. Besides, the Elderborn would cut through this lot," he gestured, taking in the mercenaries, "faster than even the Dragonslayer."

"I was joking," said Gerald. "Elderborn are a children's fable, like faeries and Demonsouled...you're not joking?"

"No," said Mazael. Wesson descended the stairs and sat at the table, panting.

The jongleur ran his fingers over his harp and began another song.

"Heart of darkness, soul of sin,

a murderer's bloody grin.

So came the boy to his fate,

dark son of a demon great."

The crowd's boisterous enthusiasm dampened. "The Song of the Demon Child" was not often sung in busy inns.

"I say, I detest that song," said Gerald.

Mazael looked up at the jongleur. "Why is that?" The jongleur's gray eyes gleamed keen and intent, his fingers dancing over the harp in accompaniment to his deep, rich voice.

"Father Marion would always recite a few verses when he saw me, citing the fate of wicked children," said Gerald.

"The child met his dark father,

before the church's altar.

'My dark child,' said the demon.

'Your glory has now begun.'"

"I hope you didn't let it bother you," said Mazael. "Most priests couldn't find their manhood with both hands."

Gerald frowned. "That's hardly an appropriate example to set for Wesson."

Mazael shrugged. "If he wants to take a vow of chastity, let him become a monk."

"'Your demon soul has power,

curse the gods, curse Amater.

Take that which is your dark right.

Spurn heaven; claim your demon might!'"

"Sing something else!" someone shouted. Others took up the cry.

The jongleur stopped. "My apologies, good sirs!" he called out, smiling. "What shall I sing for you instead? 'The Song of the Serpents', perhaps, or 'The Fall of Tristafel'?"

"What's this, a funeral?" yelled a drunken voice. "Sing something good! 'The Virgin with Five Veils'!" The jongleur took a flourishing bow and began to sing. "There was a girl with raven hair and the curves of a goddess…"

DEMONSOULED
"What a morbid fellow," said Gerald. "It's a wonder he's able to earn his bread. 'The Song of the Demon Child' and 'The Fall of Tristafel' indeed! I've never heard 'The Song of the Serpents', though. Probably some dreadful story of demons, to judge from this fellow's tastes."

"No," said Mazael. "Snakes. It tells how the god of the serpent people rebelled against heaven. In punishment the other gods took the arms and legs from the serpents and made them crawl through the dust."

Gerald shuddered. He hated snakes. "Gods be praised, the food is here."

A plump, pretty barmaid in a tightly laced dress gave them their food. Gerald thanked the woman. Mazael sent her off with a silver coin and a pinch on the bottom, earning a frown from Gerald. The jongleur continued "The Virgin with Five Veils" and soon had the mercenaries roaring along to the song. "The virgin girl danced and giggled, her body bounced and jiggled..."

Gerald admonished his squire against such revels. Mazael downed his ale and called for another.

The jongleur finished his song to thunderous applause as a storm of copper coins rained upon the stage.

"Another song!" called out a man.

"Grant me a short rest first, my generous friends!" said the jongleur, sweeping up the coins. "For you all have mighty voices, and I fear I shall ruin mine if I dared compete!" The assembled ruffians laughed and went back to their drinking. Mazael took a drink of ale to wash down some beef, draining half the tankard in three big gulps.

When he looked up, the jongleur stood over their table, a smile on his bearded face. "Pardon, my lords...but have we met before?"

Mazael frowned. "No, I don't think so."

"But...are you not Sir Mazael Cravenlock, my lord? And is your companion not Sir Gerald Roland?" said the jongleur.

Mazael's teeth clenched. He had wanted to reach Castle Cravenlock unseen. "How do you know who I am?" A quick dagger thrust between the ribs could kill the jongleur...

The jongleur tapped a finger against his jaw. "It...was at an inn in Mastaria, I believe, during Sir Mandor Roland's march against Castle Dominus. A village called Deep Creek, as I recall..."

Mazael frowned. "I remember! It was the night before the battle. That fool Sir Mandor—pardons, Gerald, but he was—spent the night celebrating at the inn. You were the jongleur he had brought from Deep Creek for his entertainment."

"I remember now," said Gerald.

7

The jongleur smiled and executed a florid bow. "Mattias Comorian, a simple musician, at your service."

"How did you come to be here?" said Mazael, indicating for Mattias to take a seat. "Mastaria is on the other side of the kingdom. I had thought most the villagers of Deep Creek slain in the battle."

"Most were," said Mattias. "I suspected that ill fortune would soon fall upon Sir Mandor. I slipped away after the noble knight had gone to bed. Not long after, the Knights Dominiar struck. I watched the slaughter for a while, then escaped to the north." He paused. "Did Sir Mandor chance to survive?"

"No," said Gerald. A shadow crossed his face. "He...ah, rose, and rallied the defenders, but he was wounded, and died soon after." Mazael concealed his contempt. Mandor had lain snoring in bed when the Dominiars attacked. Gerald's older brother caught two arrows in the gut and another in the leg. Mandor died three days later, weeping and feverish, as the remnants of his army straggled north.

"Ah," said Mattias, sipping at his ale. "My deepest condolences, my lord knight. At any rate, Lord Malden - and Sir Mazael here, I might add - prevailed over the Dominiars, and I resumed my wanderings. I visited Swordor, and spent some time in Redwater and Ravenmark shortly before the old Lord of Ravenmark disappeared. I performed in the Crown Prince's great city of Barellion for a time, and fortunately left before those riots burned down half the city. Dreadful, that. Then I traveled across the Green Plain during the succession struggle, and just in the last year made my way to the Grim Marches."

"Quite a journey," said Gerald.

Mattias laughed. His gray eyes glittered. "Ah, my lord knight, it is nothing. In my time, I have visited half the world, I fear."

"You seem to have had singular bad luck in your travels," said Mazael. "The war in Mastaria, the succession troubles in the Green Plain, the uprising in Barellion...why, it's as if troubles sprout where you walk."

"I pity I cannot make wheat and barley sprout where I walk," said Mattias, grinning. "Why, the lords of the Green Plain would shower me with riches to tramp about their fields, and I never would need work again."

Mazael and Gerald laughed. Wesson even smiled a little.

"And now, it seems, my bad luck has struck again," said Mattias. "Rumors of war sprout in the Grim Marches."

Mazael grimaced. "You must hear more than most. All we've heard are peasants' gossip, each word more outrageous than the last."

Mattias laughed. "I fear knowledgeable peasants are as numerous as flying sheep, my lord. Every mercenary in the kingdom is making for

Castle Cravenlock. The rumors say that Lord Mitor plans to rise against Lord Richard, the way the Dragonslayer rose against old Lord Adalon." Mattias frowned and continued. "Those living near the Great Forest claim that the Elderborn—" Mazael thought it odd that a jongleur would use the wood elves' proper name, "—plan to march from their forest and take bloody vengeance. And the closer you get to Castle Cravenlock, my lord, the wilder the rumors get. I met a peasant who swore that a malicious wizard was stirring up trouble. I have heard tales of ghosts rising from graveyards, and of snake-cults worshipping in cellars." Mattias snorted. "To believe these fools, you'd think that the Old Demon himself haunted the Grim Marches."

"Aye, well, my father sent us as his emissaries," said Gerald. "I know not what is happening, but with the gods' blessing, we can end these disturbances without bloodshed."

Mattias sighed and rubbed his salt-and-pepper beard. "Ah, your hope warms my heart, my young lord, but I know otherwise. When lords quarrel, the law is set aside in favor of swords. You know those peculiar blood roses that bloom in the Grim Marches? Well, the peasants say that only blood can irrigate those flowers, and we'll have blood roses as far as the eye can see before this business is done."

Mazael blinked. For a moment, it seemed as if he could see blood. Not drops or pools, or even streams, but a sea of blood stretching as far as his eye could survey. He blinked again and shook away the disturbing vision.

"What makes you say that?" he said at last.

"Your family, my lord knight, and the Mandragons have hated each other for centuries," said Mattias. "Every child in the Grim Marches knows as much. Should it come to war, and I do hope that it does not, these proud lords will settle their differences with arms, not words."

"We'll not know until we try," said Gerald, crossing his arms, "and I am determined that we shall try."

Mattias smiled. "Ah, forgive me, for I am an old, old man, and I have forgotten the hopes of youth. I wish you the best of luck, my young lord, and hope all goes well with you."

"If the gods will it," said Gerald.

Mattias's eyes glinted. "I find, my lord, that the gods favor those who make their own luck. In that spirit, let me pass along a tidbit of news to you. Sir Tanam Crowley is in the area."

"Sir Tanam Crowley?" said Gerald. "I've never heard of him."

"I have," said Mazael. "He's Lord Richard's most trusted vassal. When the Mandragons rose against my father, Sir Tanam was the first to join the Dragonslayer."

"Indeed," said Mattias. "And Sir Tanam would like to make the youngest son of Lord Malden and Lord Mitor's brother his master's ...enforced guests, no?"

Gerald's tankard slammed down on the table. "Is that a threat? Are you asking us to buy your silence?"

Mattias spread his hands. "You wound me, my lord knight! I might believe that war is coming, but that does not mean I do not wish for peace! Lords have markedly short tempers in war, I fear, and an incautious jongleur might find himself shorter by a head."

"Very well," said Gerald. "I trust you'll not spread news of our meeting?"

"It doesn't matter," said Mazael. "He could shout our names from the rooftops. If there's trouble between here and Castle Cravenlock, it'll find us one way or another."

"Then once this business has blown over," said Mattias, "I can tell my grandchildren that I spoke with two knights of the mighty noble houses of Roland and Cravenlock."

"You don't look that old," said Gerald. "You have grandchildren?"

"Oh, yes," said Mattias. His eyes sparkled with mirth. "Many, in fact."

"Jongleur!" bellowed a mercenary in a boiled leather breastplate and dirty furs. "More music, I say, more music!" The crowd took up the cry. The assembled freebooters roared for music.

"Ah, duty calls," said Mattias. "I must say, it was a pleasure speaking with you. It is good to know that someone survived the carnage at Deep Creek."

"You as well," said Gerald. Mazael nodded.

Mattias Comorian hopped back onto the stage and strummed the strings of his harp. "Let us make merry, my friends, for the past is gone and the future is dark, and all we have is today!" He pointed into the crowd. "You sir, you have a drum, and you, yes, you with the lute. Come up here, my friends, and let us make music for dancing!" The two men climbed onto the stage. Men shoved aside tables and chairs to make room. Mazael saw a good number of peasant girls from the local farms. The girls eyed the mercenaries, the mercenaries eyed the girls, and Mazael supposed that many of the girls would lose their virtue tonight in the grass behind the inn or in the hay of the stables. He hoped they stayed away from his horses.

Mattias and his conscripted musicians struck up a lively tune. The drunken mercenaries and the farm girls began to dance. Gerald looked intrigued, to Mazael's surprise. The pious knight rarely enjoyed himself. Perhaps tonight would become a first.

"I say, Mazael, I believe I will indulge," said Gerald. He stood and frowned. "Aren't you coming?"

Mazael waved a hand at him. "Go. I think I will retire early."

Gerald laughed. "You're joking. You were so eager to find a whore earlier. You might not need to. That girl, the one with the brown eyes? She has been staring at you since she came in."

"Maybe later," said Mazael. Gerald shrugged and joined the dance, Wesson following his master.

Mazael finished his ale and felt the drink warm his insides. For a moment he considered joining the dance, perhaps finding a willing girl for later, but brushed the notion aside. He felt tired and sick. Maybe the food had been bad. If so, the innkeeper would regret it.

Mazael climbed the stairs, leaving the dance behind, and pushed open the door to their room. Wesson had piled their armor and supplies in the corner, and a single narrow bed rested under the window.

He shut the door behind him, undid his sword belt, and claimed the bed. Gerald and Wesson could have the floor.

"See, Gerald?" he muttered. "You're right. There are rewards for virtue. I get the bed and you don't."

CHAPTER 2
MAZAEL MEETS SIR TANAM CROWLEY

Mazael opened his eyes and saw the sun's first rays painting the wall. Wesson lay on the floor, snoring. There was no sign of Gerald. Perhaps Lord Malden's youngest son had overcome his inhibitions.

Mazael found the chamber pot, relieved himself, and pulled on his boots. Then he picked up his sword belt and buckled it about his waist. A small mirror hung on the wall over the bed, and Mazael drew his sword and stared into the mirror.

Sunlight glimmered off the razor edge of his blade and danced off the golden hilt. The sword's pommel was a golden lion's head with ruby eyes and a roaring mouth. For four years now, Mazael had carried this blade, after Sir Commander Aeternis of the Knights Dominiar had offered it up in surrender. Mazael had named it Lion and carried it at his side ever since.

Mazael sheathed the blade and tapped the squire with his boot. "Get our armor and supplies ready. I want to leave within the hour. I'll find Sir Gerald." Wesson sighed and got to work.

Mazael stepped out into the hall, the floorboards creaking beneath his boots, but otherwise the inn was quiet. No doubt the mercenaries were sleeping off hangovers. A man lay facedown in the hallway, snoring, his trousers gone.

"Watch for splinters, friend," muttered Mazael.

He found Gerald sprawled in a bed three rooms over, tangled with the blankets. No one was with him, so far as Mazael could see. Mazael shook Gerald's shoulder. Mazael shook his shoulder, and when Gerald did not respond, he reached down and pinched the younger knight's nose shut.

Gerald came awake with a snort. "Gods, what ...blast it all, Mazael, how many times have I asked you not to do that?"

"You sleep like a stone," said Mazael. He grinned. "What did I tell you, when you were a squire? Sleep too deeply, and someone might make sure you never wake."

Gerald didn't answer. He rubbed his eyes, groaning. "Ah, the light! And my head!" His eyes bulged and he sat bolt upright. "Where ...my clothes ...oh, gods in heaven, what did I do?"

"Had a good time, from the looks of things," said Mazael.

"I don't remember!" said Gerald.

"A ripping good time, then," said Mazael.

"I have sinned!" said Gerald. "I have dishonored myself...I could have deflowered some virtuous young maid...oh, I must do penance..."

"I doubt it," said Mazael. "You get weepy when you're drunk, not lecherous. Now get up, get dressed, and get your gear. I want to get over the Northwater bridge and past the village of White Rock today."

Gerald nodded and climbed out of bed. "I shall never drink so much again."

"It's usually a good idea to stop after a while," said Mazael.

"I shall take a vow to abstain from spirits for the rest of my days!"

"Don't overdo it."

Mazael returned to his room and looked out the window. It faced to the east, and he saw the steep gully of the Northwater. A wide wooden bridge crossed the river here, the only crossing for a day in either direction.

The perfect spot for an ambush, come to think of it.

"Help me with my armor, Wesson," said Mazael.

Mazael wore light armor for a knight. He could move much faster than most men, and heavy armor only slowed him down. He wore a mail hauberk with a breastplate that had seen much use, steel plates for his shoulders, bracers for his forearms, and leather gauntlets backed wth steel disks. His helmet was the style used by the foot soldiers of ancient Tristafel, with an open face and metal flaps to protect the ears and jaw.

Gerald came in as Mazael redid his sword belt. Despite his hangover, Gerald had managed to shave, trim his mustache, and style his hair. "You're armoring yourself? Why?"

Mazael hefted a heavy war hammer with a black steel head and an oaken haft. He had taken the hammer from a dead Knight Dominiar after Sir Commander Aeternis's defeat. Sharp as it was, Lion could not cut through solid steel plate. The Mastarian hammer did an admirable job of crushing armor and smashing bone in one solid swing.

"Caution," Mazael said. He slung the hammer over his shoulder.

"With all these mercenaries streaming towards Castle Cravenlock, more than a few might decide to go bandit."

"True," said Sir Gerald. "Wesson! My armor!"

Unlike Mazael's battle-scarred armor, Gerald's armor gleamed with a mirror shine. Gerald wore a steel breastplate and chain hauberk, a mail coif, and a conical helm. Gauntlets of steel plate protected his hands, and he attached steel greaves to his legs. Over his armor he wore a blue surcoat with the gray greathelm sigil of the Rolands. His sword, a dagger, and a mace crowned with the greathelm of Roland hung from his belt. Wesson received the unenviable task of carrying Sir Gerald's heavy oak shield.

"I say, you should fight with a shield," said Gerald.

"Slows you down," said Mazael. He glanced out the window.

"Yes, but better to be slow than dead. Sooner or later, some screaming fool will come at you with an axe. What will you do then?" Gerald frowned. "Mazael, what are you looking at?"

A great plume of dust rose to the east. After a moment, he saw a column of riders cross the bridge - thirty of them, at least. The lead rider carried a banner, and a woman shared his saddle.

"Riders," Mazael said. "They're coming this way."

"Those are armored lancers," said Gerald, and his eyes widened. "That's the Dragonslayer's banner."

The banner of the Mandragons, a black dragon on a red background, flapped from the lead rider's lance. Beneath it flew a smaller banner, depicting a crow perched on a gray rock against a field of green.

"And that's Sir Tanam Crowley's banner," said Mazael. The lead riders thundered into the inn's courtyard and reined up, sweat lathering their horses.

"What do you suppose they're doing here?" said Gerald. "And at this hour in the morning? From the look of those horses, they must have been riding all night!"

Mazael spotted Sir Tanam as the knight slid off his horse. His narrow features and long nose had earned him the nickname "the Old Crow". Two of Crowley's men lifted the woman from the saddle. She wore an elegant riding gown, yet her wrists had been bound and a hood pulled over her face.

"I suspect a great many of our questions will be answered in the next few minutes," said Gerald.

"Take off your surcoat," said Mazael.

"What?"

"Do it!" said Mazael. "That prisoner has the look of a noblewoman. If Lord Richard sent the Old Crow to kidnap her, what do you think he'll do with one of Malden Roland's sons?"

Gerald nodded, pulled off his surcoat, and kicked it under the bed. Mazael heard the door to the inn bang open, followed by heavy footsteps thudding up the stairs. His hand curled around Lion's hilt. "We may need to make a run for it."

A moment later an armored man, wearing a surcoat quartered with the black dragon of Mandragon and the crow of Crowley, peered into their room. "If you're fighting men, make your way to the common room at once. Sir Tanam Crowley is hiring, and you'll have the chance to make some gold."

Mazael and Gerald nodded. The armsman moved down the hall, banging on doors and awakening slumbering mercenaries.

"Maybe that's why Sir Tanam is here," said Mazael, striding into the hall. "Perhaps Lord Richard sent him to hire away all of Lord Mitor's mercenaries."

"He could do it," said Gerald. "Not a day passes without Father complaining about the Mandragons' gold."

A half-dozen sleepy mercenaries stomped past, a pair of Crowley armsmen herding them down the stairs. Mazael waited until they had passed, then gestured for Gerald and Wesson to follow him. They stopped on the landing of the stairs, overlooking the common room.

A dozen armsmen waited in the common room with as many mercenaries. Sir Tanam stood on a table, rubbing his thin nose. He had taken off his helmet, and Mazael could have killed him with a thrown dagger to the throat. Crowley's prisoner stood behind him, two men holding her arms.

"Roger, is this all?" said Sir Tanam, his voice clipped and precise.

"Aye, sir, it is," said a soldier.

"Very well, then," said Tanam. He cleared his throat. "I am Sir Tanam Crowley of Crows' Rock, vassal to Lord Richard Mandragon of Swordgrim."

Bleary-eyed silence answered this pronouncement. Mazael leaned forward, trying to see under the prisoner's hood.

Tanam grimaced. "Lord Richard has commanded that I make for Swordgrim with all haste, and I ask for your assistance."

The mercenaries stared at him.

Tanam cleared his throat. "Paid assistance."

The mercenaries smiled.

"The Mandragons are generous to those that serve them well," said Sir Tanam. "Every man who joins me will receive three silver pieces. Every man who completes the journey to Swordgrim will receive three gold pieces."

The mercenaries' smiles widened, and the armsmen moved closer to Sir Tanam. The guards holding the woman shifted, turning her face towards the stairs. Mazael moved to the left, trying to see into the hood.

"We will journey with haste," said Tanam. "I must deliver this prisoner to Swordgrim with all speed so she may face my lord's justice. We may come under attack."

Mazael leaned over the railing to get a better look at this prisoner destined for Lord Richard's judgment.

The green eyes of Rachel Cravenlock, his younger sister, stared back at him from beneath the hood.

Her eyes widened as she recognized him.

Mazael jolted back from the railing. Through sheer will he kept his hand from flying to his sword.

"What is it?" whispered Gerald.

"My sister," hissed Mazael, his voice grating. "The damn bastard has my sister."

"Your sister?" said Gerald. "Gods, Mazael...Crowley must have kidnapped her from Castle Cravenlock. Mazael, for the love of the gods, don't do anything foolish..."

"Just follow me," said Mazael. He put one foot on the railing. "Sir Tanam!"

Sir Tanam looked up. "Three silvers are all I'm offering for hire. The gold will have to wait until we reach Swordgrim."

"A question, sir knight!" said Mazael. "What crimes has your prisoner committed?"

Sir Tanam's face darkened. "She has committed crimes against the laws of both gods and men. She has done witchcraft and practiced sorcery. Her family has ...well, regardless to say, she has well-earned her fate. Might I ask, who are you? You have the look of a knight about you. A knight-errant, perhaps?"

Mazael grinned. "Not quite. I am Sir Mazael Cravenlock. This is Sir Gerald Roland." Gerald groaned.

Tanam's eyes widened. "Mazael...Cravenlock? I thought you were still in Knightcastle." He shook his head. "Well, here you are, and for the welfare of the Grim Marches, I think you and Sir Gerald had best come with us. My lord Richard would much like to speak with you."

"I think not," said Mazael. His blood drummed in his head and his battle instrincts rose. "For your welfare you had best release my sister to my custody and go on your way."

Tanam seemed amused. "Really, now?"

"Last chance," said Mazael. "Let her go."

"No," said Tanam. "Come with us."

"I did warn you," said Mazael.

Lion flew from its scabbard. Mazael vaulted over the railing and landed in the midst of the Crowley soldiers, his sword blurring. Two men fell dead before they had even thought to draw their weapons. He heard Gerald's groaned curse and the hiss of his drawn sword. Crowley's men shouted and scrabbled for their weapons, while Sir Tanam himself bellowed commands and drew an axe from over his shoulder. The innkeeper shrieked and dove under a table. Gerald leapt over the railing, sword and shield in hand.

Mazael drove Lion through the eye slit of a helm. The man-at-arms staggered and fell, blood gushing out of his mouth. Mazael spun and parried two quick blows, riposted, and another Crowley armsman fell dead. Blood ran red down Lion's steel blade. Mazael danced through Crowley's men, laughing. They all seemed to have lead weights tied about their arms and legs. Lion felt like a part of his arm and the blood roared through his body as he sidestepped a thrust and took off an armsman's head.

It was so easy to kill them.

Someone hit him from behind with a sword. The blade didn't penetrate Mazael's armor, and he used the blow for momentum. He bashed aside one man, gutted another, jumped, and landed face to face with Sir Tanam Crowley. Sir Tanam lifted his axe, but Mazael jerked his sword up, bashing the lion's head pommel across Tanam's face. The knight fell like a dead horse, his armor clanging against the floor. The armsmen holding Rachel leapt to defend their master. Mazael killed one, wounded the other, and severed the ties holding Rachel's hands with a single slash. She looked at him, green eyes wide, a thousand questions on her face.

"Can you run?" said Mazael.

Rachel nodded. "What..."

"Gerald!" bellowed Mazael. "Let's go!"

Gerald ran for the door, Wesson at his heels. "By all the gods of all the heavens," yelled Gerald. "I swear, man, you are a lunatic!" His shield had been hacked to kindling and his shiny armor bore a half-dozen scars.

Mazael laughed and kicked down the door. A half-dozen of Sir Tanam's irate men charged after them.

The morning sun shone bright in the courtyard. A dozen more of Sir Tanam's men sat on their horses, their expressions tense and anxious. They scowled at the sight of Mazael, hands flying to their weapons.

"We're under attack!" said Mazael as he ran for the stables. "The Cravenlocks! The Cravenlocks came through the back of the inn!"

The horsemen galloped towards the door just as Crowley's other men burst out. They tangled together in a confused mass as Mazael, Gerald, Wesson, and Rachel ran into the stables, hastening to saddle the horses.

"Rachel, take my palfrey," said Mazael, vaulting into the saddle of his war horse, an ill-tempered brute named Chariot. Gerald helped Rachel into the saddle and then mounted his own war horse. Wesson claimed Sir Gerald's palfrey.

"What if they try to stop us?" said Gerald.

"Ride them down," said Mazael. Sword in one hand and hammer in the other, Mazael spurred Chariot forward. The big stallion whinnied and burst out of the stable.

Mazael heard Sir Tanam shouting, and armsmen raced towards them. Mazael hit one on the head with his hammer, while Chariot bit a second in the face. He heard the clang of Gerald's sword and a man's scream. Then they were through the inn's palisade, riding hard for the Northwater bridge.

Dust churned beneath their horses' hooves, and soon the long wooden Northwater bridge came into sight. A trio of riders waited on the bridge next to a pot of burning coals and a bundle of unlit torches. Each of the rides wore armor and bore a heavy war lance. Beneath the bridge the Northwater raged in a swirl of white foam.

"They're going to burn the bridge!" shouted Mazael. "Ride!" He kicked Chariot to a gallop, the horse thundering forward. The riders on the bridge wheeled and dropped their lances for a charge. Mazael slung the hammer over his shoulder and snapped Chariot's reins. A pair of the lancers made for Gerald, while one rode for Mazael.

Mazael stood up in the saddle, the lancer raising his weapon in response. At the last second, Mazael jumped off Chariot's side. He tucked his shoulder and rolled as he hit the ground, his armor rattling. The lancer reined up, attempting to swing around to attack. Mazael surged to his feet, Lion's hilt in both hands, and swung. The longsword hewed the horse's leg like wood, and the big animal went down with a scream. The lancer flew from his saddle and struck the ground, his armor clattering with the impact. Mazael was on him in an instant, his sword stabbing down for a gap in the armor.

He sprang back into Chariot's saddle as one of the remaining lancers broke his lance against Gerald's shield, the other circling with an axe in hand. Mazael spurred Chariot to a gallop, slammed Lion into its scabbard, and took his Mastarian war hammer in both hands.

The lancer on Gerald's right never saw Mazael coming. Mazael whipped the hammer sideways in a looping swing. The lancer toppled off his horse, head bent at a bizarre angle. The second lancer gaped at his dead comrade long enough for Gerald to finish him.

Horses galloped from the inn as the Old Crow rallied his troops. Sir Tanam looked bloody and very angry.

"Any wounds?" said Mazael.

"No," said Gerald. "Just bruises."

"Good. Over the bridge, I'll follow," said Mazael.

"What..." said Gerald.

Mazael grinned at him. "Just go."

Gerald sighed. "Madman." He spurred his horse over the bridge, Rachel and Wesson riding alongside.

Mazael leaned down, snatched a torch from the bundle, and thrust it into the pot of burning coals. Then he wheeled Chariot around, galloped onto the bridge, and dropped the torch.

Evidently it had not rained in the Grim Marches for some time, because the bridge's planks were hard and dry, and took fire at once. A wall of flame rose up behind Mazael, and Chariot whinnied and bolted to the opposite bank.

He joined Gerald and Rachel and turned Chariot around just in time to see Sir Tanam's horse shy away from the flames. Tanam stared across the river at Mazael, his expression a mixture of frustration and astonishment.

"Sir Mazael," said Sir Gerald. "You are insane. You could have gotten us all killed!"

Mazael grinned at him. "Yes, but it worked, didn't it?"

Gerald sighed and looked heavenwards.

Mazael clasped his sister's hand, careful not to squeeze with his armored gauntlet. "And you, are you all right?"

Rachel smiled at him. She had always been very pretty, and even as a child suitors had swarmed about her like flies, hoping to win her hand once she came of age. Mazael didn't know if his sister had married or not. He had left the Grim Marches fifteen years ago, and no word had come to him since. Rachel looked much the same, but there were dark circles under her eyes, and she was very pale.

"Mitor will be upset you burned his bridge," Rachel said at last.

"Mitor can bugger himself with the bridge," Mazael said. "A bridge for a sister, a small price, it seems. Now, how are you?"

"I've been better, I'll confess," she said. "But, gods, Mazael, it's so good to see you again."

"You as well." Mazael looked over the river. "We'd best be on our way before old Sir Crow decides to use those crossbows."

They galloped for the east, leaving the inn and the burning bridge behind.

CHAPTER 3
RACHEL'S APPLE

At Mazael's insistence, they rode hard for the east all day, leaving a cloud of dust in their wake. The nearest fords were a day's ride north and south of the burned bridge, but Mazael didn't want to risk encountering more of Lord Richard's minions. He permitted his companions to stop long enough to water the horses, but no longer. They rode in silence. There would be time to exchange stories later.

They passed bands of mercenaries that ranged from ragged knots of ruffians to professional companies with banners. All marched east for Castle Cravenlock. Mazael and his little band rode around them, and the mercenaries ignored them.

As the sun sank beneath the western sky, they came across one of the abandoned farmsteads that littered the Grim Marches. Only few strewn foundation stones, a pond, and an overgrown orchard remained, and Mazael pronounced the site fit for a camp. Gerald slid out of his saddle with a sigh of relief.

"Good horse," said Mazael, patting Chariot's flank. He undid the saddle and blanket, rubbed the horse down, checked the hooves, and gave Chariot another apple snared from the grove the day before. Chariot snorted but accepted nonetheless.

Rachel stumbled from Mazael's palfrey. Mazael and Gerald were both accustomed to hard riding and days in the saddle, but Rachel was not, and Gerald helped her to stand. It seemed that his sister had captured another admirer. Wesson gathered wood and grass, and soon a fire crackled within the old foundation stones.

"I don't suppose we have any of our supplies left?" said Gerald, brushing down his horse.

Mazael shook his head. "Our supplies are sitting in our room at the inn. No doubt Sir Tanam and his men are enjoying them. We'll have to make do with whatever's in our saddlebags. I hope the lady of Cravenlock will not be discontented with jerky and stale bread?"

Rachel laughed and sat down. "I would rather eat peasant fare than dine with Lord Richard at Swordgrim." She winced again. "I can't imagine how you knights can ride that hard for days on end."

"Practice, mostly," said Mazael. "You're still able to sit, at least. When Gerald first trained with a lance and hammer from horseback, he had to sleep standing up for weeks."

"Gods, don't remind me," said Gerald, rummaging through one of Mantle's saddlebags.

"Gerald?" said Rachel. She laughed. "Sir knight, I've been riding with you all day, and I don't know your name! Mazael, would you kindly make the introductions?"

"Certainly," said Mazael. "Lady Rachel Cravenlock, this is Sir Gerald Roland. Sir Gerald, Lady Rachel."

Rachel's pretty green eyes widened. "Sir Gerald Roland?" Gerald looked pleased. "Lord Malden's son, Sir Gerald?" Gerald nodded. "A pleasure to meet you, my lord knight. What brings you to the Grim Marches?"

"I was wondering much the same of you, sister," said Mazael, tearing a hard chunk of bread into four pieces.

"It's been fifteen years since we've heard from you, Mazael," said Rachel. "Then, a day and a half after I'm kidnapped by Sir Tanam Crowley, I find you here with the youngest son of one of the most powerful lords in the kingdom. That is a strange coincidence, I think."

"So Crowley did kidnap you?" said Gerald. "Gods, Mazael! What have we walked into?"

"A mess, it seems," said Mazael. "But that's a fair question, sister. I've served Lord Malden Roland for the last nine years. When Lord Malden heard rumors of trouble in the Grim Marches, he sent us to investigate."

"My father has a vested interest in the Grim Marches," said Gerald.

"He wants revenge, you mean," said Mazael. He took a bite of the stale bread and winced.

"Lord Richard did kill Lord Malden's second son, Sir Belifane," said Rachel. "And he killed our older two brothers, Mazael."

"I know," said Mazael. He hadn't liked his two oldest brothers and considered their deaths a favor. "Our brothers and Sir Belifane Roland managed to get themselves killed in battle with Richard Mandragon. Then Father marched out from Swordgrim to avenge their deaths, and what happened? Father lost, Lord Richard marched in triumph into Swordgrim, and we were left with Lord Mitor the Mushroom."

Rachel laughed.

Gerald looked puzzled. "Mitor the—Mushroom?"

"Our nickname for Mitor, when we were children," said Mazael. "When you meet him, you'll understand. So, now that you know how we came here, how did you wind up the captive of Sir Tanam Crowley?"

Rachel shivered and hunched closer to the fire. "It's...a long story."

"Considering I just tried to kill one of the Dragonslayer's sworn knights, I would like to hear it," said Mazael. He looked at Rachel for a moment. She was indeed thinner than he expected, more tired, more worn.

"It was about a marriage," said Rachel. Her eyes glimmered in the firelight.

This surprised Mazael. "You aren't married yet? I thought Mitor would have married you off the instant you came of age."

"He wanted to," said Rachel. "But he wanted to save me for the son of some powerful lord, someone with whom he could make a strong alliance."

"Bloody chance of that," said Mazael. "The Dragonslayer crushed Lord Adalon. What fool would want to ally himself with Lord Adalon's imbecile son?"

"Not many," agreed Rachel.

"Did Mitor ever get married?" said Mazael.

"He did," said Rachel. "About four years ago, to Marcelle Trand."

Mazael knew of the Trands, a noble house that had supported Lord Adalon against Lord Richard. After the Dragonslayer became liege lord of the Grim Marches, the Trands found themselves relieved of a great portion of their lands. "Lord Marcus Trand must have been desperate to foist off the girl, if he offered her for Mitor."

"He was," said Rachel. "Marcelle is a hateful woman. I imagine Lord Marcus offered her to half the noblemen in the kingdom before Mitor finally took her."

"Why would Lord Mitor marry her, then? From everything you've told me over the years, Mazael, your brother sounds a proud man," said Gerald.

"Isn't it obvious?" said Mazael. "If Mitor ever goes to war against Lord Richard, then Lord Marcus will have to stand with him." Mazael paused. "Is Mitor planning to do something so foolish, Rachel? Lord Richard is a seasoned commander, Mitor is no warrior, and Swordgrim can raise three times the men Castle Cravenlock can."

"I don't know, Mazael. I really don't." Rachel stared into the fire. "About six months ago, Lord Richard sent Sir Tanam to Mitor with an offer. Lord Richard wished to end the long enmity between our houses, and offered to join me in marriage to his eldest son Toraine."

"Amatheon and Amater!" swore Mazael.

Gerald frowned. "That's brilliant. Toraine is Lord Richard's heir. If you bore him a son, a man with both Mandragon and Cravenlock blood would rule the Grim Marches one day. That would forever end the rivalry between the house of Cravenlock and the house of Mandragon."

"Mitor refused him," said Rachel.

Silence hung over the little camp for a moment. Mazael heard the fire crackle, saw the flames dance in Rachel's eyes. "Why? Even Mitor could not be so foolish. Half the lords in the kingdom have approached Lord Richard to offer their daughters for Toraine. How could he possibly pass up such an opportunity?"

"I didn't want to marry Toraine Mandragon," said Rachel in a rush. "He's a monster. The peasants don't call him the Black Dragon because of his armor. In a village near Amritsar, a man stole one of Toraine's horses. The Black Dragon caught the thief and had him and his entire family herded out into the village square. He beheaded them all with his own sword, even a baby and an old woman, and had their heads mounted above the village gate as a warning to other thieves."

"That's monstrous," said Gerald.

"Yes, but he made his point," said Mazael.

Rachel glared at him. "Would you want me to marry such a...a monster? Would you want me take him into my bed?"

"No," said Mazael, "but I doubt Mitor had such concerns. What made him turn Lord Richard down?"

"Pride, I suppose," said Rachel. "He said it would be an insult for me to marry the son of the man who had murdered my father. And...and I wanted to marry someone else." Gerald looked disappointed.

"You did?" said Mazael. "Who?"

"Sir Albron Eastwater," said Rachel. Her eyes lit up with a feverish glow as she said the name.

"I've never met him," said Mazael. "I've never even heard of him."

"He was a mercenary who fought alongside Father against Lord Richard. After Lord Richard won, Father knighted Albron and gave him lands along the Eastwater, north of Castle Cravenlock."

"So you turned Toraine Mandragon down in favor of a knighted mercenary?" Rachel's eyes flashed. "No mockery, sister, but Mitor only allowed this to insult Lord Richard. The Mandragons must have been furious."

Rachel's lips compressed into a thin line. "You think I don't know that? I wish that Albron and Toraine's births could have been reversed. Albron is the best man who ever lived, but Toraine...I half think Toraine is Demonsouled."

"Don't tell Lord Richard," said Mazael, chewing at the stiff jerky. "Mitor's already insulted him. We needn't tell him that he was cuckolded by the Old Demon." Rachel laughed, the weariness falling from her face for a moment. "So Mitor refused Lord Richard. How did you wind up in Sir Tanam Crowley's hands?"

"After Mitor refused Lord Richard, we heard no response for months. Mitor and Sir Albron feared that Lord Richard planned war. Then a week ago, Sir Tanam returned to express Lord Richard's regrets. Mitor had no choice but to give Sir Tanam and his men lodgings for the night. They crept into my chamber, seized me, and rode off before the garrison could rouse."

"Daring," said Gerald.

"That's Sir Tanam's style," said Mazael. "He has gall, I'll give him that."

"Sir Tanam said...he said that Lord Richard had commanded that I be brought to Swordgrim to marry Toraine. I refused...and he said that I had no choice in the matter," said Rachel.

"That's odd," said Mazael. "Sir Tanam said in the inn that you were guilty of...how did he put it...doing witchcraft and practicing sorcery."

Rachel flinched. "That's a lie. I did no such thing." Her eyes darted to the fire and back to his face.

Mazael laughed. "The church and the wizards of Alborg might believe it is a crime for a woman to wield magic, but I don't care. What, did Master Othar teach you?"

"No," said Rachel, shaking her head. "No. I've had nothing to do with magic, I swear it."

Mazael shrugged. "If it matters that much..."

"You know our family's history," said Rachel. "The peasants are always ready to believe anything evil said about a Cravenlock. There are—there are enough stories already, without adding to them."

"If you feel it so important," said Mazael. He smiled. "How are Sir Nathan and Master Othar? You, Sir Nathan, and Master Othar are the only people I regretted leaving behind when I left Castle Cravenlock."

Rachel hesitated. "They...are well, I believe. Master Othar won't live much longer, I think. He's so fat, and has trouble getting around."

Mazael laughed. "Master Othar was always fat. Careful what you say, sister. Othar has outlived five men who said he had only a year left to live."

Rachel laughed. It transformed her face. Then she sobered. "Mazael, I'm sorry, but..."

Mazael felt something grab at his stomach. "What? Sir Nathan? Is he dead..."

Rachel shook her head, dark hair sliding about her shoulders. "No. Lord Mitor dismissed him as armsmaster."

Mazael blinked. "What? Mitor is a bigger fool than even I thought! Sir Nathan is the finest sword in the Grim Marches. He's better than even me! What was Mitor thinking?"

"Mitor said Sir Nathan was too old, that he needed a younger man as armsmaster," said Rachel.

"Too old!" said Mazael. This was beyond idiocy. Some of his rage must have shown on his face, because Gerald and Rachel flinched away from him. With an effort, he forced himself to calm down. "I wonder what fool Mitor found to replace the likes of Sir Nathan Greatheart?" Rachel frowned. "I'll see what Mitor has to say about this, and a great many other things."

Rachel leaned over and hugged him. "I'm so glad you've come home, brother. It's been so hard, these last few years but I know you'll set things right. You will, I know."

Startled, Mazael took his sister's hand. "I will try. Someone must stop Mitor. If he continues to follow this course, he'll bring the kingdom to bloody war."

For a moment the tired shadow crossed Rachel's features again.

Then an impish grin lit her face.

"Wait here," she said, and stood and walked towards the old trees.

"I say, Lady Rachel, come back!" Gerald said. "We risked our lives to win you free...gods only know what is wandering about in the dark."

She returned a moment later, and the object in her hand sent Mazael's mind back over the years, to the time he had first met Rachel as a child.

She had been only three. Mazael had spent most of his childhood at Sir Nathan's estates, away from his mother and brothers, who hated him, and his father, who ignored him. One day Lady Arissa, in a fit of rage, banished Rachel to Nathan's estates. The old knight ordered Mazael to greet her, a duty he found less than cheerful.

Mazael's sister arrived in a carriage escorted by a dozen knights. The child's nurse spotted Mazael and pointed him out to the little girl.

"Look, Rachel," the woman said. "That's your brother."

Rachel's face lit up, and she out something clutched in her hand.

"Want an apple?" she had said.

Mazael had missed breakfast that morning, and found himself thinking his sister was not such a worthless creature after all.

Now, twenty years later, Rachel held out another apple to Mazael. She was much taller now, and the plumpness had changed into beauty, but the smile had not changed.

"Want an apple?" she said.

Mazael laughed and took the apple.

CHAPTER 4
THREE BANDITS, TWO BOOTS, ONE WIZARD

The next day they continued riding to the east. Mazael was certain that they were well ahead of the Old Crow, but he wanted to take no chances. Rachel's abduction out of Castle Cravenlock had proven Sir Tanam's skill.

So they rode fast, the Grim Marches stretching around them in all directions, a sea of waving grasses. Mazael remembered days from his youth when it seemed like the entire world was nothing but two vast plains of green earth and blue sky. Thousands of red-and-white blood roses had bloomed among the grasses, their white petals and red interiors giving them the look of bleeding wounds in pale flesh.

Mazael remembered Mattias Comorian's prediction of war and scowled.

They passed peasant farmsteads where the farmers stood grim-faced before their houses with weapons in hand, ready to defend their homes and their daughters' virtue. More than one farmer shot ogling glances at Rachel, but no one dared anything under Mazael's glare.

Shortly after noon, Mazael reined up and turned to face his companions. "I don't want to take the road. Half the men in the last group we passed were drunk, and I saw smoke on the northern horizon an hour ago. Lord Richard doesn't need to ravage the countryside. Mitor's mercenaries will do that for him if they're not taken in hand. It's only a matter of time before some of these fools decide we'd make an easy mark."

Rachel did not seem pleased at the prospect. "Couldn't you fight through them, the way you did at the inn?"

Gerald snorted. "My dear lady, your brother is brave, but he's also

27

a madman. It was more luck and the gods' grace than our own skill that we escaped from Sir Tanam."

"None of these ruffians are mounted," said Mazael, "and we could ride through them like a wind, but with Rachel along, I'd rather not take the chance. Castle Cravenlock is two days east from here as the crow flies, but the road veers southeast to pass through the village of White Rock. If we ride straight east, we can leave the road and the mercenaries behind."

Gerald looked out over the plain. "The horses should have no trouble with the land. And once Sir Tanam crosses the Northwater, he will direct his search towards White Rock. I believe I concur, Sir Mazael."

"I'm flattered," said Mazael.

Gerald grinned. "Your brother is a madman, Lady Rachel, but he does have good ideas from time to time."

"I know," said Rachel. Mazael snorted and steered Chariot off the road, the others following.

They traveled cross-country, past small farms and villages. This region had been left untouched during Lord Richard's uprising, and most of the grassland had been plowed and cultivated. Mazael took worn cart tracks when he could find them, but there were no real roads here. When they passed farms, the peasants hurried inside and bolted their doors as they passed.

"I say, I wonder what they're all afraid of?" said Gerald.

"The mercenaries," said Rachel. "They'll tell you tales of demons and witchcraft in the night, but it's the mercenaries they fear."

"If you say so," said Mazael. "But..."

"Mazael!" hissed Gerald, pointing. "Look!"

A cloud of dust rose from one of the cart tracks. A man ran towards them, his legs and arms pumping, black cloak flapping out behind him. Behind him came three horsemen with rusty helms and battered swords. They laughed and whooped, spurring their horses closer to the running man.

"Bandits," said Mazael. He reached down, plucked his helm from his saddle horn, and dropped it on his head.

"I thought you said we would avoid any bandits," said Gerald.

Mazael grinned at him. "Stop complaining. There are only three of them."

Gerald sighed and drew his sword.

"Wait here," Mazael told Rachel. "Wesson, stay with her."

Then he spurred Chariot forward. The three bandits circled around their quarry, thrusting their swords at him, only to jerk their weapons away at the last moment. They were so focused on their fun that they didn't notice Mazael until Lion crashed through a bandit's head.

The other two bandits shouted in surprise. One came at Mazael with a rust-splotched sword. Mazael parried, rolled his wrist, and swung, Lion biting deep into the bandit's chest. The man slid from his horse, blood pumping from his wound, even as Gerald finished the last bandit with a quick thrust.

Mazael looked over the man they had rescued. He had dark hair and a goatee that came to a little spike, and wore a black coat, black books, and a dusty black cloak. A heavy pack dangled from his shoulder. His eyes darted to the twitching corpses, to Mazael and Gerald, and then back to the dead men.

"I have very little of value. Please leave me be," said the man. His voice had a lyrical Travian accent.

Mazael could have killed him so very easily.

Instead, he leaned down and tore off a bandit's cloak, wiping down Lion's blade. "What, you think we're more bandits?"

"Yes," said the man.

Mazael passed the cloak to Gerald and beckoned Rachel and Wesson over. "What sort of bandits travel with a woman and a boy?"

The man blinked. "Your armor...your armor is very beaten up." Mazael snorted. The man pointed at Gerald. "But his...his is too fine for any bandit. You are knights, yes? Please forgive me, my lord knights. My wits were addled with fear." He wiped sweat from his brow.

"Understandable," said Gerald. He cleaned his blade and tossed the bandit's cloak aside. "Tell me, if you have so little of value, why were these ruffians after you?"

The man grimaced. He pointed at his feet. "They wanted my boots." They were very good boots. "I traded my mule for them at the last village I passed...ah, Eastbridge, I believe. I told the bandits they would have to purchase their own boots, and then they tried to kill me! Over a pair of boots! I fought them as best I could, but I had to flee. And I have seen bands of similar villains coming down the north road as well. Why does the lord in Castle Cravenlock not keep the peace? What sort of land is this?"

"One on the verge of war, it seems," said Mazael.

The man's face sagged. "Oh, I knew it. I should have stayed in Alborg."

"Who are you?" said Gerald.

The man executed a small bow. "My lord knights, I am Timothy deBlanc...a...a wizard." He looked at their faces, and when he saw that Mazael and Gerald were not about to slay him as a wicked sorcerer, he continued. "Might I ask the names of those who saved my life?"

"I am Sir Mazael Cravenlock," said Mazael. "The man with the fine armor is Sir Gerald Roland. The fair lady is Lady Rachel Cravenlock," Rachel inclined her head, "and the boy is Wesson Joran, Sir Gerald's squire. Now, might we ask what a wizard is doing alone in the midst of the Grim Marches?" Mazael remembered the rumor he had heard of a wizard raising trouble.

Timothy's eyes widened. "Sir Mazael Cravenlock? My lord knight, my lady, this is...a fortuitous coincidence. I am bound for Castle Cravenlock."

"Why?" said Mazael.

"I recently completed my time as an apprentice, and the magisters sent me to study with a Master Wizard," said Timothy.

"Master Othar," said Mazael.

"You know him?" said Timothy.

"Since I was a child," said Mazael.

"The magisters said I was to study under him, and they hinted...well, perhaps, that I should take his position after he died," said Timothy.

Mazael's wrath flared. "Did they, now?"

"I meant no disrespect!" stammered Timothy. "I hope Master Othar has many fruitful years yet, but he is past seventy, and the magisters said that his health was not good."

Mazael forced himself to calm. "Your magisters can say what they like. Men have said that Master Othar would die any day now for the last twenty-five years. He is still here."

"May the gods grant him twenty-five more," said Timothy.

Mazael decided that he liked the young wizard. "Grab one of those dead fools' horses. You'll ride with us back to Castle Cravenlock. Master Othar said for years he'd like an assistant. Who am I to thwart his will?"

"Thank you, sir knight," said Timothy, snaring one of the horses. "That is very generous of you. In fact, that is what I shall name the horse. Generosity."

Mazael grunted. "What spells can you do?"

Timothy hoisted himself into the saddle with some effort. Horsemanship did not seem to lie among his skills. "Many, my lord. I know spells that can predict the weather, see distant places, communicate across vast expanses, and several others." He paused. "I also know several spells of protection...no doubt, they will come in handy here."

"Why do you say that?" said Mazael.

Timothy tugged at the spike of his goatee. "There are...many old tales about Castle Cravenlock and the surrounding lands, my lord knight."

Mazael waved his hand. "Yes, yes, witchcraft and demon worship and all that. Surely that doesn't worry you?"

"There is no witchcraft at Castle Cravenlock," said Rachel. "None. It's a slanderous story the Mandragons spread."

"I...ah...do not doubt it, my lady," said Timothy. "But it is the recent tales I fear. The peasants say the dead rise from their graves at night and slay the living. And there are darker tales, as well. Ah...my lady, I know that Lord Cravenlock would never succumb to such a base deed, but they say that some of the villagers near the castle practice the old worship of the San-keth."

"San-keth?" said Gerald. "What is that? I've never heard that word before."

"Serpent people," said Mazael. "Remember how I told you about the Song of Serpents? 'San-keth' is the formal name of the serpent people." He laughed. "I doubt they're much more than a song. I've never seen one."

"A myth dreamed up by some addled peasant," said Rachel.

"They're very real, my lord," said Timothy. His voice became quiet. "Or, at least they were, at one time. I saw some of their writings during my studies at the citadel of Alborg. Vile books, vile, full of blasphemies. I hope you are right that they do not live. But if they do, then it is the duty of the wizard to protect mankind from such monsters."

Mazael doubted that Timothy could defend himself from mosquitoes, but nodded nonetheless.

"My lord knight...I have a spell I can cast, if you wish. It is...an eye, one that will let me see if any enemies approach us," said Timothy.

Mazael gestured. "By all means."

Timothy slid back out of the saddle and landed with a thump. The wizard rummaged through his pack and produced a heavy book, a twist of copper wire, a quartz crystal, and other oddments. Timothy wrapped the wire around the crystal and muttered a chant under his breath. Mazael recognized the spell. He had seen Master Othar cast it as a boy, and some of the wizards who had accompanied Lord Malden's armies into Mastaria had used it. The spell bestowed some sort of clairvoyance on the caster. It worked, he knew that for a fact. It had saved their lives after the Dominiars' crushing victory over Gerald's idiot brother Sir Mandor.

"Brother, I will withdraw," said Rachel. "I find this distasteful."

Mazael frowned. "Why? You saw Master Othar do magic often when we were children."

Rachel blinked, and looked as if she wanted to weep for a moment. Then she turned her horse and rode off a distance.

"That was strange," said Gerald.

"Women," agreed Mazael.

"You know, there are two horses left," said Gerald. The dead bandits' horses wandered nearby, picking at the ground. "I'll take one, and you take one."

Mazael laughed. "As I recall, I slew two bandits, you one. By rights, I should get both horses."

Gerald scowled. "You gave one of your horses to the wizard."

"No, Timothy earned it by staying alive. So...I suppose, if you want to get petty about it, I get a horse and a half, and you get the remaining half," said Mazael.

"What am I supposed to do with half a horse?" said Gerald.

"Eat it," said Mazael.

Gerald grimaced. "I had enough horse in Mastaria after Grand Master Malleus routed Mandor!"

"Your father has more horses than the Lord of Swiftheart," said Mazael. "But, because I am a compassionate soul, I'll give you my half of the second horse."

Gerald laughed. "You're too kind, I say."

Mazael smirked. "I know."

Timothy finished his spell. The crystal shimmered, rainbow light flashing from its facets, and he tucked it into his coat. "The spell is complete," he said.

"Good," said Mazael. "Any enemies nearby?"

Timothy's eyelids fluttered. "Ah...no. There are some peasants in that house," he pointed, "watching us...I suppose they were afraid to come out when they saw the bandits. Other than that...there is no one nearby."

"Splendid," said Mazael. "Let's keep moving. Rachel! You can come now. The wizard's done being distasteful." Rachel rode to rejoin them, ignoring Timothy. Mazael offered Timothy a shrug and set Chariot to a walk.

They passed the peasant farmhouse. One of the fields behind the house had been left fallow for the season, and blood roses filled its furrows. It resembled one great wound, hacked and stabbed by thousands of knives. Mazael remembered Mattias Comorian's words, and shivered despite himself.

CHAPTER 5
IN THE MONASTERY'S SHADOW

"I say, Mazael, I thought we had another day of travel. Is that the castle already?" said Gerald, squinting at the massive structure brooding at the top of the hill. A thick mist had risen up that morning, swirling around their horses' hooves like fingers of cloud. The fortress loomed out of the murk like a grim stone fist.

Mazael gave a curt shake of his head. "No."

Here the land rose up into one of the Grim Marches' few craggy regions, worn spurs of gray granite jutting from the earth like jagged teeth. The rocks sported no lichen or moss, but instead tough weeds and small, rugged trees. Small brooks trickled through the hills, flowing their way to an eventual rendezvous with the Northwater.

Last night, Mazael had stopped at a dozen farmhouses to ask for lodgings. Two had turned them away, and the rest had refused to even open the door. At the last house, he had heard an old woman screaming out a prayer for Amatheon to protect her from the Old Demon. Disgusted, Mazael and his companions had bedded down beneath a tree. Unable to sleep, Mazael had kept watch most of the night, leaving him tired and irritable.

Gerald, who had seen Mazael in darker moods, was undaunted. "That fortress is a strong place. If it does not belong to your family, then who dwells there? Look at the way the ground slopes towards the walls! Fifty men could hold that place against an army. I cannot believe that it lies simply abandoned."

Mazael yawned. "It doesn't. That's a Cirstarcian abbey."

Gerald frowned. "The Cirstarcians? But...they're the most powerful monastic order in the kingdom. Your pardon, Mazael, my lady...but Castle Cravenlock is something of a backwater."

Mazael laughed. "So are most of these lands."

"Why would the Cirstarcine Order establish an abbey so far away from the great cities?" said Gerald.

Rachel shrugged. "Who knows, Sir Gerald? The Cirstarcians are meddlers by nature. I cannot count the number of times Mitor has flown into a rage after meeting with an emissary from that abbey." She gazed up at the walls with unblinking green eyes.

"The gods only know. And so do the Cirstarcians, I suspect," said Mazael. "The Cirstarcians have been there as long as anyone can remember."

Timothy smiled. "The Cirstarcians have always been a friend to wizards," he said. "With the exception of the Arminiars, every other monastic or militant order in the Church condemns wizardry."

Mazael grinned at him. "Conjuring the dead and lying with succubi and all that?"

Timothy grimaced. "If I had a copper coin for every peasant who believes that twaddle—I—well—I'd have more gold than Lord Richard himself."

"You'd need quite a few peasants for that," said Mazael. They rode between two crags of weathered granite.

Part of Mazael's mind - the dark part, the part that plotted how to kill everyone he met - realized it was the perfect place for an ambush.

Timothy jerked in his saddle and nearly lost his seat. His horse whinnied, tried to bolt, but Mazael wheeled Chariot around and put a firm hand on Generosity's head.

"What is it?" said Mazael. For a moment, he thought Timothy had been hit with a crossbow bolt, and the blood started to thunder in his temples...

"My lord knight," said Timothy. "There are men watching us, from the monastery. Six, I think." His hand clutched at the wire-wrapped quartz crystal.

Mazael looked up at the fortress wall. "Are there, now? Well, let them look. It's their road, after all. They can stare until their eyeballs shrivel, for all I care, so long as they don't try to stop us." He scratched Generosity behind the ears. The horse's ears perked up. "Next time, try to keep your saddle. Sir Gerald and I didn't rescue you from the bandits to have you break your neck."

Timothy's smile turned sheepish. "I fear that I have little experience with horses, my lord knight. And I sensed their presence...suddenly, that's all."

"We'll work on your horsemanship later," said Mazael.

"Mazael, let's go," said Rachel. "I don't trust the Cirstarcians. Any number of those monks have been to Mitor's court and they could recognize me. The Cirstarcian monks support Lord Richard. I'd rather not have them deliver us to Swordgrim."

Mazael frowned. "Since when do monks abduct travelers from the road?"

"My lady," said Timothy. "The Cirstarcians are legendary for their reclusive nature. They are likely watching us to make certain we are not one of the mercenary bands plaguing the countryside. If we leave them alone, they will let us pass in peace."

Rachel glared at the wizard. "Let's go. The gods only know what goes on behind those monastery walls. I'd rather not find out. Please, let's ride before they find us."

Mazael contrasted the smiling, cheerful girl he remembered with the suspicious woman he saw now. When had Rachel grown so fearful? For the first time, Mazael found himself wondering what had happened to Rachel since he had left.

What sort of woman she had become.

"I think the wizard is right," said Mazael, "but if it troubles you that much, yes, then we'll go from this place with all speed."

Rachel sagged with relief. "Thank you, Mazael."

They continued along the hill path and the monastery soon vanished into the mists behind them.

"A pity we couldn't stop," said Gerald. "I would have liked to make prayers at the monastery."

"There's a chapel at Castle Cravenlock," said Mazael. "You can make your prayers there."

"True," said Gerald. "But it's been so long since I've been at a proper church for a proper prayer."

Mazael shrugged. "The gods are eternal. I'm sure they'll wait two days for your prayer."

Gerald made a sound that was a curious mixture of a laugh and a sigh. "You never did care much for the gods, did you?"

Mazael laughed. "You've known me for—what—ten years now, and you've just realized it? I thought I trained you to be more perceptive."

"You know what I mean," said Gerald.

Mazael shrugged. "So what? If the gods exist, then they either ignore us, which is fine, or they take interest in the lives of men, in which case they are obviously cruel."

"That's impious," said Gerald. "A knight is sworn to be pious."

Mazael laughed. "Actually, my father tapped me on the shoulder with his sword and shoved me out the door. You remember, Rachel? After Lord Richard defeated him, my father wanted no one to interfere with Mitor the Mushroom's inheritance. He gave me a sword, a horse, knighthood, and told me to leave and never return."

Rachel frowned. "Our father was a good man."

"Oh, I don't doubt that," said Mazael. "Generous and kind, but weak and none too bright. Gerald, did you know that Lord Adalon had twice the men Lord Richard did? My father could have sat in Swordgrim and waited for Lord Richard's army to starve. Winter was coming. Instead, he marched out to meet Lord Richard in battle. He didn't want to seem a coward, you see. As Rachel said, Lord Adalon was a good man, but he was no commander. Lord Richard tore his army to shreds, killed my two older brothers, and took Lord Adalon captive. Now, what sort of gods allow a weak man like my father to lead his land to ruin?"

"Evil comes from men, and good from the gods," said Gerald.

"And now it might happen again," said Mazael. "Instead of Lord Richard Mandragon rising against Lord Adalon Cravenlock, Mitor will rise against Lord Richard. Unless I talk some sense into the fool, Lord Richard will crush the Cravenlocks once again." Mazael smirked. "Like father, like son."

They rode in silence for a moment.

"Mitor could win," said Rachel.

Mazael stared at her. "Mitor? Defeat Lord Richard the Dragonslayer? And just how would he do that? A pact with the Old Demon and all the powers of darkness? His soul for the Grim Marches?"

"Mazael, that's not funny," said Rachel.

Mazael sighed and scrubbed his fingers through his beard. "Very well. How in the name of the gods do you think Mitor could possibly defeat Lord Richard?"

"Mitor's no battle commander, like you said, but he has men who could serve him as one. Lord Marcus, Sir Nathan, Lord Roget of Hunter Hall," said Rachel.

"Lord Marcus Trand is, as I remember, a bootlicking toad," said Mazael. "Lord Roget is a scholar, not a warrior. And Sir Nathan...Sir Nathan could lead an army against the Dragonslayer...but Mitor considers him too old, remember?"

"Sir Albron could lead Mitor's army," said Rachel. Her face beamed at the mention of her betrothed. "He's as good a fighter as Sir Nathan. He could defeat the Dragonslayer."

Mazael doubted it. "Even if he could, what would he fight Lord Richard with? Mitor could probably call, say, ten thousand men to his banner. Lord Richard could easily call twenty thousand, maybe even twenty-five. Your Sir Albron had best be a damned fine commander, if he's going to face those odds."

"When we fight," said Rachel, "we won't just have the men of Castle Cravenlock and the other lords. The Knights Justiciar will fight with us."

"The Justiciars?" said Gerald. His lips twisted into a frown beneath his moustache. "What do they see in this? Most of their land is west of my father's holdings."

"Yes," said Mazael. "But they hold estates in the Grim Marches as well."

"Lord Richard has been stripping away those estates from the Justiciars and bestowing them on his followers," said Rachel. "When...if Mitor rises against Lord Richard, the Justiciars will follow him!"

"Really?" said Mazael. "If that happens, then the lords of the Stormvales will rise and join Lord Richard, along with the lords of the Green Plain. The Castanagents of the High Plain will come to join Mitor, along with Lord Malden Roland and all his vassals. The lords of Travia will probably become involved as well. If Mitor decides he wants to be liege lord of the Grim Marches, he might be able to do it, but he'll rip the kingdom apart for years of bloody war..." For a moment Mazael saw an image of a vast, bloody sea. Chunks of meat floated in the gory ocean, and something within him found the sight beautiful. He shook his head and his vision cleared.

"Why does the prospect of war trouble you so?" said Rachel. "Mitor just wants to take what belongs to our family."

"The Mandragons held the liege lordship of the Grim Marches before the Cravenlocks took it from them," said Mazael, "and they were descended from the old kings of Dracaryl."

"So?" said Rachel. "The Grim Marches belong to the Cravenlocks, Mazael. It belongs to us. Mitor wants to take back what is ours."

"No," said Gerald. "Pardon, my lady, but it is wrong. I saw much of war in Mastaria. Good men were slain on both sides. I slew good men, loyal and brave, with my own blade. I will face war again if I must...but only for a true and good reason. Lord Mitor is already a powerful lord. Let him be content with what he has. Those who are discontent with the gods' blessings may find those blessings taken away."

"My lord knight, if I may speak?" said Timothy. Mazael nodded. "I agree with Sir Gerald. I was a boy when the princes of Travia contended for the throne. I was young, but I remember the war very well...the fires, especially. The gods have mercy, the fires...my brother and my mother burned to death when raiders torched our house. If my lord knight would forgive my frank tongue...if Mitor would bring such death and misery to the Grim Marches, with no reason but his own power and prestige...then...then...he is much a murderer as those who threw the torches through the windows of my father's house."

"Don't worry, wizard," said Mazael. "I prefer honest men to liars."

"They were just peasants," said Rachel, so softly that Mazael almost didn't hear her. For a moment he wanted to shove her from the saddle, until chagrin restored his control. What was he thinking? This was Rachel, his sister, his only friend growing up. What was wrong with him?

She would never have said such a thing as a child.

"Perhaps a war is unavoidable," said Gerald.

Mazael thought of the war, and excitement tingled through him, the fingers of his sword hand clenching. He could defeat Lord Richard. He could lead Mitor's army and cast down the Dragonslayer and his son. What could stop him? What enemy had ever stood against him? But what would Sir Nathan and Master Othar say about this? He thought of their words, as he often did when the path seemed unclear.

"Sir Gerald is right. Timothy is right," Mazael said. "If Mitor starts this war he'll have the blood of thousands on his pudgy hands. Nobles and 'just peasants' alike."

Rachel flushed. Mazael thought it made her look healthier. "I...that was a heartless thing for me to say. I should know better. I do know better. I'm sorry."

Mazael smiled. "You've had a hard few days. Sir Tanam did kidnap you, after all."

"Yes," said Rachel, "but...that defeat killed Father. He died five years after you left. Mother died less than a month later. They wasted away, Mazael, they wasted away from shame. Father and Mother both made Mitor promise to restore the house of Cravenlock to its old glory."

Mazael recalled his first clear memory of his mother. He had been no more than three or four years old. He had come into her bedroom and seen Lady Arissa crying, her green eyes puffy with tears. The sunlight shone through the window and glinted off her hair. He remembered that very clearly, the glint. When she saw him, she screamed in rage and pushed him out the door. He fell and cracked his head on the hard stone floor, raising a lump. Master Othar tended the lump, but Mazael had cried and cried. He cried for days. When he stopped crying, he no longer cared what his mother thought or did.

"You loved our parents, I know," said Mazael. "But, Rachel, sister, they were both fools." She started to protest. "You know that. You loved them, fine. Don't follow their path to ruin."

"Perhaps you're right," said Rachel. Her voice held little conviction. "Maybe…"

"My lord knight!" said Timothy. He swayed in his saddle and managed to seize the pommel. Generosity gave out a frustrated grunt. "Someone approaches!"

All thoughts of family and dead parents vanished from Mazael's mind. "Where?" he said. His hand curled around Lion's hilt.

"From the south," said Timothy. He regained his balance and pointed. A narrow path came down between two crags and intercepted their trail. "Just one."

Mazael frowned. "Just one?" Timothy nodded. "Well, let him come."

Mazael reined in Chariot at the fork in the path, reined up, and waited, Gerald at his side.

A horseman appeared in the mists, riding a gray mare. The rider was lean and slender, clad in an old green cloak with the hood pulled up, and armed to the teeth. Two daggers waited in his belt, the hilt of a bastard sword rose over his shoulder, and the staff of an unstrung longbow rested over the saddle horn. Mazael watched the man closely and frowned. The shape of the leg was wrong, the hip too curved. The rider was a woman.

The woman reined up the lean mare.

"Waiting for me?" she said, and pulled back her hood. Black hair hung loose over her shoulders, and her eyes were an odd shade of blue. Mazael had only seen that color once before, as a boy, when Sir Nathan had taken him to the mountains. The ice topping some of the mountains had been that strange, rich shade of blue. He could not place her age. She could have been anywhere from fifteen to forty.

"We were waiting for you," said Mazael. "I didn't know if you were friend or foe. With these bandits loose through the countryside, it seemed safer to be cautious."

The woman grinned. "Ah. You don't know if I'm friend or foe, yet you sit here talking?"

"You could try to rob us," said Mazael. "You wouldn't like the results."

She laughed. "Is that so? Well, let's see who you are, then we'll see if we're friends or foes." She pointed at Rachel. "She's a Cravenlock."

Rachel stirred. "How could you know that?"

"The eyes," said the woman. "They're green. Only Cravenlocks have eyes like that." She frowned. "I don't know you, nor do I know the man with the mustache, nor do I know that red-faced fellow with the goatee."

"Very well," said Mazael. "I am Sir Mazael Cravenlock. This is Sir Gerald Roland. The man with the goatee is Timothy deBlanc, a wizard, and the boy is Wesson Joran, Sir Gerald's squire."

"Sir Mazael Cravenlock?" said the woman. "You don't look like a Cravenlock. You're something of a hero in the Old Kingdoms."

"And why is that?" said Mazael.

"The Knights Dominiar conquered the Old Kingdoms. When you defeated Sir Commander Aeternis at of Tumblestone, you broke the main strength of the Dominiars. It was all Grand Master Malleus could do to hold onto Mastaria, let alone fight the war with the Old Kingdoms."

Rachel looked at Mazael with admiration. "That was you? When the Mastarian war ended, we heard it was Sir Mandor Roland who led Lord Malden's army to victory against the Knights Dominiar, at cost of his life."

Mazael shrugged. "Sir Mandor had been dead for three months by then. Lord Malden decided to credit the victory to his son."

"Wiser men know better, Mazael," said Gerald.

The woman laughed. "The Dominiars crushed Lord Malden north of Tumblestone, Sir Gerald. Your father undoubtedly wanted a Roland besides you to have a victory."

"So, who are you, and how do you know all this?" said Mazael.

The woman smiled and did a mocking little bow from her saddle. "I am Romaria Greenshield, of Deepforest Keep." That explained her unusual garb and knowledge. Deepforest lay within the Great Southern Forest, isolated and surrounded by the dense forest and the Elderborn. Visitors rarely came to the keep, and rumors swirled around the Greenshields. The men of Deepforest Keep lived and traded with the Elderborn, it was said, and adopted their ways as well. The peasants whispered that the women of Deepforest lay with the Elderborn, producing half-human, half-Elderborn abominations.

"Deepforest Keep!" said Rachel. "There's no such place!"

Romaria grinned, her smile mocking edge. "Oh, there is. I should know. After all, I spent many years there. Now Castle Cravenlock...is there such place as that?"

Gerald laughed, and Rachel blushed. "You needn't be rude."

"What brings you this far north?" said Mazael. Chariot's nostrils flared, sniffing at Romaria's mare, and Mazael yanked at the reins. "Stop that."

Romaria laughed. "Don't blame him. My little mare's in heat. I suspect they'll be at each other if we give them the chance."

"And then you'll have to walk all the way back to Deepforest Keep, leading a pregnant horse," said Mazael. "We can't have that."

"Oh, I don't plan on leaving Castle Cravenlock for some time. After all, I came all this way," said Romaria. "My father, Lord Athaelin, sent me to visit Castle Cravenlock in his name."

"Why?" asked Mazael.

Romaria looked towards the east. "My father believes there is something wrong near Castle Cravenlock. He says that dark magic haunts the countryside."

Timothy looked troubled. "There are...such things, my lord knights and my lady. Some wizards turn against their oaths and seek forbidden knowledge. The magisters execute those that seek such dark arts...but even the magisters cannot police every wizard in the kingdom."

"That's rubbish," said Rachel. "Rumors spread by addle-brained peasants and slanders told by drunken jongleurs."

Romaria raised an eyebrow. "I've seen this dark magic. In the barrow fields near Deepforest, I saw a corpse claw itself free from the grave." Her voice was calm, but her blue eyes grew distant. "It killed three of my father's men before they took down the creature. It took fire and magic to kill the monster." She smiled at Rachel. "Now, Lady Rachel, are you calling me addled?"

"No," said Rachel, her voice angry. "I'm calling you a liar."

Romaria laughed. "You might not see such things in your safe castle...but you'll see them soon enough, if it's not stopped."

"The only troubles I've seen here are court intrigues," said Mazael. "Sir Tanam Crowley kidnapped Lady Rachel less than a week ago, under Lord Richard's orders."

"My father's told me of old Sir Crow," said Romaria. "How did Lady Rachel here manage to get away from the likes of Sir Tanam?"

"Sir Mazael and I...ah...had something of a hand in it," said Gerald.

"I see," said Romaria. "My father believes that a renegade wizard is responsible for the troubles we've experienced. Perhaps our problems and yours have a common root?"

"Nonsense," said Rachel. "Utter nonsense. There is no wizard, no dark magic. The real enemy is Lord Richard Mandragon and his murdering son. Can't you see that?"

Mazael raised his hand. "No. I'll hear her out. Gerald and I have dealt with rogue wizards before, during my service with Lord Malden. A wizard's trickery might be at work here...no insult, Timothy."

"None taken, my lord knight," said Timothy. "Such a schemer does not deserve the title of wizard."

"Lord Athaelin sent me to warn Lord Mitor, and to find and kill this wizard if necessary," said Romaria.

"Mazael, I can't believe you're listening to this!" said Rachel. "Sir Tanam is scouring the countryside for us, and Lord Richard is probably marching towards Castle Cravenlock with an army as we speak, and you sit here listening to this...this wild woman!"

Romaria's mocking grin returned. "Wild, am I? What does that make you? Tame? Helpless?Helpless enough to let Sir Tanam spirit you away in the dark of the night?"

"Enough," said Mazael. "I don't care if you're right. Insult my sister again, and I'll see to it that all your talk of wizards and walking corpses falls on deaf ears. Understand?"

Rachel glowered, but Romaria only sketched a shallow bow. "If you wish."

"So, you think a rogue wizard is behind all this turmoil?" Mazael said. "What do you intend to do if you find him?"

"That's simple enough," said Romaria. "A man that would summon such abominations as I saw does not deserve to live. I will kill him."

"With what?" said Mazael. Her flippant confidence annoyed him, but it also appealed to him. In some strange way, she reminded Mazael of himself. "Do you have magic?"

Romaria smiled. "I do."

"Witchcraft!" hissed Rachel.

Mazael looked at his sister. "Weren't you complaining two days ago that Sir Tanam had accused you of that?"

Timothy looked interested. "You can cast spells, Lady Romaria?"

"Oh, a few," she said. "Watch." She leaned forward and her fingers plucked at Mazael's ear. His hand lanced for his sword, but she leaned back, something glittering in her fingers. Romaria grinned and flipped a silver coin in her fingers.

Timothy's disappointment was plain. "That is not magic, my lady. Simple trickery. Any street charlatan could do the same."

"Quite true," agreed Romaria. "But show me a street charlatan who can do this..." She balanced the coin atop her hand, closed her eyes, and swung her fist in a slow circle. Her lips moved in silent words and the fingers of her free hand waggled. Then her blue eyes opened wide, and she thrust her hands in Timothy's direction. A spray of silver coins, dozens of them, burst from her fingers and rained across the path. Then Romaria snapped her fingers, and the coins vanished in a flash.

"And I'll eat your horse," she finished.

"Illusion," said Timothy. He tugged at the spike of his beard. "I was never very skilled at illusion."

"Very impressive," said Mazael. "But what use is it? Will you throw illusionary coins at this renegade? Can you use that sword over your shoulder?"

"Better than you could, I imagine," said Romaria.

Mazael grinned at her. "We'll see."

He had Lion free from it scabbard in an instant, the blade arcing for her head. Romaria could not possibly get her heavy blade out in time to block his strike. Yet she did. Lion clanged against her sword, and the gray light of the overcast day flashed from the steel of their naked blades.

"Sir Mazael!" said Gerald, grabbing Mazael's arm. "Have you completely lost your mind? You just attacked a traveler, a woman, on the road!"

"He didn't attack me," said Romaria. "His sword was an inch too far to the left. It would have missed me entirely. Sir Mazael just wanted to see if I was all talk and no action."

"Not bad," said Mazael, sliding Lion back into its sheath.

"You, sir, are mad," said Gerald.

"Oh, undoubtedly," said Mazael. "Lady Romaria, will you accompany us to Castle Cravenlock?"

Rachel looked shocked. "You...you can't be serious! She's wild, and she knows magic...a woman!"

"Three swords have a better chance than two," said Mazael. "And she knows how to use that ugly sword of hers, I'm sure of it."

"Why not?" Romaria said. She turned her coin over in her fingers, an odd light in her eyes. "Maybe I can shock your lord brother Mitor into action."

Mazael thought of what Mitor would say when he met her and laughed. Rachel was right. Romaria Greenshield was wild. But she was no wilder than Mazael himself.

"After all, Rachel," Mazael said. "If Mitor starts this war, we'll need every sword we can find."

CHAPTER 6
THE TOWNSMEN'S WELCOME

The mist cleared, and Mazael set a hard pace for Castle Cravenlock. Soon the clouds broke, the setting sun flooding the hills with light and shadow. Mazael watched the shadows, expecting each to hold a hidden enemy, but none appeared. Night fell, and Mazael called for a stop. Better to rest and delay a night than to have a horse break a leg in the darkness.

They set up camp at a small hollow in the base of a weathered hill. Timothy cast a spell to make a six-inch jet of flame burst from his finger and started the campfire. Wesson saw to the horses while Mazael pulled out the scanty remains of their supplies.

He saw a flicker of movement atop the hill. A large black hunting cat perched on the rocks above, firelight glinting off a yellow eye. Before Mazael could shout a warning, Romaria spun, her arms a blur, and an arrow sprouted from the cat's skull. It twitched and fell forward, landing with a meaty thump at the edge of the hollow.

"What was that?" said Rachel.

"A good shot," said Mazael.

Romaria grinned and lowered her bow. "That, and supper."

They skinned the cat and had fresh meat. Mazael and Gerald had long ago learned to eat when food was offered, and Romaria looked almost catlike herself in satisfaction. Rachel turned pale when they skinned the cat, excused herself, and went to sleep.

"Women have little stomach for the sight of blood," said Gerald.

"That so?" said Romaria around a mouthful of meat. Mazael snorted laughter.

"Lady Romaria is correct," said Timothy. He pulled a chunk of

44

hot meat from a bone. "All wizards are trained as physicians. If you've ever attended a woman in childbirth...well, it is not a sight for those with weak stomachs."

"I'll take first watch," said Romaria.

"Why?" said Mazael.

"I can't sleep in this country," said Romaria. "The gods only know what wanders this land at night."

"Mercenaries, bandits, and hunting cats," said Mazael. "You've already taken care of the cat, so I suspect you'll have little difficulty with the other two."

"Mercenaries and bandits don't scare me," said Romaria. "An arrow through the eye will fix them, just like the cat. It's the walking dead, the zuvembies, that frighten me." She looked out into the darkness. "Night's their time."

"An arrow through the eye will stop a dead man?" said Mazael.

Romaria snorted. "Not likely. But dead men burn, just the same as the living." She pointed at the fire. "I mean to keep that going all night. It'll keep away the animals, and if any of the zuvembies rise tonight, fire will ward them off."

"Pardon, Lady Romaria, but what was that word you used? Zuvembie?" said Timothy. "I speak five languages, yet have never heard that word."

"It's Elderborn" said Romaria. "In Caerish, it means...oh, 'demon corpse', or 'dead devil'. Not an exact translation, but you get the idea."

Timothy blinked. "You know the Elderborn?"

Mazael laughed. "She said she was from Deepforest Keep, didn't she?"

Romaria grinned. "Know them? I grew up with them. Who do you think taught me to use a bow like that? Lord Richard's crossbowmen? The Elderborn have long been allied with Deepforest Keep. We look out for each other. In fact, they were the ones who first warned us of the dangers. Their druids sensed a disturbance. Not long after, the first zuvembie rose from the barrows."

"Mitor won't believe you," said Mazael.

Romaria leveled a flat glance at him. "Is that so? Do you believe me?"

Mazael thought it over. "I think I do. You don't seem the sort to make up a wild tale. And Gerald and I saw a necromancer conjure up a shade once, before we killed him. That's not the sort of thing you forget. I know such things exist. But Mitor won't believe you."

"Why not?" said Romaria.

"He's a fool," Mazael said. "And you're a woman."

"I noticed," said Romaria.

"Mitor will look at you and see a woman carrying a man's weapons and wearing a man's clothes. At best, he'll laugh at you. At worst, he'll have you imprisoned for obscenity," said Mazael.

"Yet you believe me," said Romaria. "Why?"

Mazael laughed. "I had better teachers. My father was a kind fool and my brother is a cruel fool, but I don't think it runs in the blood. Master Othar and Sir Nathan taught me otherwise."

"Sir Nathan Greatheart is a good man, and a friend of my father," said Romaria. "In Deepforest, some of the Elderborn still tell the story how he helped save the Tribe of the Wolf when he was a young man."

"He and Master Othar taught me near everything I know," said Mazael. "I was a wild, undisciplined, violent fool." He grinned. "I suppose I still am."

Gerald took a sip from his waterskin. "No, you're just mad."

Mazael laughed. "My mother hated me and my father ignored me. It was as if they wanted me to be cruel and lawless. I don't know what would have become of me were it not for Sir Nathan and Master Othar." He looked at the sleeping form of his sister. "And Rachel. Gods, if it weren't for those three, I would probably have been another Toraine Mandragon."

"Well, it is quite late," said Gerald. "I shall turn in."

"I'll keep the fire burning," said Romaria.

"Why not prepare some fire arrows?" said Mazael. "If this...whatever you called them, these walking dead men show up, you can just shoot them full of flaming arrows. No need to get close with a burning brand."

Romaria stared at him for a moment, and then laughed. "That is a good idea! I should have thought of it myself." She pulled strips of rags from her saddlebags and began to wind them around a few of her arrows.

Mazael rolled himself up in his cloak and went to sleep.

The morning dawned bright and clear and hot, and they resumed their eastward wide.

"There," said Mazael three hours later. "There's Castle Cravenlock."

The castle sat at the edge of the hill country. overlooking a broad swath of cultivated land along the banks of the Eastwater. It perched atop the easternmost of the gray granite crags, its towers grim and strong, its walls crowned with battlements. The banner of the Cravenlocks, three crossed swords on a field of black, flapped over the castle towers. Mazael also saw the red rose on white of Lord Marcus Trand, the brown bow on green of Lord Roget Hunterson, and other banners. Mitor had visitors.

"Home," Rachel said.

"A formidable fortress," said Gerald.

"Ugly place," said Romaria. Rachel shot a furious glare at her.

"I tend to agree," said Mazael.

"I don't see a gate," said Romaria.

"The barbican's on the other side of the castle," said Mazael. "The main road from White Rock and the other villages leads through the town. We'll take that way."

They rode past herds of grazing sheep, and the shepherds gaped. Mazael grinned. He could imagine that two knights, a woman dressed in man's clothing, a Travian wizard, a noblewoman, and a boy squire made quite a sight. They rounded the base of the hill and Cravenlock Town, an overgrown village of four thousand people, came into sight, smoke rising from hundreds of chimneys. The main road passed through the town's gates, and Mazael Cravenlock came home after fifteen years.

The peasants teeming the narrow streets parted before them. A murmur of whispers rose up as they recognized Lady Rachel, a buzz of surprise spreading through the crowd.

Mazael frowned. Why were so many people on the streets? At this time of day, they should have been in their fields or workshops.

"Lady Rachel!" he heard one man say. "She's come back."

Mazael stared at the peasants. He saw worry on their faces, and lines from years of hard labor. But most of all, he could saw the fear. Suddenly Romaria's tales of zuvembies didn't seem so outlandish.

"That Sir Mazael," another man said. "He must've rescued her. He could outwit the Old Crow, too. He killed the Grand Master of the Knights Dominiar, I heard it myself!"

"Who's the handsome knight, the one with the golden hair?"

"That strange woman...wearing a sword?"

He heard another voice, just at the edge of his hearing, that made his skin crawl. "Sir Mazael's come back...he'll set things right, he'll put an end to this bloody business..."

Romaria flipped a silver coin over her knuckles. Her hands moved with fluid grace through the gestures of the spell she had used yesterday. She thrust out both hands and threw handfuls of silver coins into the crowds. A gasp went up, and Mazael saw that the coins were real, this time.

"How does she do that?" said Gerald as the peasants thronged around the coins.

Mazael shrugged and waggled his fingers. "Magic."

They rode into the town square and Mazael reined Chariot up.

"What in the hells?" Mazael said.

Little wonder such a crowd had gathered.

A gallows rose in the center of the square. A dozen Cravenlock armsmen stood around it in a ring, holding back the crowd with their spears. Some of the peasants screamed curses, and the town looked on the edge of a riot.

The gallows had nooses and trapdoors for eight people, and each noose held an occupant. The necks of a plump man and a stout woman filled the first two, the man's eyes bulging huge with fear while the woman wept. An ancient woman stood next to them, the noose holding down her white hair. Two pretty young women and three children filled the other five nooses. The oldest child looked Wesson's age, the youngest about three years or so.

"Mazael!" said Gerald. "Those are children! What in the gods' names are those soldiers doing?"

A fat man in the armor and tabard of a captain stepped to the gallows. "Hear all you loyal subjects of Lord Mitor Cravenlock, Lord of Castle Cravenlock and liege lord of the Grim Marches!"

"Liege lord?" said Mazael. "What nonsense is this?"

"Know you all that these men, women, and children are traitors, and guilty of treason against Lord Mitor!" continued the captain. "Hence they have earned their deaths."

"How does a child commit treason?" said Gerald.

"Rachel, what is this?" said Mazael.

Rachel's face went white. "I...I don't know," she said. "I don't come to the town often, and..."

A gleeful grin spread across the captain's face. "If any of the condemned would like to beg for their lives, they may do so."

The stout man and woman screamed at the captain, begging for their children's lives. The pretty younger women wept and offered to give him what he wanted while the children sobbed.

"For gods' sakes, Mazael, we've got to stop this," said Gerald. "But there are fifty soldiers here. Don't do anything mad..."

The fat captain smirked, and Mazael's rage found a focus.

"What is the meaning of this?" Mazael roared.

The peasants took one look at his face and hastily backed away.

The fat captain spun, his jowls quivering with anger. "Who dares..." His eyes widened as he saw Mazael, then they narrowed again. "Who are you? You dare interrupt these proceedings of justice?"

Mazael pointed at the quivering children. "You call this justice?"

"Seize him!" yelled the captain. Gerald groaned and spurred his horse to Mazael's side.

Lion glimmered in Mazael's fist. "Try," he said, his voice calm. Something in his face made the Cravenlock armsmen back away.

"Now, who the hell are you?"

The man's face glowed with rage. "I am Captain Brogan. When Lord Mitor hears of this, he'll have your head!"

"I am Sir Mazael Cravenlock," said Mazael, "and threaten me again, and I'll give Mitor your head."

Brogan's eyes widened. "Sir...Mazael? Forgive me, my lord knight, I didn't recognize you."

Mazael waved Lion at the bound prisoners. "Now, explain to me how a little girl commits treason?"

"My lord knight," said Brogan. "It grieves me to bring you ill news, but your sister was kidnapped less than a week ago. Sir Tanam Crowley came in good faith as Lord Richard Mandragon's emissary and spirited Lady Rachel away. These vermin," he pointed at the prisoners, "aided the treacherous Old Crow in his escape!"

"They did not!" said Rachel, riding to Mazael's side. "Sir Tanam abducted me with his own men. No one from castle or town helped him! These people are innocent!"

"Lady...Lady Rachel?" Brogan said. "But how? Sir Tanam..."

"Sir Mazael and Sir Gerald rescued me from Sir Tanam," said Rachel. "They cut through his men and took me before Sir Tanam even knew what was happening. Just two, against Sir Tanam's thirty, when you and all the armsmen of Cravenlock couldn't keep me safe!"

Jeering laughter rippled through the crowd, and Brogan snarled. "They are guilty of treason nonetheless!"

Chariot stepped towards Brogan. "And what treason would that be?" said Mazael.

Mazael saw the panic begin in Brogan's eyes.

"The child!" Brogan screamed, pointing at a girl of ten or so. "She sang a treasonous song, 'Lord Mitor the Mushroom Lord.'"

"My lord knight!" screamed one of the young women. "That's..."

"Silence!" said Brogan.

"Let her speak," said Mazael. "You did, after all, ask any of the condemned if they wanted to beg. What's your name?"

The young woman's face was puffy from tears. "I'm...I'm Bethy, my lord knight. I work for master Cramton, who runs the Three Swords Inn."

"Cramton is the fellow in the noose over there, I assume," said Mazael, pointing at the fat man.

"Yes, my lord," said Bethy.

"So, what happened?" said Mazael.

"She's a liar!" bellowed Brogan.

"Shut up," said Mazael. "Bethy, what happened?"

"It was like this," said Bethy. "Me and Lyna work in master

Cramton's inn. We wait on the patrons and tend the bar. Captain Brogan and some of his men come in yesterday, start smashing up tables and stealing ale. Master Cramton tells them to stop. Captain Brogan says master Cramton should shut up if he knows what's good for him. He said that master Cramton should hand over me and Lyna...for his men. Master Cramton said no. Captain Brogan then says that's treason, and arrests us all, even master Cramton and his wife and his little ones."

"That so?" said Mazael.

"Lies," said Brogan. "These peasants hate the strong firm hand of justice that rules them, so...so they spread slander and falsehood..."

"For the last time, shut up," said Mazael. He pointed at the man-at-arms holding the lever. "You. Cut them loose. They can go back to their inn."

The man-at-arms stammered. "My...my lord knight, we...Captain Brogan commanded us to burn the Three Swords inn to the ground."

"So," said Mazael to Brogan. "The innkeeper refused to let you rape his barmaids. That's treason, now? And because of this crime, you burned down his inn and tied him and his family to a gallows? Oh, yes, the firm hand of justice indeed."

"Who are you to tell me what to do?" said Brogan. "You ride in here after fifteen years and strut about so high-and-mighty! I kept order in Lord Mitor's name. You wouldn't know the first thing about keeping order, about justice, if it hit you in the face!"

Brogan never saw it coming. Mazael ripped Lion's point through Brogan's throat, the captain's eyes bulging as blood gushed from his mouth. He collapsed to the ground, drowning in his own blood.

"And neither would you," said Mazael.

The Cravenlock armsmen gaped, fingering their weapons.

Gerald sighed. "Oh, this is off to a dreadful start."

Mazael tore off Brogan's cloak and used it to wipe down Lion's blade. "I mean to have words with this new fool of an armsmaster, Sir Albron." Rachel's eyes flashed. "Sir Nathan would never have let something like this happen." An armsman shouted and ran at Mazael. Mazael rammed the palm of his hand into the armsman's face, sent him sprawling.

"Anyone else have any objections?" said Mazael, glaring at the armsmen. None of them did. "Good." He pointed. "You."

"Sir?" said another armsman.

"Cut them loose. Since Brogan saw fit to burn down their inn, they'll have to come with me back to the castle. I mean to see that they get reparation," said Mazael.

"Cut them loose?" repeated the armsman.

"Now!" said Mazael. The soldier leapt up the gallows and sawed at the ropes with his dagger. Cramton stumbled free from his noose and ran to his wife and children.

"Form up!" yelled Mazael to the armsmen. "You will provide an escort for Lady Rachel back to Castle Cravenlock."

"Oh, my lord knight, thank you, thank you," wailed the innkeeper's wife, clutching her children. "Oh, thank you, thank you."

"We did no treason, my lord knight," said Cramton, sweating and weeping. "I just wanted to do right by my workers, I did."

"The gods sent you," Bethy declared. "The gods knew we were innocent, so they sent you."

Mazael snorted. "Come long. Here, now. If the woman can't walk, Sir Gerald and I have two extra horses. She and the little ones can ride."

"I can take one up here with me," Romaria said.

Eventually, the innkeeper's wife, so overcome by relief that she could not walk, mounted with her youngest child on one of the dead bandits' horses. Bethy went on the second horse, another child on her lap, while Romaria took still another with her. By then the milling mass of Cravenlock men had managed to form up in an escort. Romaria started to amuse the children with another coin trick.

"Go," said Mazael.

Cramton walked next to Mazael's horse and babbled thanks. Mazael nodded, his thoughts dark. Things were indeed wrong at Castle Cravenlock. He had just seen firsthand evidence of it. For the moment, he didn't care about Rachel's story of impending war, or Romaria's tale of dark magic. The idiocy, the brutality of the armsmen, bothered him the most. Oh, yes, he would have words with Lord Mitor over this, and with this fool Sir Albron Eastwater.

CHAPTER 7
THE BROTHERS' REUNION

Castle Cravenlock stood on a war footing.

Mazael saw camps of mercenaries arrayed around the base of the castle's rocky hill, some standing in precise military order, others little more than a hodgepodge mess of tents and latrine ditches. At least three thousand men all told, Mazael reckoned. Nearby a blue banner with a silver star, the standard of the Knights Justiciar, flapped over a camp of five hundred men. Next to the Justiciar camp rose the banners of Lord Marcus Trand and Lord Roget Hunterson, their camps holding at least another two thousand men.

Mitor meant to challenge the might of Swordgrim with this rabble?

Spearmen patrolled the castle's ramparts, looking down as Mazael and the others rode up to the gates. Armsmen guarded both the gate and barbican, while crossbowmen waited atop the wall.

Mazael reined up before the gates.

"Halt!" called a man from the ramparts. "Who comes?"

"Gods almighty!" swore an armsman. "That's Lady Rachel with him!"

"I am Sir Mazael Cravenlock!" said Mazael, standing up in his stirrups. "Behind me are Sir Gerald Roland of Knightcastle, Lady Romaria Greenshield of Deepforest Keep, and the wizard Timothy deBlanc. And no doubt you recognize Lady Rachel Cravenlock?"

"My gods!" exclaimed the gate's lieutenant. "Sir Mazael, Sir Tanam Crowley abducted Lady Rachel a week past! For you...to come with..."

"How do you think Lady Rachel won free?" said Mazael. "Do you think the Old Crow let her go?"

"Open the gate!" said the lieutenant. "Lord Mitor will want to meet with his brother and sister at once."

"He damn well better," muttered Mazael.

The castle's portcullis rattled up, and Mazael rode into Castle Cravenlock's courtyard and came home.

It was almost exactly as he remembered. A new roof had been put upon the stables, and three additional forges stood against the curtain walls, but nothing else had changed. The earth beneath Chariot's hooves remained a mixture of hard-packed dirt and grassy patches, and the servants, peasants, and armsmen going about their business in the courtyard could have been the same men Mazael had seen fifteen years ago.

Someone touched his elbow. "Welcome home," said Rachel.

Mazael laughed. "Yes, but I rather doubt home is glad to see me."

Grooms hurried forward to take their mounts, and Chariot bared his teeth. Mazael handed the reins over, and the big war horse deigned the grooms to lead him.

"You ought to have that horse gelded, you know," said Romaria. She slid down from her mare's saddle. "He's hasn't stopped sniffing at my poor mare."

Mazael snorted. "Why would I want to do that? A gelding's no good in battle."

"A gelding would be easier to control," said Romaria.

"Yes," said Mazael, "but a gelding wouldn't bite the faces off my enemies."

A young boy in a page's livery ran forward. "Sir Mazael Cravenlock," he said in a high voice. "Lord Mitor commands your presence and the presence of your companions in the great hall at once."

"There's gratitude," said Mazael. "I bring back his abducted sister and he cannot even rouse himself to come meet me?" The page flinched. No doubt Lord Mitor was not often questioned. "Very well. Tell him we will come presently."

The page bowed and ran off.

"Master Cramton, accompany me," said Mazael. He turned to the Cravenlock armsmen. "Make certain his family is comfortable. If they give me a single word of complaint, I'll take you back down to those gallows and hang you myself. Oh, and try not to burn down any more inns while you're at it?"

"Shall...shall some of us escort you to the great hall?" said an armsman.

"I know the way," said Mazael.

He started for the great hall. Some of his mood must have shown on his face, and servants and armsmen alike melted out of his way. Mazael climbed the steps to the central keep and walked through the anteroom. The massive double doors to Castle Cravenlock's great hall stood open.

The great hall had been built in imitation of the vast vaulted naves of the high cathedrals. Delicate pillars supported the ribbed roof, and crystal windows stretched from floor to ceilings. The banners of the Cravenlocks hung from the ceiling and balconies. The lord's dais stood at the end of the hall, and a long table rested at its foot for the lord's councilors. Both dais and table stood empty.

"Where is everyone?" said Mazael.

A herald's voice rang out from the balconies. "All hail for Mitor Cravenlock, Lord of Castle Cravenlock, and liege lord of the Grim Marches!"

"Oh dear," said Gerald.

Lord Mitor Cravenlock appeared from the lord's entrance behind the dais, the hem of his embroidered robe trailing against the floor. Unlike the castle, Mitor did not look as Mazael remembered. He looked worse. His face was milk white, and dark bags encircled his bloodshot green eyes. Sweat plastered his lank black hair to his pale scalp, making him resemble a poisonous mushroom, while his belly strained against the front of his robe. Mitor sat in the lord's chair, his bloodshot eyes fixed on Mazael and Rachel, and did not speak.

"All hail of Marcelle Cravenlock, lady of Castle Cravenlock and wife of Lord Mitor!" boomed the herald.

Mitor Cravenlock's wife and Marcus Trand's daughter was a thin woman in a rich green gown. As far as Mazael could see, she had no curves at all. She looked at Rachel with open contempt, and sat down with serpentine grace besides Mitor.

"Marcus Trand, Lord of Roseblood keep, vassal to Lord Mitor!"

Lord Marcus, built like an ale keg, looked nothing like his daughter. Muscles rippled beneath his fine tunic, yet Mazael saw the cringing sycophancy in his eyes. He took a seat at the table beneath the dais.

"Roget Hunterson, Lord of Hunter's Hall, vassal to Lord Mitor!"

Lord Roget was a thin, stooped man with a long white beard and a bald head who looked as if he had not gotten much sleep.

"Sir Commander Galan Hawking, Commander of the Justiciar Knights of the Grim Marches, and Lord Mitor's honored guest and friend!"

Sir Commander Galan gleamed, light reflecting from the polished silver of his breastplate. His blue cloak with its Justiciar silver star flowed out behind him, and he moved with the grace of a stalking lion. Once Lord of Hawk's Reach, Galan had supported Lord Adalon against Lord Richard. But Lord Richard had won, Galan's younger brother Astor became lord of Hawk's Reach, and Galan found himself shipped off to the Knights Justiciar. He had done well in the order, it seemed, but Mazael saw bitterness in the Sir Commander's eyes.

"Sir Albron Eastwater, armsmaster of Castle Cravenlock, vassal to Lord Mitor!"

Sir Albron looked like the sort of muscled, handsome knight that rescued pining damsels in jongleurs' bawdy tales. His skin was tanned, his face chiseled, his eyes clear and strong. Sir Albron wore a black surcoat embroidered with the three silver swords of Cravenlock. A plain longsword with a leather-wrapped hilt hung from his belt. Mazael wondered if Sir Albron knew how to use that blade. Sir Albron smiled when he saw Rachel, and she returned the smile tenfold.

Mazael saw Romaria staring at Sir Albron as well, her eyes intent, and suppressed a laugh.

"Simonian, wizard of Briault, advisor to Lord Mitor!"

"A foreign wizard...my lord knight, he wouldn't have been trained at Alborg," whispered Timothy. "He could have learned dark arts. Briault is a land of warlocks and necromancers."

Romaria looked away from Sir Albron and frowned.

"Of Briault?" said Mazael to Rachel. "You didn't tell me that Mitor had hired a foreign wizard."

Rachel blinked. "I...I forgot."

A man wrapped in a voluminous brown robe followed Sir Albron. He wore a bushy gray beard, and unkempt iron-gray hair encircled his head like a lion's mane. His eyes were brown and muddy, the color of a pond choked with silt. He reminded Mazael of someone, but he could not place the recollection. Simonian's murky eyes fixed on Mazael for a moment, and then he sat at the councilors' table.

The herald banged his staff against the floor three times to signal the beginning of court.

"You," said Lord Mitor, his voice rusty.

"Correct," said Mazael.

"What are you doing here?" said Mitor. "Why are you here? Father sent you away fifteen years ago. Why did you come back?"

"Why did I come back?" said Mazael. "I'm gone for fifteen years, I rescue your sister from the likes of Sir Tanam, and return with her to Castle Cravenlock, and that's all you have to say?"

"Will you tolerate this questioning from your younger brother?" said Lady Marcelle.

"I am lord of Castle Cravenlock," said Mitor. "Not you. You do not question me."

"My lord," said Sir Albron. His voice was melodic. "Sir Mazael has accomplished a great feat! My men scoured the countryside and we found no trace of Sir Tanam. I had feared her lost to Lord Richard's clutches. And now Sir Mazael has returned your sister, my dear betrothed," a flush of pleasure rose in Rachel's cheeks, "to our arms. We should greet Sir Mazael with gratitude, my lord, not with suspicion and angry accusations."

"Indeed," said Lord Roget. "Lord Mitor, Sir Mazael has rescued your sister. He may very well have saved the Grim Marches from another bloody war."

"Don't speak foolishness, old man," said Mitor. "There will be war." Gerald's frown deepened, and Timothy tugged at the spike of his beard. "I am the rightful liege lord of the Grim Marches. My father was liege lord, and I am his heir. Lord Richard Mandragon is a usurper and a craven murderer, and I mean to see him cast down. I may even kill him myself."

The thought of Mitor facing battle-hardened Lord Richard in single combat was absurd. Mazael could not stop his laugh.

Lord Marcus's ruddy face darkened. "See, my lord! He laughs at you. Your own brother laughs at you. This is unacceptable, I say, unacceptable. How do we know Sir Mazael had no hand in Lady Rachel's abduction? Yes, perhaps he had her kidnapped, and then returned her to raise his standing in your eyes?"

Lord Roget grimaced. "Pardons, my lord of Roseblood, but that is absurd!"

"Is it?" said Sir Commander Galan. "My own brother stood by and did nothing while Lord Richard stripped me of my lands and titles. This Sir Mazael is no different."

Marcelle reared up like a venomous snake. "Perhaps Rachel and Mazael both are traitors, hmm? For all we know, they both could be in league with..."

"Silence!" Gerald's voice rang across the hall. "Is this how courtesy is done in the Grim Marches? Perhaps the men of Knightrealm and the High Plain are right to call this a land of barbarians. My brothers and I have had our differences, but we always spoke to each other with courtesy. And Sir Mazael has done more than speak, my lord of Cravenlock! We cut through Sir Tanam's soldiers and whisked away Lady Rachel. Sir Mazael has returned with him your kidnapped sister, and you greet him with accusations? What madness is this? What utter madness? I half-think Lady Rachel would be better off in the hands of Sir Tanam Crowley!"

Shocked silence followed Gerald's speech.

Simonian's harsh laughter broke the silence. "Well spoken, my lord knight," he said, speaking with a guttural Briaultan accent. "Honest counsel is often rare at Castle Cravenlock."

Marcelle's thin lips twisted with fury. "You...you dare..."

Mitor raised a spindly hand. "No, my wife. Sir Gerald...is right, I fear. I see his father Lord Malden has raised him very well, yes. Very well, brother. I apologize."

Mazael grinned. "Accepted."

"Now, please...tell me why my brother and...lawful heir...should return so suddenly, without warning, after fifteen years?" said Mitor. His hands twitched in his lap.

Mazael frowned. "Lawful heir?" And then it hit him. Mitor had no children. Though it was hardly surprising, given how fertile Lady Marcelle looked. If Mitor had fathered no children, Mazael was the rightful heir to Castle Cravenlock and its lands.

And that mean Mitor feared Mazael had returned after all these years to kill him and claim Castle Cravenlock. And why not? Mitor was fat and weak. Mazael could run up the dais and tear his older brother into a dozen pieces before his councilors could react.

But Mazael did not want Castle Cravenlock.

"Very well, my lord brother," said Mazael. "First, I didn't know I was your lawful heir. I haven't heard anything about Castle Cravenlock since I rode out the barbican without looking back. I had assumed that you would have had a brood of squalling sons by now, but it appears that I was wrong." Lady Marcelle's expression was nothing short of venomous. "Second, I have been in service to Lord Malden Roland, you've heard of him, no doubt, for the last nine years. It was only at his command I returned to Castle Cravenlock. Lord Malden had heard rumors of the difficulties in the Grim Marches, and sent me with Sir Gerald to investigate and report back to him. And third, the matter of Lady Rachel's rescue. As I said, I knew nothing of the troubles. I happened upon Lady Rachel and Sir Tanam at the inn near the Northwater bridge. Sir Tanam claimed he was taking Lady Rachel back to Swordgrim for crimes of witchcraft and sorcery. These were obviously false charges, so I cut through Sir Tanam's men, burned the bridge behind me, and rode for Castle Cravenlock."

Mitor did not look pleased. "You...you burned the bridge? I shall have to pay to have it replaced..."

"I brought Lady Rachel back, and you're quibbling about a damned bridge?" said Mazael.

"You destroyed my property!" said Mitor. "Do you have any idea how much it costs to raise a bridge over those rivers? I shall expect remuneration."

"I brought you sister back, fool," said Mazael. "That is remuneration enough, I should think!"

"You do not call the Lord of Castle Cravenlock a fool," said Marcelle.

"Shall I lie to the Lord of Castle Cravenlock, then?" said Mazael.

Mitor stood. "You..."

Simonian folded his gnarled fingers beneath his bearded chin. "My lord Mitor...in my homeland of Briault, it is often said that everything carries a price. You can have your heart's desire, so long as you pay for it. A wooden bridge...well, is that not a small price to pay for your sister's life?"

"Yes, but..." said Mitor.

"After all, suppose for a moment that Sir Tanam had delivered Lady Rachel to Lord Richard at Swordgrim. You would have been at Lord Richard's mercy," said Simonian. The wizard seemed almost amused at the prospect.

"I am at no one's mercy!" said Mitor. "I am the liege lord of the Grim Marches...the rightful liege lord! If my sister had to die to further my cause, then so..." Rachel flinched, and Mitor's voice trailed off. Mazael knew full well what Mitor had meant to say, and he hated him for it.

The cavorting amusement never left Simonian's eyes. "My lord Mitor, your brother has done you great service in returning Lady Rachel. Lord Richard could have forced Lady Rachel to marry his son Toraine. Or, he could have demanded you submit to him at doom of your sister's life. And if you had refused, if your sister had to die to further your cause...what lord or knight would have followed you then? If you had forsaken her, why, you could forsake them."

"You mock my honor?" demanded Mitor.

"Of course not, my lord," said Simonian. "I know that you are the most honorable of men." Mazael sensed the mockery in his words. Couldn't Mitor hear it? "But do the lords of the Grim Marches know it? My lord, by returning your sister, Sir Mazael has overcome all these difficulties! Now all the kingdom knows Sir Tanam and his lord the Dragonslayer as kidnappers and oath breakers."

Mitor sighed. "Ah, Simonian...as always, you are correct. Truly, you are the wisest of my advisors."

The mocking glint never left Simonian's murky eyes. "I live but to serve you, my lord."

"We must have a feast tonight," said Mitor, settling into his high-backed chair. "Yes, a great feast, a celebration of thanksgiving to the gods for bringing Lady Rachel back to us."

"And Sir Mazael," said Sir Albron, smiling. "He must be honored.

I fear he had a greater hand in returning my betrothed than did the gods."

"Yes, yes of course," said Mitor, waving a hand. "Honor Sir Mazael. And we must also show the might of Castle Cravenlock for the Grim Marches to see! Lord Richard the great Dragonslayer has been shown as a betrayer who sends his knights to kidnap weak women. Yes, I am liege lord of the Grim Marches, and we shall show it for all the kingdom!"

"Is that wise?" said Mazael. "Between the combined forces of Castle Cravenlock, Hunter's Hall, Roseblood Keep, the Justiciars, and the mercenaries, you will have just under ten thousand men. Lord Richard can call twenty, maybe twenty-five thousand to his banners."

Sir Commander Galan laughed. "I can bring another two thousand sergeant foot soldiers and mounted knights from the Justiciar estates under my command. Besides, Lord Richard is a usurper and a murderer. Our cause is just! We cannot lose."

Mitor smiled. "Lord Alamis Castanagent has pledged nothing, but the liege lord of the High Plain has no love for the Mandragons. He will come to support me, yes. And your own father, Sir Gerald, your father burns for justice on the Mandragons. Lord Malden would stand with the Old Demon if he went to war against Lord Richard!"

Gerald frowned. "My father wants justice for Sir Belifane, yes, but he is not a foolish man. He will not rush into war." Mazael knew better. Lord Malden hated Lord Richard, and would drag the kingdom into war to bring the Dragonslayer down.

Mitor smirked. "We shall see, yes. Sir Albron, please see Sir Mazael and Sir Gerald to guest rooms..."

"There are a few matters we must first discuss," said Mazael.

Mitor scowled. "What? It had best be important."

Mazael gestured at Cramton. "This is master Cramton, an innkeeper...a former innkeeper...from the town."

"I assumed he was one of your servants," said Mitor. "Well, why should I care?"

"Your soldiers burned his inn," said Mazael, "and when I rode into the town, I found them preparing to hang master Cramton and his family."

"Well, what did they do to warrant hanging?" said Mitor.

"Captain Brogan had accused them of treason, of aiding Sir Tanam..."

Mitor waved a hand. "There it is, then. Why is this peasant fool still alive?"

"He committed no treason," snapped Mazael. "Captain Brogan and his men tried to rape Cramton's serving girls. He refused to allow it, and so Brogan imprisoned Cramton and burned his inn!"

"Sir Mazael is right," said Rachel. "Master Cramton and his family and his workers had nothing to do with my kidnapping. It was entirely the work of Sir Tanam and his men."

"I commanded my men to keep order in the town," said Sir Albron, his voice calm and pleasant. "How they carry out their orders is of no concern to me, so long as they are carried out."

Annoyance flashed across Mitor's face. "If this peasant's workers refused to service my soldiers, that, too, is treason!"

"No, that is arson and murder!" yelled Mazael. "I killed Captain Brogan for..."

Mitor lurched out of his seat. "You killed Brogan? You killed one of my armsmen? How dare you? Who do you think you are, to ride into my town and my lands and kill my soldiers?" Cramton shrunk down into himself.

"Who do you think you are?" roared Mazael. "A lord is supposed to do justice for his people! And where is the justice in murder and fire? Your armsmen, bandits, I'd call them, torched this man's inn and tried to hang his family. Children, Mitor, they tried to hang children! You were complaining about remuneration? I demand you pay it to master Cramton for the loss of his inn!"

"Demand?" said Mitor, his voice shrill. "You demand nothing of me! I am Lord of Castle Cravenlock and liege lord of the Grim Marches! You are a landless knight! You demand nothing of me, and certainly demand nothing for damned peasants!"

"You call yourself a lord, then be a lord!" said Mazael. Red rage howled through him, and he wanted to draw Lion, run up the dais, and kill every last one of those fools before the guards could react. "Do you know what a lord is who won't do justice? A bandit, a thug in an oversized robe! So, go ahead, Mitor, gorge yourself and get drunk and call yourself liege lord and ignore your people. And when Lord Richard comes for you, they'll rise up for him, and the Dragonslayer will mount your head above his gates." He cast his glare over the council table. "Alongside the heads of your fool advisors!"

Sir Commander Galan and Sir Albron reached for their swords, while Simonian only smiled. Lord Marcus got redder. "You dare insult me so..."

"Shut up, you bag of wind!" said Mitor.

For a long moment Mitor and Mazael glared at each other.

Mitor looked away first. "Very well. Remuneration. So be it. One hundred crowns."

"That's all?" said Mazael.

"We have need of servants here in the castle. The peasant and his family can work here until their inn is rebuilt," said Mitor. "I trust you are satisfied."

"My...my lord is generous," said Cramton, staring at the floor.

"Yes. See that you don't forget it," said Mitor.

"Why is Sir Nathan Greatheart not armsmaster?" said Mazael. "He kept the armsmen of Castle Cravenlock in better order than this Sir Albron."

"Sir Nathan is too old," said Mitor. "He is incapable of carrying out my orders. That fat slug Master Othar, as well. Simonian serves me far better." Mitor smiled. "He can do things that Othar could never dream of..."

Mazael took another step forward. "If you had them killed..."

"Of course not!" shouted Mitor. "No! I did no such thing! They are in my service, under my protection. They serve here still. When war comes, I will find some post suitable for Sir Nathan's skills. Guarding the baggage, perhaps."

"Very well," said Mazael. "There is one more matter. While on the road west of here, near the Cirstarcian monastery I met Lady Romaria Greenshield, of Deepforest Keep, who wishes a word with you."

Romaria gave another strange glance to Sir Albron and stepped forward. "My Lord Mitor."

"Lady Romaria," said Mitor. He snickered. "Or is it Lord Romaria? I find myself unable to tell, from your garments." Mitor's councilors all laughed, save for Simonian.

Romaria smiled. "A beardless man in a long robe, and one who has fathered no children as well. What shall I make of that? I was looking for Lord Mitor...but I seem to have found a eunuch instead. Pray tell, where shall I find the Lord of Castle Cravenlock?"

Mitor slammed a fist down on the arm of his chair. "Watch your tongue, woman. You are in the presence of civilized men, not the wood demons and the barbarians of your home."

Romaria laughed at him. "I assumed I was in the presence of courteous men, but it appears that I was wrong. Sir Gerald Roland was correct. Did you learn your courtesies from a toad? Shall I return to Deepforest Keep and tell my father Lord Athaelin that you would not speak with me? Perhaps I should pay a visit to Swordgrim next."

Mitor's thick lips pulled back in a snarl.

"My lord," said Simonian. "It would be wise to gain the friendship of Deepforest Keep. Lord Athaelin's lands border on your own. When you march to fight Lord Richard, Athaelin could make a powerful friend...or a dangerous enemy."

"I am the liege lord of the Grim Marches!" said Mitor. "I do not need to ask for Lord Athaelin's friendship. It is mine by rights. And if he refuses it...why, then I shall have to take it."

"I did not come to offer my father's friendship," said Romaria. "I came to bring you his warning."

"Oh?" said Mitor. "So now the Lord of Deepforest Keep threatens me? Does he truly wish my wrath so much?"

A smile twitched across Romaria's face. "Oh, no, Lord Mitor. Your wrath is something that keeps my father awake long into the night, I am sure. But I came to bring a warning of the danger you face, not threats."

"And what dangers do I face?" said Mitor. "Asides from having queerly dressed women strut through my castle, that is."

"Something far more dangerous than I," said Romaria, "and that is saying quite a bit. Dark magic is loose in your lands, Lord Mitor. The dead rise from their graves and walk the earth, and no one is safe at night. My father believes that a renegade wizard is to blame." She looked at Simonian for that.

Silence answered her pronouncement. Then Lady Marcelle began to chuckle. Soon Lord Mitor laughed, and the rest of his councilors joined him. Simonian only smiled at Romaria over his folded hands.

"The dead live, eh?" snorted Sir Commander Galan. "If that is so, then should you not be on your knees praising the gods for such a miracle rather than wasting Lord Mitor's time?"

"These...creatures...do not live," said Romaria. "They are dead things, given a semblance, a mockery, of life through dark necromancy."

"So, the dead walk in my lands," said Mitor. "Bah! You say they were raised by dark magic. Who wielded this dark magic, eh?"

"Some wizard, some renegade," said Romaria. "Perhaps from Briault."

"I confess!" said Simonian. "I am the guilty party! I had hoped to use these walking dead men as an entertainment at Lady Rachel's wedding!" A fresh gale of laughter answered his jest. Even Rachel chuckled.

Romaria smiled. "Laugh if you wish, Lord Mitor...but I assure you, when you see these creatures with your own eyes, the laughter will stop."

"I have heard enough," declared Mitor. "I will not be made mock in my own hall. Corpses crawling from their graves? Bah! If you come to bring me lies, woman, why not bring some more interesting ones...gold falling from the sky, perhaps, or a forest where jewels grow upon trees?"

Romaria's smile grew thin. "Because gold does not fall from the sky, nor have I found any trees that bear gems in place of fruit. I bring you no lies, Lord Mitor...ignore my warnings at your peril."

"Enough," said Mitor. "This audience is over. I wish a private word with my sister and with Sir Albron. Once we are finished, Sir Albron will escort our...guests...to their chambers. Now, be gone."

Rachel climbed the steps to the dais, and Sir Albron took her arm. For an instant revulsion touched Rachel's features, and then she smiled. Mitor's guards came forward to escort Mazael and his companions from the hall. The audience was over.

CHAPTER 8
RACHEL'S LOVE

"That went well," said Gerald.

"I hope you're joking," said Mazael. He looked over Castle Cravenlock's courtyard, watching as the servants and armsmen went about their business. "If you aren't, then your wits have gone addled."

"I confess, Mazael, for years I thought your stories about your brother were exaggerations," said Gerald, "but now I see that you were generous! There is no way that Lord Mitor could hope to defeat Lord Richard in battle."

"Sir Gerald is correct," said Romaria. "Such a slug as Lord Mitor isn't fit to rule a dunghill, let alone the Grim Marches."

Mazael snorted and turned to Cramton. "I'm sorry Lord Mitor would not pay more. The wreck of your livelihood deserves more than one hundred crowns."

Cramton gave Mazael a wan smile. "It will do, my lord knight. After all, I am grateful to the gods we live at all! Thank you, my lord knight, for everything. If you ever need a favor, just come to me or my own. We can't ever repay you."

"I'll remember that," said Mazael. He caught a passing armsman by the elbow. "Take this man to his family. See that they're given comfortable quarters. Lord Mitor has promised them work in the castle. Once they are settled in their new chambers, take them to the head steward."

The armsman started to sneer a response, then got a good look at Mazael's face. He bowed and hurried away with Cramton.

"Idiot," said Mazael. "What sort of fools has this Sir Albron Eastwater trained?"

"Numerous fools," said Sir Gerald. "We saw quite a few in the town."

"Sir Nathan would never have allowed these ruffians into the garrison," said Mazael. "Maybe that's why Mitor dismissed him. My brother seems to want bully boys in his armies, not soldiers."

"Aye," said Gerald, "and how long do you think those bully boys will stand up to Lord Richard's horsemen?"

"I fear we're going to find out," said Mazael. "Lady Romaria, I regret my brother's rudeness."

Romaria shrugged. "You warned me, didn't you? In truth, I expected little help from him. If I'm to find this renegade necromancer, I shall have to do so on my own."

"What of this Briaultan wizard, this Simonian of Briault?" said Mazael. "Do you think it is him?"

Gerald laughed. "Lord Mitor has surrounded himself with...ah, how did you put it, Mazael? A covey of clucking hens? Likely Simonian is likely another clucking fool."

"No," said Mazael. "He's no fool. I think he has his own game."

"What would it gain him to unleash dark magic in the lands of the lord he serves?" said Gerald.

"Who knows? It would be part of some wizard's trickery, no doubt," said Mazael. "Once again, no insult, Timothy."

Timothy smiled. "Once again, none taken, my lord knight."

"You were staring at him rather oddly, my lady," said Mazael. "Both him and Sir Albron. My sister seems infatuated with the fool. Don't tell me he's drawn you into his spell as well."

Romaria laughed. "I prefer real men in my bed, not crowing roosters or clucking hens." She shrugged. "I can't say why. There was something strange around them. I couldn't tell you what it was. They were just...odd."

"Well, Simonian is strange enough," said Mazael. "I'll wager this Sir Albron Eastwater is just another fool..."

The door behind them creaked. Mazael spun, saw a hulking shadow in the doorway, and his hand shot to Lion's hilt. Then the shadow stepped forward and resolved into Sir Albron Eastwater.

He smiled, exposing brilliant white teeth. "I see you were speaking of me." He looked at Mazael and frowned. "Did I startle you? My apologizes." Rachel followed him, her arm in his.

"No need for apologizes," said Mazael. "Preparedness...is something I have been taught with great force, time and time again."

Sir Albron laughed. He did not look as young as Mazael had thought. Wings of silver rose from his temples, and fine lines chiseled his face. He was a big man, but moved with a light grace, as if he didn't carry the weight of his muscle and bone.

"Ah, I know it well," Albron said. "I have seen my share of wars as well."

"Albron is a great fighter," said Rachel. She stared up at her betrothed with worshipful adoration, all trace of her earlier revulsion gone.

"Is that so?" said Mazael.

Sir Albron smiled. "Lord Mitor has given you guest quarters in the King's Tower." That was good, at least. The King's Tower held the most comfortable rooms in the castle. "I would be pleased to tell you my history on the way, if you're curious."

"I should like that," said Mazael. He wondered what sort of man had replaced Sir Nathan Greatheart as armsmaster of Castle Cravenlock.

"This way," said Sir Albron.

"I know the way," said Mazael. "I used to live here."

Sir Albron laughed. "Of course...I had forgotten." He walked towards the King's Tower, Rachel on his arm. "Sir Gerald and I have something in common. We both come from Knightrealm."

"You do?" said Gerald. "From where do you hail?"

"Krago Town, south of Ironcastle," said Sir Albron.

Gerald frowned. "Krago Town?" he said. "I fear you have me, Sir Albron. I have never heard of the place."

Albron laughed. "Few have, indeed. There's not much there. It lies on the north end of the swamplands between the hills of Stillwater, the Great Southern Forest, and the Mastarian Mountains."

"I know of the region," said Gerald, "but I don't recall ever visiting. It has something of an ill reputation. I did meet a noble from that region once, Lord Alfred Karagon. Unpleasant fellow, as I recall."

"That is not surprising," said Sir Albron. "The main road from Knightcastle does not pass through Krago Town, and the surrounding lands are full of thick swamps. Naturally all sorts of queer tales have sprung up over the years." He laughed again. "And if you've met Lord Alfred, then the bad reputation of Krago Town is secured. He really is quite an unpleasant old fellow, to say the least."

"How does a knight from a backwater become armsmaster of Castle Cravenlock?" said Mazael. "That's a tale for the jongleurs, certainly."

"Doubly so," said Albron, "for I was not born noble. My mother was a milkmaid, and my father worked in tanner's shop, you could say. I fear I grew up with the crudest of country boors. I took service with Lord Alfred's guard, maintaining the peace, chasing bandits, and slaying the Karwulf monsters when they raided over the Stillwater hills."

"The Karwulf are not monsters," said Romaria. "They're different from humans, aye, just as the Elderborn, but that doesn't make them monsters."

Albron smiled. "You speak truly, my lady. But you of Deepforest Keep have a different way. You have lived in harmony with the forest peoples since...why, since the old kingdom of Dracaryl fell to the Malrags. But we of Krago must defend our own lands in our own way."

Romaria frowned, but said nothing.

"At any rate," said Sir Albron, "I served as an armsman in Lord Alfred's guard until the uprising began on the Grim Marches fifteen years past. When Sir Belifane called for men to accompany him to Castle Cravenlock, I volunteered and rode with him. And then Lord Richard rose up against Lord Adalon, and I saw more of war than I ever did in Krago Town. Sir Belifane and Lord Adalon fought well," Mazael held back his laugh, "but in the end it was for naught. Sir Belifane was slain and Lord Adalon defeated. But your father, Sir Mazael, was a good and kindly man. I saved his life during the battle, and in return, he knighted me and gave me lands along the Eastwater. When Lord Adalon died a few years later, I swore to his son Lord Mitor, and have served him ever since."

"Indeed a tale for the jongleurs," said Mazael. He thought how a man like Mattias Comorian would mock the tale. "Yet how did you become armsmaster? I thought that Sir Nathan Greatheart had filled the post most admirably."

Sir Albron sighed. "Sir Nathan was growing older, Sir Mazael. I know that you thought most highly of him, yet Lord Mitor felt he could no longer adequately carry out his many duties."

"Mitor felt?" said Mazael. "Mitor doesn't know which end of a sword is the blade and which is the hilt. He knows less about war than my father."

"Perhaps," said Albron, "but he is the Lord of Castle Cravenlock, and his judgment is the correct one."

Mazael frowned. "Why did Lord Mitor choose you as the new armsmaster?"

Sir Albron shrugged. "Experience, mostly. I had fought in the battles of Lord Richard's uprising. And loyalty, perhaps. I had served Sir Belifane to the bitter end, and was sworn directly to the house of Cravenlock." That explained it. Sir Nathan would never have given a fool like Brogan an officer's rank. "Sir Nathan was a good man, and loyal...it was most kind of Lord Mitor to let Nathan live out his remaining years in peace."

"It's a good thing Sir Nathan still has years remaining," said

Mazael. "I think you could take a lesson from him."

"Mazael!" said Rachel.

"Is that so?" said Albron, smiling. "I understand you are a most accomplished knight, Sir Mazael. I would be pleased to take any advice you can offer."

"The armsmen I saw in the village were an undisciplined mess. You heard what I said to Mitor," said Mazael.

"I did," said Sir Albron. "In all truth, Sir Mazael, I thought the criticism was unwarranted."

"And why is that?" said Mazael. "Brogan tried to rape Cramton's barmaids, burned his inn, and tried to kill his family when he refused. Cramton's youngest daughter is three. Three, Sir Albron! Tell me, do the armsmen of the Cravenlocks now swear to terrorize innocent children as part of their oath?"

Sir Albron smiled. "Hardly. Yet...peasants are an undisciplined, unruly...filthy lot. They are much like...oh, small children, I suppose, or frightened little mice that scurry about and spend their time pursuing cheese. That is why the gods created the nobility, Sir Mazael. The peasantry needs a strong, firm hand."

"Interesting words, coming from a man who was once a peasant himself," said Romaria.

Albron flashed his brilliant white smile at her. "Yet I improved myself, and rose above my meager beginnings. Most peasants...alas, are incapable of such. Ah! Here were are."

The King's Tower loomed above them like a granite fist. "Sir Gerald, you have been given the apartments on the top floor as Lord Mitor's honored guest," said Sir Albron. "Lady Romaria, the chambers on the fourth floor are yours. A wardrobe has been provided. I suggest you dress and prepare yourself for the feast. Sir Mazael, your rooms are on the third." Sir Albron bowed and disengaged himself from Rachel's arm. "My lady, my love, I must be on my way. Duty calls." He bowed, kissed her fingers, and set off in a quick walk for the stables.

"What an utter ass," said Mazael.

"He is not!" said Rachel.

"I'm sure he has many fine qualities," said Mazael. "Perhaps he will display them someday." Rachel glared at him and stalked away.

Sir Albron mounted a horse and rode for the barbican. His steed moved with a light walk. Mazael frowned. Sir Albron was a big man ...yet the horse...

"What is it?" said Gerald.

"The horse," said Mazael, shaking his head. "It's moving too fast for a rider Sir Albron's size. Ah, perhaps he's lighter than he looks."

Romaria laughed. "It wouldn't surprise me if those bulges in his arms were clumped rags." Timothy snorted and covered his mouth.

CHAPTER 9
MAZAEL'S FATHERS

Mazael examined his reflection in the silvered looking glass. He wore boots, clean trousers, and a tunic. Over his shoulders went a black cloak embroidered with the three-swords sigil of Cravenlock.

The quarters Mitor had given them were comfortable enough. Tapestries covered the stark stone walls, depicting scenes of Castle Cravenlock's past glories, and a large double bed rested against one wall, covered with a feather mattress and an enormous pile of pillows. A huge paneled wardrobe, a large desk, and a pair of chairs made from red oak and carved with Cravenlock sigil stood against the walls. Mazael had spent the greater part his life sleeping on cold ground under the stars and found the chambers excessive. Gerald, though, was right at home.

Mazael picked up his worn sword belt and wrapped it around his waist. Lion dangled from his left hip and a dagger rested on his right. Lion was ornate enough for a feast and dagger was necessary as an eating utensil. He grimaced and rubbed his beard. He was rarely adverse to feasting, revelry, and wine. But eating at Mitor's table would leave a sour taste in his mouth.

But there was nothing to do but to get on with it. With luck, he and Gerald could depart for Knightcastle within a week. He felt a twinge of anger when he thought of Rachel. She had changed in the last fifteen years, and not for the better. Her betrothal to smiling Sir Albron Eastwater proved that.

Mazael shook his head and left his chambers, intending to see if Gerald was ready yet. Gerald took more time to primp than the vainest of noble ladies.

He rounded a curve in the staircase and almost walked into Romaria. She stumbled, and his hand shot out and caught her arm.

"Gods of the earth," swore Romaria. "You're fast." She grinned. "I thought I was going to have a headlong tumble."

"We can't have that," said Mazael. Her bare arm felt warm and soft under his fingers, despite the corded muscles beneath her skin. She wore a gown of patterned green and blue fabric that left her arms bare. It suited her very well. Around her neck was a stole of black fur. Mazael laughed.

"What?" said Romaria. She did not try to pull away from him.

Mazael reached up with his free hand and fingered the black fur. "It seems you've found more than one use for that cat."

Romaria grinned. "I cleaned it this afternoon." Her smile turned mischievous. "So, are you going to let go of my arm...or do you want to take a different sort of tumble together?"

Mazael slid his hand over her shoulder and onto her other arm. "Right here, against the wall? Direct, aren't you?"

"What, would you have me play the blushing virgin?" said Romaria.

"You? I didn't think so?" said Mazael. He wanted to kiss her.

"So perceptive," said Romaria. "For a man, that is. And so good with that fancy sword, and so fast. I think you might be worthy of me."

"I should hope so," said Mazael.

Romaria smiled. "Your friend would be shocked if he saw us."

"Gerald shocks easily. I've tried to train him out of it," Mazael said. Romaria's strange ice-blue eyes sparkled, a flush spreading through her pale cheeks. "Gods, you have lovely eyes."

"Do you say that to all your women?" said Romaria.

"No, I usually say 'how much for the night?'" said Mazael.

Romaria went silent, and Mazael realized that he had blundered.

Then she laughed, her shoulders shaking with amusement. "You would, wouldn't you? What a strange man you are! It wouldn't surprise me if you'd had every whore from here to Knightcastle, yet you put your life on the line for those peasants in the town. You stood up to Mitor, when no one else was brave enough."

Mazael shrugged. "Mitor's cruel and stupid. What right does he have to terrorize his peasants? As for the whores, well, I have urges, as does any man, and the women need to eat, as does anyone. I always pay them triple what they ask. I can afford it, and it seems only fair."

"How generous. The Church should make you into a saint."

Mazael laughed. "Somehow, I doubt it."

"I wonder if you're the one the Seer saw," said Romaria. "I wouldn't mind that, not at all." Her voice had that odd note of fear again.

"Who?" said Mazael.

Romaria's grin reappeared, as wicked as the flashing edge of a sword. "No one." She leaned up, gave him a quick kiss on the lips, and pulled away. "At least...not yet."

"I'm disappointed," said Mazael. "Could you trip again?"

Romaria laughed. "Maybe later. After all, we wouldn't want to shock Sir Gerald."

"I suppose I'll see you at the feast, then," said Mazael.

Romaria grinned. "I look forward to it." Then she was gone.

Mazael leaned against the wall and blew out a sigh. He'd had numerous women in his life, but never an encounter quite like that. Then again, he'd never met a woman like Romaria before.

He shook his head. Nothing clouded the mind like lust, and he needed his wits clear for Lord Mitor's feast. After a few moments, he put Romaria from his mind and climbed the stairs. He thought of what Gerald would have said if he had seen them together and laughed.

A moment later he reached Gerald's door. "No, no," he heard Gerald say. "Fetch that tunic...no, the blue one, I say!"

Gerald stood before the mirror, his torso bare. His hair and his mustache had been trimmed with razor precision, his boots polished to mirror sheen. His sword lay across the bed, sharpened and polished.

Wesson stood at the wardrobe, digging through a pile of tunics. He gave Mazael a despairing glance.

"Ah...good...Sir Mazael!" said Gerald, shaking out a tunic. "I didn't expect you so early."

"Actually, I'm late," said Mazael.

Gerald pulled the tunic on, stared at his reflection, shook his head, and pulled the tunic off. Wesson stifled a groan.

"Really?" said Gerald. "So soon? Were you delayed?"

"What?" said Mazael. "I suppose so."

Gerald grunted. "Say, Wesson, hand me the, ah...red one. Red and blue usually go well together." Wesson grunted and began to dig through the pile of tunics.

Mazael sat on the edge of the bed. "This is fastidious, even for you."

"Well, I haven't mentioned it before," said Gerald. "But my father considered arranging a marriage for me with one of the ladies in the southern half of the Grim Marches."

A chill tugged at Mazael. He glanced out the window, and lurched to his feet, eyes wide. A sea of blood covered the plains surrounding the castle, churning in froth-crowned waves, splashing and staining the castle walls...

"Mazael?" said Gerald. "Is something wrong?"

Mazael blinked. He saw the plains and the town through the window, and nothing more. "What...nothing. I almost sat on your sword, that's all."

Gerald laughed. "That would make for an unpleasant wound."

"What were you saying about a marriage?" said Mazael. He sat in one of the chairs, away from the window.

Gerald scrutinized his reflection, tugged at his mustache, and smiled. "Well, I am the only one of my father's sons to remain unwed. Before he sent us to the Grim Marches, he suggested that a marriage with one of the daughters of the southern Marcher lords might lie in my future."

Mazael laughed. "So, a future Lady Roland might feast in Mitor's hall tonight?" A gleam came into his eye. "I hear that Lord Marcus has another daughter."

Gerald shuddered. "The gods forbid! If she's anything like her sister, I fear that I would rather join a celibate order."

"You realize, of course, it's all intrigue?" said Mazael. "Your father would marry you to my sister if she wasn't betrothed already. He wants an alliance with the Cravenlocks, should they rise up against the Mandragons."

Gerald sighed. "Wesson! My surcoat, please. I'm well aware of that. You have something of an advantage over me, I fear. You left Lord Mitor's household, so your brother has no hold over you and cannot command you to marry." Mazael shuddered at the thought. "Yet you are not one of my father's vassals, nor are you of his blood. You could marry whomever you wish. You could marry a comely peasant wench, and no one would object, though I imagine the court would whisper."

Mazael snorted. "Once you've been hit with a sword a few times, words lose their sting."

"Truly," said Gerald. "Yet I must marry as my father commands, and I can only hope for a wife who does not have the countenance of a sow and the temperament of a porcupine."

"Good luck," said Mazael.

"A pity your sister is already betrothed," said Gerald, pulling on his surcoat, the fine blue cloth embroidered with the greathelm of Roland in silver thread. "She seems quite a proper lady, and is very comely, to boot. Wesson, my sword and belt, please."

Mazael tugged his fingers through his beard. "Betrothed to that smiling fool Sir Albron. You ought to court her anyway. Gods know you'd make a better husband. Sir Albron would likely stand there and smile while you wooed her away."

Gerald tucked his dagger into his belt. "Well...I agree with you, but it hardly seems honorable..."

"Honorable," said Mazael. "Albron has all the honor of a jackal. I wonder if Rachel is merely infatuated. She gets cow-eyed whenever he comes near."

Gerald tossed a blue cloak over his shoulders with a flourish. "Well, that's a consideration for later. Right now, there is a feast with food and wine and music awaiting. I, for one, do not want to keep it waiting any longer than necessary."

Mazael laughed. "Then by all means, let's go."

They descended the steps of the King's Tower. Mazael passed the spot where he had walked into Romaria and grinned.

Only a thin line of light glimmered in the western sky when they entered the castle's courtyard. The doors to the central keep stood open, torchlight spilling out. Six armsmen in formal armor stood on either side of the doors, and four other men waited nearby. One lumbered ponderously, while the other moved with fluid grace. Mazael turned towards them, a smile spreading across his face.

"Who is it, Mazael?" said Gerald.

"Sir Gerald Roland," said Mazael, "may I introduce Master Othar, court wizard of Castle Cravenlock, and Sir Nathan Greatheart, armsmaster...former armsmaster, of Castle Cravenlock...and the men who managed to keep me from getting killed as a child."

Master Othar boomed laughter. Six feet tall and half as wide, a tangled white beard covered his double chin. Othar walked with the ponderous majesty of a lumbering elephant, barely using the cane in his meaty right fist. The much shorter and thinner Timothy deBlanc walked after him.

"Well, boy!" said Othar. "You've gotten taller."

"And you've gotten fatter," said Mazael.

Othar laughed and slapped his belly with his free hand. "Aye, boy, so I have! At my age, I reserve the right to eat any damn thing I want. Sir Nathan here has been telling me that he expects my heart to burst any day now for the last twenty years. Well, my heart's still pounding along just fine." He laughed again. "Though I do expect I'll make a misery for the gravediggers when I finally go."

"That is not something to jest about," said a deep voice. Sir Nathan Greatheart was lean and gaunt. Deep lines marked his weathered face, and ropes of sinewy muscle corded his arms. The hilt of a two-handed greatsword, bigger than Romaria's bastard blade, rose from over his shoulder. A young man, Nathan's squire, Mazael assumed, stood behind the old knight. "I have been admonishing you to take better care of yourself for twenty years. I cannot recall a single time when you heeded my advice. Mazael."

"Sir Nathan," said Mazael.

"Sir Mazael, I should say," said Nathan. He smiled, something he did rarely. "You have earned that title. Even here, we have heard tales of your exploits during the Mastarian war."

"Thank you," said Mazael.

"Sir Nathan and I have been visiting the villages north of here for the last few days," said Othar, "raising fresh men for Lord Mitor's army. When we returned earlier today, it seems you were the talk of the town. According to one peasant, you cut your way through a thousand Mandragon soldiers and snatched Lady Rachel from their grasp."

"It was more like thirty," said Mazael. "And Sir Gerald helped."

"And then, when you return in triumph to Castle Cravenlock, you save an innocent innkeeper and his wife from unjust execution at the hands of a cruel knight," said Othar. "Sounds like a jongleur's song, boy! You have had a few busy days. I told you, Nathan, this one's destined for legend."

Remembering the sorry scene made Mazael angry all over again. "Captain Brogan was a cruel fool. He should have been scraping dung from the stable floors, not commanding men. And for Albron to give a man like that free reign in the village, gods, that went from mere foolishness to stupidity."

"Albron and I have our disagreements," said Nathan. "The appointment of Brogan stands among them."

Othar snorted. "It's possible that the gods have made worse men, but not many."

Mazael grunted and looked at the sky. The stars had begun to come out. "How are things here, really?"

"What do you mean?" said Othar.

Mazael made a see-saw motion with his hand. "I talk to Rachel and get one version of events. I talk to Mitor and get grandiose ramblings. I talked to Sir Tanam, briefly, and he accused Rachel of witchcraft and sorcery. What is happening here, truly?"

Sir Nathan sighed. "Mazael, things have not been well at Castle Cravenlock since Lord Richard rose up against your father Lord Adalon. You know that."

Mazael nodded.

"In truth, I think things have not been well here since Lord Adalon married Lady Arissa Dreadjon, your mother. No man was more kind and generous than your father, Mazael, but he was weak. It shames me to say it of the lord I served for most my life, but he was not a man of strong will, a quality Lady Arissa possessed in abundance. She rode over him without mercy. Were it not for her, I believe Lord

Adalon would have surrendered the liege lordship of the Grim Marches to Lord Richard without struggle," said Sir Nathan.

"Oft times the sorrows of the present are rooted in the miseries of the past," said Timothy.

"Ah...the writings of the magister Aristor. I see you are familiar with the works of the great wizards. Very good, young man," said Othar. Timothy beamed.

"What is happening now?" said Mazael. "The Grim Marches were peaceful when I left."

"I thought Mitor would be content as Lord of Castle Cravenlock," said Nathan. "Then that whispering schemer Simonian came..."

"No," said Othar. "It began earlier, when Albron came..."

"You are right," said Sir Nathan. "Albron came to Castle Cravenlock six years ago..."

"Six years?" said Mazael. "Albron told me that he had fought in the uprising, and received his knighthood from my father."

Nathan grimaced. "A lie. Albron is full of them. He may have fought in the uprising. Thousands did. But he did not set foot in Castle Cravenlock until six years past. He took service as an armsman. Somehow he gained Lady Rachel's favor, and Lord Mitor knighted him after a year. I wanted him gone from the garrison. The man had less truth in him than a thief. Yet he courted Lady Rachel, and she insisted that he stay."

"Then Simonian came," said Othar. "Watch yourself around that one, Mazael my boy. He's sly and powerful. It would not surprise me if he knows black arts."

"Simonian came three years past," said Nathan. "I urged Lord Mitor to banish him. Foreign wizards are notorious for knowledge of dark arts. From time to time the magisters simply assassinate those they suspect of practicing forbidden magic. It is legal for them to do so, sanctioned by both Church and king. I feared Lord Mitor would become caught in Simonian's eventual fall."

"Mitor bobs his fat head up and down whenever that wizard speaks," said Mazael.

"Lord Mitor made him court wizard," said Othar, scowling, "but he carries out none of the duties. Simonian is often gone for weeks at a time. I continue on, as I always have, and neither Simonian nor Lord Mitor seems to care. After a few months of this, Lord Mitor demanded harsher taxes of the local peasantry to pay for his mercenaries. Sir Nathan protested, calling it banditry. So Lord Mitor dismissed him..."

"And replaced him with Sir Albron Eastwater. A liar, but a liar that would carry out Mitor's instructions without question," said Mazael.

"Yes," said Sir Nathan.

"Are Albron and Simonian in league together?" said Mazael.

Othar shrugged. "It is possible. If they are, Simonian is the greater. When they disagree, Albron always backs down."

"What about this business with Sir Tanam Crowley and Rachel's abduction?" said Mazael.

"Gods," swore Sir Nathan. "If Albron and Lord Mitor had listened to me, it would never have happened. Albron had holes in his guards that an army could stroll through. And if Lord Mitor hadn't planned to take Crowley captive..."

"What?" said Mazael. Rachel certainly hadn't mentioned that. "Rachel told me that Lord Richard had sent Crowley to offer Toraine Mandragon in marriage. Mitor rebuffed him, Sir Tanam rode back to Swordgrim, returned to begin dickering, and rode away with Rachel!"

"That's almost what happened," said Othar. He pulled a battered wooden pipe from a pocket of his robes and stuffed it with tobacco leaves from his belt. A brief spell kindled the pipe, and Othar took a long pull, sighing in satisfaction. "Lady Rachel neglected to add that Lord Mitor planned to capture Crowley and hang him in the town's square."

"Gods of heaven!" said Mazael. "If he had...nothing could have stopped war. Lord Richard and the Black Dragon would have fallen on Castle Cravenlock like a storm out of hell. Mitor would find himself dangling from a gibbet. Gods! Sir Tanam might have seized Rachel out of fear for his life!" Mazael wanted to kill someone. Preferably Mitor

"Oh, yes," said Othar, puffing on his pipe. He wiggled his fingers, whispering a spell, and the smoke rising from his pipe formed the ghostly image of a noose. "Simonian and Sir Albron had been telling Mitor lies of grandeur for years...how he deserved the liege lordship of the Grim Marches, how Lord Richard was nothing but a murdering usurper..."

"Yet they failed to remind Lord Mitor how the Dragonslayer spared his life," said Nathan. "Another man would have killed every one of the Cravenlocks."

"Truly," said Othar, "but tell that to Lord Mitor. Simonian and Albron have filled his head to bursting with these foolish dreams. I'm afraid this business with the Old Crow has sealed the matter. There will be war. Lord Mitor will charge Lord Richard with the abduction of Lady Rachel...and Lord Richard claims..."

"What?" said Mazael. He thought of Sir Tanam's charge of "witchcraft and sorcery", Romaria's tales of walking dead men, and Othar's suspicions of Simonian. Something clicked together in his head. "What does Lord Richard claim?"

Othar raised an eyebrow. "He claims that members of House Cravenlock are practicing ungodly witchcraft and unholy sorcery. Utterly absurd, of course..."

Mazael shook his head. "No, it's not. It's not Mitor or Rachel or Marcelle. It's Simonian who's doing this 'vile sorcery'. On my way to the castle, I met a woman named Romaria Greenshield..."

Nathan blinked. "One of Lord Athaelin's sisters?"

"His daughter," said Mazael. "He sent her north to find and deal with a renegade wizard. She claims that dark magic is loose in the Great Southern Forest, that corpses...zuvembies, she called them, rise to kill. I'm inclined to believe her. She seems a remarkable woman."

"Mazael suspected before that a 'wizard's trickery' lay behind the troubles," said Gerald. "No insult, of course."

"None taken," said Othar and Timothy together.

"I would not find it hard to believe that a creature like Simonian traffics with demons and conjures dark magic," said Sir Nathan.

"Then let us march into the great hall and put an end to him right now," said Mazael.

"I taught you better than that," said Sir Nathan. "We have suspicions, but no proof. Lady Romaria claims to have seen dead men rising. The folk of Deepforest Keep are known for strange things. Master Othar and several other visiting wizards have scoured Castle Cravenlock and the surrounding lands for dark magic and have had found nothing. For all we know, Lord Richard has seized upon this tale of witchcraft to rid himself of Lord Mitor once and for all. The Dragonslayer has mercy in him, but far more ruthlessness than compassion."

"You're right," said Mazael. "But if Simonian is here for a benevolent purpose, I'll believe it when I see pigs flying over the castle."

"I as well," said Sir Nathan. "But we have suspicions, suppositions, and rumors. Not fact. We may believe what we will, but Lord Mitor will never believe us without proof."

"Damnation," said Mazael.

"Speaking of messes," said Master Othar, "why did you come back to Castle Cravenlock? You were always good at staying out of the messes of other people...but you had an unfailing tendency to create messes of your own, as I recall."

Mazael laughed. "That's true enough." He told Sir Nathan and Master Othar everything that had happened in the last few months.

"So, Lord Malden plans to involve himself our mess?" said Othar.

"I expected as much," said Sir Nathan. "Lord Malden has never forgiven Lord Richard for his son's death. Pardons, Sir Gerald, but

Lord Malden would welcome vengeance against Lord Richard."

"None taken, Sir Nathan," said Gerald. "I know my father. But I am sure he will see reason."

"And Lord Alamis Castanagent will not sit by while a war rages on the eastern borders of his lands," said Sir Nathan. "And if Lord Alamis involves himself, then so will every great lord in the kingdom."

"The king would have to take a hand," said Othar.

Sir Nathan sighed. "And then we will have war across the kingdom."

Mazael blinked. For an instant he saw blood gushing from within the castle keep, bursting from the windows, and pouring down the stone walls in crimson rivers. He blinked again and shook his head.

"Is something amiss?" said Sir Nathan.

"No," said Mazael. "I've been suffering from headaches recently."

Othar laughed. "Too much ale, I'll warrant."

"Do not project your bad habits onto Sir Mazael," said Sir Nathan.

"No, it's not ale," said Mazael. "I haven't had enough to make me drunk since I left Knightcastle."

"I could give you an elixir," said Master Othar.

"If they still trouble me tomorrow," said Mazael.

"Let us speak of happier things," said Sir Nathan. "Master Othar and I have not seen you in fifteen years, Sir Mazael, and the gods have decided to bring us together again. Let us commiserate and share what has happened over the years."

"Truly," said Othar. "All this talk of war and necromancy spoils my appetite. A man can't eat properly when he's worried."

Sir Nathan raised an eyebrow. "That has never stopped you before."

Othar shrugged. "It is the principle of the matter."

"Indeed. Sir Mazael...there is something I would ask of you," said Sir Nathan.

"What is it?" said Mazael.

"Come here, Adalar," said Sir Nathan. Nathan's squire stepped forward. The boy was about thirteen, with brown eyes, a narrow face, and a grave expression.

"This is your son!" said Mazael.

Nathan smiled. "Yes."

"But you were certain that you and Lady Leah would never have children," said Mazael.

A shadow passed over Nathan's gaunt face. "I...was wrong, it seems. Leah conceived a year or so after Lord Richard's victory. Nine months later she gave birth to Adalar. The...birth went hard. Othar tended her, and she lived through it, but..."

"It took most of her strength," said Othar, holding his pipe in one hand. "I thought she would pull through...but, the gods have mercy, she died five months later."

"I'm sorry," said Mazael. He remembered Sir Nathan's wife very well. She had always given Mazael a treat when he had accompanied Sir Nathan to his keep.

"The gods give with one hand and take with the other," said Nathan. "It had always been her fondest wish to have children." Nathan looked away for a moment. "Regardless, I have a request to ask of you, Sir Mazael. I ask that you take Adalar for your squire."

"Squire?" said Mazael. "Why me? Surely you could find some great knight to take Adalar as a squire. I am sworn to Lord Malden, and spend most my time riding about fulfilling his commands..."

"That is why I want you to take him as your squire," said Sir Nathan. "I have raised my son as best I know how, and now it is time for another knight to complete his training. You are the best knight for that task. Granted, you are often reckless, and have several bad habits." Gerald smiled. "But you are the best sword, the best fighter, I have ever met. And you fulfill the true spirit of a knight's vows, as your actions against Sir Tanam and Brogan show. Too many knights are hollow suits of armor, following the letter of vows they do not believe."

"Sir Albron Eastwater," said Mazael.

Nathan nodded. "Aye. He offered to take Adalar as his squire. Do you think I would entrust my son's training to that one?"

That decided Mazael. "Very well." He drew Lion. "Kneel." Adalar knelt, his head bowed. Mazael spun his sword and placed the flat of the blade on Adalar's left shoulder. "Adalar Greatheart," he said. He tried to remember how the oath went.

Fortunately, it came. "Do you swear to serve me in all things, to obey me without question, to care for my weapons, mounts, and other possessions, and to pay me due respect?"

"Yes, sir knight," said Adalar. His voice cracked on the second word. The boy grimaced and spoke again. "Yes, I swear, Sir Mazael."

Mazael tapped Adalar and switched the blade to the boy's right shoulder. "And I swear to feed and keep you, to train in you in the use of weapons and horses, and to teach in you in all the ways of a knight. Do you accept my oath?"

"Yes, Sir Mazael," said Adalar.

"Splendid," said Mazael. He sheathed Lion and pulled his dagger from his belt. He offered it hilt first to Adalar. "Well, get up, Adalar. You're a squire now."

Adalar took the dagger and stuck it through his belt. He was smiling. "Yes, Sir Mazael. Thank you."

"I'd offer you congratulations," said Gerald, "but I fear you'll come to regret this, after the first time Sir Mazael decides to charge an army by himself."

"Hilarious," said Mazael.

"Wesson should be glad for the reprieve, since he will no longer have to squire for both of us," said Gerald.

"Yes, Sir Gerald," said Wesson. Mazael could not recall ever hearing such sincerity in the boy's voice.

"I am proud of you, my son," said Nathan.

Othar clapped his free hand on Adalar's shoulder. "Very good, my boy! I have no doubt you'll make a splendid squire. You take after your father that way." The old wizard grinned. "You'll make a far better squire than Sir Mazael was, I'll wager."

"No challenge there," said Mazael.

Othar laughter. "Ha! If Sir Mazael rides you too hard, boy, come to me and I'll tell you about the time he broke the leg of Lord Willard Highmarch's eldest son."

Adalar's eyes widened. "You did, Sir Mazael? Robert Highmarch is lord of Highgate now."

Mazael had forgotten about that. "The fool had it coming. His father's armsmaster hadn't trained him to guard for blows below the waist."

"Lord Willard was furious, as I recall," said Sir Nathan.

"Why? I did him a favor. It's good someone taught Robert Highmarch that lesson. If I hadn't, I doubt Lord Willard would have ever had any grandchildren," said Mazael.

Sir Nathan cleared his throat. "Perhaps we should go to the great hall. Lord Mitor will be waiting on us...or upon you and Sir Gerald, rather."

"I wouldn't mind making Lord Mitor wait a little longer, in truth," said Gerald. "I wish my father would meet Lord Mitor before deciding his course. I do not doubt that speaking with Lord Mitor in person would drastically change my father's opinion regarding certain matters."

The guards bowed as they stepped through the keep doors. Lord Mitor, his wife, and his advisors waited within the anteroom to the great hall, clad in their richest finery. Mitor looked like a pear in his green doublet, and Marcelle's gown somehow made her look more vulpine. Rachel was beautiful in a green gown that matched her eyes, but Mazael thought Sir Albron's arm around her waist ruined her appearance.

Simonian of Briault stood in the corner, still in his rough brown robes, shadows playing across the craggy planes of his face. Mazael saw the amusement in his murky eyes.

Lord Marcus quivered with indignation. "You are late! One does not keep the liege lord of the Grim Marches waiting!"

Mitor waved his hand. "Bah! One does not keep you waiting for your food, that is what you mean to say, Marcus. Sir Mazael has merely ensured that we enter a few moments late, as is appropriate to our high stations."

"That's exactly it," said Mazael.

"I was afraid you were not coming, Sir Mazael," said Rachel.

"Why? I wouldn't miss this for all of Lord Richard's gold," said Mazael.

Simonian laughed. "That is generous of you, my lord knight. Richard Mandragon has quite a lot of gold."

Mitor's bloodshot eyes narrowed. His pallor was worse than it had been this morning. Mazael wondered if Mitor was drunk. "That is my gold, by rights."

"Truly, my lord," said Simonian. "Lord Richard shall soon learn that, to his everlasting sorrow. But if your humble servant may make a suggestion, should you not commence with the feasting? Your subjects within the hall grow anxious, my lord, and wish to bask in the light of your wisdom."

Flatterers and liars, Mazael thought.

"Do not presume to advise Lord Mitor, sorcerer," said Sir Commander Galan.

Simonian bowed his head. "Forgive me, my lord knight, but I cannot wield sword and shield as you do, or lead armies, or inspire the masses. I can only serve my lord as best I can."

"Do not concern yourself, my friend," said Mitor to Sir Commander Galan. "Simonian only seeks to serve me...and I seek to restore the Justiciar order to its ancient rights in the Grim Marches once I am liege lord. Therefore, we are all of one purpose, no?"

Sir Commander Galan looked anything but pleased. "Very well, Lord Mitor."

"Let us proceed, then," said Mitor. "Mazael, you and Sir Gerald will join me at the high table, as befits my brother and a son of Lord Malden Roland."

"Really," said Mazael. "What of Sir Nathan and Master Othar? They have served the house of Cravenlock well all their lives. Surely they deserve a seat at the high table?"

Mitor snorted. "They are old and have outlived their usefulness to me." Mazael saw Adalar tense at the insult to his father, but the old knight remained calm. "Do not quibble with me, Mazael. After all, once Lord Malden comes to my cause, yes, we shall all indeed be of one purpose."

Sir Nathan bowed. "If you will excuse me, my lords, Master Othar and I must find our places at the benches. Adalar, remain with Sir Mazael."

"Yes, Father," said Adalar.

"Now, shall we feast, or shall we stand here and talk all night?" said Mitor. "Tell the herald to begin."

Armsmen threw open the double doors to the great hall. Mitor's herald banged his staff against the marble floor thrice and called out the names. "Lord Mitor Cravenlock, lord of Castle Cravenlock and liege lord of the Grim Marches. Lady Marcelle Cravenlock, his wife!" Mitor and his wife marched arm in arm down the aisle between the low tables, almost appearing regal.

"Lord Marcus Trand, lord of Roseblood Keep!"

"Mazael," said Rachel, "I'm sorry we exchanged harsh words earlier today. You were only trying to tell me the truth...at least, the truth as you see it...and there are so few people who will be honest with me."

"Now, Rachel," said Albron. "If Sir Mazael has offended you, he should apologize to you, not the other way around." He smiled at Mazael. "True knights should remain courteous to ladies at all times."

"Lord Roget Hunterson, Lord of Hunter's Hall!" Old Lord Roget sighed and began the long shuffle down the great hall.

"Knights are also supposed to speak the truth at all times," said Mazael. "Didn't Lord Mitor...oh, wait, Lord Adalon...tell you that when he knighted you?" Mazael had the satisfaction of seeing Albron's eternal smile turn sour.

"Sir Commander Galan Hawking, Justiciar Knight, Commander of Justiciar Knights in the Grim Marches!" Sir Commander Galan adjusted his blue cloak with a flourish and marched into the hall, boots clacking against the stone floor.

Sir Albron laughed. "Now, now, Sir Mazael. You're setting a poor example for young Adalar Greatheart. We should not bicker like this. It is most unseemly."

"Did Lord Adalon tell you that?" said Mazael. "That would be an interesting trick, since you never met him."

"Mazael," said Rachel. "Please, stop this. Albron will be your brother-in-law within the year."

"Truly," said Sir Albron. "There's no need for such pettiness. I have no doubt that you have a few embellishments in your personal history. Did you really defeat Sir Commander Aeternis in the Mastarian war? Oh, wait, my mistake. That was Sir Mandor Roland, as I recall. And that sword with such a pretty gold lion's head for the hilt? A trophy of battle, or a bauble picked up in some Knightport vendor's stall?"

"Sir Albron Eastwater, armsmaster of Castle Cravenlock, and his betrothed, Lady Rachel Cravenlock, sister of Lord Mitor!"

"Ah," said Albron. "Duty calls. Well, I shall see you at the high table, Sir Mazael, Sir Gerald." He marched away, Rachel on his arm. Mazael wanted to ram Lion into the man's back. Rachel gave Mazael a single sad glance over her shoulder, and then walked with her betrothed to the high table.

"What a remarkably loathsome little man," said Gerald. "Wesson, take note. When you are a knight, never act as Sir Albron did."

"I must apologize for Sir Albron," said a gravelly voice. Simonian stepped out of the shadows. "He has risen high most quickly. Seven years ago he was a common mercenary. Now, he is armsmaster of Castle Cravenlock and betrothed to Lady Rachel. I fear his pride has risen just as high. He is almost unmanageable at times."

"Lord Mitor does not find it so," said Mazael.

Simonian laughed. "Indeed. Why would Sir Albron bite the hand that feeds him? So long as Lord Mitor's star rises, Sir Albron will rise with it."

"Until this ship starts to sink," said Gerald. "Then Albron and all the other rats will swarm out."

This seemed to amuse Simonian. "I had not viewed in that way, my lord knight."

"Sir Gerald Roland, son of Lord Malden Roland!"

Gerald straightened. "Well, that's it, I suppose. Come along, Wesson." Gerald strode down the hall, scrutinizing every noblewoman in sight.

"And what of you, wizard?" said Mazael. "What stripe of rat are you?"

Simonian smiled. "You are direct, are you not? I imagine Sir Tanam Crowley found that out quite well. No doubt our fair young Lady Romaria has accused me of all sorts of vile necromancy. And I shudder to think what Sir Nathan has told you."

"How would you know?" said Mazael.

Simonian spread his callused hands wide. "My lord knight, you know better than that. When there's a plague, or a famine, or a woman births a deformed child, who is first to catch blame? Why, the wizard, of course. The common folk of Briault always believed such twaddle. And a foreign wizard...even better! Fetch the oil and the torches!" Simonian sighed. "I fear I am misjudged and misunderstood on every turn. I am a simple servant. I simply wish to help Lord Mitor reach his full potential, the heights of greatness."

"Really," said Mazael. "I have difficulty connecting Mitor with greatness."

Simonian sighed. "As do I." His murky eyes glimmered. "But you, my lord knight, you're different, aren't you? You always have been, I judge. That fine sword must dance like lightning when you wield it. Who has ever been able to stand against you? None, I should think. Killing comes so naturally to you. And you enjoy it, do you not? Yes, I can see it in your face, in your eyes."

Mazael wanted to draw Lion and silence the wizard. But another part wanted to listen. "What are you babbling about?"

"Potential," said Simonian. "Mitor is nothing. But you, Mazael Cravenlock, you could be so much more. The herald will call your name soon. When he does, why not march up to the dais, draw that magnificent blade, and separate Mitor's ugly head from his fat body?"

Mazael saw it clearly. He saw himself stride up to Mitor, saw Lion flash from its sheath, and saw Mitor's head roll and bounce down the hall.

"Think of it," murmured Simonian. "You could become a greater lord that Mitor ever was. You can end your sister's absurd betrothal to that strutting fool...marry her to your friend Gerald, perhaps. And Mitor deserves to die, does he not? And you want to kill him, I know you do. I see it in your face. You would enjoy it. Do it."

Mazael looked into the hall. He saw Mitor sitting at the high table, fat and weak, his harridan wife perched besides. Around him, Mitor's covey of fools and allies sat and babbled, Rachel caught in their midst like a rose in a ring of thorns. His gaze wandered down the hall and settled upon Sir Nathan and Master Othar. Yes, Mazael could kill Mitor, but what would they say? What example would that set for Adalar?

"What sort of lying serpent are you?" said Mazael. "Mitor's advisor, indeed! What game are you playing? I'll warrant you're the one behind all the rumors of witchcraft and necromancy I've heard!"

"No serpent, I assure you," said Simonian.

"I ought to tell Mitor all this," said Mazael. "Let's see how he reacts when he's confronted with real treason."

Simonian's amusement increased. "He'd never believe you. You do realize that he's terrified of you?"

"Get out of my sight," said Mazael, "else I'll kill you, and deal with the consequences later."

Simonian flinched, then his smile returned. "Yes...I rather believe you would." He bowed and departed for the great hall.

"Sir Mazael Cravenlock," boomed the herald, "brother of Lord Mitor."

"Adalar," said Mazael.

Adalar didn't answer.

"Adalar!"

Adalar twitched. "What...oh, my apologizes, Sir Mazael. My...my attention wandered." He frowned. "Where did everyone go?"

"To the feast," said Mazael. "Didn't you see?"

Adalar's frown deepened. "I...I suppose not."

Mazael stared after Simonian. "Go to your father, and tell him that I gave you permission to attend with him."

"Are you not coming?" said Adalar.

"I feel ill," said Mazael. "The prospect of eating with that pack of serpents is enough to steal anyone's appetite."

"As you command." Sir Nathan had trained Adalar well. The boy walked through the doors and went to his father's side.

Mazael walked out into the comforting coolness of the courtyard. His stomach churned and his head ached, and he felt so tired. Gerald will laugh at this tomorrow, Mazael thought. He went to the King's Tower to find his bed.

CHAPTER 10
THE DREAM

Mazael stood atop the castle's curtain wall and looked over the land.

The Grim Marches had become a desert of cracked earth. The plains lay blasted and dead, the swollen sun hanging in a blood-colored sky. A jumble of broken stone and burned timbers marked the ruins of the town, bleached skeletons strewn about the ruins.

"It all ends like this, eventually."

Mazael turned. "Father?"

Lord Adalon Cravenlock stood next to him. He looked as Mazael remembered, gray-haired and thin, his face careworn. "Yes. I am."

"No," said Mazael. "You're dead. You've been dead for more than ten years."

"True...but I live on through my sons." His voice was sardonic. He had never taken that tone in life. "Come, my son, let's go for a walk. We can catch up, you and I. We have so much to talk about."

"This is a dream," said Mazael.

Lord Adalon nodded. "Most likely. Would you care to find out?" He walked along the rampart wall, Mazael following. Lord Adalon carried a black staff topped with a silver raven, the sun flashing like flame from the dark wood.

Lord Adalon swept his arm out over the wall. "Look at it! An improvement, I'd say."

"The people are dead," said Mazael. "The land is a desert. You have a strange idea of improvement."

Lord Adalon roared with laughter. "Now, if I had a copper coin for every time someone told me that...why, I could buy the world. Several times over. Not strange, my boy, not strange, correct."

"And why is that?" said Mazael.

"Because they're all dead," said Lord Adalon. "Every last one of them. They destroyed each other. It always happens. It always ends this way. The heavens fell when the demons rose up. And again and again men build nations, and destroy themselves in war. Tristafel. Dracaryl. The Kingdom of Storm. All mighty nations, now nothing more than dust." He laughed, his tired eyes sparkling with delight. "Do you know something, Mazael? Do you know something, my son?"

"What?" said Mazael. Lord Adalon had never spoken like this.

"They say dark sorcery ruined Tristafel." Lord Adalon grinned. "But...do you know what? They brought themselves down. The Tristafellin invited in the Great Demon. The wizards wanted more magic. And they created the Demonsouled. They destroyed themselves." He swept his black staff over the plain. "It doesn't matter, my boy. No matter how strong an empire is built, no matter how great a kingdom becomes, those nations are still built of mere men, and mere men always end like this. In utter ruin."

"Why are you speaking this nonsense?" said Mazael.

Lord Adalon smiled. "Come with me."

He hurried down the rampart stairs. The castle's courtyard lay desolate and empty. Something gleamed in the courtyard's scorched dirt, and Lord Adalon bent and picked up a silver dagger. His eyes blazed, and his wrist snapped.

The dagger hurtled for Mazael's face.

"Catch!" said Lord Adalon.

Mazael's right hand snapped up. He caught the dagger by the hilt. The blade quivered an inch from his eye. He threw it aside and reached for Lion.

Lord Adalon laughed. "Hold your wrath. I knew you would catch it."

"How?" said Mazael.

"How old are you now, Mazael? Two-and-thirty years? Getting older, aren't you? When I was that age, I started to slow down. My eyes began to blur, my hands began to shake, and I couldn't move so fast."

He laughed harder. "But not you, my son! Not you! You've only gotten faster. And stronger as well. A fellow your age should start to feel it...aches just beginning in his bones, death starting to chew just a little. But not you. What a fighter you are, Mazael! What a man! No wonder the lady desires you so."

Mazael blinked. Romaria Greenshield stood next to his father, clad in a low-cut black gown. He saw the curves of her breasts and the shape of her hips.

Lord Adalon walked around her, running his hand over her bare shoulders. "She wants you, yes, but she's terrified of you. And you don't even know why, do you?" His fingers tangled in her dark hair. "She's very beautiful, with hair like night...and those eyes. You've never seen eyes like that before, have you? I find her too scrawny, myself. I prefer a woman with more to squeeze. Like your mother, for instance. But Romaria is such a formidable woman. So skilled with that bastard blade. Yet she's helpless against you."

Romaria's bastard sword gleamed in her hand, and she charged him. Mazael snapped his sword out of its scabbard and parried. A dozen blows flashed in half as *many seconds. Then Romaria's sword went flying, and she fell backwards upon the ground, chest heaving with her breath. She raised her arms, as if inviting Mazael to take her.*

"Helpless," *said Lord Adalon.* "They're all helpless against you. That primping dandy Sir Gerald Roland, Sir Nathan the Dull, even the Dragonslayer himself...what are they, next to you? Nothing." *He crooked a finger.* "So sorry to tear you away from your pretty half-breed, but we have a walk to finish. After all, you can take her when you wake up. One more stop."

Romaria vanished. Mazael sheathed Lion and followed his father across the courtyard. Lord Adalon jumped up the keep steps and rapped on the door with his staff. The great doors shuddered and opened with a loud groan.

"Come along, now!" *said Lord Adalon, his voice cheerful.* "There are a few more people I'd like you to meet."

The great hall was empty, the vaulted ceiling arching away into darkness. The high windows glowed a dull red. The metal-shod butt of Lord Adalon's staff clicked against the polished stone floor. He spun to face Mazael. "Tell me, my boy! What do you think?"

"Think of what?" *said Mazael.*

"This! All of it! Lord Mazael, Lord of Castle Cravenlock...now how does that sound, eh?" *Lord Adalon slammed the butt of his staff onto the floor. Ghostly images flitted past, the lords and knights of the Grim Marches came to swear fealty to Lord Mazael Cravenlock. Lord Adalon rapped his staff again, and the images vanished.* "And the only thing that keeps Sir Mazael from becoming Lord Mazael is the feeble fluttering of Mitor's shriveled heart."

"No," *said Mazael.* "I won't kill him."

Lord Adalon snorted. "And why not?"

"Because Sir Nathan and Master Othar taught me better than that," *said Mazael.*

Lord Adalon howled laughter. "So they say it's wrong, then?" *He pointed his staff towards the dais. The silver raven's eyes were red, glowing crystals.* "Come then! Let us just see whose life you have so generously spared!"

They walked to the end of the hall, to the lord's dais.

Mitor Cravenlock sat in the lord's seat, his belly bulging against his fine clothes, his arms and legs like twitching sticks. Rachel sat next to him in the lady's seat, pale and lovely.

"Older brother, younger sister," *said Mazael's father.* "Lord Adalon's baby children!" *He sneered.* "I am so proud!" *He tapped Mitor's stomach with the head of his staff.* "Look at this weakling. I doubt he could lift your sword, Sir Mazael." *Lord Adalon twined the fingers of his free hand in Mitor's hair and yanked back his head.* "And so stupid. So very, very stupid. Lord Richard might mount this head above his gates. I wouldn't. It would make a hideous eyesore." *He let Mitor's head drop and circled to Rachel.*

"And the Lady Rachel Cravenlock," said Lord Adalon. He grinned and caressed her cheek with a finger. "Pretty, yes. But I doubt there's a thought in that comely little head that wasn't put there by Sir Albron! You know, Mazael, if he told her to jump from the castle walls, why, I'm quite certain she would do it! Now wouldn't that be a sight to see?"

"Be quiet," said Mazael.

Lord Adalon laughed. "Oh, that's right! She was your best friend for a time...your only friend. And look what's she's become. Lady Rachel is a vase painted bright on the outside, but empty and dead on the inside." Lord Adalon licked his lips and waggled his eyebrows. "And wanton...do you think she loves Albron for his charming conversation? For his grace and charm? Certainly not! No, she wants him, she lusts for him..."

"Quiet," said Mazael.

Lord Adalon's laughter shrieked off the vaulted ceiling. "Feeling angry, my boy? Want to take that fine sword and ram through my lying heart?" Lion glimmered in Mazael's hand, and Lord Adalon's grin stretched from ear to ear. "Don't kill the messenger! It's very bad form. Is it my fault Mitor is a cruel weakling? Is it my fault that Rachel is an empty-headed little flower?" He leveled his staff at Mazael. "And you're so different from them, aren't you? So much stronger, so much faster, so much better...why, it's hard to believe that you came from the same father."

"Quiet!" roared Mazael.

"They hate you," said Lord Adalon. "Mitor would sell you for power. And Rachel...ah, poor Rachel, how she's drifted from you..."

Mazael swung Lion. The sword sheared through Mitor's neck, his head rolling down his chest to land on his lap. Mazael snarled and hacked again and again, Lion ripping and tearing into Mitor's flesh. Blood sprayed everywhere, pooling on the floor, staining the chair, covering Mazael's arms. The scent of Mitor's lifeblood filled him with satisfaction and a yearning for more.

Lord Adalon laughed as Mitor's corpse fell in pieces to the floor. Mazael kicked the bloody chunks aside and stalked towards Rachel. She screamed, arms raised in front of her face. Lord Adalon's laughter rang in his ears. Mazael brought Lion arcing down towards her head...

He woke up, screaming.

Mazael's breath heaved in his chest, sweat dripping down his face, his stomach roiling and twisting. For a moment he could not remember where he was. He stumbled out of bed just in time to empty his guts into the chamber pot.

"Gods," he said. "Mitor does disagree with me." He found a clay pitcher of water on the desk and drained most of it to wash the bitter taste out of his mouth. His stomach lurched, but the water stayed down.

Mazael caught sight of his reflection in the mirror and grimaced.

He had gone as pale as Mitor. Blood covered his hands, red and thick and gleaming...

He gaped down at his hands. They were clean.

"A dream," he said. "That's all. A dream."

He walked to the window, half-expecting to see endless desert wastes and a burning sun. Instead he saw the castle courtyard and the grasses of the Grim Marches. He heard laughter and music from the great hall. Mazael had never given a damn what Mitor thought and wasn't going to start now. But tomorrow he would make peace with Rachel. The dream had been too real. He remembered the way Rachel had screamed, and how he had enjoyed that scream and the fear in her eyes...

"A dream," Mazael said. He went back to bed.

CHAPTER 11
ARMSMASTER

Sunlight rose over the eastern horizon of the Grim Marches and spilled across the plain.

Mazael walked the courtyard ramparts, as he had every morning of his youth. The bleary-eyed night watchmen bowed or offered a salute as he passed. Word of Captain Brogan's fate had gotten around.

Mazael felt better. Sleeping from sunset to sunrise would do that. He bit into the apple had taken from the castle's orchards.

The memory of the strange dream had faded. Most likely it had come from his anger at Mitor and Rachael. And he had been living off travel rations for a month, and a month of travel rations would sicken anyone. And Mitor Cravenlock could upset the strongest stomach.

He flicked the apple's core into the courtyard. Another few days and he would depart Castle Cravenlock and leave Mitor to his ruin. But what would become of Rachel when Lord Richard crushed Mitor's delusions of liege lordship? Mazael considered abducting her himself and taking her back to Knightcastle. She would be better off at Lord Malden's court than in the clutches of Mitor and Albron Eastwater.

Mazael decided to consider it later. Sleep had slowed his muscles, and he needed morning sword practice to loosen them.

"Sir Mazael?"

Timothy deBlanc climbed up the rampart stairs, his black cloak fluttering in the wind. On the collar and shoulders of his black cloak he wore a variety of small metal badges marked with different sigils. Each sigil represented a magical spell he had learned.

"You're up early," said Mazael.

"Revels...ah, do not agree with me, my lord knight," said Timothy.

"We appear to share that preference."

"I enjoy a feast as well as any man," said Mazael. "But I prefer my own company to that of certain others."

"I cannot hold drink very well, I must confess. I left quickly. Yet Master Othar had already drained four tankards of ale!" said Timothy.

Mazael laughed. "He's not what you expected?"

"No, my lord knight," said Timothy. "Ah...I do not mean that as an insult, please understand. He's skilled in the magical arts. In just the last afternoon, he showed me a dozen ways to improve upon my spells."

Mazael nodded. "Lord Mitor should have kept him as court wizard."

"Oh, certainly," said Timothy. "Master Othar is a skilled master wizard, but this Simonian of Briault...Simonian is...unknown."

"Simonian is a lying schemer, you mean to say," said Mazael. "Lady Romaria thinks he is the wizard she seeks."

"It is possible," said Timothy. "Briault is full of practitioners of dark arts, warlocks and necromancers...or so I've read. I've never actually been there." He coughed into his fist. "I...ah, well, it's a terrible breach of etiquette, but my curiosity got the better..."

"What?" said Mazael.

"I cast one of the minor spells before I left the feast. One to sense the presence of magic," said Timothy. "Simonian has a spell resting upon him."

Mazael frowned. "What sort of spell?"

"I...don't know, my lord knight," said Timothy. "I didn't recognize it. And I feared Simonian might notice me, so I released my spell before I could seek further."

"That was likely wise," said Mazael. He remembered the gleeful amusement in Simonian's eyes. "He seems dangerous. If he suspected you of meddling, I doubt he would spare you harm."

Timothy tugged at his beard. "I've lately had no shortage of men trying to kill me."

"I'll have to tell this to Master Othar," said Mazael. "He likely has a spell that can reveal more about Simonian. Thank you."

"Yes. And...there is another reason I'd like to speak with you this morning, my lord knight," said Timothy.

"Well, out with it," said Mazael.

Timothy cleared his throat. "Ah...I would like to swear to your service...if you'll take me, that is."

Mazael frowned. "You mean Lord Mitor's service?"

Timothy shook his head. "No, Sir Mazael. Your service."

"Why?" said Mazael. "I thought you had come all this way to learn from Master Othar."

"Well, yes," said Timothy. "But Master Othar hardly needs help executing his duties. And he is a good man, my lord knight...but this castle..." He shrugged. "I do not like it here. That is all I can say."

Mazael laughed. "You're not alone in that, wizard. Go on."

"And..." Timothy shrugged. "I would rather serve you, my lord knight, than swear to your brother Lord Mitor." He sighed. "The gallows in the town...I have seen many such executions in my life. I always wanted to put a stop to it, but I had not, and still do not have, the power. Sir Mazael, you are the sort of man who has that power, and I would follow you."

Mazael snorted. "Don't fill your head with notions of chivalry and adventure, wizard. My life is a hard one. If you swear to me, you'll spend your days riding back and forth on Lord Malden's errands in fair, and usually foul, weather, with bad food."

"I understand," said Timothy. "I spent most my youth sleeping under trees, and I slept in a bare stone cell during my time at Alborg."

"If you're determined...well, then, who am I to turn away help?" said Mazael. He drew Lion. "Kneel." Timothy knelt, and Mazael laid the flat of the blade on the wizard's right shoulder. "Timothy deBlanc, wizard of Travia, do you swear to be my true and faithful servant?"

"Yes, Sir Mazael," said Timothy.

"In return, I swear to provide you with food, clothing, and the protection of my sword. Do you accept this oath?" said Mazael.

"Yes," said Timothy.

"It's done, then," said Mazael. He offered his hand and helped Timothy back up.

"So quickly?" said Timothy.

Mazael frowned. "The full version of those oaths are longer. I don't have the time or patience to recite them, even if I could remember them. First a squire and then a wizard. I'll have a bloody court of my own by the time I return to Knightcastle." He frowned. "Speaking of which, here's your first task. Find where my squire has gotten..."

"Oh," said Timothy. "He's over there."

Adalar Greatheart jogged up the rampart stairs. Mazael could have killed the boy with a quick push and a long fall to the courtyard, but he pushed the thought out of his mind.

"I went to your rooms, Sir Mazael," said Adalar, "but you weren't there."

"I rose early," said Mazael. "Take a room in my chambers in the King's Tower."

"Would that be inconvenient?" said Adalar.

Mazael snorted. "Inconvenient? There's room to quarter an army in the King's Tower."

"Thank you, Sir Mazael," said Adalar. "I'll move my possessions in at once..."

Mazael waved his hand. "Do it later. Now, you can tell me where Sir Albron keeps morning arms practice." He frowned. "Sir Albron does have morning arms practice, doesn't he?"

"Of course," said Adalar. "It is held over on the other side of the castle, in the courtyard between the armory and the barracks."

"Let's go."

Below them, Castle Cravenlock came awake as servants hurried to their duties. Squires and grooms descended on the stables. The watch changed, tired night guards going for their beds, while rested men came to take their places on the ramparts. Singing rose from the castle's chapel, and a deep red glow and the sound of ringing metal came from the forges. Suits of chain mail rested on wooden stands, while completed swords and maces leaned against the forges' walls. The smell of cooking bread rose from the kitchen, and Mazael's stomach rumbled. Perhaps he would pay a visit to the kitchens later.

They made a complete circuit of the castle's walls and came to the stretch of rampart overlooking the yard between the barracks and the armory. Two hundred armsmen milled about, bearing wooden practice weapons, Sir Albron directing them. Further down the battlements, Mazael saw see Sir Nathan and Master Othar. Rachel stood with them, her eyes on Sir Albron. Mazael grimaced, stiffened his resolve, and went to join them.

"Father," said Adalar.

"Adalar. Sir Mazael," said Nathan. Rachel's hands clutched at her sleeves.

"Sir Nathan," said Mazael.

"I trust you are well? Adalar told me of your sickness," said Nathan.

"I'm well enough," said Mazael. "After a night of sleep and emptying my guts into the chamber pot, I feel fine."

"A pity you missed the feast, boy," said Othar. He rapped the tip of his cane against a battlement. "A man should never pass up an opportunity for fine food and strong drink, I say."

"You ate and drank to disgraceful excess, as always," said Nathan.

"Absolutely!" said Othar. "I'm an old man, Sir Nathan. I want to enjoy my last years on earth. If I'd wanted a life of austerity, I'd have joined the Cirstarcians."

"I'm older than you," said Nathan.

Othar waved a meaty hand. "Yes, yes, obey your elders and all of that." He winked at Adalar. "My boy, let me give you a piece of valuable advice. Just because a man is your elder does not necessarily mean that he is your better."

"I know," said Mazael, thinking of Mitor.

"Do not poison my son's mind," said Nathan.

Othar rolled his eyes. "Poison? You wound me, old friend. I just want to insure that the boy has proper appreciation for the gift that is life." He slapped Mazael on the shoulder. "Now, if it wasn't for me, Mazael would be as dry and dull as you."

"Somehow I doubt that," said Nathan.

"Besides, if we do not enjoy life, then all that is left is our worries and cares," said Othar. He frowned. "And there are so many of those."

"Lady Rachel," said Mazael, "how are you this morning?"

Rachel smiled, her eyes fever bright. "I...I am well. And you?"

"Fine," said Mazael. "Where is Mitor?"

"Lord Mitor...does not usually rise before noon," said Rachel. "Nor the lady Marcelle."

Othar snorted. "Bah! And you say I drink to excess, Nathan."

"I left early, as well," said Rachel. "Albron and Mitor often discuss matters of state during the meal. I find that leaves me with little appetite."

"That's understandable," said Mazael, "considering 'matters of state' just gave you three days in the company of Sir Tanam Crowley."

"I wanted to rise early," said Rachel. "Albron likes it when I come to watch him train the men."

"Does he, now?" said Mazael. "Rachel, I think you're making a mistake, marrying him. But I suppose it's your mistake to make."

"It's not a mistake!" said Rachel. "You just don't know him as I do."

"And how well do you know him?" said Mazael. "I hope better than I, for what I saw was not very complimentary."

"He's...a hard man to really know," said Rachel. "But...inside, he's very brave, and very daring."

"But not brave enough to go after Sir Tanam to get you back," said Mazael.

Rachel had no answer for that.

"A brave man inside," said Othar, shaking his bearded head, a strange look on his face. "If you'll excuse me, I had best retreat to my workroom. Lord Mitor will have a thunderstorm of a hangover when he awakes. I had best have some medicinal elixir prepared."

Mazael spat. "Lord Mitor has seen fit to make Simonian his court wizard. Is a medicinal elixir out of reach of his great arts?"

Othar shrugged. "I do not know. Besides, Simonian left on one of his 'errands' shortly after the feast. No one has seen him since."

"Will you need my assistance?" said Timothy.

Othar laughed. "My boy, I prepared medicinal elixirs decades before you were born. I do believe I shall be fine." He left, his cane thumping against the ramparts.

"Mazael," said Rachel, "I know we don't agree on everything, but you are right about Simonian."

"I am?" said Mazael.

"I don't know about all these rumors of dark magic and the like," said Rachel, "but he is a very dangerous man. His eyes give me nightmares, sometimes. And he's...powerful. He does things I don't think any other wizard could do."

"I see," said Mazael.

Rachel's voice fell lower. "I...I think Mitor should send him away, but he'll never listen to me. Please, Mazael, stay far away from Simonian. It's been so hard, here...if something were to happen to you, I think I would go mad."

Mazael remembered the amusement in the wizard's flat gaze as he spoke of Mitor's death. "I'll do what I can," he said.

"He's doing that wrong, you know," said a woman's voice.

Mazael's hand fell to Lion's hilt as he whirled. Romaria Greenshield stood behind them. Mazael hadn't heard her approach. She wore again her trousers, boots, tunic and worn green cloak, though a suit of steel-studded leather armor covered her torso. The hilt of her bastard sword poked out over her shoulder.

Her grin cut like a dagger's edge. "Did I startle you?"

"I nearly cut you in two," said Mazael.

A flicker of fear flashed across Romaria's blue eyes. Mazael wondered if her bravado covered something else.

"You nearly tried to cut me in two," Romaria said.

"I don't try. I do," said Mazael. He remembered how her skin felt and he grinned. Then he remembered the dream and his smile faded.

"You did startle us," said Sir Nathan. "Your skill at stealth must be considerable."

Romaria smiled. "Thank you. It's hard to keep in practice, but I try." She bowed. "I am Romaria Greenshield, of Deepforest Keep."

Nathan bowed in return. "I had hoped to speak with you. I saw you at the feast, but did not have the opportunity. I am Sir Nathan Greatheart. Is your father well, my lady?"

Romaria's eyes widened. "Sir Nathan Greatheart?" She smiled. "Yes, he is well. In fact, he told me to give you his greetings, should I happen to meet you."

"You know Lord Athaelin?" said Rachel. "But I didn't think

anyone knew the Greenshields. Until I met Romaria, I thought Deepforest Keep legendary."

"Lord Athaelin and I knew each other in my youth," said Nathan.

Romaria laughed. "You saved his life, you mean."

Nathan shrugged. "I happened to be in the right place at the right time."

"My father tells it differently," said Romaria.

"Knowing him, no doubt," said Nathan. He watched her for a moment. "Is something amiss?"

Romaria pointed to the courtyard. "Sir Albron. Those men are a mess."

Rachel's eyes flashed. "Albron does his best."

"Then despair for the future of Castle Cravenlock," said Romaria. "Half those men aren't holding their weapons correctly. The other half at least have correct grips, but haven't the slightest idea what to do with a blade."

Nathan grimaced. "I have offered to assist Sir Albron with training, but he has rebuffed my aid."

"He needs it," said Mazael. "Sir Tanam's crows could take this lot. Lord Richard's veterans would annihilate them. If Mitor plans to go to war with Sir Albron training his soldiers..."

"Mitor will win," said Rachel. "You'll see. He hasn't told you..."

Mazael frowned. "Told me what?" Rachel blanched.

"Sir Mazael, I say!"

Sir Albron walked towards the rampart stairs. "Are you going to join us?" His smile widened. "I have heard so much about the daring of Sir Mazael. Is it true, or does the great knight spend all his time in the company of women and old men?"

"Albron!" said Rachel. "Please."

Mazael laughed. "Sir Albron, this old man did a better job of training Cravenlock armsmen than you ever could. As for the company of women, I think Lady Romaria could split your head down the middle."

"Oh, flattery," said Romaria. A chorus of laughs burst from the armsmen, and Sir Albron silenced his men with a smiling glare.

"Easy to say standing up there," said Albron. "Why not come down here and prove your words?"

"I think I will," said Mazael. "Adalar, Timothy, with me."

"I shall join, as well," said Nathan. "Perhaps you can teach me a few lessons, Sir Albron."

"And I," said Romaria.

Rachel gaped. "Lady...that's...that's hardly proper."

Albron laughed. "A woman? Lady Romaria, you mock me."

Romaria grinned at him. "Indeed? Consider this, Albron. If your men can defeat a woman of Deepforest Keep, then Lord Richard's armies won't even be a challenge."

Albron shook his head. "I won't have it. In the barbarian wilds, women might waddle about in a man's garb and with a man's weapons. But you are in civilization now, Lady Romaria, and you will act in a civilized fashion."

"No," said Sir Nathan. "If Lady Romaria possess a tenth part of her father's nature, Sir Albron, then I would rather stand with her to death then spend an hour with the likes of you."

Albron's face hardened, and for a moment fury seem to rise off him in waves. His smile returned, but Mazael was certain he had glimpsed Albron's true feelings. Perhaps Rachel had as well.

"Well, then," Albron said. "Humiliate yourself, Lady Romaria, if you wish. Stand with her, Sir Nathan, and prove yourself an old fool. It matters not to me. I did warn you. Come down, then, and let us practice the blades."

CHAPTER 12
SWORD DANCERS

Mazael descended the rampart steps alongside Sir Nathan and Romaria, followed by Adalar and Timothy.

"Cease!" Albron said. The armsmen stopped fighting, the clack of wooden swords fading. "Now it is time to watch and learn from a true master of the blade. Sir Mazael has bravely volunteered to fight me."

"Oh, have I?" said Mazael. "Such a brave act."

Another flicker of rage shadowed Albron's face, and he gave orders to the armsmen. "Give your practice blade to Sir Mazael. You and you with the wooden bastard sword. Relinquish your weapons to Sir Nathan and...the lady." Three armsmen ran forward. Mazael took a practice longsword made of heavy wood with a lead core. It was heavier and shorter than Lion, but Mazael had used far worse weapons.

He unbuckled his sword belt, Lion swinging in its scabbard. "Adalar, hold this for me."

"Perhaps Sir Mazael needs a bit of a primer, before he has to face me," said Albron. "We wouldn't want the great knight to overtax himself."

"Albron," said Rachel. She had come down from the ramparts. "Mazael is Lord Mitor's brother and his guest. Please be more polite."

Albron laughed. "My dear, how do you worry! There's no need to involve yourself in this. It is a matter for men. I only have Sir Mazael's best interests at heart."

Mazael smiled. "I'm sure you do."

"Lady Romaria first, Sir Mazael," said Albron. "After all, a mere woman should be no challenge for such a great fighter as yourself?" Romaria watched Mazael with intent blue eyes. "Or maybe the women of Deepforest Keep are just as wild as the wood demons!"

"Albron!" hissed Rachel. She fell silent at his glare.

"I'd be honored," said Mazael. "Romaria is a skilled opponent, I've seen that for myself. I could use a challenge today." He shrugged. "I doubt I'll find one fighting you."

Shocked silence rose from the soldiers.

"Very well, then!" said Albron. "Watch closely, men! See if you can learn anything from the fighting of a wild woman!" More laughter rose up.

Romaria stepped towards Mazael with the wooden bastard sword in hand, her eyes like blue ice. She moved with the grace of the hunting cat she had killed in the hills. Mazael wanted her, drawn to her in a strange way he had never experienced before. She wore her usual confident grin, but Mazael saw something in her face. She was afraid of him.

Mazael raised his sword to a guard stance. "This wasn't the sort of tumble I had in mind."

Romaria took her sword in a two-handed grip. "Who knows? A good fight always gets my blood up. And no man can see the future...or so I hope." Again he heard the fear in her voice.

Mazael stepped towards her. "What are you afraid of?"

Her eyes flashed. "Not anything. Not you." Her sword blurred towards his chest, and Mazael barely got his parry in place.

"Ha!" Albron shouted. "This cat has claws!" Then Romaria's attack drove all distractions from Mazael's mind.

Her sword spun and stabbed for Mazael's head. Her grip shifted from two hands to one and then back again. His sword worked circles as he blocked Romaria's blows. Mazael parried a low blow, and Romaria twisted her wrist, the dulled tip of her longer sword nicking against Mazael's leg.

Romaria laughed. "First blood, mine!"

Mazael grunted and sidestepped, Romaria's thrust shooting past his hip. His sword blurred in a two-handed swing for Romaria's shoulder. She parried, but the force of his strike knocked her back. Mazael drove into the opening, sword flashing for her throat. But Romaria regained her balance, and beat back Mazael's attacks. He hammered at her again and again, and so caught her off-guard when he fell to one knee and thrust at her legs. Romaria jumped aside, but Mazael's sword banged into her knee.

"Second blood, mine," said Mazael.

Romaria grinned at him. "Second blood, second best."

"Let's find out," said Mazael.

Romaria flew at him. Her thrust flowed into a swing and then into a two-handed chop. Mazael blocked and parried, the wooden sword vibrating in his hand. His breath came rapidly, his heart pounding in his chest. Romaria was better than good. She was masterful. He had not fought anyone this skilled in years.

Mazael was enjoying this.

Romaria's attack played out without landing a single hit, and Mazael launched his own attack. He threw a flurry of two-handed swings at Romaria's head, forcing her to take the bastard sword in both hands to block his heavy blows. Mazael finished the attack with a high swing aimed for her head, and Romaria raised her sword to parry. But his swing had been a feint, and he reversed the momentum of his sword, sending it for her stomach. Few fighters would have seen it coming. But Romaria did. Not only did she block the blow, she turned her sword and clipped Mazael on the forearm. Mazael jerked away, his forearm stinging from the hit.

Romaria laughed, her blue eyes were ablaze. "Two for me, and one for you."

Mazael stepped back. "First blood doesn't matter. What matters is the last blood!"

Mazael rushed her, driving a lunge at her heart. Romaria sidestepped and batted his sword aside, splinters flying from the battered practice swords. Mazael turned her parry into an attack and twisted his sword around to strike at her legs. Romaria parried low, and Mazael sent his next attack high. His attacks and parries merged with Romaria's, joining together in an intricate, blurring dance. Mazael moved with Romaria, fighting on instinct and trained reflexes, without thought, thrust left, thrust right, parry high, parry low, block, riposte, swing high, swing left, swing right...

Their swords came together with a great crash, the crosspieces jamming against each other. Mazael shoved forward and tried to push Romaria off balance, but she held her ground. They strained against each other, close enough that Mazael could feel Romaria's hot breath on his face, that he could smell her sweat. Mazael couldn't lower his blade, but neither could Romaria.

"Stalemate," said Mazael.

"Think so?" said Romaria.

Mazael almost leaned forward and kissed her. "Unless you have some trick even I've never heard of."

Romaria's grin widened. "Tricks, is it? You are in for a surprise!" She pushed backwards and broke free from their clinch. Mazael brought his sword up, knowing she could not regain her balance in time...

Romaria's free hand flew through an intricate gesture, and she vanished.

Mazael's mind overrode his shock. He remembered her tricks with the coins. She could do magic. Wizards knew how to make themselves unseen.

He moved his sword in a sweeping parry just as Romaria reappeared before him, beating aside the sword point darting for his throat, and brought his sword down in a two-handed swing. Their swords crashed together and shattered with a tremendous crack. The blades splintered into pieces, the leaden cores falling to the ground.

"A stalemate!" said Albron.

A thunderous cheer rose up from the armsmen. Mazael saw their rapt, amazed expressions.

"Now it's a stalemate," said Mazael.

An expression of relief washed across Romaria's face. "That's good to know."

Mazael frowned. "Why?"

Romaria smiled. "You're no more skilled than I am."

Mazael snorted. "Just why is that important?"

Romaria put a finger over his lips. "You'll see." She stepped away from him, and he watched her go, entranced.

Albron's voice jerked Mazael out of his reverie. "Well fought, Sir Mazael! A stalemate against a woman. Indeed, I see your reputation is not exaggerated. But let us see how you do against a real opponent."

"Adalar," said Mazael. "Another sword." The squire fetched another wooden blade from the rack. Mazael took the sword and raised it to a guard position. His heart beat rapidly, but he was not tired.

He wanted to fight this liar who had usurped Sir Nathan's place.

Albron swung his own wooden sword. "Are you ready?"

"Yes," said Mazael. "Perhaps you'll learn a lesson or two."

Albron came at him before he had finished speaking. Albron's sword spun, flashed high, then low, then high again. Mazael shifted his sword to a two-handed grip and parried. He beat aside a thrust from Albron, side-stepped, and riposted. Albron danced away. The armsmaster was deadly quick. Mazael tossed his sword to his right hand.

Albron came at him again, slashing for Mazael's chest. Mazael parried and shoved, pushing with all his way. Albron stumbled, and Mazael's sword lanced out. Albron jerked back, quick as a snake, but not before the wooden blade kissed his left shoulder.

The impact made an odd scraping sound.

Mazael grinned. "First blood. Good thing we're not using steel swords."

Albron snarled. "I'm waiting for that lesson."

"Then I'll give it to you."

Albron whipped his sword over his head and brought it whistling down. Mazael blocked, the rapid crack-crack-crack of strained wood filling his ears, and twisted his wrist. Albron's sword scraped to the ground, and Mazael's blade shot up, the point aimed for Albron's face. Albron jerked back, but the pommel struck him hard enough to make his teeth click. Mazael reversed his sword and struck for Albron's throat. The other knight danced away.

Albron went on the attack, his sword reaching for Mazael's neck. Mazael could not parry in time, so he rolled, tumbled past Albron's legs, came to one knee, and gave the knight a solid hit across the back of his legs. A gasp of wonder rose from the watching soldiers.

Albron turned, growling, before Mazael could rise and hacked a vicious two-handed blow. Mazael parried high and caught the strike above his head. Albron hammered at Mazael like a smith pounding iron. Mazael parried every blow, his arms and shoulders aching from Albron's pounding.

Mazael took a chance and rolled to the side. Albron's overbalanced and stumbled as his blow missed, and Mazael shot to one knee and drove his sword forward. Albron twisted to the side, but Mazael's sword smacked into his hip, and Albron fell. Mazael jumped to his feet and brought his sword down in imitation of Albron's two-handed blows. Albron jerked to the side and regained his feet.

Mazael tossed his sword from hand to hand as Albron backed away.

"First, second, and third blood," said Mazael. "A very good thing we're using wooden swords."

Albron's sneer said more than words. He ran at Mazael with a noticeable limp.

Albron was good, but his skills lacked something. Mazael was not surprised when Albron began to repeat the same attack routine over and over again. It was if he knew all the thrusts, parries, and blocks, but had never used them before. Albron fought as one who had been trained by the best tutors, but who had never before lifted a blade in mortal combat.

Albron swung high twice, his handsome face contorted with exertion. Mazael beat aside the reaching blade. Albron reversed the momentum of his sword, bringing it around in a high loop for Mazael's head.

But Mazael moved, and Albron's sword swished over his head. Mazael took his sword in both hands and swung into Albron's guard. His sword crashed down on Albron's wrist. Albron bellowed, his practice sword flying, and Mazael thrust to finish the fight.

The dull tip of his wooden sword plunged into Albron's stomach, and six inches of splintered wood disappeared into Albron's belly. Mazael felt the sword scrape against bone. It was impossible. The wooden sword couldn't have impaled Albron. Yet Mazael saw it with his own eyes. Mazael waited for Albron's face to pale, for the blood to gush from his mouth and his stomach.

Instead, Albron shook his head and stepped free.

Mazael's eyes darted from the tip of his sword to Albron's stomach. No blood marked the wood.

"How?" said Mazael.

"You ought to know," said Albron. "After all, you did win. I didn't even hit you once. Well...fought." His eyes were hard and angry.

"But I saw the sword go in!" said Mazael. "I felt it scrape against your spine! You ought to be bleeding to death."

Rachel ran to them. "Albron! Oh, Albron, you're hurt!" She frowned. "You're...but...I saw Mazael run you through."

Albron laughed. "Ah, you worry for me so. No need. Your brother can't kill me."

"But I saw the sword go in," said Mazael.

Albron shrugged and a put an arm around Rachel's shoulders. "Men see many strange things in the heat of battle. Most like your sword caught up in my clothes."

Mazael stared at Albron. "That must be it." He had seen the blade go in. He had felt it scrape against bone. Mazael had felt that scrape a hundred times before in battle. "That must be it, I suppose."

"You must be more careful, Albron. If you were to die...well, what would we do, then?" said Rachel.

Albron jerked his arm away. "Wither and perish. If you'll excuse me, I have business." He stalked from the practice field, Rachel trailing after him like a faithful dog. Mazael wiped sweat from his brow as Romaria and Sir Nathan came to join him.

"What a remarkably chivalrous loser," said Romaria.

Adalar took the battered wooden sword and handed him a clay pitcher, and Mazael drank. "What a bad swordsman, you mean. The man has potential, I'll give him that. But he doesn't know..."

"It's as if he learned perfectly how to use that sword yesterday," said Romaria, "but hasn't been able to practice the skill."

"Yes. That's exactly it," said Mazael, handing the pitcher back to Adalar. "It's like his hands but not his mind knew how to use a sword."

"I noticed that, as well," said Sir Nathan.

"Fighting with the blade is an art," said Romaria, pushing a stray strand of hair from her face. "It combines mind and body and spirit. Albron's body knew that art, I saw ...but his mind and spirit did not."

Mazael stared after Albron. "And that sword. I saw it go into his belly. I would swear it."

Sir Nathan frowned. "I thought it had, for a moment. But he stood. A man could not stand after taking such a wound." He shrugged. "Besides, you were fighting with dulled wooden blades. You would have to fall with the sword beneath you to drive it into flesh."

"I saw it as well," said Adalar.

"As did I," said Romaria. "So did half the garrison, I would wager."

Timothy cleared his throat. "Ah, my lord knights and lady, if I may speak? Sir Mazael, it concerns the matter we spoke of earlier ..."

"Go ahead," said Mazael. "I trust everyone here."

"Why, how flattering," said Romaria.

"My lord...I observed, discreetly, of course, during your fight that Sir Albron carries an enchantment about him," said Timothy.

Silence answered his pronouncement.

"As well?" said Romaria. "Who else?"

"Simonian of Briault, my lady," said Timothy. "He and Sir Albron have similar spells cast upon them."

"What sort of spell?" said Mazael.

"I do not know," said Timothy.

"Could you determine who had cast the spells?" said Romaria.

Timothy shook his head, flustered. "Ah...no, Lady Romaria. I have yet to develop my skill to such a high degree."

"A spell of protection," said Mazael. "I knew that sword had gone in. Albron must have had some magic to keep him safe from injury."

"Then who cast the spell on him?" said Romaria.

"Could Othar have done it?" said Mazael.

Nathan shook his head. "I doubt it."

"That would leave Simonian," said Romaria.

"Perhaps Albron is Simonian's creature," said Mazael.

Sir Nathan shrugged. "It is possible."

"More wizard's trickery," said Mazael. He remembered Simonian's casual request for Mitor's death.

Sir Nathan frowned. "You may be right, Mazael. But we have no proof. We cannot act without proof."

"What are you going to do?" said Romaria.

"Find proof," said Mazael. "But first, I'm going to find breakfast."

Romaria smiled and touched his arm. "I think I'll join you."

CHAPTER 13
MAZAEL VISITS THE KITCHENS

"Sir Gerald!" said Mazael.

Sir Gerald descended the steps to the chapel, his sheathed longsword's pommel flashing in the morning son. Wesson trailed after, bearing Gerald's shield.

"Sir Mazael," said Gerald. "I missed you at the feast. What detained you?"

"I fell ill," said Mazael.

"You? You never take sick," said Gerald. "Are you sure you are well?"

"I feel fine now," said Mazael. "You missed morning practice, Gerald."

"I wanted to attend morning prayer," said Gerald with a sigh.

Mazael laughed. "Why so glum? Confessing your sins puts you into a better mood for hours."

Gerald scowled. "You should try it." Romaria snickered. "No, what upsets me is the chapel's condition."

The ancient chapel dated back to the old kingdom of Dracaryl. The massive building had stone walls, high, narrow windows, and a domed roof. The three interlocked rings of Amatheon, Father of the Gods, rested atop the dome. "It looks fine to me."

"The outside does, yes," said Gerald. "These old chapels were built like fortresses. In Dracaryl I suppose they were built to take blasts of dragon fire. It's the interior that troubles me."

"What about it?" said Mazael.

"A mess," said Gerald. "I've rarely seen such open disrespect, Mazael! The floor looks as if it was used to stable horses. The pews are dusty and have been carved with all manner of vile obscenities. And those priests, and those acolytes." Gerald shook his head. "I've never seen such an ill-trained bunch! They stumbled through the liturgy. I doubt they even know more than five or six words of High Tristafellin."

"Mitor was never one for piety," said Mazael.

"Your whole family seems that way," said Gerald.

"That's insulting," said Romaria.

Gerald shrugged. "Mazael is hardly the most pious of men, but he's not a blasphemer. Lord Mitor borders upon it."

"Perhaps we'll be fortunate and the gods will strike Mitor dead," said Mazael.

"Let's leave this place," said Gerald. "I do not like it. No doubt Lord Mitor is awaiting us for breakfast."

Mazael laughed. "I doubt it. Lord Mitor feasted last night. He might rouse himself in time for supper, though I wouldn't wager on it."

"Lord Mitor reminds me of Wesson's father," said Gerald. "They call him Lord Tancred the Tankard. I've seen him drink like a fish. But Lord Mitor and Lady Marcelle." Gerald shook his head. "I've never seen a man drink so much. It was as if they drank to escape all the demons of all the hells. And the court followed suit. Such debauchery. And I shudder to think what followed in the hay lofts and in the dark corners."

Mazael laughed. "We need to find you a wife."

"Why?" said Gerald.

Mazael laughed harder and clapped him on the back. "Let's go get breakfast."

He led Romaria and Gerald around the back of the chapel and towards the kitchen's rear door. He felt eyes on him as he walked. Servants faltered in their stride and armsmen gaped.

"They're staring at us," said Gerald.

"No," said Romaria. "They're staring at Mazael. They saw the way he fought."

"That's hardly new," said Gerald. "Sir Mazael has always fought well."

"Yes, but he defeated Sir Albron in sword practice," said Romaria.

Gerald whistled. "That will raise attention."

Mazael snorted. "It shouldn't. It wasn't impressive. Yes, yes, I know, Romaria. If I could defeat him, then the great and powerful Lord Richard should have little difficulty vanquishing Albron."

"Is Lord Mitor incapable of leading his own armies?" said Romaria.

Mazael snorted. "What do you think? In armor, Mitor would look like a pear in chain mail."

They came to the back of the kitchens. A stout old woman brandished a broom, herding a trio of clucking chickens back into an old coop. Mazael felt heat radiating from the ovens, and he stepped through the back door. The kitchens were vast, a dozen ovens ablaze as cooks labored to feed the castle's armsmen, servants, and nobles.

"Sir Mazael!"

Mazael turned. A young woman in a soot-stained apron approached. Her sweat-stained clothes stuck to her body. It made for a pleasant sight.

Especially since when Mazael had last seen her, Bethany had a noose around her neck.

"Do you remember me?" said Bethy. "Or do you go about saving women and children so often that it's all another day's work to you?"

Gerald laughed. "You'd be surprised what occupies Sir Mazael's days, lady."

"And how are you faring in the kitchens, Bethy?" said Mazael.

Bethy sighed. "Well enough, I suppose. Master Cramton has taken over the kitchens." The fat man bellowed orders on the other side of the room. "Lord Mitor had no one running things, if you can believe it. I miss the old inn, though."

"At least you're alive," said Romaria.

"That's true," said Bethy. She grinned, her teeth white in her sooty face. "I saw you beat Albron, Sir Mazael. You whipped him right and good."

Mazael shrugged. "It wasn't hard."

"Aye, I've never seen a man fight like you, so I have!" said Bethy. "And if there's ever a man that deserved a good whipping, it was that Sir Albron."

Mazael thought of Rachel. "I couldn't disagree."

Bethy's eyes sparkled. "But, oh, the way you and the lady fought!"

"You fought a woman?" said Gerald.

Romaria turned on him. "So? He couldn't beat me."

"He couldn't? But...it...is not chivalrous," said Gerald.

"I'd never seen anything like it, Sir Gerald," said Bethy. "They moved together, and so fast, so...graceful, it was like watching a great ball, where the lords and ladies wear their silks. Except it was swords, instead of silks, I suppose."

"She beat you?" said Gerald, incredulous.

"Oh, no, my lord handsome knight," said Bethy. "No one won. It was a stalemate, just like in the songs."

"Songs? I wonder what Mattias Comorian would say of that," said Mazael.

"Who?" said Romaria.

"Just a jongleur I met," said Mazael, wondering what had brought him to mind.

"Their swords crashed together," said Bethy, "and then they shattered, and all that was left was the splintered hilts. I'd never seen anything so wondrous as that fight, so I have. Neither had half of those armsmen, too, the way they stood about with their mouths hanging open." She snorted. "It's the likes of them that are supposed to defend us from the Dragonslayer lord? I'm betting that if Sir Mazael and the Lady Romaria stood together, they could fight his army themselves."

"A pity I missed this," said Gerald. "The gods know I wouldn't have missed much by passing up on morning prayers."

Bethy wrinkled her nose. "Bah, I don't hold with that lot, those chapel priests with their mutterings. They spend half their time drunk and the other half staring at me and the other girls as if they'd like to see us with no clothes." She winked at Gerald. "Of course, you do too, but with you, it's different." Wesson smothered a snicker.

"But..." said Gerald. "I most certainly...I didn't, I mean—"

"Oh, but I'm being rude!" said Bethy. "Why, you likely came here for food, not to listen to me babble! Master Cramton would bellow my ears off if he saw me standing about chattering with you hungry. Let me run and get you some food." She winked at Gerald again and hurried off, leaving the young knight speechless.

"Sir Mazael is right," said Romaria. "He does need to find you a wife."

Gerald sighed.

"And what of you, Sir Mazael?" said Romaria. "Have you no plans to wed?"

Mazael laughed and looked over the bustling kitchen. "I doubt it."

Gerald laughed. "My father will likely find some pretty but brainless minor noblewoman for you. You're almost two-and-thirty. He has said that it was past time you married."

"I doubt it," said Mazael. "Your father acts only for power and prestige. Were I Lord of Castle Cravenlock, he'd offer his daughter."

"The Elderborn believe that marriages are fate, the joining of two hearts," said Romaria.

"Not from what I've seen," said Mazael. "Marriage is about lust and money. Love is a ploy for the jongleurs' songs."

"I am not hungry. Excuse me," said Romaria.

"She's a strange woman," said Gerald, tugging at his mustache.

"Yes, but I don't hold it against her," said Mazael. Women either bored him or inspired lust, but he had never met anyone like her before. And he had never met anyone who could have fought him to a standstill.

Bethy returned, bearing hollowed heels of bread filled with steaming beef. "Here you are." She smiled at Gerald. "I put a bit of extra in yours."

"I'm sure he's flattered," said Mazael. "Anything to drink?"

"Oh!" said Bethy. "I'd forgotten." She disappeared into the chaos of the kitchen and returned a moment later with a pitcher of ale. "Now, drink up."

"Gladly," said Mazael. He drained a large part of the pitcher and handed it to Gerald. "Thank you."

"Oh, you're welcome," said Bethy. "For you, we'd prepare a feast, we would! Besides, with Lord Mitor sick as an old dog from too much drink, we needn't worry about preparing his breakfast."

Gerald snorted. "That's hardly appropriate!"

Bethy smiled at him. "Oh, but it's true, isn't it? I bet you tell the truth all the time, don't you?"

"A knight must strive to act honestly and honorably at all times," announced Gerald.

Bethy laughed. "Oh...so they swear," she said. She shook her head. "But give me a copper coin for every one that doesn't...why, I'd have more money than the Lord Dragonslayer. But you and Sir Mazael, you're different. This isn't your place." Her eyes darted back and forth, and her voice fell to a whisper. "Lord Mitor and Lady Rachel and Sir Albron and...that wizard, the Briaultan fellow...they're all bad sorts, all of them."

"Not Rachel," said Mazael. "What are you saying?"

"Leave," said Bethy. "Right now. This isn't a good place. I don't think you're welcome here. You take Lady Romaria and your squire and your friends and leave and don't ever come back."

"What are you talking about?" said Mazael.

Bethy paled. "I've...said too much...I'm just babbling...I'm a bit tired..."

She spun and ran away.

CHAPTER 14
ROMARIA'S TALE

Mitor's head exploded from his shoulders in a shower of gore, his body crumpling. Mazael sneered and kicked the head aside. Blood pooled on the marble floor, gleaming like liquid ruby, and Mazael heard Lord Adalon's laughter.

Rachel screamed and backed away. Mazael raised Lion, blood dripping down the sharp blade...

He awoke with a strangled scream, sweat dripping down his jaw. For a moment he thought he saw Rachel's severed head lying its pool of blood, the green eyes staring at him...

"Sir Mazael?" Adalar stood near the bed.

"What?" said Mazael, his voice a rasp.

"I heard you shouting..." said Adalar.

"Nothing," said Mazael. "It was nothing. Go back to sleep." He stood and tried to find his boots. "I'll take a walk. The night air will clear my head."

"If...if you say so, Sir Mazael," said Adalar. The squire turned and went back to his chamber. Mazael wondered what he had shouted out in his sleep. His head ached, worse than any hangover he had ever had, and he shut his eyes and pressed his hands to his temple. After a few moments, the pain faded. He reached for his sword belt, remembered the dream, and let his blade fall.

He climbed the stairs to the top of the King's Tower. A wooden ladder reached the tower's turret, and Mazael pulled himself onto the roof. The cool wind blew past him, tugging at his cloak and running chilled fingers through his hair. Mazael leaned against the battlements. He could see the land for miles around, the stars blazing overhead.

"What's wrong with me?" Mazael said.

Killing came easily to him. He had often entertained the notion of killing Mitor. But the dreams were so vivid. He could still see the blood staining the marble stairs, could still smell Mitor's fear. And Rachel...gods, he loved Rachel, he had never wanted to hurt her, not even now.

It was Castle Cravenlock. He had memories here, some good, many dark. It was good to see Sir Nathan and Master Othar and Rachel again. But Mitor had grown from a cruel, lazy boy to a cruel, foolish man. No wonder Sir Nathan had given Adalar to Mazael as squire. The old knight likely wanted his son far away when Lord Richard dealt with Mitor's rebellion.

Mazael decided to leave tomorrow. He would leave Mitor behind, he would leave the scheming Simonian behind, and he would leave the dreams behind. Let Mitor smash himself against the Dragonslayer. He would take Rachel with him tomorrow, whether she wanted to come or not. Better that he drag her to Lord Malden's court than to leave her here in the grasp of a creature like Sir Albron.

Something scraped against the stone.

His hand shot to his sword hilt but banged against his hip, and he berated himself for leaving his sword in his room. He reached for his boot and yanked free a short dagger. Mazael peered over the battlement, glimpsed a dark form making its way across the roof of the keep.

Could the wealthy Lord Richard have hired assassins? Mazael tucked the dagger into his belt, vaulted onto the battlements, and jumped. His boots hit the roof of the keep with a slap. The dark form spun, and Mazael raised the dagger for a throw.

It was Romaria. She wore tight-fitting trousers and a tunic with the sleeves cut away. Her marvelous eyes widened in fear as she saw him.

Then she recognized him and amusement almost replaced the fear. "Good to see you, too."

"What in the gods' name are you doing? I could have killed you."

Romaria shrugged. "Everyone dies. I could ask the same of you."

"I saw you," said Mazael. He slid his dagger back into its boot sheath. "I could not sleep. I came out to the tower's roof to think and saw you crawling about. That wasn't a good idea, my lady. And you still haven't told me what you're even doing up here."

"I like to climb things," said Romaria.

"Climb things?" said Mazael.

"I find it relaxing," said Romaria.

Mazael's annoyance evaporated. "You would, wouldn't you? Just don't fall. Give the guards some warning, first. I would be displeased if someone put a crossbow bolt through your chest."

"Would you?" said Romaria. "Flattering. And the guards didn't see me. Lord Richard could march his whole army into the castle, and Mitor wouldn't notice them until his hangover passed."

Mazael laughed. "Gods, I suppose you're right."

Romaria tossed her head, hair sliding over her shoulder. "And they couldn't hit me. You saw the way they stumbled over each other this morning. I doubt they could hit the side of the castle..."

He noticed something.

Her voice broke off as Mazael stepped towards her. A dozen expressions flashed across her face, and for a moment she trembled like a deer mesmerized by a wolf.. Mazael reached for her neck, pushing back her thick black hair to reveal her ears.

They came to delicate points.

"Who are you?" said Mazael. "You don't look like one of the Elderborn. But you move like one, and those eyes..."

"I am who I told you I am," Romaria said. "Romaria Greenshield, the daughter of Lord Athaelin of Deepforest Keep."

"Are the Greenshields all Elderborn?" asked Mazael.

"No," said Romaria. "My father is human, but my mother was the Elderborn high priestess. I have the blood of both races."

"How did that happen?" said Mazael. He drew back his hand, his fingers lingering on the skin of her neck. "I thought the two races never mated with each other."

"It's always been this way," said Romaria. "The old Dragon Kings of Dracaryl sent the first Greenshield to the Great Forest to conquer the tribes. Instead he made a peace with them and took the high priestess to wife...though they rarely have children. It's been that way ever since, for thousands of years. Deepforest Keep has outlasted Malrag invasions, the great Holy War, and a dozen other battles." She smiled. "It will outlast Lord Mitor and Lord Richard, and even you and me."

"Why do you hide it?" said Mazael.

"I didn't want to," Romaria said, "but I know how the peasants feel about the Elderborn...wood demons and other nonsense. And even the other Elderborn believe 'half-breeds' are...inferior." Her eyes turned flinty for a moment. "You don't think that, do you?"

Mazael kissed her on the forehead. "What do you think?"

Romaria kissed him back on the lips. "I knew it."

Mazael snorted. "Gods forbid I should agree with Mitor."

Romaria laughed. "And if you do, should I kill you?"

"Probably," said Mazael. "At least, you should try."

"You ought to kill Mitor," said Romaria, "and save us all a

horrible amount of bloodshed."

Mazael frowned, remembering Simonian's words. "I won't kill Mitor. I don't like him. I detest him, in truth. But he's my brother and I can't kill him."

"I was half-joking," said Romaria. "He would never survive the Ritual of Rulership."

"What's that?" said Mazael.

"It's a test," said Romaria. "When the old lord of Deepforest Keep dies, his heir undergoes the Ritual in the druids' caverns under the Keep. It's a test of strength of will and strength of body. No one knows what goes into it, save the heir and the druids. If the heir succeeds, he walks out of the caverns as the new Lord of Deepforest Keep. If the heir fails...well, he doesn't walk out at all, and the nearest blood relation takes the Ritual."

"Sounds efficient, I suppose," said Mazael.

"Oh, it is," said Romaria. "It ensures that only one worthy takes the mantle of ruling." Her smile turned mocking. "Deepforest Keep has never had a lord like Mitor."

"Then your home's the better for it," said Mazael. "What's it like?"

"What?" said Romaria.

"Your home," said Mazael. "Deepforest Keep."

This time Romaria's smile held no mockery. "It's the most beautiful place in the world. The castle's been built with the trees, over the years. Great oaks taller than this castle form the pillars of the great hall. The town, humans and Elderborn alike, live in the trees, in houses built within the branches. And the gardens...the druids blessed the gardens with their earth magic. You'll never see larger fruits and vegetables, Mazael, no matter how long you live and how far you travel." Starlight glinted in her eyes. "I've visited the Old Kingdoms in the south and Travia in the north, and many places in between, but there is nowhere more beautiful than my home."

"Perhaps I'll see it for myself, one day," said Mazael.

"Where's home for you?" said Romaria.

"Home?" said Mazael. "I never gave it much thought." He shrugged. "Not here, that's for certain. Knightcastle, maybe...but I've rarely stayed there more than four months out of the year. My home is on the road. I've spent most of the last fifteen years riding from place to place."

"You were a knight-errant?" said Romaria.

Mazael nodded. "My father turned me out after Lord Richard's victory."

"Where have you traveled?" said Romaria. "You must have seen most of the kingdom."

Mazael shrugged. "Here and there. Through the Stormvales and the Green Plain, and then I rode with the Iron Lancers of Barellion."

"What's the most beautiful place you've seen?" said Romaria.

Mazael thought it over for a moment. "Stillwater...the lands and castle of Wesson's father. It's this little valley in the Knightrealm hills, near the River of Jarrsen. The mists come down from the hills in the morning ..." He shook his head. "But I think the most beautiful thing I've seen is you."

Romaria looked away. "Flatterer. You really mean that, don't you?"

"I do," said Mazael. He laughed. "Gods help me, I do. I don't know why. But I do."

"He told me I would meet you," said Romaria, voice distant.

"Who?" said Mazael.

"The Seer," said Romaria.

"Who is that?" said Mazael.

"He's a druid, I suppose. I don't know," she said. "He's a Elderborn and has no other name. We all call him the Seer. He has visions. They come true."

"Is he some sort of wizard?" said Mazael.

"No. A druid," said Romaria. "There's only one Seer born every generation...for the Elderborn, that's around a hundred and fifty years. He receives his powers and his mantle in a ceremony." She closed her eyes and took a deep breath. "When Father sent me north, to find the wizard raising the zuvembies, the Seer...the Seer told me I would meet you."

"How would he know that I was coming?" said Mazael.

"I don't know," said Romaria. "He said I would face a demon...and that I would meet you." Her voice became hysterical. "He said...he said you were a man with a lion's fang for a sword, who could move faster than any other, and could kill any man...and that you...that I would..."

And to Mazael's astonishment she began to cry. He took her in his arms, and her face fell against his shoulder. It had been a very strange day. He held her and tried to think of something to say.

Romaria sniffled and wiped at her eyes. "Gods, look at me."

"What did he say?" said Mazael.

"I...don't...I don't want to talk about it now," said Romaria. She managed a feeble smile. "I just hope that for the first time the Seer was wrong."

Mazael laughed. "When I was in Barellion, this old gypsy woman predicted that I would rise to great power and fame. Unless spending my nights sleeping on cold ground is greatness, she was wrong. Your Seer is probably no better."

"I hope you're right," said Romaria.

"Come with me," said Mazael.

Romaria laughed. "What?"

"Come with me," said Mazael. "Mitor's a sinking ship. Lord Richard will crush him and most likely he'll kill your dark wizard. I'm leaving tomorrow, and taking Master Othar and Sir Nathan if they'll come. Why don't you come with me? You've seen the Old Kingdoms and Travia...why not see the rest of the kingdom? I would like you would come with me." He could not believe what he had just said. He wondered what Lord Malden would say when he saw Romaria Greenshield. Mazael decided that he didn't care.

"I can't," said Romaria. "I would like to, but I must stay. I was sent to kill this dark wizard, and that is what I mean to do. You have to stay, as well."

"Why?" said Mazael.

"Because if you had seen a zuvembie, you would know that whoever would raise such a monstrosity must be stopped," said Romaria. "And you can't leave. This is your family, where you were born. I know you don't care for Lord Mitor, but I think you loved your sister, once. Will you leave her to the mercy of Lord Richard?"

Mazael was silent. "I don't know. She's changed."

"Then stay," said Romaria.

Mazael kept silent and stared out over the courtyard.

"I think I shall retire," said Romaria. "Climbing up the keep is tiring."

Mazael reached out and took her hand. "I'll stay. Don't go. I haven't been sleeping well, lately."

Romaria smiled. She stayed.

CHAPTER 15
MITOR'S PLANS

"Lord Mitor commands your presence at once in the great hall," said the page.

Mazael stared at the boy. "Does he, now?"

The page's face whitened. "Ah...he sent me to tell you, Sir Mazael, if you please."

Mazael waved a hand. "Go. Tell him I shall be there shortly."

The page ran from the room. Mazael yawned, leaned back in his chair, and scrubbed his fingers through his hair. He had not slept at all last night. That was fine. If he did not sleep, he did not dream.

Timothy returned, bearing a clay cup filled with a vile-smelling black fluid. "It is ready, my lord knight."

Mazael took the cup and sniffed. "What is it?"

"A southern elixir made from the beans of a wild plant," said Timothy. "It is called coffee. I understand it is quite popular among scholars."

Mazael sipped at it. "Tastes vile."

"It does," said Timothy.

"Will it keep me awake?" said Mazael.

"Oh, yes," said Timothy.

Mazael shrugged and drained the cup in one long draught. The black liquid burned like hot pitch going down. "Strong stuff. Thank you. Adalar!" Adalar handed Mazael his sword belt. Mazael rose, exited his chambers, and started down the stairs. The wizard and the squire followed him.

He found Gerald waiting in the courtyard, with Wesson standing behind him. Gerald's armor had been polished, and the leather of his

DEMONSOULED

sword belt and boots gleamed. No doubt Gerald had kept Wesson quite busy last night.

"You look awful!" said Gerald.

"And a fine morning to you, as well," said Mazael.

"I mean no insult," said Gerald. "You look ill again, Mazael. You should speak with Master Othar."

"I've spoken to a wizard," said Mazael. He felt the aftertaste of the coffee. Gods, that was foul stuff. "I'm fine. I didn't sleep well last night, that's all."

"He didn't." Romaria stepped out from the entrance to the King's Tower. She wore her traveling clothes and her worn green cloak. "I should know. I was with him."

Color flushed Gerald's cheeks. Mazael heard Wesson's ribald snicker. "Ah...I see...I did not mean to pry..."

Mazael laughed. "Never mind, Gerald. Let's go see what Mitor wants."

They crossed the courtyard and entered the anteroom to the great hall. A herald in Cravenlock livery raised a hand for them to halt. Mazael walked past, and left the flustered herald behind.

Mitor stood at the high table with Marcelle, his advisors, his allies, and his vassals - Sir Commander Galan in his armor, Lord Marcus and Lord Roget in their finery, Albron in his mail, Rachel at his side. And Simonian, watching Mazael with a smile. Mazael wanted to sprint up the dais and gut the wizard, but he did not. Perhaps Sir Nathan and Master Othar's presence stopped Mazael. They stood with Mitor and his advisors on the dais.

Mitor's bloodshot eyes locked on Mazael. "It is customary to wait for the herald," he said.

Mazael strode up the dais. "You did summon me here, my lord brother. Should the business of the Lord of Castle Cravenlock wait upon mere formalities?"

Sir Albron smirked. "Is it customary for a landless knight to ignore his lord brother's preferences?"

Lord Marcus puffed up. "Lord Mitor is your elder and your lord, Sir Mazael! It is your duty to heed his wishes."

Simonian drummed his gnarled fingers on the table. "Sir Mazael may speak wisdom, my lord."

"What?" said Mitor and Marcus.

"Have the great men of history waited upon mere formality when events moved about them?" said Simonian. "No, my lord, they moved with speed and acted with decisive power! Now history taps upon your shoulder, my lord, and it is time for you to seize the liege lordship of the Grim Marches."

Mazael heard Mitor's teeth grinding. "Very well. Come here, Mazael. There are events afoot that we should discuss."

Mazael and his companions stepped up to the dais. The wrist of Albron's sword hand had been bound with a bandage. Mazael wished he could kill Albron and Simonian both and have done with them.

"I have just received word," said Mitor. "Lord Richard has marched from Swordgrim."

Dead silence answered his announcement.

"With him is the entire might of Swordgrim, nine thousand foot and horse," said Mitor. "Marching with him are Sir Tanam Crowley," he shot a sour glance at Mazael, "Sir Commander Galan's brother, the Lord Astor of Hawk's Reach, the Lord of Drakehall, the Lords of Highgate and the other mountains passes, for a total force of perhaps twenty-two thousand men."

"My Lord Mitor," said Lord Roget. "Our own hosts number under ten thousand fighting men. The Dragonslayer brings two armsmen for every one of ours. How can we hope to defend against him, let alone defeat him?"

Lord Marcus sneered. "You doubt our Lord Mitor?"

"No need to fear, old man," said Sir Commander Galan. "My brother Astor is a traitor and a usurper. The gods are on our side. More importantly, I bring the might of the Knights Justiciar to deal with this traitor Richard Mandragon. Two thousand sergeant foot and Justiciar knights, and ten thousand more once I inform the Grand Master in Swordor that we stand to regain our ancient estates!"

"Sir Commander," said Sir Nathan. "The forces of the Justiciars are scattered across the kingdom, and your two thousand, however strong, are still only two thousand. By the time your order marches, they will arrive to see the Mandragon banner over Castle Cravenlock."

"Have you lost your courage, old man?" said Sir Commander Galan.

"I have lost my youth," said Sir Nathan, "in the service of Lord Adalon and Lord Mitor, but I have gained the experience of years. My lord Mitor, I beg that you heed my words. Meeting Lord Richard in open battle is folly."

"Folly, eh?" said Mitor, waving his spindly hand. "Well, we shall see what is folly! My father had twice the men that Lord Richard did, and the Mandragons defeated him nonetheless. Now the tables are turned, yes? Lord Richard has twice the men, but justice and the gods are on our side, and we shall prevail! Besides, Sir Albron shall lead my host, and he has a few tricks for the mighty Dragonslayer."

"He had better," said Romaria. "Else you'll get to personally explain to Lord Richard why you are the rightful liege lord of the Grim

Marches."

Mitor's face soured. "When I want your counsel, woman, I shall ask for it."

"She is right and you know it," said Mazael. "Unless you have some brilliant strategy, Lord Richard will tear your army to shreds."

"Do not fear, Sir Mazael," said Albron. His smile turned wolfish. "I plan to kill Richard myself and present his head to Lord Mitor."

"Oh, I should like to see that," said Mazael. "Especially with the broken wrist."

"Enough," said Mitor. "I did not summon you here for advice, Mazael. I will not entrust my plans to a brother who has not visited his home in fifteen years. I have a task for you. I hope you can carry it out."

"What sort of task?" said Mazael.

Mitor waved him over. A detailed map of the Grim Marches had been laid out across the table, its corners weighed down by empty wine goblets. The map was old, but accurate. The towns and villages that had been destroyed in Lord Richard's uprising were underlined in red ink, while additions and notes had been made in Master Othar's firm hand.

Mitor tapped a thin finger on Swordgrim. "Lord Richard marches for us. I shall face him and crush him. But if I am to do so, then my flanks and rear must remain secure."

Mazael snorted. "What threat do you face from behind? The Castanagents and the Rolands will support you. The lords of the Green Plain might side against you, but they would have to march around the Dim Mire. The nearest army, other than Lord Richard's, will take weeks to arrive. The only threat you face is Lord Richard."

Mitor smirked. "Oh, is that so? Well, it seems your reputation is inflated. You forgot a potential foe."

Mazael laughed at him. "Then enlighten me, my lord brother."

"Oh, not them," said Mitor. He reached across the map and tapped Deepforest Keep.

They stared in silence at the map.

"What is this?" said Romaria. "You mean to make an enemy of Deepforest Keep? That is not a wise course. I..."

"Bah!" said Mitor. "Deepforest Keep? What is there that any lord would wish to rule? Trees? Perhaps some rocks, with a bit of moss, as well? And if Lord Athaelin does side with Lord Richard, what shall he send, hmm? Wenches painted up to be war-women like you, my lady?"

Romaria's smile was chill. "You should hope not, my lord Mitor. You had best keep your guards close. If one of those war-women would get past them, I fear that you would not live long."

"Must your brother bring this odious creature to court?" said Marcelle. "I fear her stench is quite overpowering." Romaria ignored her, which seem to infuriate Marcelle all the more.

"You said you do not wish an enemy in your flank," said Mazael. "Why make one now, by offending Lord Athaelin's emissary and daughter? Rein in your wife, my brother, lest her lips make you an enemy."

"How dare you mock me?" said Marcelle.

"How dare you mock my daughter?" bellowed Lord Marcus, shaking a fist.

"Have him removed," said Marcelle. "He does not mock me. No one mocks me."

"Ha!" said Mitor. "Even if they are right? You talk too much, woman. Remove yourself. You are giving me a headache."

Marcelle staggered. "What...but...but he..."

Mitor fluttered his fingers at her. "Go. This is not business for a lady, but a matter for men. You as well, Rachel."

A dozen expressions fluttered across Marcelle's face, rage, pride, hate, and a deep and profound misery. Mazael almost felt sorry for her. Was it Rachel's fate to end as Marcelle had, married to a proud wretch? Marcelle descended from the dais, shot a venom-filled glance at Mazael, and then glided from the throne room. Rachel looked relieved as she slipped out through the lord's entrance.

"I must apologize for my daughter," said Lord Marcus. "She has always been proud..."

"Quiet," said Mitor. He pointed at a servant. "You, bring me wine!" The servant scampered from sight. "Sometimes I envy you, brother. You have not had to marry. All women are base creatures, full of cunning and envy and deceitful tricks."

"No," said Mazael. "Not all."

Mitor sneered. "All. Your savage woodland woman can stay. After all, she is no proper lady."

Romaria looked at Marcelle's retreating back. "I should hope not."

Mitor ignored her. "I do not speak of Deepforest Keep as the enemy in our flanks. After all, not one man in a hundred knows the place exists. No, it's the wood elves who threaten us. The Elderborn, as the wizards and the scholars call the creatures."

"The wood elves?" said Sir Nathan. "My lord, that is absurd. The Elderborn venture out of their forests only when their lands are threatened. War looms with Lord Richard in the north, not in the south. The only village near the Great Southern Forest is White Rock. The others were destroyed during Lord Richard's uprising."

Romaria shook her head. "Sir Nathan is right. The Elderborn

have no reason to make war on Castle Cravenlock. I doubt that the tribes know, or care, who rules the Grim Marches."

"Your father sent you, did he not?" said Mitor.

"My father sent me to find the dark wizard," said Romaria. "I learned about the other troubles riding through the countryside."

Mitor smirked. "Oh, we may have found your dark wizard, Lady. It seems your father does not know his neighbors as well as he may think."

"We have all heard the rumors," said Simonian. "The dark creatures that hunt the night, the disappearances, the tales of sorcery. It is all hogwash! It is the wood elves, I say."

"That is hogwash," said Romaria. "The Elderborn don't creep through the night and kidnap peasant farmers from their hovels."

"Lord Richard has hired them, most likely," said Albron. "He fears to face Lord Mitor's might in open battle, and has sent these sneaking wood demons to harass his lands."

"And just why would the Elderborn work for Lord Richard?" said Romaria.

Simonian shrugged. "Who can say? The wood elves are wicked creatures, full of fey enchantment and devilish cunning. Perhaps they commit atrocities for amusement. Or perhaps they have kidnapped innocent men and women from their homes for sacrifice to their demon gods."

"The Elderborn do not worship demon gods," said Romaria.

"We should not trust her words, my lord!" said Albron. "After all, by her own word, she has dwelt in the forest of these creatures all her life. Perhaps they have bewitched her."

"Bewitched?" said Romaria. "I tell you the truth, and you call it bewitchment? If I hand you a fistful of gold, will you call it dung?"

"Enough!" said Mitor. "I will not listen to a wild woman quibble with my armsmaster! My armsmen have seen these wood elves prowling the edge of the forests near White Rock." He pointed at Romaria. "You have been sent north to chase a dark wizard, yes? Well, you were sent to chase your own neighbors. A pity you did not stay at Deepforest Keep. You would have saved yourself a long journey."

"You believe that the Elderborn raid your southern border and are responsible for the rumors?" said Mazael. "Why is this my concern?"

"You were always blunt," said Mitor. "The wood elves and whatever dark sorcery they practice are an irritant, nothing more, but an irritant I need removed. I must have my full attention focused upon Lord Richard and his vassals."

"I still fail to see why this is my problem," said Mazael. "You need the wood elves removed? You have no lack of willing servants. Albron certainly seems eager. Or why not Lord Marcus? Let him serve you in deed as well as fawning word." Lord Marcus sputtered, but Mazael ignored him.

"I need them at my side," said Mitor. "But you, my brother, you appeared out of nowhere, as if the gods had sent you to my cause. So, this is what I would have of you, Mazael. I will give you some men. Take them south and drive these wood elves from my land. We have all heard tales of your exploits in the Mastarian war. Now let us see if they were truth or mere lies."

Mazael frowned. "No."

"No? You would tell me no?"

"I just did, didn't I?" said Mazael. "No. I don't believe the Elderborn are behind these troubles."

Mitor's flabby face twisted with rage. "You...you believe the ramblings of this wild wood woman..."

"She's more credible than you," said Mazael. "When was the last time you left Castle Cravenlock? I doubt you would know a Elderborn from a zuvembie."

Mitor's bloodshot eyes bulged. "You defy me?"

"You want to start a war with the Elderborn tribes, then find someone else to do it. I won't," said Mazael.

"You are my younger brother," said Mitor. Flecks of spittle flew from his lips. "You will do as I command."

"I am sworn to Lord Malden Roland," said Mazael, "not you. I obey him, not you. Someday, I will obey Lord Malden's eldest son Sir Garain, or Sir Tobias, or if death takes them both, then Sir Gerald. But not you."

Mitor's voice was a harsh whisper. "Careful where you tread, brother. The steps are perilous."

"Is that a threat?" said Mazael.

"Oh, no," said Mitor. "But remember, then...that you are in my castle, in my lands, surrounded by ten thousand of my men. You're right, of course. I cannot command you. But I can strongly suggest that you follow my requests."

Mazael drummed his fingers against Lion's hilt. "You suggest, then, hmm?"

"Enough!" said Sir Nathan. "Sir Mazael, my lord Mitor, we have enough enemies without bickering amongst ourselves. We do not know who or what is behind these rumors. It might be dark magic and walking dead, as Lady Romaria claims. It might indeed be the Elderborn. For all we know, it might be Sir Tanam and his crows, or raiders searching for plunder. I propose we send Sir Mazael to search out the cause of these rumors and to deal with them, since we do not know what is really happening."

"My lord knight," said Simonian. "I believe that is folly. My divinations have revealed that the Elderborn are indeed behind these dark tidings."

Master Othar cleared his throat with a deep rumble. "Is that so? Well, Master Simonian, I have cast my own divinations, and they have reached different results than yours. The Elderborn are not behind these tidings...although my divinations have revealed some very interesting things."

Simonian laughed. "Ah, you wizards of Alborg limit yourselves, my friend, to such minor magic. Just give me the chance, and I will teach you spells the likes of which you have never imagined."

"I prefer not," said Othar. "I would not enjoy burning at the stake for practicing dark magic."

Simonian sounded amused. "The magic I practice is not dark, oh, no...just merely different." His muddy eyes shifted to Timothy. "And what of you, my young friend? You are young, not yet set in your ways. Learn from me, and I'll show you magic no man of Alborg has seen in generations."

Timothy tugged at his beard. "Ah...no, thank you."

"Ah," said Simonian. "A pity. The young are so unwilling to learn, these days. I have so much to teach."

Master Othar smiled. "You have nothing I need learn."

"We shall see," said Simonian.

"Enough!" said Mitor. "I have neither the time nor the patience to listen to wizards gloat about their learning! Very well, Sir Nathan, despite your advanced age you yet have some wisdom about you."

Sir Nathan bowed stiffly. "Thank you, my lord."

"Mazael, if you will not go out to hunt the wood demons, then go and...investigate," said Mitor. "I will give you four hundred of my best men. Take them, go south, and do not return until you have found and dealt with these rumors of dark magic. I care not who or what is the cause. Most likely Simonian is correct and it is these wood demons. But find it and deal with it." He fluttered his fingers at Mazael. "Now, leave me. I must consult with my captains. Sir Nathan, you will see to the arrangement of the troops and accompany Sir Mazael. Sir Albron, Simonian, with me." Mitor walked through the lord's entrance with Simonian and Albron. Sir Commander Galan marched away, while Lord Marcus and Lord Roget looked like dogs abandoned by their masters. Mazael glanced at them with contempt and turned to Gerald.

"That went well," said Gerald.

Mazael frowned. "Oh, did it? Mitor's given me four hundred men to go and chase rumors. How could it possibly have gone any better?"

"He's getting you out the way," said Romaria.

"What do you mean, my lady?" said Gerald.

"Mitor's never shown any concern about the zuvembies and their master before," said Romaria. "Now he's told Mazael to go hunt them. He's getting you out the way, Mazael. For whatever reason, he doesn't want you here over the next few days."

"Why?" said Mazael.

Romaria shrugged. "I don't know. Between Albron and Simonian and your brother, this place has more secrets than a courtesan's diary." She looked at Sir Nathan. "And he has sent you away, as well. He doesn't trust you or Mazael."

"Perhaps I should refuse him," said Mazael.

"No!" said Romaria. "You and Sir Gerald and Sir Nathan may think this fight between Lord Richard and Mitor is important. But finding this necromancer and his zuvembies is more important by far."

"I thought you believed that Simonian raised these creatures," said Mazael.

"I do. Or, at least, he and Albron are allied with the necromancer," said Romaria. "Hear me out. I know that a wizard can use an enchanted object to track the enchantment's caster."

Master Othar grunted. "It is true. If you could bring me a bone from one of these undead creatures, I have a spell that could trace the necromancy back to its caster."

"I suspect that all that has befallen us recently, the difficulties with Sir Tanam, the coming war with Lord Richard Mandragon, and these creatures are all tied together in some wizard's trickery," said Sir Nathan.

"But to what purpose?" said Sir Gerald.

Nathan shrugged. "The wizard knows, the gods know, but I do not. It is up to us to discover."

"But if you find and destroy a zuvembie," said Othar, "then we can find out who is behind it."

"Simonian, most like," said Timothy. "I do not like that man, and I have told you about the enchantments I sensed upon him and Sir Albron. You should see the way the servants react to his presence. The castle's dogs howl at him as if he were a wolf!"

"Perhaps he's not a man," said Gerald. "Perhaps he's a ghost...or a demon."

"Perhaps Demonsouled," said Romaria.

Mazael laughed. "You believe in Demonsouled?"

Romaria shrugged. "I believe in the gods, I've seen a zuvembie. After seeing such a creature, Demonsouled are not so hard to believe."

"Milady Romaria is correct," said Timothy. "I told you how I saw San-keth writings at Alborg. I have read of darker things, as well."

Master Othar fumbled for his pipe. "The boy's right, of course. Why, in this very castle, a thousand years past, the histories tell of a lord that led a cult of serpent worshippers."

Mazael shrugged. "There may be serpent people, there might be serpent kissers, and there may be Demonsouled, but right now I have more immediate problems. Chasing ghosts, zuvembies, and Elderborn, for one." He turned to Sir Nathan. "I'll start gathering the necessary supplies and arms. We can depart by noon, I believe, if you..."

Sir Nathan held up a hand. "No. Lord Mitor gave you the command."

Mazael sputtered. "Me? But you, you're..."

"Older?" said Sir Nathan.

Othar lit his pipe with a burst of magical flame from his finger. "Aren't we all."

Nathan sighed. "I had noticed, thank you, Othar. Sir Mazael, I am no longer armsmaster of Castle Cravenlock. I am just another knight in the service of the Cravenlocks. You are Lord Mitor's brother. He has seen fit to give you the command." He smiled and a glint came into his eyes. "Besides, I have heard you led Lord Malden Roland's armies well in the Mastarian war. I should like to see how well you have learned those lessons Othar and I tried to teach."

Othar snorted. "Tried to pound into his head, you mean."

"We shall see," said Nathan.

Mazael sighed. "Very well. I suppose if Mitor intends to lay blame on someone, it had best be me. I don't plan to remain here long. Gerald, Sir Nathan. Go to the barracks and round up our four hundred men. You know the garrison best, Sir Nathan, pick men you would trust, and not fools like Brogan. Gerald, then go to the armory and select the weapons. Adalar, go with him, you can learn...what are you grinning at?"

"This reminds me of Mastaria," said Gerald, "after you took command."

Mazael snorted. "Pleasant memory, too, isn't it? Marching through mud and rain with Grand Master Malleus's army dogging our heels. We can reminisce later. Get going."

Gerald grinned and marched off, followed by the squires.

"It will take me a few hours to find the best men," said Sir Nathan. "Sir Albron scattered those who displeased him."

"Take all the time you need. Timothy, assist him," said Mazael. Sir Nathan nodded and left with the wizard.

Romaria cleared her throat.

"I suppose you'll want to come, too," said Mazael.

Romaria smirked. "This concerns my home and my people, lord knight. You couldn't stop me from coming. And I will find this wizard and his creatures, and I will kill them."

"Then I won't try to stop you," said Mazael. "I hope to leave by midday." Romaria left, leaving Mazael alone with Master Othar.

"I'd like you to come," said Mazael. "If we do indeed find zuvembies or some necromancer, I'd like your spells with us."

"Bah," said Othar. "I'm too old and too fat for much traveling. I pity the horse that would have to bear my arse. Besides, young Timothy is more than adequate to the task."

"Timothy is...well, Timothy is not you," said Mazael.

Othar boomed laughter. Puffs of smoke drifted towards the ceiling. "Of course he's not! I'm pleased to see all the effort we expended to teach you perception didn't go to waste." Mazael grimaced. "In seriousness, though...do not underestimate that young man. He survived the war of Travian succession. He knows his way around a fight. Timothy deBlanc has some depths, I think, that will surprise you."

"I hope so," said Mazael, "though I don't wish to test that claim in a battle."

Othar took a draw on this pipe. "I would go with you, boy, if I could. Fat and old I may be, but a good adventure still gets my blood up. But...I can't leave, not right now."

Mazael frowned. "Why not?"

Othar sighed and tapped the stem of his smoking pipe against his jaw. "Nathan's right, you know. There's more to all this. It's like one of pretty young Romaria's coin tricks. You see depths within depths, until you're not sure what's really there." He sighed. "She is a fine young woman. I wish I was thirty...well, forty years younger."

"What do you mean?" said Mazael.

Othar hooted. "Do you mean I have to explain that to you? Ho, ho, ho! You always were a lusty lad, I thought you would have bedded a wench or three by..."

"No!" said Mazael. " Master Othar, say what you mean, and say it plain."

Othar sighed. "I have a theory, more of a suspicion. No proof, not yet, at least. The entire thing could prove to be some fantasy of smoke, mirrors, and balanced cards. Do you know what begins tomorrow?"

"No," said Mazael.

"A new moon. Or the Black Nights, as they're called by some circles," said Othar. "I will have a chance to test my theory. I'm wrong, most like. Gods, I hope I'm wrong."

"Wrong about what?" said Mazael.

Othar chuckled. "Nothing, most likely. I will tell you my suspicions when you return, and we shall have a good laugh, my boy, at the foolish ravings of an old man!" His old face hardened. "But if I'm right...if I'm right...gods, Mazael...you think Timothy's stories about old dark books are bad?"

"What are you talking about?" said Mazael.

"I can't tell you," said Othar. "Not yet, anyway. But when you return, and if I'm right, then we'll take some steps, you and Sir Nathan and I. By all the gods, we'll take steps."

The old wizard turned and left.

CHAPTER 16
WHITE ROCK AND RIDE

Mazael left Castle Cravenlock three hours later at the head of four hundred men. To his surprise, the armsmen were disciplined and tough, with shaven faces and well-maintained armor and arms. Perhaps it wasn't so surprising; Albron surrounded himself with bootlickers, cowards, and thugs, while the good men were left to rot.

The village of White Rock lay two days' ride southwest of Castle Cravenlock, and Mazael led his men along the main road. A pity that the Old Crow had likely headed north for Swordgrim by now. Mazael would have liked to renew their acquaintance now that he had four hundred armed men at his back.

He planned to travel south to White Rock and to question the villagers. White Rock sat on the main road to Castle Cravenlock, and the village had seen every traveler for the last few months. Mazael hoped that the village was still there. He knew that some of Mitor's mercenaries would not hesitate to burn and rape White Rock off the map.

They rode past many fields and hamlets, the farmers staring at them with suspicious faces. Bit by bit the cultivated fields changed to empty
plains filled with blood roses. Past the cultivated lands near Castle Cravenlock the land was empty but for the ruined villages destroyed during Lord Richard's uprising. They made camp the first night in one of the ruins. Romaria insisted that they light dozens of watch fires, and kept watch almost all night.

But they saw nothing, whether human foe or eldritch creature.

The next day they broke camp and continued their ride along the road. What few peasants they saw fled indoors.

"We are not welcome here, it seems," said Gerald.

Mazael grimaced. "Not surprising. With a lord like Mitor, how can you fault them?"

When night fell, they made camp in the open. Romaria lit her fires and kept watch once again. No foes showed themselves.

They came within sight of White Rock before noon on the third day.

"Look at those fortifications," said Gerald. "Heavens above, Mazael, we saw smaller castles in Mastaria!"

A palisade of sharpened wooden logs encircled the small village, straddled by wooden watch platforms. A ditch had been dug at the base of the palisade wall and lined with fire-scorched wooden stakes. Large patches of earth beneath the wall had been blackened by flame.

"The mercenaries," said Gerald. "The villagers must have raised the wall for defense."

"Perhaps they have memories of the last war," said Sir Nathan. "Many unprepared villages were destroyed."

"No," said Romaria. "Not mercenaries. See those burned spots? They built that wall to keep out zuvembies."

"They built that wall to keep someone out," said Mazael. "Let's find out who. Adalar, the banner. The rest of you, wait here."

Adalar raised up the banner Mitor had given them before they departed, a black field with the three crossed swords of Cravenlock.

Mazael spurred Chariot towards the gate, Adalar following, and reined up about thirty paces from the wall. "Hello, the gate!"

A ragged peasant farmer stood over the closed gate, crossbow in hand. "Who are you and what's your business here?"

"I am Sir Mazael Cravenlock," said Mazael.

His words caused a stir atop the walls. Men rushed atop the crude ramparts, bearing crossbows, spears, and even pitchforks.

"Cravenlock!" said the peasant. "We've already paid our taxes, and we've only enough food to last until the harvest. Leave us in peace."

"I am not here for your gold or your grain," said Mazael. "We have heard rumors of disturbances. I have been sent to investigate."

"Investigate!" said the man. He spat over the wall. "You know full well who brought this darkness down on our heads, you and the castle lordlings!"

"Shut your mouth!" said another man. "You'll bring them down on us!"

Mazael laughed and held out his hands. "If I had come to kill you, you'd all be dead already. Who is in charge here?"

"Don't see why you'd need to know," said the first man.

"Gods, grow some sense!" said the scarred man. "Sir knight, Sir Albert Krondig holds this village. When we heard rumors that Lord Dragonslayer was going to war against Cravenlock again, he had us build the wall." The man forked his first and fourth fingers and spat through them. "Damned good thing he did. Right after that...those hell-spawned creatures started coming down on us."

Mazael saw Romaria sit straighter. "Creatures?" he said.

"You heard me right," said the scarred man. "Creatures."

"Laugh all you want," said the first man. "You'll laugh no more when they come for you, when these demons turn on those that summoned them!"

"What are you babbling about?" said Mazael.

"He wouldn't know," said the scarred man. "You said you're Sir Mazael, right?"

"Yes," said Mazael. "Get on with it."

"The Sir Mazael that went off to fight the Mastarian war?" said the first man. "The Sir Mazael that killed a hundred Dominiars and defeated
their Grand Master? That Sir Mazael?"

Mazael snorted. "Close enough, once you take away the jongleurs' exaggerations."

"That Sir Mazael!" said the first man, his eyes still wide. "Gods!"

Mazael realized he would get nothing useful from this lot. "Can you send word to Sir Albert that I would like to see him?"

"Aye, that I will," said the scarred man. "Sir Albert and Brother Silar like to see you, I'm thinking. You can come in, but only you and four
others."

"Four?" said Mazael. "I already said I wasn't here for your gold, your grain, or your women!"

"That you did," said the scarred man, "but we're not for trusting anyone from the castle these days."

"Knowing my brother, I'm not surprised," said Mazael. "Very well, give me a moment."

The scarred man gestured with his crossbow. "Go ahead."

Mazael and Adalar rode back to the waiting lines of armsmen.

"They seem suspicious," said Gerald.

"No. It's the zuvembies," said Romaria. "You heard them, they mentioned creatures."

"They blame Lord Mitor?" said Mazael. "What does that mean?"

Sir Gerald shrugged. "It's not uncommon for the peasants to blame every misfortune upon their lords."

"There have always been a number of legends surrounding Castle

Cravenlock," said Nathan.

Romaria laughed. "Not surprising. That place looks like the dark wizard's tower from a children's tale."

Mazael snorted. "They can blame these creatures of theirs on Simonian or whatever necromancer has raised them. When Lord Richard's army comes and burns their homes, steals their crops, and rapes their women, they can blame that on Mitor." He wheeled Chariot around. "Sir Nathan, I'd like you to accompany me. They may know of you. If they do, they'll undoubtedly respect you. Romaria, come as well. You've seen these creatures. You can see if their descriptions match your observations. Gerald, watch my back."

Gerald snorted. "Your back doesn't usually need watching."

"Timothy, come as well," said Mazael. The wizard sat atop the horse Mazael had given him. "Use your arts to watch for any ambush. And keep an eye out for any magic."

Timothy nodded, closed his eyes, and began spell casting. He tumbled a piece of quartz wrapped with silver wire across his fingers. The crystal glowed when he finished his spell, and he tucked it away in his pocket.

"What spell did you use?" said Romaria.

"Ah...one to sense the presence of foes," said Timothy. "The spell to sense the presence of magic is far simpler."

"Good," said Mazael. "Now let's go meet Sir Albert and this Brother Silar."

Mazael felt the villagers watching him as he rode closer, fear on their faces. Not surprising, given the brutality he had seen Mitor display. The crude gates opened with a groaning creak, and Mazael rode Chariot into the village.

The scarred man waited for them. "Sir Albert and Brother Silar will see you in the church."

White Rock's church was a looming edifice of dark stone, similar Castle Cravenlock's chapel with its thick walls, high windows, and domed ceiling. The three interlocked rings of Amatheon adorned the dome's crest, and over the iron-banded doors rested the weathered bronze symbols of Joraviar the Knight and Amater the Holy Lady. Mazael reined Chariot up before the church and waited for the others to dismount. When they had, he pushed open the church's doors and strode inside.

The only illumination came from the narrow windows and the altar candles. Mazael smelled the old wood of the pews, and he saw specks of dust dancing in the thin beams of light. Two men stood before the altar. One was old and leaned on a cane for support, his face a labyrinth of meandering wrinkles, left eye masked beneath a yellow film. Despite his age, the old man wore chain mail, a sword, and a green tabard embroidered with a pair of coins and a shield.

The other man was younger. His leathery skin was weathered, and what little hair he had left had been cropped to stubble. He wore a coarse brown robe, and the rings of Amatheon hung from his rope belt alongside a strangely shaped star.

The man was a Cirstarcian monk.

The old man stepped forward, his cane clicking against the stone floor. "Sir Mazael Cravenlock, I assume. My men told me of your coming. Well met. I am Sir Albert Krondig. I do not know your companions, I fear."

"Then I shall have to rectify that," said Mazael. "This is Sir Nathan Greatheart, former armsmaster of Castle Cravenlock, Sir Gerald Roland, youngest son of Lord Malden Roland, Lady Romaria Greenshield, of Deepforest Keep, and Timothy deBlanc, a wizard."

"A wizard," said the man in the monk's robe. "That is well. With all that has transpired here, a wizard's skills would be most welcome."

"Well met, all of you," said Sir Albert. "Ah, I recognize you now, Sir Nathan. I remember the tournament Lord Adalon held at Swordgrim to celebrate his marriage. That must have been thirty-five years past."

Nathan laughed. "Forty-two, more like it."

"Sir Nathan was a humble squire then," said Sir Albert. "No more than a lad of fifteen or sixteen, I'll warrant. He won the squires' melee. I remember it well."

"You did quite well at the lance, I recall," said Nathan.

Albert laughed. "Hardly. Ah, but thank you, sir knight. It is well to remember the good times in these dark days." He gestured at the monk. "This grinning fool is Brother Silar, a monk of the Cirstarcine Order."

The monk laughed and bowed. "Sir Albert is too kind. I have been called much worse in my day."

"The Cirstarcine Order is famous for taking a hand in the kind of troubles we have been lately experiencing," said Sir Albert. "The monastery sent Brother Silar as an emissary to aid us. The good brother and I have known each other for some time. Despite his rampant foolishness, the man has been a great help."

"Speaking of those troubles," said Mazael. "That's quite an impressive palisade you've got. Why did you build it?"

Sir Albert's face tightened with anger. "You would know, my lord knight."

"Just why is that?" said Mazael.

"You came from the castle," said Sir Albert.

Mazael sighed and pounded a fist into his leg. "Sir Albert, I shall be blunt. Until last week, I hadn't set foot in the Grim Marches for fifteen years. And in these last weeks, I've seen my sister abducted by one of Lord Richard's vassals, bands of pillaging mercenaries roving the countryside, and heard rumors that dead men stalk the plains at night. Do you know something, Sir Albert? I'm damned tired of people assuming I know what's going on, and I want some bloody answers!" His voice had risen to a shout, and he forced himself to calm down. "Lord Mitor seems to think that the Elderborn are behind the rumors."

Sir Albert looked incredulous. "Sir Mazael, I beg your forgiveness...but Lord Mitor is a fool."

Nathan flinched. "That is treason."

"Regrettably, truth and treason are often one and the same," said Silar. "In this case, doubly so."

"Lord Mitor could not have chosen a worse time to begin this uprising against the Dragonslayer," said Albert. "It is folly of the worst sort. He should be sending for the magisters of Alborg and the Masters of the Cirstarcine Order to combat this evil. Instead, he fritters away his men and his gold raising an army to fight the Mandragons. He stripped away the best men from the villages. All that is left are the old men, the injured, and women and children to fend off..."

"To fend off what?" said Mazael.

"You really don't know, do you, my lord knight?" said Albert.

"That's what I just said," said Mazael. "Lord Mitor says they're Elderborn. Sir Albron thinks they're wandering bandits. Lady Romaria thinks they're zuvembies..."

"Zuvembies?" said Silar. "Demon-corpses? Yes, that's quite apt. I called them animations, but 'zuvembies' is a more apt description of the necromancy that raised these fiends."

"I had best start at the beginning, I fear," said Sir Albert. "Will you take offense if I sit? My bones are old, and they ache terribly this time of year." He sighed. "Or any other time of the year, for that matter."

Mazael gestured at the pews. "By all means."

They sat in the pews. Gerald started to fold his hands and bow his head on reflex. Mazael hid a smile as the younger knight shook his head and sat up.

"This misery all began about six months ago," said Sir Albert.

"Six months?" said Gerald. "Mazael, wasn't that when Lady Rachel said that Sir Tanam first came to Castle Cravenlock to offer Toraine Mandragon's hand?"

"It was," said Mazael. "Sir Albert, please continue."

Sir Albert frowned. "I had heard nothing of that, though we of White Rock soon had our own concerns." He shifted in his seat. "In truth, Sir Mazael, I am uncertain how to broach this."

"Well, get on with it," said Mazael. "I'd rather have the ugly truth than some perfumed lies."

Sir Albert cleared his throat. "As you wish. About that time we started hearing some dark rumors about Castle Cravenlock."

Sir Nathan frowned. "What sort of rumors?"

"If the tales could be believed, a cult of serpent worshippers had arisen at Castle Cravenlock," said Sir Albert.

"What?" said Sir Nathan. "That's absurd. I have seen no such thing."

"Regardless," said Sir Albert. "Travelers went to Castle Cravenlock and never returned. The peasants saw strange things happening at night. Some even claimed that Lord Mitor and Lady Marcelle were the high priest and priestess of that cult, and that Lady Rachel had promised herself in marriage to the dark powers."

"Absurd," repeated Sir Nathan.

"These rumors have their foundations in fact," said Silar. "According to the histories of my order, Castle Cravenlock has been home to three separate San-keth cults. In fact, the castle was raised by the serpent worshippers. According to legend, the house of Cravenlock was founded when the younger brother of the high priest turned away from the dark path and slew his entire family and all the cultists. In fact, that is what Cravenlock means in bastardized Tristafellin... betrayer's sword. My home monastery was founded to keep watch over the castle so no cult would rise again." A wry smile formed on his lips. "It appears we failed."

"An interesting tale," said Mazael. "But what of it? You speak of history a thousand years dead. It is the present that concerns me."

"I will speak of that later," said Sir Albert. "The troubles started a soon after we first heard of the cult. It began with a pair of courting peasants who crept out of the village for a tryst. Their bodies were found the next morn. At first I assumed the hunting cats, or a pack of wolves from the forest. Then people began disappearing in the village, snatched out of their homes. And there were sightings of creatures, monsters out of the priests' descriptions of the fires of hell."

"What do they look like?" said Romaria.

"Like dead men, my lady," said Albert. "I've seen many corpses in my days, I fear. That is exactly what these things look like. Walking corpses, rotting and foul and torn. Their eyes and mouths glow with a sick green light. They are slow, and shamble along, but they are as strong as ten mortal men."

"Necromancy," said Timothy. Gerald made a sign to ward off evil.

"Aye," said Romaria, "that matches the things I've seen near Deepforest Keep."

"I ordered the palisade constructed," said Albert. "We were fortunate to have finished it before Lord Mitor stripped away the most able-bodied men for his armies. We also lit watch fires at night, and they seem to keep the creatures away. Fire has the power to end their wretched existence. Mortal weapons cannot touch them. We killed, if you can say that, several of the creatures with flaming arrows. Yet we can still see their eyes watching us out of the darkness of the night." The old knight shook his wrinkled head. "I am too old. Would that I had died before I had seen such evil. The wars of men are one thing, but this is a violation of heaven's laws."

"What does this have to do with a San-keth cult at the castle?" said Mazael.

"Necromancy goes hand and glove with these cults," said Silar. "It is one of the foul arts the serpent god teaches his people and his race. I believe that the cult is raising these creatures."

"A cult?" said Mazael. "Romaria and the druids of Deepforest Keep believed it to be one man, a renegade dark wizard or necromancer."

Silar shrugged. "That would not surprise me. Often only the high priest, or an actual San-keth cleric, possesses power enough to perform such dark arts."

Sir Albert frowned. "Do you suspect anyone?"

"Yes," said Romaria and Mazael together.

"Simonian of Briault, a wizard Mitor has employed in his court," said Romaria.

Sir Albert did not recognize the name, but Silar's dark eyes widened.

"You know the name?" said Mazael.

"Oh, yes," said Silar. "Yes, indeed. Most of my order and certainly all of Briault does. Simonian was a necromancer and a warlock of the worst sort, one who consorted with the dead and with demons in equal measure. He terrorized Briault for decades until the Briaultan lords united to fight him. My order had a death mark on him. We assumed that he had died in the fighting. It appears that we were wrong."

"Your order isn't right too often, is it?" said Mazael.

Silar grinned. "All too true, I fear. We try our best, but alas, we are mortal and prone to error of all sort."

"If Mitor's Simonian is the same man you described," said Mazael, "then he is undoubtedly the wizard raising these creatures."

"Perhaps," said Sir Albert. He hesitated. "My lord knights...have you considered that Lord Mitor brought him here with just that purpose in mind?"

"What do you mean?" said Mazael.

"Lord Richard Mandragon's army is twice the size of Lord Mitor's," said Albert. "Lord Richard's potential allies can reach the Grim Marches with greater speed, as well. It..." Albert fell silent.

"What my friend is unable to say," said Silar, "is that my order believes Lord Mitor Cravenlock invited the San-keth and Simonian to Castle Cravenlock to help defeat his enemies."

"That's absurd," said Mazael after a long pause.

"Why?" said Silar.

"Because," Mazael said. "Because...Mitor's a fool, but... even he could not do something so wretched."

"It wouldn't surprise me," said Romaria.

"Besides," said Mazael. "How could Mitor even know where find these San-keth?"

"Because," said Silar. "Your mother brought the cult to Castle Cravenlock in the first place."

"That is treason," said Sir Nathan. "Dare you say that Lord Adalon or Lady Arissa involved themselves in such filth, I will..."

"Lord Adalon had nothing to do with the San-keth," said Silar. "It was Lady Arissa who brought the serpent priests to Castle Cravenlock, to assure her husband's success against Lord Richard. It was her undoing. Did you know that Lord Richard rose up because he knew of the San-keth cult? We Cirstarcians knew, Lord Richard knew, and yet Lord Adalon never did, the poor old fool."

Mazael shoved to his feet. "My father was a kindly fool, but even he could not have missed something so dark!"

"Ah, but he did," said Silar. "History doesn't repeat itself, you know, but certain patterns do. Lady Arissa consorted with dark powers to try and hold her grip on power. She ruled Lord Adalon, you know that as well as I. And now her son Lord Mitor consorts with those same dark powers to regain his father's title. And once again Lord Richard marches to meet the armies of the house of Cravenlock."

"This is madness," Mazael said. "Even if Mitor was cunning enough to ally himself with the San-keth, Rachel...Rachel would never stand by to something so vile..."

Silar sighed. "Sir Mazael, your sister is not the girl you grew up with, just as you are not the boy you were. You said you had left the Grim Marches for fifteen years, correct? Much can happen in fifteen years. Much can change."

Mazael mastered his rage before he drew his blade and slew the old man and the monk. "Do you have any proof?"

Silar grimaced. "None. Yet."

Mazael sat back down. "Then this is all supposition. Simonian is the cause of all this. You said your order had put a death mark on him. He is playing some trickery on Mitor, I don't doubt it. Gods, I should have simply killed him."

"You may yet have the chance," said Sir Albert. "My lord knights, I am honor-bound to tell you. I have seen enough. When Lord Richard's army comes, I plan to stand with him."

"Now, that is treason!" said Gerald.

Mazael's words caught in his throat. He wished that he had stayed in Knightcastle. Everything the old knight and the monk had said rang true in Mazael's mind. He could almost believe it of Mitor and his harridan wife. But there was no way Rachel could have been involved in something as twisted as a San-keth cult. There was no way. He felt tired. He felt like killing someone.

He remembered how bitter his mother had become. Had she truly worshipped the god of the serpents? She had had no use for him, but had often spent time with Mitor. Had she drawn him into her perversion? He could believe it of Mitor, perhaps, but not Rachel.

"Fine," said Mazael. "Stand with Lord Mitor, or stand with Lord Richard, it means naught to me. And if that's all, we'll be going."

CHAPTER 17
PARLEY

They rode over White Rock's splintering drawbridge.

"We should go back," said Gerald.

Mazael glared at him. "Why?"

Gerald met Mazael's gaze. "Because Sir Albert and Brother Silar could have told us much more. Sir Albert has dealt with these creatures from the beginning."

"So has Romaria," said Mazael.

"True," said Gerald. "But Brother Silar is a Cirstarcian. He has access to all the histories of his order. He could help us."

"No," said Mazael. "The Cirstarcians will support Lord Richard. Silar said as much."

"Would that be such a bad thing?" said Romaria.

Mazael reined Chariot up hard and turned the big horse around. Romaria had to snap the reins to keep her mount under control.

"What did you say?" said Mazael.

"Everything the old knight and the monk said seems plausible," said Romaria. "I've only been at Castle Cravenlock a few days, yet even I have seen your brother for a wretch."

"I don't disagree," said Mazael.

"If Mitor is willing to plunge the Grim Marches into years of death and blood for the sake of his pride, what's to keep him from selling his soul to the San-keth?" said Romaria.

"That's different," said Mazael.

"How?" said Romaria.

"Because," said Mazael, "Rachel would never go along with him."

"Your sister agrees with him on all other matters," said Romaria.

Mazael's fist tightened on Chariot's reins. "We're going."

"We should stay," said Romaria.

Mazael stared at her. "If we did, we would sign the death warrant of the village, do you realize that? Mitor has gathered an army of thousands. If he learns that Sir Albert means to declare for Lord Richard, Mitor will raze White Rock. You thought what Brogan did was bad? White Rock would make that seem like a actor's farce."

Romaria frowned. "I...hadn't thought of that." Her eyes flashed. "But surely you don't mean to abandon the search for the zuvembies..."

"Of course not," said Mazael. "We'll camp out in the open this night. If the creatures are at hunt, they'll find us. We'll ward them off with fire, destroy one, and take its remains back to Castle Cravenlock. This talk of a San-keth cult is all hot air. Simonian is behind this business, I believe. Master Othar will cast his spell over the remains and prove that Simonian raised the creatures. With luck, I can also prove that our honorable Albron Eastwater is Simonian's lackey."

"A fine plan," said Romaria, "but what of Lord Richard, and what of this war Mitor seems intent on starting?"

Mazael grinned. "It's like I told Sir Gerald, back at the Northwater inn." Gerald groaned. "We'll take things one step at a time."

They rode back to the armsmen waiting beneath the Cravenlock banner. The men milled about, gripping their weapons. Mazael spotted the captain he had left in charge and rode over.

"I thought I told you to keep the men in order," said Mazael.

The captain flinched. "I did, my lord knight! Or so I tried. You ordered scouts and outriders be kept out at all times. One of them has come back with a report."

"Report of what?" said Mazael.

The captain's face tightened. "There are creatures approaching, my lord."

"Creatures?" said Mazael, turning to Romaria. "I thought you said the zuvembies came out at night."

Romaria frowned. "They do."

"No!" said the captain. "Not zu...zuh...not those. Wood elves, my lord. Wood demons out of the Great Southern Forest to raid the countryside! Lord Mitor was right! The wood demons have allied with Lord Dragonslayer against us."

"Ridiculous!" said Romaria.

"Begging your pardon, my lady, but I can only tell you what I see," said the captain.

"Do you have any idea why a band of Elderborn would have ventured this far north?" said Mazael.

Romaria shook her head. Dark locks spilled from the hood of her cloak. "No. The northernmost tribes in the forest are the Tribe of the Wolf and the Tribe of the Oak," she said. "And they're probably looking for us."

"Why?" said Mazael.

"The Elderborn are the best scouts and trackers in the world," said Romaria. "If your scouts saw them, then they wanted to be seen."

"The men did say the wood demons—" the captain flinched under Romaria's furious glare, "—the wood elves were headed this way."

"Yes, but why are they coming for us?" said Mazael.

Romaria shrugged. "Gods only know. The Elderborn do as they will, when they will it. It's possible they're here to hunt down zuvembies." She hesitated. "If they are, and they've the same reasoning as Sir Albert's...then they've likely come to kill us."

"Amatheon and Amater," Mazael swore. "If they're so eager to pin blame on the Cravenlocks, why don't they go and pay a visit to Mitor? I haven't set foot in the Grim Marches for the last fifteen years. Romaria, come with me, you'll know these Elderborn and how to deal with them. Adalar, you'll come as well, as standard-bearer. I shall take our fifty lancers on horse. If it comes to blows, we can either run for it or ride them down. Sir Nathan, Gerald, take command of the remaining men and follow us at a distance. If battle seems likely, come to our aid."

Sir Nathan grimaced. "This does not bode well. The presence of Elderborn hunters in the Grim Marches will lend credence to Simonian's claims. Lady Romaria, do you truly believe the Elderborn have come to make war?"

"I don't think so, Sir Nathan," said Romaria. "But if they believe Lord Mitor is responsible for raising the zuvembies, they could do anything."

"I've no intention of waiting here to find out," said Mazael. He pointed at a scout. "You will show us the way. Gerald, Sir Nathan, give us a few minutes and then follow. Let's ride."

They rode away across the plains. Scattered trees stood here and there, casting long black shadows across the waving grasses. The clouds began to break up, shafts of sunlight stabbing down.

An hour later, the scout pointed. "There, my lord, I can see them."

"They're waiting," said Romaria.

The ground rose in a low hill topped by a ring of eroded boulders. An ancient statue, some forgotten monument, stood in the center of the ring. Mazael could saw figures waiting atop the hill, tall, slim shapes clad in gray mantles.

"The Tribe of the Wolf," said Romaria.

"Do you know of them?" said Mazael.

Romaria nodded. "They're the northernmost of the tribes. They visit Deepforest Keep from time to time."

Mazael could feel their gazes. "Would they know of you?"

Romaria brushed a stray lock of hair back into her hood. "They might. The morgans...ah, the chiefs, you would say, have often visited Deepforest Keep."

Mazael decided. "Then let's go meet them." He ordered the men to wait, and rode forward with Romaria. Details became visible as they drew closer. The Elderborn wore trousers and vests of animal skins and mantles of gray wolf fur. Their features were angular and sharp, with large eyes and slender ears that rose to delicate points past their hair. Their knives and spears had blades of chipped obsidian, but their great bows looked deadlier than any Mazael had ever seen.

One of the Elderborn stepped forward as Mazael and Romaria's mounts trotted up the hill. His mantle of wolf fur was silver, his skin weathered and marked with many scars. His eyes were a deep, unsettling purple, and he carried an oaken staff in his sinewy left hand.

Romaria reined up. "Dismount," she said, her voice soft and respectful. "This is Morgan Sil Tarithyn, Mazael. The ardmorgan...the high chief...of the Tribe of the Wolf."

Mazael slid from the saddle and put his hand over Chariot's face to keep the skittish horse from acting up.

Romaria walked to the ardmorgan, bowed before him, and began to speak in a melodic, rhythmic tongue. Sil Tarithyn answered, repeating many of the words Romaria had said. His voice was rough and soft, like a stone rasping on steel. Then the ardmorgan said something else, and all the Elderborn burst into laughter.

"What did he say?" said Mazael.

"I'll tell you later," said Romaria.

"Greetings, war-knight Mazael of Cravenlock," said Sil Tarithyn in the kingdom's common tongue.

"Ah...greetings to you as well, ardmorgan of the Tribe of the Wolf," said Mazael.

The old Elderborn grinned. "Romaria has told you of the Mother's People, I see. That is well." He tapped the earth with his staff. "We know of you, war-knight. In the south, the tribes speak of the defeat of Malleus, and how the humans who revere the Mother were saved."

Mazael smiled. "You attribute too much to me, I fear. My lord wished to seize some of the Dominiars' lands for himself. Concern for the Old Kingdoms meant nothing to him."

Sil Tarithyn chuckled. It made Mazael uneasy. "You will learn, war-knight. You will learn."

"Learn what?" said Mazael.

Sil Tarithyn did not answer.

"With respect, ardmorgan," said Mazael. "Why have you come here? It is unusual for any Elderborn to come to the plains, let alone for the ardmorgan of the Tribe of the Wolf."

Sil Tarithyn watched him for a while. Mazael met that violet, inhuman gaze and did not blink.

The old Elderborn nodded. "The Seer was true, when he said you were to be feared."

The Seer? Was that the same Seer Romaria had mentioned?

"I do not understand," said Mazael.

"You will, young one," said Sil Tarithyn. "You know why we have come. The daughter of Athaelin has told you. Dark sorcery defiles our land. The shells of those who have moved onward are raped by this necromancy and forced to walk the temporal world once more."

"You mean the zuvembies, I assume?" said Mazael.

Sil Tarithyn's face tightened. "Say not that word! It speaks of demon magic. We have come to remove that word, war-knight, to make this sorcerer face the Mother's wrath. We have come for justice."

"Do you know who raises these creatures?" said Mazael.

"Not who," said Sil Tarithyn. "What. The San-keth have returned to this land. Fifteen turns of the sun have passed since they were defeated. Yet they have returned to our land to spread their filth once more. It is the people of the Serpent who spread this poison across the land, who blaspheme the Mother with their unholy ways." His face seemed a mask of wrath. "And the great dark one has come back with them, that monger of lies and the weaver of deceits. He was here in the days of your father, do not doubt it, before the Slayer of Dragons destroyed his web of lies."

"My father?" said Mazael. "You can't mean that this San-keth cult and this dark one were here during Lord Richard's uprising..."

"I say what I mean, young one," said Sil Tarithyn. "The dark one wears many faces and many names. His is the power to trick and deceive, to wear lies as one of the Mother's People wears a garment. And the San-keth have been in this land during many turns of the sun, many turns. They built the stone house of your family, the castle of Cravenlock. It is the curse of your family. Always there is one to defeat the serpent people. Yet always there is one to invite them back. Much misery has been wrought from the house of Cravenlock."

"I don't believe this," said Mazael. "First Krondig and now you?

How do you know all this?"

"The Mother has told us, young one," said Sil Tarithyn. "And you know it in your heart and in your soul. You know the truth."

"Do I?" said Mazael. "And what truth is that?"

"The nature of your house," said the old Elderborn. "The darkness in their souls, the blight in their hearts."

"Oh, truly?" said Mazael. "I'm a Cravenlock, as well. Your people are fingering those bows so eagerly. Why not give them the chance to try feathering my blighted black heart? I wouldn't advise it, though."

"Mazael!" said Romaria.

"You are not like the others," said Morgan Sil Tarithyn. "Your soul is not black. Your heart is fire and your sword arm is power, but you are not tainted. Not yet."

"Tainted," said Mazael. "What does that mean?"

"You know," said Sil Tarithyn, and all at once Mazael remembered the dreams. "The daughter of Athaelin knows it true, as well." Romaria looked away.

"Mitor thinks you're behind the zuvembies," said Mazael. "He blames you."

"The Lord of Cravenlock is unworthy," said Sil Tarithyn

"We agree on that," said Mazael, "but he's a powerful unworthy, one with many soldiers. My original task was to slay any Elderborn I found north of the Great Southern Forest."

"A task you do not carry out," said Sil Tarithyn.

Mazael snorted. "Mitor and I share parents, that is all. And sometimes I even doubt that."

"Then what is your purpose, coming here?" said Sil Tarithyn.

"Master Othar, the wizard of Castle Cravenlock, has a spell that can trace an enchantment back to its caster," said Mazael. "My purpose is to destroy a zuvembie and take its remains back to Castle Cravenlock. Then I will know who has raised the creatures, and I will kill him."

"You do not believe in the San-keth," said Sil Tarithyn. "Who do you believe is responsible for these heinous acts?"

"Simonian of Briault," said Mazael. "An outlander wizard. I believe he is the necromancer."

"So you do," said Sil Tarithyn. "Perhaps you have it true. But do you have the why?"

"Why?" said Mazael. "I don't care why."

"To defeat your enemy, you must know him and know his reasons," said Sil Tarithyn.

Mazael snorted. "Why or not, he'll still die on my blade."

"Perhaps," said Sil Tarithyn. "What do you mean to do now?"

"Make camp," said Mazael, "and wait for the zuvembies to arrive. If they are so numerous as Sir Albert and that Cirstarcian monk fear, they'll come."

The ardmorgan considered this. "Your plan is sound. We shall make camp alongside you."

Mazael snorted. "Even if I am in error?"

Sil Tarithyn's gaze flashed like purple fire. "The creatures are more of a threat to us than you, war-knight. You live walled away in your stone houses. We live under the stars in the leafy houses of the Mother's trees. No child of the Mother is safe in the night while these creatures walk. The necromancer can be made to face justice later. For now, it is well that we destroy his abominations."

"I'm glad we agree," said Mazael.

Sil Tarithyn said something to his warriors in his own tongue. The Elderborn began to sharpen stakes and wrap oil-soaked rags around their arrows. Mazael saw the fifty lancers Mitor had given him approaching, and behind them the men with Gerald and Nathan.

"Your men approach," said the ardmorgan. "Go to them. We have yet a few hours before the sun goes to his rest and the moon awakens. We shall speak later," said Sil Tarithyn

Romaria bowed. "Thank you for your wisdom, ardmorgan. I shall try to remember what you have said this day."

"Go," said Sil Tarithyn, "and may peace find you."

"I doubt it will," said Mazael, "but thank you for the thought, nonetheless."

Mazael and Romaria rode down the hill as the Elderborn began raising a camp of their own. Chariot sniffed at Romaria's mare, and Mazael grimaced and tugged on the big horse's reins.

"What did the ardmorgan say?" said Mazael. "That made his men laugh?"

Romaria flashed a smile. "He said he thought that my mare was not the only one in heat."

Mazael blinked, but they rejoined the lancers before he could think of a response, and together they rode to rejoin Sir Nathan and Gerald with the footmen.

"How did it go?" said Gerald.

"Splendidly," said Mazael. "Their leader offered me a nonsensical string of riddles for answers. He seems to believe this idiocy of a San-keth cult as well. Nonetheless, they want these creatures destroyed. They will help us."

Sir Nathan shifted in his saddle. "You have a plan, I take it."

"Aye, I do," said Mazael. He waved an arm. "These creatures, by all reports, only come out in the night. Well, we'll give them something to hunt. We will make camp at the base of that hill, dig a trench around it and ring it with stakes and torches. The crown of the hill and that ring of boulders will make an excellent archery platform for the Elderborn. If these zuvembies attack, we'll greet them with fire and arrows."

"And then we will take some of the remains back to Castle Cravenlock for Master Othar's arts," said Sir Nathan. "Well thought."

"I hope so," said Mazael. "What was it you told me once? Words are idle, but hands are busy? Time to put that practice. We've work to do."

"Very good," said Sir Nathan.

CHAPTER 18
THE DEAD THAT WALK

The land was scorched and black, as if some great fire had turned the world to ash. Twisted black clouds writhed beneath a bloody red sun. Mazael walked past the crumbling foundations of ruined houses and the blackened corpses of long-dead villagers. He saw a cratered pit filled with writhing, snapping snakes, their fangs dripping with venom. A pair of wretched creatures, twisted serpents with human heads, crawled out of the pit. Mazael drew Lion and slew them both.

"Interesting, is it not?"

Mazael turned, black ichor sliding down Lion's length. Lord Adalon stood nearby, his lips twisted in a cavorting smile. Again he held the black staff crowned with a silver raven.

"What?" said Mazael.

"How little we know of our origins," said Lord Adalon. The snakes hissed and snapped, but could not climb out of the pit. "Most men know from whose loins they sprang. A few know their parent's parents and a little of their history. The great houses can trace their lineage back for centuries, even millennia." He laughed. "But do any of them truly know their origins? Do they?"

"The gods made men," said Mazael.

Lord Adalon grimaced. "How very puerile. What were the gods thinking, eh? Likely they regretted their acts of creation the next morning. But you, Mazael, my boy, where did you come from? That's the question that must occupy us now." He gestured at the pit of snakes. "You came from this, you know."

Mazael looked into the pit. "This?"

"Not literally, of course," said Lord Adalon. "Think of it as a circumstance, one of many that led up to your birth." He grinned, his teeth yellow and crooked and sharp. "That was such a happy day. I was so proud. You'll make me prouder yet, before I'm done. And, ah, your fair mother." His vicious grin widened.

"Pregnancy gives a certain glow to a woman, wouldn't you say? But when you were born...oh, my son, how did she cry. You must have been such a disappointment. She even tried to kill you. Pulled a pillow over your little wrinkled red face, tried to smother the air from your flapping little lungs..."

"Stop this," said Mazael. *"I don't want to hear it."*

Lord Adalon laughed. "The truth always hurts, doesn't it? But it will make you free. Free as a bird, free as the heavens...free as a demon."

"Go away," said Mazael. *"You're dead, Father, or have you forgotten? Go and leave me in peace."*

Lord Adalon's laughter redoubled. "Dead? Oh, no, not dead. Certainly there are many who pray for my demise." He snapped his fingers. "Let's take another walk, shall we? I do so enjoy our little strolls together. Who knows? You might even find it instructive."

They walked together across the blasted land, their boots raising puffs of black dust.

Lord Adalon hummed to himself. "I've always been fond of music. It can lift the spirit and soothe the soul, but it can also pull men down to murder, madness, and despair. Not that they've ever needed much help, of course. I think a little music to accompany our walk would be pleasant. Don't you?"

He waved his staff. The air shimmered, and a lean, hawk-nosed man with a silver-shot black beard and gray eyes appeared. It was Mattias Comorian, the jongleur from the Northwater inn.

Lord Adalon snapped his fingers. "Play, I say!"

The jongleur obliged.

"Heart of darkness, soul of sin,

a murderer's bloody grin.

So came the boy to his fate,

dark son of a demon great."

"I've always loved that song," said Lord Adalon. *"Don't you? No? A pity. I must confess, I've never liked the ending. Too inaccurate. How often have you seen a man proclaim the gods in the face of certain death? But, who knows? Perhaps I'll yet have a chance to write a different ending."*

"Leave me in peace," said Mazael. *"Go away."*

Despite the sun's glare, the air was cold. Mattias Comorian continued to sing.

"His demon soul within him rose.

He slew and cast down his foes.

Blood stained red his killing blade.

Death and fear his kingdom made."

"Peace, my son?" said Lord Adalon. "Is that what you want? I'm disappointed in you. Peace is a shelter for the cowardly, a place where weaklings can hide in the shadow of the strong." He looked at Mazael. "You weren't born for peace."

Castle Cravenlock loomed ahead of them, bleak and empty as the rest of the land, its windows black eyes in walls of dead rock.

"The child met his dark father,

before the church's altar.

'My dark child', said the demon.

'Your glory has now begun'."

Lord Adalon waved his staff at the castle. "This is where you were born. More, it is where you were conceived. It is where you began. It is where you grew up. And it is where you will embrace your destiny, your true self."

"This is nonsense," said Mazael.

"'I renounce you!' said the demon child.

'You lie, you destroy, you defile!

In the name of heaven, get...'"

Lord Adalon grimaced. "Silence." Mattias Comorian vanished in a flash of light. "A fine song, but such an execrable ending." He grinned, a black, rough tongue licking at his jagged teeth. "But let's write a different ending to this song, shall we?"

He snapped his fingers, and the world swam around them.

Mazael found himself standing before the altar of Castle Cravenlock's chapel, the domed ceiling draped in shadow. Dust caked the altar, and debris littered the floor. A peculiar stench, a mixture of excrement and snake scales, hung in the air.

"Look," said Lord Adalon.

Rachel, Mitor, and Arissa Cravenlock stood motionless on the dais, their green eyes empty and uncomprehending. His mother looked more peaceful than

Mazael remembered.

"Here!" said Lord Adalon, spreading his arms wide. "Here is where it all began, right where you are standing. There the Lady Arissa Dreadjon became the Lady Arissa Cravenlock." He smiled and climbed the dais steps to stand besides her. "How she hated the man she had married! She wanted power. To her, Lord Adalon was a weak, sniveling wretch. It was so easy for her to dominate him. Yet she too was weak. She brought down the house of Cravenlock with her machinations."

"Why should I care?" said Mazael. "That was fifteen years past."

"Ah," said Lord Adalon. He reached out and squeezed Arissa's shoulder. "Your mother was a beautiful, lusty woman, even wanton. I still think of her fondly, from time to time. But don't you see? No, of course not, they never do, not at first. The events of the past cast a long shadow."

He ruffled Mitor's lank hair. "Look at her children. They're just like her. They both want power they cannot wield. Mitor wants the liege lordship of the Grim Marches. But he has no idea how to attain it. And Rachel." Lord Adalon stroked a lock of her hair. "She has grown into a beautiful woman. I might even take her into my bed. If she survives what is to come." He laughed. "But she's no different than her mother. Softer, perhaps, but no different."

"That's not true," said Mazael.

"Is it?" said Lord Adalon. "No doubt you'll have the chance to discover it firsthand." He descended the stairs and faced Mazael. "But you, my son, you are different."

"What do you mean?" said Mazael.

"Arissa's children are smaller simpering versions of herself," said Lord Adalon. "They lust for power. But they are flawed. They are unable to attain what they desire. You're different. You're my son, after all. They are weak, but you are strong."

"I don't care," said Mazael. "This is madness. I want nothing to do with it."

"Do you?" said Lord Adalon. "Do you know what happens to the strong when they refuse to use their strength? Mitor fears you. For all her beauty, the Lady Arissa was a petty little soul. How she hated you! You were a reminder of her failure and the price she had to pay for it. And Rachel. Do not doubt that she will kill you if you stand in her way." Lord Adalon laughed. "Such a fine family, eh?"

"Be quiet and go away," said Mazael.

"You still don't believe me," said Lord Adalon. "Ah, pity. The young are ever slow to take instruction from their elders." He rapped the butt of his staff against the dirty stone floor. "It is time for a lesson."

Mitor and Lady Arissa shrieked. Black daggers flashed in their hands, the blades glistening with green poison, and they leapt at Mazael.

Mazael had Lion in his hand in less than a heartbeat. He stepped to the side as Mitor stabbed at him, drops of poison falling from the dagger. Mazael parried *his mother's stab, shoved her back, and spun on Mitor, Lion's blade ripping across his chest. Mitor attacked still, screaming as he raised his dagger high. Mazael's next slash opened Mitor's throat and half his chest. Mitor staggered and fell, landing in his own blood.*

Lord Adalon laughed.

Mazael's mother screamed as she attacked him, a poisoned dagger in either hand. Mazael's sword angled left and right to beat off her attacks, fine droplets of poison splattering on the floor. For all her fury, Lady Arissa moved so slowly. Blocking her attacks was like batting aside feathers.

Arissa stabbed her daggers at Mazael's face, and he spun past her. She lost her balance, her legs tangled in her skirts, and Mazael plunged Lion into her back. Arissa screamed, howling like a dying dog. Mazael put his boot to her back, wrenched his sword free, and she fell lifeless to the ground.

"So easy," said Lord Adalon. "They tried with all their fury and strength to slay you...and it amounted to naught. They are nothing before you. They deserved to die, did they not? Was it not satisfying to make them suffer?"

Mazael looked at the bloody corpses. "Yes."

"Splendid!" said Lord Adalon. "But there's one more Cravenlock, isn't there?"

Mazael turned and saw Rachel, the shadows gone from her face.

"Rachel," he said, smiling.

"Dear brother," she said.

Mazael never saw the dagger coming until Rachel had plunged it into his chest. Hot blood bubbled through his lips as he screamed, Rachel's laughter ringing in his ears.

"You see?" said Lord Adalon. "You're more powerful than her. But if you don't destroy her, she will take what you refused."

Blackness welled up in Mazael's vision, blood choking his throat...

He jerked awake with a gasp in his rolled-up cloak. The stars shone bright above him, the smell of smoke in the air. He remembered the   camp, and the Elderborn, and how he had taken the opportunity to get some sleep...

He could still feel the pain. He pawed at his chest, feeling for the dagger's hilt, for the blood. Instead he felt the sweat-soaked fabric of his tunic.

Someone lay down besides him.

An arm encircled his chest. A hand reached over, cupped his chin, and tilted his head to the side. Mazael stared into Romaria's ice-blue eyes.

"Another dream?" she said.

Mazael tried to speak, but his tongue and throat were too dry. He managed a nod.

"I saw you thrashing like you'd taken a fever," said Romaria. "And you're sweating like a man on his deathbed."

"It," said Mazael. "It was not pleasant."

"Tell me," said Romaria.

"No," said Mazael. Her hair tickled at his face. "No."

Romaria touched his lips with a finger. "The Seer told me that a man can't carry his burdens alone. They will weigh him down and destroy him. Or his soul will twist under their weight."

"It was the same as the others," said Mazael. "I saw my father, my brother, and my sister. But my mother was there. My father talked, taunting me and telling me to kill the others. Mitor and my mother tried to kill me. I slew them. And then Rachel came to me, I reached for her...and she...she..." He swallowed and closed his eyes. "She stabbed me in the chest."

"Here." Romaria handed him a waterskin. He spilled some, sloshing his beard and tunic, but the rest was blessedly wet in his dry throat.

"What's happening to me?" Mazael said. "Gods. These dreams. Am I going mad? I've had them, every night, for nearly the last fortnight. I am going mad. I've heard tell of men who saw visions that drove them mad. Is that what's happening to me?" A fire lit in his mind. He wanted to draw his sword and start killing things.

His hand curled around his sword hilt, and leaned she forward and kissed him.

Shock pushed everything else from his mind. Her hands clasped the side of his head and pushed his face into hers. When Romaria released him, her blue eyes were ablaze. The fire went out in Mazael's mind. For a moment he felt old and tired, but with Romaria pressed against him, the feeling did not last long.

"No," said Romaria. "Not a monster." She grinned. "You're half-mad and arrogant...but you're a good man, all the same. Not a monster. Would I kiss a monster?"

"No," said Mazael. He twined his fingers through her hair and tugged her face back down. "I don't think you would."

He kissed her again. She looped her other leg over his body and straddled him...

"Mazael!"

Gerald's voice jerked Mazael back to reality. Romaria's head snapped around, her eyes widened, and jumped to her feet. Mazael felt a momentary impulse to strangle Gerald. Instead he lurched to his feet, pulling Lion up with him. Gerald ran towards them, Wesson and Adalar trailing after. A cold wind whistled through the camp, tugging at their cloaks.

"What is it?" said Mazael.

"You'd best come quickly," said Gerald. "Timothy says something is happening, and the wood elves are in a frenzy. And...and the light, gods, Mazael, the light..."

All thoughts of dreams, murder, and Romaria fled from his mind. "Then let's go. Adalar, my armor!" Adalar handed him the quilted tunic and chainmail, and Mazael pulled it over his head as they ran.

He had ordered a trench dug in a half-circle at the base of the hill. Torches ringed the trench, their light flaring and sputtering. Armsmen stood ready, crossbows clutched in their hands. Mazael spotted Sir Nathan and Timothy and hurried to join them.

"What's happening?" Mazael said

Timothy pointed. "Nothing good."

Flickers of pale green light danced in the darkness surrounding the camp.

Timothy made a chopping gesture with his right hand. "My lords...that light is necromancy." Romaria sheathed her bastard sword and strung her longbow.

"Crossbowmen to the front!" roared Mazael, pulling on his leather gauntlets. "Footmen, lancers, hold the torches, keep them burning!"

The wind pulled the torches' flames into long dancing ribbons. Armsmen ran forward, carrying quivers of crossbow bolts wrapped with oil-soaked rags, while Timothy pulled a short copper tube from his black coat. The green lights focused into hundreds of tiny pinpricks, and Mazael glimpsed shambling forms in the darkness.

Then something stepped into the circle of torchlight.

"Gods have mercy," said Gerald.

The thing that shambled towards them had once been a living man. Its skin was gray and limp, with long tears revealing rotten muscles and pockmarked bones. Its hands were twisted, the fingertips ending in black claws. The creature's face was a skull sheathed in rotting flesh. A ghastly green radiance shone from the empty sockets, mantling its head and shoulders in an emerald corona.

"Zuvembie," said Romaria.

"Fire!" said Mazael.

But the crossbowmen stood frozen with fear.

Romaria shoved an arrow into a torch, the head tacking flame. She fitted the arrow, pulled, and released. It shot through the air with a trail of smoke and thudded into the zuvembie's chest. Flames licked at its ragged clothes, and a low moan escaped the creature's yawning mouth.

Romaria's shot broke the armsmen' paralysis. A dozen of crossbow bolts slammed into the zuvembie. The green light vanished as flames burst from its eyes, and for a moment longer it shambled towards them, wreathed in flame. Then it collapsed, its body disintegrating in a spray of embers and smoldering bones.

A frantic cheer went up from the terrified men.

"Well," said Gerald, pale-faced. "That wasn't so difficult."

Another zuvembie lurched out of the shadows, followed by five more, and then dozens and dozens of the creatures streamed out of the darkness. Green light danced in their skulls, and their combined glow outshone the torches.

"Fire!" roared Mazael. "Shoot them down, fire, fire!"

A storm of blazing crossbow bolts lanced out. They smacked into dead flesh and set the zuvembies ablaze..

"Keep firing!" said Mazael. He drew Lion and seized a torch in his other hand. "Any get too close, use the torches to push them back!"

A flight of Elderborn arrows flew from the top of the hill with a hiss, trailing ribbons of fire, falling into the zuvembies like burning rain. Flesh ignited and corpses turned transformed into walking candles.

But the creatures still shambled forward.

"My lord knight," said Timothy. "You, ah, may wish to step back." He raised the copper tube and began to chant. Both ends had been plugged with cork.

Romaria's eyes widened. "Do it! Get back from him!"

Mazael had seen the havoc a wizard's war spells could unleash and did not need a second warning. Reddish-orange light flared about the tube as Timothy gestured over it. He plucked the cork free, raised the tube, and covered his eyes.

A huge gout of orange-yellow flame blasted from the tube. The flames roared over the trench, incinerated the torches and the stakes in its path, and rolled into the advancing zuvembies. Four were blown apart, and a dozen others took fire. Within seconds, half the zuvembies burned, vanishing in the spreading flames as the grasses burned. Several men made signs to ward off evil, staring at the young wizard.

"My," said Timothy, panting. "That worked rather well." His legs went limp and he stumbled. Mazael ordered the armsmen to take him to safety.

The crossbowmen fired with renewed vigor. Burning bolts ripped through zuvembie flesh, while storms of Elderborn arrows raked at them. Romaria fired and fired, and every burning arrow seemed to take a zuvembie through the skull.

Zuvembies went up like walking candles, flames shooting from their empty skulls. They stumbled, lurched, and then fell, the hungry fires eating their flesh. The few that reached the trench were clubbed back with torches.

Gerald grinned. "It's working!"

Then the earth beneath Gerald's feet exploded. A skeletal hand gloved in moldering gray skin shot from the dirt ,wrapped about his ankle, and yanked him to the ground. An instant later a shoulder and the top of a skull emerged from the earth, the eyes glowing green. The ground beneath Mazael's feet quivered as animated corpses clawed free from long-forgotten graves. Chaos erupted as men screamed and pulled away from hands and arms rising beneath their feet.

Gerald lashed at the hand with his sword, but his blade bounced away from the bone as if he had struck a bar of iron. The undead things might burn, but steel could not harm them. Zuvembies shook free from the earth, men screaming in terror as weapons bounced from undead flesh.

Gerald shouted in pain as the hand tightened around his leg.

Mazael acted without thought and brought Lion down in a whistling arc, the weapon hot and alive in his hand, as if something long-dead had awakened within the blade. Lion sheared through rotting skin and crumbling bone, and the hand fell twitching. Mazael slashed his sword around in a backhand, the steel flashing blue in the night, and split the zuvembie's skull like a rotten melon. Blue fire flashed in the creature's eye sockets and extinguished the green glow, dusty bones and leathery flesh falling to pieces.

"Gods," whispered Gerald.

Lines of blue light glimmered in Lion's razor edges, tiny sapphire flames flashing in the metal. The glow spread, blue flames blooming along the sword's length. Mazael felt something old and powerful thrumming through his sword. Something that raged with fury, something that wanted to destroy the zuvembies.

Mazael agreed.

Three zuvembies shuffled towards him, fresh blood staining their black claws. Gerald gave a cry of alarm and raised his damaged sword in guard, but Mazael cut through the zuvembies like flame through chaff. He took an arm off at the shoulder, reversed his cut to shatter the zuvembie's chest, and spun to decapitate another. With every hit, the power within his sword grew, the blade's glow blossoming into shimmering azure flames. When he split the third zuvembie from crown to crotch, Lion exploded with blazing blue flames.

"Amater have mercy," said Gerald. "What is..."

"I don't know," said Mazael. Some instinct tickled his brain. "Hold up your sword."

Gerald complied, and Mazael tapped Lion's tip to the younger knight's blade. Blue flame leapt to dance in a shimmering corona around Gerald's sword. The glow was not so intense as Lion's, but it was there.

Gerald held up his weapon. "It is a miracle."

"I don't care what it is so long as it stops zuvembies," said Mazael, touching Lion to Wesson's mace and Adalar's shortsword.

Gerald nodded, and they plunged into the fray, their squires following.

Mazael's ordered camp had fallen into chaos. Men screamed and cursed as they grappled with zuvembies. The battle-fury came on Mazael, and the world blurred and slowed so that the already slow zuvembies seemed like granite statues. An armsman fell to his knees before a zuvembie, blood streaming down his face.

Lion plunged through the zuvembie and disintegrated the creature's emaciated chest, bone and leathery skin dancing with blue flames. The wounded armsman gaped at Mazael. Mazael slapped Lion against the flat of the man's broadsword. The armsman flinched, grinned, and then sank his glowing weapon into the skull of another zuvembie.

Then he saw Romaria nearby. A quartet of zuvembies pushed her towards the trench, their black claws darting and stabbing for her. She fought, her sword blurring around her, but the creatures advanced nonetheless.

Mazael took Lion in two hands and split the nearest zuvembie in half. A zuvembie seized Romaria, its claws brushing at her face. Mazael's sword took off its hand, its arm, and then its head in rapid slashes, and then he and tapped Romaria's sword with his own, set her blade to dancing with sapphire flames. She went on the attack, her sword twisting and weaving as she carved chunks from a zuvembie. The creature took another step before it fell, azure fire threading into its shriveled flesh. Mazael slashed Lion through the neck of the last zuvembie. The thing's head rolled across the trampled grass and torn earth.

Romaria laughed. "The gods of the earth, Mazael! That sword is out of legend. It was made to destroy things like this!"

"Then let us use it," said Mazael.

Together they cut a swath through the zuvembies, fighting back-to-back. Zuvembies crumpled before Mazael, the fires of his blade burning through their flesh and extinguishing their necromancy. He slapped Lion against the weapons of every armsman he saw, and soon dozens of blue lights flickered in the battle. Romaria's every strike ripped through a zuvembie, and Sir Nathan smashed his greatsword down, hammering a zuvembie to pieces. Mazael saw Timothy chanting and gesturing, loosing invisible force to throw the zuvembies to the ground, where armsmen with flashing broadswords fell upon them.

Burning arrows slashed down from the Elderborn, and smoke and ash filled the air.

"White Rock! White Rock!"

Mazael heard the thunder of hooves and the distinct twang of short horse-bows. A score of men on horseback riding around the base of the hill, Silar the Cirstarcian monk among them, fitting an arrow to a short bow.

The Cravenlock armsmen rallied and formed a fist of steel around Mazael. They drove towards the trench and pushed the remaining zuvembies between the Elderborn longbows and the horse archers from White Rock.

The creatures did not last long.

Mazael cut the last zuvembie down with a vicious slash. The fires on his sword flickered and went out, while the glow on the armsmen's weapons faded away.

The battle was over.

The sudden silence seemed deafening.

Mazael touched Gerald's shoulder. "Find out how many we lost." Gerald nodded and rammed his sword back into its sheath. "Timothy, that was explosive."

Timothy grinned and wiped soot from his brow. "It does come in handy, my lord knight. I think I'll sleep for a week now, but it does come in handy." He coughed. "You seem to have magic of your own."

Mazael looked at Lion. "So it seems. I wish I'd known of it earlier." Where had the Dominiars found such a weapon? "I'll have Master Othar examine it when we return to Castle Cravenlock." He kicked a charred leg bone. "We now have ample proof now that the Elderborn had nothing to do with these disturbances."

"Aye," said Timothy.

"Gather up some bones and ashes at once, so Master Othar will have something to examine," said Mazael. "I'd hate to have done all this for naught."

"Aye, my lord knight," said Timothy.

Sir Nathan approached, wiping ashes and bone chips from the length of his greatsword. "Well fought."

Mazael grimaced. "I'll not know until Sir Gerald tells me how many men we lost."

"Your plan held well," said Sir Nathan. "You couldn't have known that the creatures would rise from the earth like that."

Mazael smacked a fist into his palm. "My plan can go to hell. It did, in fact."

"You responded well," said Nathan.

"The sword responded well, you mean," said Mazael. "I've not the slightest idea what happened."

Sir Nathan shrugged. "Nor do I."

Ardmorgan Sil Tarithyn and his Elderborn descended from the hill. "A great triumph," he said. "The Mother is pleased with our actions." He glanced at Lion. "I did not know that any still possessed weapons with the magic of old."

"Neither did I, for that matter," said Mazael. Gerald returned with Romaria. "How many?"

"Twenty-six," said Gerald, "with perhaps another thirty wounded. Most should make it. Timothy is tending them."

"Burn the shells of those who moved onward," said Sil Tarithyn.

"What?" said Mazael. "Why?"

"The ardmorgan speaks true," said Romaria. "They've been in contact with the necromancy. If we do not, they'll rise again come nightfall as zuvembies."

"Then burn them," said Mazael. The White Rock men dismounted and made their way towards him with Brother Silar in their lead. "But we'll see to it later. Right now, we have wounded to tend. I'd also like to know how the men of White Rock arrived so fortuitously."

"Alas, I fear it was the gods' grace and dumb luck more than any meager skill on our parts," said Silar. "Sir Mazael, Sir Gerald, Sir Nathan, my lady Romaria, and..." He bowed to Sil Tarithyn, and said something in the Elderborn tongue, and Sil Tarithyn answered in kind.

"How did you come to be here?" said Mazael. "We're grateful for your help, certainly, and it came at a good time. But why did you come?"

"Sir Albert sent us after you," said Silar. The monk grinned. "He's heard rumor of you before, Sir Mazael, and figured you would meet with the creatures, whether you sought them or not. He knew now was the time to deal a strong blow to these devils."

Mazael looked over the smoldering battlefield. "It seems that he was right."

"Besides, I knew you would come under attack," said Silar.

"What?" said Mazael. "How?"

"You said Simonian of Briault serves Lord Mitor as court wizard," said Silar. "I saw the man near White Rock an hour after you departed."

"How could you have known him?" said Mazael. "Have you ever seen him?"

"No," said Silar. "But my order has a death mark on him, as you no doubt recall. His description states that he has tangled gray hair, an unkempt beard, and eyes that seem like pits of boiling mud."

"That's him," said Mazael.

"He's the man I saw," said Silar. "He traveled alone on horseback past the village. The stink of necromancy hung about him, and he wore some sort of enchantment. I don't think he meant to be seen. I approached him. He rode off before I could reach him."

"This is his doing," said Romaria. "He convinced Mitor to send you out after the Elderborn, then he went to use his dark arts to raise zuvembies."

Mazael cursed. "It seems to fit. Gods, I knew I should have killed the old wretch when I had the chance. And I may yet have the opportunity." He gestured at the charred ruin lying all about them. "Master Othar has a spell that can trace an enchantment back to its caster."

"Let me accompany you back to Castle Cravenlock," said Silar.

"Why?" said Mazael.

"There is a San-keth cult near Castle Cravenlock, Sir Mazael, if you believe it or not," said Silar. "And a man like Simonian of Briault makes them very dangerous, indeed. Perhaps you're correct, and this is all the necromancer's doing. But if you're not, then the superiors in my order must know the extent of the threat."

"Very well," said Mazael. "I mean to leave for Castle Cravenlock by midday tomorrow. You can ride with us." He touched Lion's hilt. "But if it is Simonian who has raised these things, I'll kill him when I lay eyes on him and deal with the consequences later."

CHAPTER 19
THE RIDE HOME

The stink of burned flesh filled Mazael's nostrils.

The sun climbed over the eastern horizon, red-orange light spilling over the plain. Mazael held out his sword, sunlight glittering off Lion's golden pommel. The blade was the work of a master swordsmith, but seemed normal in all other respects. Timothy's spell of magical detection had sensed power within it, but the wizard had been unable to determine the nature of the sword's magic.

"Let's put this Cirstarcian learning of yours to the test," said Mazael. Brother Silar ran two fingers down the length of the blade. "Do you recognize it?"

Silar winced and pulled his finger back. "Sharp."

"I could have told you that. Do you recognize it?" said Mazael.

"Aye, I do," said Silar. "The sword is Tristafellin."

"That's what I thought," said Romaria. "The magic of ancient Tristafel. I've heard legends of such swords. I'd never thought to see one, though."

"I can tell you more than that," said Silar. He tapped Lion's pommel. "This is the sigil of a group of knights founded in Tristafel's last days. They called themselves the Knights of the Lion, dedicated themselves to fighting the Demonsouled and the San-keth that had corrupted Tristafel. Sir Mazael, this sword was made to destroy dark magic. The wizards allied with the Knights of the Lion made magical weapons for them, working spells of power into the folds of the steel."

"Then that sword is valuable beyond price," said Timothy. "No spells of such power have survived."

Mazael reversed Lion and slid it into his scabbard. "A lot of good it did these Knights. Tristafel is no more, last I heard."

"True," said Silar, "but remnants of Tristafel survived in the kingdoms of Knightrealm and Dracaryl and Cadlyn and Caria. Sir Gerald's own distant progenitors, ancestors of King Roland of Knightcastle, were Knights of the Lion."

"He's right, Mazael," said Gerald. "Do you remember a battered old shield hanging in Knightcastle's hall? You've seen it, I'm sure. It has the lion sigil."

"The Knights of the Lion and their wizards, allied with the High Elderborn, confronted the Great Demon and the San-keth high priests in Tristafel," said Silar. "The city was destroyed, and the Great Demon and the Knights slain, but the Knights of the Lion saved our world. Were it not for them, the San-keth, the Demonsouled, and the Malrags would have overrun everything."

"But the Old Demon," said Sir Nathan, "the firstborn child of the Great Demon, eldest of all the Demonsouled, escaped to wreak havoc in the world. I've heard the same story, Brother."

"History, not story," said Silar.

"Fascinating," said Mazael, "but story or truth, I care not."

Silar scratched at his chin. "You ought to, sir knight. That sword just saved our lives, did it not? The shades of the Knights were undoubtedly pleased to see that sword battle dark magic once more."

"It was farsighted of those wizards to let Lion bestow some of its enchantment when touched to another weapon. I couldn't have destroyed all the zuvembies myself," said Mazael.

Silar frowned. "That was strange."

"Beyond the obvious?" said Mazael. "How so?"

"Weapons of magical power are rare," said Timothy. "It is unheard of for a magical weapon to transfer its power in such a manner."

"You said the spells of enchantment were forgotten," said Mazael. "It's been centuries since Tristafel fell. The sword could simply have powers you never considered."

"True," said Silar. He smiled. "We Cirstarcians are strange ones. Our stated mission is to praise the gods and to preserve knowledge. And we do, don't doubt. But our true purpose is to hunt down and destroy creatures such as the zuvembies. Magical Tristafellin weapons are valuable to us. We've collected a few, some quite similar to your Lion. None of them can temporarily bestow their power the way your sword did."

Mazael shrugged. "So what? It seemed logical enough at the time. Fire spreads, does it not? My blade had taken afire. So I thought to spread the fire and drive back the zuvembies."

"Aye," said Silar. "Suppose your own will made the sword's power spread?"

For a moment, it seemed as if Silar's face was a mask of crimson blood, his eyes white and staring and dead. Mazael blinked, and the momentary vision vanished.

"My own will?" Mazael said. "That's absurd. You said the sword's magic awoke in response to the necromancy that raised the zuvembies."

"It did," said Silar. "But you exhibited control over that magic. Suppose you have some sort of innate power?"

Romaria flinched.

"Power?" said Mazael. "You speak nonsense. I am not a wizard. The only power I've ever wielded is that of the sword."

"There are different sorts of magic than that of Alborg," said Romaria.

"Most certainly true," said Silar.

"Sir Albert was right," said Mazael. "You are mad."

Silar laughed. "The good knight was right, I fear, but this is no delusion. Hear me out, Sir Mazael, if just for a moment. Consider yourself. I have trained in fighting arts all my life, and seen more than my fair share of war, but I have never seen anyone fight like you. You move like lightning."

"I had good teachers, that's all," said Mazael, "and a great deal of hard experience."

Sir Nathan laughed. "Sir Mazael, you do me too much credit. You have surpassed my teaching, I fear."

"He's right, you know," said Gerald. "I fancy myself skilled with the blade, but if I practiced every hour of every day for ten years, I still could not hope to defeat you."

"I'm faster, that's all," said Mazael.

"Is it?" said Silar. "Suppose you do have some sort of magic, Sir Mazael, a magic that is unconscious and follows your will? You worked to become a warrior. You have become a formidable fighter. And now in your need, when the zuvembies rose to slay us, you exerted command over the magic of the sword."

Mazael thought it over. Chills ran up his spine as he remembered the bloody dreams. He remembered how, since he had first begun practicing with a wooden blade, he had always known exactly how to kill his enemies. He looked at Romaria and saw the fear on her face. Why did she fear him? He was tempted to leave, take her with him, kidnap Rachel from Castle Cravenlock, and ride far away.

He wondered what was happening to him.

"It doesn't matter," said Mazael.

Silar blinked. "Why do you say that?"

"The sword has magic. Perhaps I do as well. Right now I have more pressing concerns than some mystical power. If this sword has power, it will make it all the easier to kill Simonian."

"Easier, yes, but still dangerous," said Silar. "Simonian of Briault is a dangerous man. You should not face him alone."

"I don't intend to," said Mazael. "I will have Sir Nathan with me, and Sir Gerald, and Lady Romaria, and Master Othar. And Lord Mitor and his armsmen, once I show them the truth of Simonian."

"Assuming that Lord Mitor does not already know," said Silar. Mazael glared at him, but Silar did not look away.

"Come," said Mazael. "Let us return to the camp. We will do what we must when the time is right. Until then, it is pointless to worry."

Smoke still rose from the pyre. Four more men had died during the night. Mazael had followed Sil Tarithyn and Romaria's advice and ordered them burned. He did not like the idea of burning the bodies of his men like garbage, but he not like the idea of their corpses rising as zuvembies even more.

"I mean to rest the men until midday," said Mazael. "We'll march until sunset, sleep the night, and continue on our way. They are exhausted. I'd rather not have them dropping in their tracks."

Gerald yawned. "I'd rather not drop in my tracks, as well."

"Then we shall deliver the remains of a zuvembie to Master Othar," said Mazael. Timothy had already packed away scraps of bone and lumps of ash in his saddlebags. "He will discover who raised the zuvembies, and then we'll have an end to this business."

"I hope you are right," said Silar, "but I believe that you are wrong."

Mazael shrugged. "We'll see, won't we?"

"What will you tell Mitor about the Elderborn?" said Romaria.

"The truth," said Mazael. "What do they have to hide? Sil Tarithyn and his warriors helped rid Lord Mitor's lands of dangerous creatures. They should have his gratitude. Perhaps he'll even send them a reward."

Romaria grimaced. "I doubt that. He'd rather send them fire and sword and call it justice."

"He can't send them anything if he cannot find them," said Mazael. Sil Tarithyn and his Elderborn had left a few hours after the battle. Mazael had been more than happy to see him go. He had not liked the ardmorgan's cryptic references to the return of the serpents.

"Get something to eat and then get some rest, all of you," said Mazael. "That goes for you as well, Sir Nathan."

Sir Nathan smiled. "Aye, as you command."

Mazael found an empty spot in the camp and fell into a deep, exhausted sleep. Dreams tormented his rest, visions of blood and death. Rachel laughed as she plunged a dagger into his heart. The dead rose and killed, their clawed fingers gleaming crimson. He awoke gasping and sweating, and as he did, Romaria lay down against him, her arm across his chest. He went back to sleep. This time his rest was blessedly free from visions.

At midday, the men from White Rock saddled up and returned to their village, leaving Silar behind. Mazael ordered the men north. They made good time, brown dust rising up in a cloud like a banner of smoke.

They camped in the same meadow as before. Again Mazael fell asleep with nightmares of carnage, and again he awoke to find Romaria lying against him. After that he was able to fall into peaceful sleep.

He began to think that without her presence the dreams would drive him mad.

The next day of their journey was peaceful. Gerald was in high spirits, joking with Adalar and Silar and Romaria. Mazael rode silent and grim.

They stopped that night in the ruins of the same village where they had camped earlier. Mazael sat at the edge of the ruins, his back against a crumbling stone wall. He did not want to sleep. Then Romaria came and sat next to him, her head on his shoulder, and they fell asleep together.

Mazael dreamt dreams of a different sort that night. He was alone with Romaria in a deep forest glen, the trees towering high overhead. He felt happier than he could ever remember feeling. Romaria kissed him, her mouth hot against his. They fell together against the grass, kissing and tugging at their clothing.

Mazael awoke that morning refreshed, feeling better than he had in days. Yet the darkness of the dreams still gnawed at him. Romaria lay against him, looking at him with sleepy eyes. He wanted to kiss her and act out the dream, but the camp was already awake.

They reached Castle Cravenlock late in the afternoon, as the setting sun painted the castle's walls a deep red. It reminded Mazael too much of his dreams. A sea of fresh tents had gathered about the castle's rocky hill. More mercenaries, come to fight beneath the banner of the Cravenlocks.

"The storm clouds are gathering," said Silar. "I fear they shall break into a storm of blood."

"There's time yet," said Mazael. "Master Othar will give us proof that Simonian is a lying serpent."

"Aye, I hope so," said Silar. "Yet I've seen the same sort of storm, fifteen years past."

No sentries challenged Mazael as he rode through Cravenlock town and up to the castle gates, and he scowled at further evidence of Sir Albron's negligence.

The guards posted at the castle's barbican straightened as Mazael approached. "Sir Mazael!" called one.

"Where is Master Othar?" said Mazael. "I must speak with him at once."

The guard hesitated. "Lord Mitor has made Simonian court wizard, and..."

"I said I wanted to speak with Master Othar, not Simonian!" said Mazael. "Where is Master Othar?"

"My lord knight, I'm sorry. Master Othar died in his sleep three nights past."

CHAPTER 20
OTHAR'S FUNERAL

"How do they say he died?" said Mazael, sitting in his rooms in the King's Tower. A drop of red wine fell from his the goblet and splashed against the table.

"Ah...that his heart burst, my lord knight," said Timothy. Mazael squinted at the wizard through blurred, aching eyes. "It would not have surprised me. He was very fat, my lord knight, and old. I am sorry to be so blunt, Sir Mazael, but that was how he was probably going to die."

Mazael waved the goblet. "No. Always tell me the truth, Timothy. Tell me what you wish. So long as it is the truth, I'll not fault you for it, ever."

Timothy bowed. "Thank you, my lord knight."

"So they say his heart burst," said Mazael. "Has anyone examined his body?"

"No," said Timothy. "It would be the task of the court wizard to do so. But Master Othar cannot examine himself now, and Simonian will hardly do it."

"Can you cast the spell?" said Mazael.

"What spell is that?" said Timothy.

Mazael finished his goblet, cursed, and reached for the wineskin. "The spell to determine the nature of an enchantment and trace it back to its caster. Can you cast it over the remnants of the zuvembies?"

"I know the spell, yes," said Timothy. "But I do not possess Master Othar's skill. I cannot trace back the magic."

Mazael bellowed and flung the goblet against the wall. Timothy flinched wine splashed across the wall and soaked into the carpet. Mazael closed his eyes and clenched a fist.

"Convenient," said Mazael.

"My lord knight?" said Timothy.

"Men have said that Master Othar would die within the year as long as I can remember," said Mazael. "And now, just as we are about to deliver the remnants of a zuvembie for his inspection, he dies. Convenient?"

"Do you suspect murder?" said Timothy.

"I don't know what I suspect," said Mazael. "He told me something, right before we left. He said he would have answers when we returned. I should have...I should..."

"My lord knight," said Timothy. "No man can see the future. You cannot torment yourself over what you might have done..."

Mazael gave a weak grin. "Yes, yes, I know all that, do what you can in the here and now. Master Othar taught me that, you know." He reeled in his seat for a moment, but managed to hold his balance. "Well, this is what I intend to do about the present. It is still early. The funeral will not take place for another few hours or so. Go to the corpse, and examine it."

"My lord knight?" said Timothy. "That is..."

"Desecrating the corpse?" said Mazael. "Othar wouldn't have cared, and neither do I. Examine the body. See if you can determine how he died, and see if magic caused his death."

"You suspect Simonian?" said Timothy.

"I'd be a fool not to," said Mazael. "Once you are finished, search Master Othar's chambers. He suspected something, and I want to know what."

"I shall," said Timothy.

"Thank you," said Mazael. "Get started. Leave me."

Mazael spent a long time staring at the wall, his head spinning. He watched the wine droplets slide down the stones. Like blood, he thought. Blood in his dreams, in the battlefield, and now here at Castle Cravenlock...

"My lord knight?"

Adalar stood in the doorway. "Are you well?"

"No," said Mazael.

"You spilled your wine," said Adalar. "I shall clean it up at once..."

"No!" said Mazael. "This mess was mine and I'll tend to it. If I teach you anything, Adalar, always clean up your own messes. Now, fetch me a fresh tunic. I'm drunk and half-mad, but I must look passably decent for the funeral."

"I will, Sir Mazael," said Adalar. "I am very sorry about Master Othar."

"You are, aren't you?" said Mazael.

"He was always very kind to me, my lord knight," said Adalar. "Father was often gone on many tasks for Lord Mitor. I spent as much time with Master Othar."

"Well," said Mazael. "If your father wouldn't kill me for it, I'd give you some wine, and we'd raise a toast to one of the finest men who ever lived."

"There's some water," said Adalar.

"That will serve," said Mazael.

Adalar poured, they raised the clay cups, and they toasted the memory of Master Othar.

"Now, run and fetch a fresh tunic," said Mazael. He rubbed his aching temples. "And see if the kitchens still have some of that coffee Timothy brewed."

Adalar bowed and left.

Mazael leaned into his chair, images swimming across his blurring vision. He saw Master Othar standing before him twenty years past. He heard the wizard's booming laughter. He remembered learning to read under Othar's eye. He remembered. No matter how drunk he got, he could not forget.

"Sir Mazael?"

Adalar stood in the doorway with a tunic and a steaming clay jug in hand. "I found the coffee. Some of the kitchen workers have taken to it. There was plenty to spare."

"Splendid," said Mazael. He raised the jug and drained it in a single draught. It burned like hot oil and tasted like dirt, but it filled him with fresh energy. He pulled off his old tunic and yanked the fresh one over his head. "Sword belt." Adalar handed him his sword belt, and Mazael buckled it on. "Thank you. You're a better squire than I deserve."

"I am only doing my duty," said Adalar.

Mazael snorted. "And you're your father's son, I see. Take that as high praise. Well, let's go. I'll not be late, not for this." They descended the stairs, Mazael taking care to keep his balance. What a fine example he had set for Adalar. He walked into the courtyard and squinted at the morning glare.

"Mazael."

Rachel stood next to the door, clad in a black gown, her green eyes puffy and red.

"My lady Rachel," said Mazael. "What can I do for you?"

"Is this what we've come to?" said Rachel. " 'My lady Rachel?' You were my best friend once."

"You've changed," said Mazael. "And so have I."

"We've gotten older...that's all," said Rachel. "I'm so sorry about

Master Othar."

"Are you?" said Mazael. "I thought magic was distasteful."

Rachel blanched. "It...that was ill-spoken of me."

"And where's Sir Albron?" said Mazael. "I'd have thought he'd have wanted to come gloat ..."

Rachel slapped him. She was not strong, but Mazael's knees nearly folded from shock. Adalar made a strangled sound.

Rachel jerked back from him. "How dare you? You can't judge me, you don't know what I've had to do! Albron didn't want me to come, Mazael, he told me to stay in my quarters. But...I...Master Othar was so kind to me when I was younger, but now I'm so alone, I've had no one to turn to but Albron..." Her voice began to break with sobs. "And you, what have you had to endure? You've ridden from one end of the kingdom to the other. I've left Castle Cravenlock once in the last ten years, and that with Sir Tanam Crowley! You haven't had to stay with Mitor and his insults or that miserable, stone-hearted shrew Marcelle, you haven't, you haven't seen..." Rachel broke down completely.

Mazael reached for her, and she flinched and collapsed weeping into his arms. Mazael wanted to cry himself. For Master Othar, for her, or for himself, he could not have said.

But no tears came.

"I'm sorry," said Rachel.

"What for?" said Mazael.

"I shouldn't have hit you, I shouldn't have wailed like this," she said. "It isn't proper."

"Don't," said Mazael. "I should apologize, not you. I haven't been fair. I don't know what you've had to endure this last fifteen years. Perhaps I made another mistake, as well."

"What?" said Rachel.

"I should have taken you with me when I left," said Mazael.

"That would have been grand," said Rachel, scrubbing tears from her eyes.

"I still can, you know," said Mazael.

"What...oh, no, Mazael, I can't..." said Rachel.

"Why not?" said Mazael. "What's here for you? Mitor? Marcelle? Simonian of Briault? They're little enough. They'll be swept away like chaff when Lord Richard comes. Come with me, Rachel. There's nothing here for you or for me. Leave Mitor the Mushroom to his plots and webs. It will all come crashing down on him. We could go from here to Knightcastle, if you wish, with Sir Gerald. Lord Malden would welcome you. Or to Deepforest Keep with Romaria."

"I would...I can't," said Rachel. "I am pledged to be married, Sir

Albron..."

"Damn Albron!" growled Mazael. "Open your eyes! Neither he nor Mitor lifted a finger when Sir Tanam and his crows flew away with you in their beaks! The man's a leech who rode Mitor to power. And what will happen when the Dragonslayer takes Mitor's head? The leech will fall off and shrivel."

"Mazael, don't say those things!" said Rachel. "Even if I did leave, who else could I marry? Toraine Mandragon? Or his brother, the one they call the Dragon's Shadow? I'm almost five years past twenty!"

"It would be easy to find you a husband in Knightrealm," said Mazael. "There are hundreds of unmarried knights. Most of them are far better than Albron. You know he's a wretch, Rachel, you do. More than that, you know he's a liar."

For a long moment she stared at him, wavering.

"Yes," she whispered at last. "He's lied to you, he's lied to Mitor, he's lied to me. About everything. But you don't know him, Mazael, not truly. You don't know what he can do. He could win this war, even against the Dragonslayer."

"What can he do?" said Mazael. "Tell me."

"I can't," said Rachel.

"Why not?" said Mazael. "Do you think I'm afraid of him? I bested him once and I'll do it again. What's his secret, Rachel? Tell me."

Rachel's eyes flickered with doubt. There was fear on her face, and despair, but the beginning of a dawning hope. "He...Mazael, he's..."

"Rachel! I say, there you are!"

Rachel jumped as if burned.

Sir Albron stood behind her, his eyes glittering like cold jewels. "I've been looking all over for you. Where have you been?"

"Rachel..." said Mazael.

Rachel tugged away from him and went to Albron's side. "I was here. You needn't have looked. You know where I was going."

Albron sighed and stroked her hair. "You want to go the funeral, yes? Well, you shouldn't. It will make you sad. You are much prettier when you're cheerful."

Mazael stepped closer, Lion's scabbard tapping against his leg. "She is not to give respect to the dead, to a man who taught her and raised her?"

Albron smiled. "Precisely so, Sir Mazael. Master Othar is dead. Dead and no longer able to defy Lord Mitor's wishes, as he had so often. It is probably a mercy, I think. After all, the man was so fat, and so old. Had he lived for much longer, he would have been in great discomfort. You ought to say a prayer of thanksgiving."

Fire flashed in Mazael's mind. "Pray that I do not act as I feel I ought."

Albron smiled. "Pray? Why, I pray every day. I am very pious, after all. More than you, I'd imagine. You see, Sir Mazael, that is the difference between us. You always seek to stand on your own with no allies, relying on your own formidable skills. But I am wise enough to recognize my weakness." He took Rachel's arm. "I turn to my deity for my strength. Come along, Rachel."

"He can't command you," said Mazael. "You haven't married him yet."

"Oh, but she will," said Albron. "Won't you, my dear? And our lady Rachel of Cravenlock is a confused soul at times. I know what is best for her. Now, come along. We shall go back to your chambers and pray upon this." He walked away, pulling Rachel along with him. She cast one glance over her shoulder at Mazael, and then followed Sir Albron.

Rage pounded through Mazael's skull. It was all he could do to keep from drawing his blade and ramming it between Albron's shoulders, and perhaps Rachel's, as well...

Mazael shuddered and raised his sword hand away from Lion's hilt. "No."

"Sir Mazael?" said Adalar. "You...do not look well. Are you ill?"

"No," said Mazael. "Not ill." He watched Rachel and Albron go. "Come."

Mazael's headache faded by the time he reached the chapel's doors. It was as if the rage had burned through him and incinerated his pains.

Sir Gerald, Sir Nathan, and Romaria waited for him at the chapel's doors. Sir Nathan looked ten years older. Master Othar had been the old knight's best friend. Mazael wanted to pull Romaria close and not move for a long time.

"Mazael," said Gerald. "A dark day, this."

"I only knew him for a short while," said Romaria, "but I even I could see that he was a good man."

"Aye," said Mazael. "He was. He gave me much, taught me much, that I could never repay."

"He will be missed," said Sir Nathan.

The chapel was as bad as Gerald had described. Dust and debris littered the floor, the tapestries and altar cloths worn and threadbare. The narrow windows and the few sputtering candles did not give much light.

"Such fine temples the Amathavians keep to their gods," said Romaria.

Master Othar's closed coffin rested on a bier before the altar, between burning candles in iron stands. Mazael stared at the coffin. Why had he ever returned to the Grim Marches? Save for Master Othar's teachings, Rachel's friendship, and Sir Nathan's hard lessons, he had known little else but misery here. Now Master Othar was dead, and he no longer knew Rachel.

There were a few others present. Master Cramton, his family, and his workers greeted Mazael at the door.

"A good man," said Cramton. "He was always good to us townsfolk." Bethy gave Mazael a sad smile, and he managed to nod in answer.

They sat and the service began. The acolytes were a sorry bunch in their dirty and threadbare robes, and the presiding priest seemed drunk. The man began the prayers for the dead, his voice stumbling over the archaic High Tristafellin used by the Amathavian Church.

Sir Nathan rose. The priest backed away as the old knight approached, but Sir Nathan did not spare him a glance. He began to recite the prayers himself, speaking the intricate words of High Tristafellin with ease. The priest slunk away, his acolytes following. Mazael only understood a few words of the long prayer but bowed his head nonetheless.

Sir Nathan had chosen the pallbearers from the armsmen he trusted. They marched from the decrepit chapel in a slow procession. They would stop in the castle's vaults and inter Master Othar's mortal remains in a stone tomb.

Mazael stopped in the courtyard and watched them march towards the vault. He could not go with them. He knew he should come out of respect, but he could not do so. The grief filled his mind, second only to his rage. If Master Othar had been murdered, Mazael would find the murderer and ram Lion down his gullet.

Mazael wandered away, head bowed. He walked beneath one of the keep's balconies and heard his brother's voice.

"Are they done yet?" said Mitor.

"No, my lord," came Simonian's voice. "They have gone to the vaults for the internment ceremony."

"Bah," said Mitor. "The man had outlived his usefulness years ago. What has he done to merit internment in my chapel and in my castle?"

"I have found, my lord, that people are far happier when customs are observed," said Simonian.

"Customs," said Mitor. "When I am liege lord of the Grim Marches, I shall do away with a great many customs, you can rest assured! Funerals for useless, fat wizards among them. Had I my will, I would have tossed the corpse out into a field and left it to rot."

"You should have had Othar's body ground up and used as rations for your troops," said Simonian.

"Hah!" said Mitor. "I like that!" He laughed. "No doubt it would provide for many meals!"

"And the blubber," said Simonian, "could have illuminated this castle for many months."

Mitor laughed. "Undoubtedly. But I find more favor with your first idea. We should have made a meat pie out of his carcass and had it served to my wretched brother at dinner the next day." He roared with laughter. Mazael drew Lion with a silent snarl.

"My lord, you must take care with Sir Mazael," said Simonian. "He schemes to replace you."

"Oh, yes," said Mitor. "Him and that fool the Dragonslayer. Well, they shall see! I don't need Mazael to claim the liege lordship. I don't need Marcus Trand and Roget and those other fools. I don't need Lord Malden's help. I shall take the liege lordship myself. It is my right, I have the power to do so. It is mine!"

"Yes," said Simonian. "They'll all see in the end, won't they, my lord?"

"They will!" said Mitor. "The old fool Nathan and my damned brother and the great and high Lord Dragonslayer will see! That fat wizard has already seen. But the others...oh, they will see, Simonian, and soon."

Mazael rammed Lion into its scabbard and stalked away. Rage burned through him, and he felt as if he would explode with it. Images flashed through his mind in rapid succession. He saw Simonian dying upon Lion's point, saw his sword plunging into Mitor's chest...

The air blurred, and Timothy appeared out of nothingness. Mazael had Lion at the wizard's throat before his mind caught up to his reflexes.

He lowered Lion. "Don't startle me!"

"I...ah...yes, I see," said Timothy. "I should have known better."

"What have you found?" said Mazael.

"A number of things," said Timothy.

Mazael frowned. "Why were you invisible?"

"Prudence," said Timothy. "Lord Mitor placed a guard around Master Othar's chambers. I doubted they would allow me entrance if I simply asked. So I placed a sleeping spell on them and used my invisibility enchantment to sneak past."

"Clever," said Mazael.

"It worked," said Timothy. "The guards didn't see me." He smiled. "They should be waking up shortly."

"What did you find in Master Othar's rooms?" said Mazael.

Timothy swallowed. "Much. On his desk were old scrolls. One was a history of the Demonsouled. Another told of the history of the San-keth race." He tugged at his beard. "And...there was one other scroll, very old. He had it locked in a chest beneath his bed. I could not read the language, but I recognized it. It was written in the San-keth tongue, my lord. The ink was dried blood, and the parchment some sort of skin. Human, perhaps."

"Where would he have gotten these things?" said Mazael.

"The scrolls...their seal was the star of the Cirstarcine Order," said Timothy. "Most likely he borrowed them from the library of the nearby monastery. I may also have found Master Othar's journal."

"You did? What did it say?" said Mazael.

"I could not open it," said Timothy. "It was sealed shut and warded with a powerful protective spell."

"Could you not dispel it?" said Mazael.

"I tried," said Timothy. "Master Othar's magic was too strong. A more powerful spell might suffice, but it would have taken several hours to ready. I feared I did not have the time."

"That was wise," said Mazael. "What of his body? Were you able to examine it before the funeral?"

Timothy's face turned fearful. "Aye, I did, my lord knight."

"What do you find?" said Mazael.

"Master Othar did not die naturally," said Timothy. "He was murdered."

The words thundered through Mazael's skull. "How?"

"Magic," said Timothy. "I was not able to learn exactly how, but..."

"Well?" said Mazael. "Out with it!"

"It was necromancy, my lord knight," said Timothy. He took a step back. "A killing spell. The residual power was focused around his chest. The magic was similar to the arts used to raise the zuvembies, though I have not the skill to discern if both spells were cast by the same man."

"Necromancy," said Mazael. "The word is bastardized Tristafellin, true? 'Death magic'?"

Timothy nodded, staring at Lion's blade. "Aye, Sir Mazael, but please, do not do anything rash..."

"Death," said Mazael. His fury had left anger behind, had become something different, something throbbing with power. "Well, there will be more death today before I am finished. Thank you, Timothy. You've been most helpful." His voice was calm. He could have been discussing supper.

"My lord knight," said Timothy. Mazael ignored him, and stalked across the courtyard, making for Lord Mitor's chambers.

CHAPTER 21
FURY

"Stop!" said a Cravenlock armsman. "Sir Mazael, you cannot draw steel..."

"Where is Mitor?" said Mazael.

"By Lord Mitor's command," said the armsman, reaching for his sword hilt, "no one may carry bared steel in the castle."

"Where is Mitor?" said Mazael.

"I warned you!" said the armsman, drawing his blade, his two companions doing likewise. "Little wonder Lord Mitor ordered watch kept over you! Take him!"

Mazael drove Lion's hilt at the armsman's face, knocking him to the floor. The other two armsmen spread out in the wide corridor leading to Mitor's chambers. Yet they moved so slow, so terribly slow, and Mazael stepped around the first thrust and brought the flat of Lion's blade hard on the nearest armsman's head. The man's eyes bulged, rolled up, and he crumpled to the floor.

The last man was more skilled than his fellows and managed to attack. Mazael parried, shoved, and slammed the man against the wall, his sword clattering against the floor. The armsman went rigid as Lion's razor edge came to rest against his throat.

"Where," Mazael said, "is Mitor?"

"I don't know!" said the armsman. "He went with the wizard!"

"Simonian," said Mazael. He considered killing the guards, and rejected the idea. He wanted Mitor and Simonian, not these wretches, and let the guard fall.

Then he kicked open a side door and strode up the spiral steps. Another door opened into a broad balcony on the main keep's side.

The floor had been torn up and filled with dirt, and a rich garden grew here. A vibrant young oak tree rose in the center, surrounded by all manner of flowers and quite a few blood roses. Lord Adalon had made a gift of the garden to Lady Arissa for their wedding. She had never used it.

There was another door on the far side of the garden, one that led to the keep's upper levels. Mazael barred the door behind him. The Cravenlock armsmen would try to stop him from killing Mitor and Simonian, but they would come too late.

And if they did reach him...why, he would just have to kill them too.

He strode to the upper door and paused as voices came through the wood.

"You must come, my lady! He's gone mad from grief, I swear it. I've seen such things before. The gods only know what he will do!" It was Timothy.

"I knew it." Romaria's voice shook. "I saw it in his face. I should have...the Seer warned me. Go and find Sir Gerald and Sir Nathan."

"My lady," said Timothy. "Sir Mazael's lost his wits! He'll kill..."

"Go!" said Romaria.

The door opened, and Romaria entered the garden, her blue eyes fixed on him.

"Move," Mazael said. She was blocking the door.

"Why?" said Romaria.

"Mitor's a wretch. Simonian killed Master Othar. Now, move!" roared Mazael.

"How do you know?" said Romaria.

Mazael growled. "How do I know?" he said. "What do you care? Out of my way!"

Romaria didn't move. "Why are you doing this?"

"Why? They killed Master Othar!" screamed Mazael. "I'll mount both their heads above the castle gates! If you don't move, you can join them!"

A muscle in Romaria's face ticked. "No. You're doing this for revenge. If you do this now, in the...state you're in, you'll damn yourself forever."

"Are you an Amathavian nun to prattle proverbs at me?" said Mazael. "Or are you with Simonian?" The possibility made perfect sense. "Yes, you're scheming with him, you were part of this, weren't you?"

Romaria shook her head. "No."

"Prove it," said Mazael. "Move."

"No," said Romaria. "Don't do this, Mazael. Listen to me..."

He ran at her instead, Lion flashing.

Romaria moved almost as fast, her bastard sword blurring into her hand. Mazael plunged his sword's tip at her head, reversed momentum, and brought it stabbing down for her belly. She parried, the swords meeting with a tremendous clang.

"Stop this!" said Romaria.

Mazael didn't hear her. The volcanic fury in his mind had found an outlet, and it felt good. Mazael's only thought was to kill.

Romaria's sword danced in time to Mazael's, her stance shifting, her grip shifting from one-handed to two-handed and back again. Mazael could not follow her movements fast enough to find an opening. He locked their swords together on the next parry and shoved. Romaria was fast and agile, but he was stronger. Romaria stumbled, her back slapping against the keep's wall.

Romaria ducked his next thrust, and Lion sheared through her cloak and slid into a gap between two stones. He roared and tore the sword free, slashing for Romaria. But she slid free from her cloak, her blade stabbing towards his gut. Mazael parried, but the flat of her blade smacked into his thigh.

"Stop this!" said Romaria. "Mazael, the Seer, I didn't tell you all..."

He ignored her and chopped towards her skull, their blades locking in a parry. Mazael shoved again, but this time she jumped back. He lost his balance for a moment, and Romaria counterattacked, her sword opening a shallow cut against his ribs.

"Mazael, please, stop this!" said Romaria. A drop of his blood slid down her sword. "You don't know what this is doing to you..."

His next attack brought Lion high, low, and then arcing for her throat. Romaria pivoted, but she was too slow. Lion scraped along her collarbone, but blood flared crimson against her pale skin. Mazael laughed and went for the kill, but she spun out of his reach.

"Brother Silar was right!" she yelled.

Mazael spun and came at her, his sword slashing at her from every angle. Yet somehow she parried every one of his attacks. She turned one of his strikes, her sword point biting at his arm.

"You have magic!" said Romaria. "Don't you see? Silar was right!"

He almost killed her. He whipped his sword at her face. Romaria jerked back, but she was almost too slow. For a moment Mazael thought he'd slain her, but she circled to his left, and he roared with frustration.

"It's out of control," said Romaria. "Your power's devouring you. The rage... it's not natural. It will burn you out from the inside..."

Mazael worked Lion through a high slash and then a low thrust. Romaria blocked and batted aside his stabbing blade. She thrust at him, and her sword nicked his hip, drawing blood.

"Stop this!" said Romaria. "It will destroy you."

"You can't stop me," said Mazael.

"I can't," said Romaria. "But you can. Please, just put down your sword..."

Mazael slashed at her, holding Lion in a two-handed grip, and she jumped out of reach.

Romaria's eyes flashed. "Then fight!" She turned his next attack and spun around him. Mazael dropped Lion low to parry, but she whirled her hilt and stabbed at his chest. He managed to parry, but the edge of her blade gashed his arm. Her furious assault did not relent. The sparks in her eyes turned to fire, and her sword was everywhere. Despite his speed and strength, it was all Mazael could do to parry. She drove him across the balcony, over the tangled roots of the tree, through the flowers and the grasses.

Romaria's attack drove him to the edge of the battlements. Her fury began to play out, her chest heaving with breath, sweat streaming down her face. Mazael felt filled with life and power.

Soon she would tire and make a mistake.

He parried another of her attacks, and this time she was too slow. He shoved at her, and she stumbled. Romaria tumbled backwards and went into a backwards fall. Mazael stalked after her, sword raised high, and she vanished.

He smiled. He had seen this trick before.

Romaria reappeared before him. Mazael stepped around her attack and rammed Lion into her throat. Her blue eyes bulged, and blood gushed from her torn neck. Crimson bubbles foamed in her mouth as she tried to scream, and she collapsed to the ground.

And Mazael's rage vanished.

His head pounded, every heartbeat sending waves of pain through his skull. He felt old and weary. For a moment, he could not remember where he was.

Then he saw Romaria's dying body lying at his feet, and he remembered.

Mazael fell to one knee. He saw the blood pooling beneath her. He saw it smeared along the length of his sword and dripping from his fingers. Lion fell from his grasp. All he could see was the blood. He tried to reach for her.

"Oh gods..." said Mazael. "Oh gods, no. No, no, no. What have I done..."

A lance of slithering pain spread through his gut. Mazael doubled over and vomited. He wheezed and coughed, drops of spittle hanging from his lips.

He looked up, dreading the sight.

Romaria was gone.

He stared at the empty stones, confused beyond the capacity for thought. What had he done? What had happened?

A warm hand fell on his shoulder. He looked and saw Romaria kneeling besides him, one hand gripping his shoulder, the other holding her heavy sword. The skin of her throat was smooth and unbroken.

Mazael couldn't believe it. He reached a trembling hand for her face and felt the smooth skin, felt the blood pulsing through the veins of her neck. "How...I....I killed..."

"It was an illusion," said Romaria. Her smile was weak. "I didn't show you all my tricks."

"Tricks?" said Mazael. His tongue felt like lead. "But...I killed, gods, I killed..." His voice shook. He felt something wet in his eyes. "I killed...I tried to kill you. And Simonian. And Mitor...I tried so hard to kill you. Gods, gods, I'm going mad...what's happening..."

The world lurched, and Mazael felt all the strength got out of him. His head struck the stone floor, and a wave of fire washed through his brain. He heard Romaria's voice once more before the darkness closed over   him.

CHAPTER 22
TWO HALVES

"Get up."

Harsh light stabbed into Mazael's face. The stench of rotting vegetation and old snakeskin filled into his nostrils. Something hard prodded his side. "Up, I say! Can't lie about. There's too much to do!"

Mazael. sat up. A swollen bloody sun painted the sky crimson, and the balcony garden had died. The oak tree was scorched, the flowers crumbling ashes, and the earth gray powder.

Lord Adalon stood over Mazael, his black robe hanging from his thin body like a flowing shroud. Red fire glinted in his green eyes, and his fingers drummed against the black staff with its silver raven statuette.

"Up, now!" Lord Adalon said. He tapped Mazael's leg with his staff. "Up! Nothing has ever come from lying about like this."

Mazael stood. He felt no pain. His stomach was settled, and there were no wounds on his arms and chest.

"Now, why would you think yourself hurt?" said Lord Adalon. A cold wind blew from the plains, whipping his robes like black wings.

"I don't know," said Mazael.

"You needn't be so grim!" said Lord Adalon. "You almost learned a most important lesson. The next time, you'll learn."

"Learn what?" said Mazael.

His father grinned. "Your fellow half-breed will soon discover the deep flaw in trickery. It is most effective, but only once." He laughed. "Fool me once, shame on you. Fool me twice, shame on me. And fool me thrice, a man who can be fooled thrice is liable to be snatched up by the Old Demon!" Lord Adalon snapped his fingers.

"I don't know what you're talking about," said Mazael.

"You do!" said Lord Adalon. "You killed her, didn't you? You can hide nothing from me. Rather, you would have killed her, if not for her simple spells." His smile displayed jagged yellow teeth. "You will learn to defeat those."

Mazael remembered how Lion had sunk into Romaria's throat. "No...I didn't...no, she lives..."

"She does," said Lord Adalon. "You cannot hide from the truth, Mazael. You cannot deny your nature. You thought you had killed her."

"Yes," said Mazael, "but...but I..."

"You enjoyed it," said Lord Adalon. "Not the killing itself, but the power."

"No," said Mazael.

Lord Adalon sighed. "Don't lie to me, my son. That power is yours. And such a little thing, too. The power of death." He made a fist. "You have the potential for so much more. Any fool can kill. But your potential is limitless."

"No," said Mazael.

"You can do anything," said Lord Adalon. "Who can rule over you? Mitor? The Dragonslayer? They are nothing to you. The power of death, the power of command is yours. You must simply take it. Claim it and make it your own. Throw down Mitor and throw down the Dragonslayer. Do it or they will destroy you."

"I...I...no," said Mazael. Something seemed horribly wrong. "No."

"Do it," whispered Lord Adalon. "Or they will kill you just as they killed Master Othar."

A thread of killing rage ignited in Mazael's mind.

Lord Adalon's laughter rang in his ears. "Is that the crack in your armor? Yes, Master Othar, so just, so wise. What good did it do him?"

"Be quiet," said Mazael. The burning thread grew.

"Is the truth so hard?" said Lord Adalon. "They will do the same to you, unless you embrace your strength. Killing is woven into the very fabric of your soul! Use it. Fat Othar had no real power. You do. What is to stop you from using it?"

Mazael wavered. Was his father right? His hand clenched around Lion's hilt.

Mitor and Simonian would pay for Othar's death.

A sharp scent filled Mazael's nostrils.

Lord Adalon's lined face contorted with rage. "She dares..."

A jolt of agony shot through Mazael's head.

He woke up and found himself lying in the balcony garden, the oak three spreading its leaves over the flowers. Romaria knelt next to him, a small stinking vial in her hand.

"Gods...Romaria..." he said. Nausea roiled in his gut.

"Hush, now," said Romaria. "Drink this. I had Timothy bring it." She handed him a heavy flagon smelling of the foul-smelling concoction wizards favored in their medicines. Mazael drank and swallowed the bitter stuff in huge gulps. It helped settle his stomach.

Romaria set the flagon down. "You had another dream, didn't

you?"

Mazael closed his burning eyes. "Yes." His voice had an edge he did not like. "See? I was right. The dreams. They're driving me mad. I am mad."

"No," said Romaria.

Mazael laughed. "No? How can you say that? I tried to kill Mitor, and then..." He remembered the blood gushing from her throat. He felt something wet slide down his face, and realized he was crying. "I tried to kill you. I did kill you, or I would have, if...what have I become?"

"No," said Romaria. "You're not mad, Mazael. I haven't told you everything."

"Everything?" said Mazael. "Of...what?"

"Of what the Seer told me," said Romaria. "I haven't told you all of it, not by half." She swallowed. "He...Mazael, I've told you how the Elderborn and the humans both feel about half-breeds." Her fingers twitched. "It's deeper than that. Half-breeds are absolutely despised. Humans and Elderborn are forbidden to create children together. My father made a mistake, and I was born. My mother was horrified."

"Sounds familiar," said Mazael.

Romaria almost smiled. "We have that in common, you and I. The laws say that parents must slay any half-breed child as purification for their sin. My mother was adamant. My father didn't want to, but felt he had no choice. But the Seer intervened."

"What did he say?" said Mazael.

"The Seer told them that if they slew me, they would damn themselves and all of Deepforest Keep. You see, I was destined to save them," said Romaria.

"Sounds like mummery," said Mazael.

Romaria laughed. "Oh, I wish it were. He told them his prophecy, the same prophecy he told to me when I went into the druids' caves thirty years later."

Mazael was surprised. He had thought her younger. "What was this prophecy?"

"I told you part of it," said Romaria. "He said I would meet a man who could kill any other man. But let me start from the beginning. I've told you half-breeds are despised. We only possess half a soul."

"Absurd," said Mazael. "That sounds like some of the lies priests tell to squeeze another copper coin from their benefices."

"Aye," whispered Romaria, "but this is true. Do you know what will happen to me? It's happened before with half-breeds who weren't killed at birth. I will rot away. It always happens, sooner or later, and there's no way to reverse it. Thirty years, forty years, fifty, my body will crumble away from the inside out and so will my mind. I will die in agony and dementia." She shrugged. "I never really worried about it. Everyone dies, after all. I learned the sword and the bow and spent most my time to the south, visiting the Old Kingdoms. I worked as a scout and a tracker, and none could match me. I suppose I planned to die that way, killed by an arrow or sword or some wild beast."

Mazael sat up. The pain in his head had vanished, and his stomach no longer felt as if it had become home to a thousand twisting snakes. "What happened? Why did you go back to Deepforest Keep?"

"Thirty is the age of maturity for Elderborn," said Romaria. She looked away. "Father sent a messenger for me."

Mazael snorted. "I'd have told him to go to hell."

Romaria smiled. "You would have. I'd never hated my father. He had always supported me, even if he couldn't allow me to live at Deepforest Keep. And the Seer asked me to come, as well. He had saved my life." She took a deep breath. "I returned, and I met the Seer in the druid caves. He told me his prophecy."

Mazael flexed the fingers of his wounded arm. "What did he say?"

"He said I had to go to Castle Cravenlock," said Romaria. "By then, the zuvembies had risen in the forest. But the Seer told me I had to go north to face a demon."

"A demon?" said Mazael.

"A demon," said Romaria. "He said that I would face that demon with the help of another. Someone like me. Another who had only half a true soul." She looked at him, her eyes full of fear and wonder. "A man who fought with a lion's tooth in his hand, who moved like lightning, a man who could kill any other man."

Mazael blinked. "Me?"

Romaria nodded.

Mazael snorted. "You needn't worry about it. My mother was a serpent and my father a coward, but they were both human. Your Seer was wrong."

"No," said Romaria. "I have only a half a soul. But your soul...your soul has power. The Seer said as much."

"Power?" said Mazael.

"You do," said Romaria. "It's always been in you. When have you ever lost a fight? It was always with you, but beneath your awareness, I think. And now something's caused it to manifest. You aren't mad. It's this magic, this dark power within you. It is rising within and consuming you."

"I think I'd rather be mad. I don't believe it...I don't want to be believe it," said Mazael.

Romaria pointed at his chest. "Look."

Mazael lifted his torn tunic and looked at the cuts Romaria had given him across his ribs.

The wounds were knitting themselves together, the flesh crawling and twisting. He watched as the wounds turned from an angry red to a soft pink. Within minutes, the cuts had healed.

"What sort of power?" said Mazael, his voice hoarse.

"Dark power," said Romaria. "Demon power."

"Demon power?" said Mazael. "Am I Demonsouled, then?"

"I don't know," said Romaria. "Even the Seer didn't know. He said you had to fight it. You would battle it for possession of your soul. You would master it, he said, or else it would dominate you, consume you, and turn you to something else."

Mazael looked at the fading cuts on his arm. His exhaustion had vanished, and his hangover had passed. A mad urge seized him, and he yanked his dagger from his belt and slashed it across his left palm. Romaria grabbed his wrist, but Mazael stared at his palm. The blood flowed for a moment, but then the wound began to close. He felt a deep itching in the flesh of his palm as the skin crawled back together. He and Romaria sat and silence and watched.

Within a quarter hour, the wound had vanished.

"Did your Seer say anything else?" said Mazael, voice shaking. He remembered all the stories he had heard of Demonsouled. Descendants of the Great Demon, cursed with demon power in their souls that drove them made even as it bestowed great strength. Children and young men who had exhibited strange powers and who had tried to kill their families wives, and sisters. He had never believed those stories. They were just myths, after all, like San-keth cults.

"One other thing," said Romaria. "He said our fates rest in each others' hands. He said that I must save you, and that you must save me, or we will both be lost forever."

"Don't leave me," whispered Mazael. "I can't face this myself. If it weren't for you, I would have slain Mitor and Simonian and likely half the castle."

Romaria nodded and took his hand. "Only if you promise not to leave me."

"I do," said Mazael. They sat together for a long time.

He looked at his healed hand and thought of Demonsouled.

CHAPTER 23
THE OLD CROW ROOSTS

Mazael awoke to pounding at his bedchamber door.

He had fallen asleep in one of the room's great overstuffed chairs, Romaria curled besides him. She had sat up beside him until he slipped into exhausted stupor, and for some reason her presence kept the nightmares away.

Mazael wanted to kiss her. He dared not. Rage had unlocked the demon within his skull. What if passion did the same? He was afraid for her. He was afraid of himself.

How far he had fallen. A month ago he had feared nothing.

The pounding redoubled. "Sir Mazael!" came Adalar's voice, faint through the thick wood. "Sir Mazael, you must come at once!"

Romaria's eyes fluttered open. "We have company."

"He wouldn't come for nothing," said Mazael. Suppose the madness took him and he slew Adalar in his rage? How could he face Sir Nathan?

Mazael rose pushed the door open.

"Sir Mazael," said Adalar. "Lord Mitor commands your presence in the courtyard at once."

"Why?"

"We'd best go, Mazael." Gerald waited behind Adalar with Wesson at his side, clad in his finest surcoat. "You'll never believe who's come to pay Lord Mitor a visit."

Mazael strode into the stairwell and looked out the window. A band of armored lancers sat atop their horses within the barbican. One of the lancers held a tall standard, flying a banner with a black crow clutching a craggy rock in its talons.

The banner of Sir Tanam Crowley.

Mazael swore. "Crowley. Is he mad? Mitor's liable to give him a swift axe to the back of the neck."

"He only brought fifty men," said Gerald. "There was some commotion. The guards nearly opened fire on sight. Sir Tanam said something, and they went to fetch Lord Mitor instead." Gerald frowned. "Perhaps he went mad. Surely he knows Lord Mitor will exact vengeance for Lady Rachel's abduction."

"Oh, he's here for a reason, all right," said Mazael. "Lord Richard's reasons. Lord Richard is up to something here, don't doubt it. Adalar, get my armor and my sword belt. Gerald, send Wesson to get Timothy. Lord Richard's younger son is supposedly a skilled wizard, and he could have sent other wizards as well. It's possible there's some trickery here."

Adalar retrieved Mazael's weapons and armor, Wesson returned with Timothy in tow, and they descended the stairs of the King's Tower. Lord Mitor and his court waited near the keep, surrounded by two hundred armsmen in Cravenlock colors. Sir Nathan stood with the armsmen, and Simonian waited in Mitor's shadow. Mazael wondered why Mitor had been foolish enough to allow Sir Tanam to inside the castle.

Sir Tanam sat atop his horse with his lancers. His face was still bruised.

"Sir Tanam!" called Mazael. "How unexpected to see you once again."

Sir Tanam grinned a gap-toothed smile and rode over. "The same to you as well, Sir Mazael. I'd not expected to see you at all. My lord Richard was most displeased."

"I can imagine," said Mazael. "Two men and a boy making off with his prize."

"Dreadfully embarrassing," said Sir Tanam. He scratched at his nose. "Gods, that aches. You punch like a mule, you know."

"Will you now take the opportunity for repayment?" said Mazael.

Sir Tanam laughed. "Gods above, no. War is war, after all. You could have killed me, and I certainly would have killed you had I the chance, so I'm grateful to have gotten off with a few bruises and a sore jaw."

"My brother might be forgiving. I am not," said Mitor. Sir Albron stepped to his side, Rachel waiting behind him. "Might I remind you, Old Crow, that you broke my good faith when last you visited my castle? You abducted my sister. It was only through good fortune that Lady Rachel was returned to me. Why should I not repay your betrayal with death?"

Sir Tanam shrugged. "For one, Lord Richard commanded me. He seems to think that your sister is consorting with dark powers." Rachel tensed, and Albron's smiling gaze fixed on the Old Crow.

"Liar!" said Rachel.

Albron stepped forward, his hand resting on his sword hilt. "You besmirch the honor of my betrothed. That is most discourteous."

Sir Tanam laughed. "Discourteous? You wrong me. I have never been discourteous to a lady."

"You did kidnap her," said Mazael.

"Well, true," said Sir Tanam. "But we were very courteous about it."

"Enough!" said Mitor. "I will not listen to you mince words with my armsmaster!"

Sir Tanam frowned at Albron. "Your armsmaster? Sir Nathan looks younger than I recall."

Mitor ignored the jibe. "You did these crimes at the command of Richard Mandragon? Well, those accusations are a lie, a vicious slander. Lord Richard is my vassal, I am the liege lord of the Grim Marches!"

Sir Tanam scratched his nose. "Lord Richard disagrees, my lord."

"Indeed?" said Simonian. "Men oft believe the strangest things, my lord knight."

Sir Tanam looked at Mitor. "Oh, truly."

Mitor sneered. "Let your precious Lord Richard slander. Let him lie until he runs out of breath. I'll take him to task soon enough. I am the rightful liege lord of the Grim Marches. Richard Mandragon is a traitor and a usurper. I shall enforce my justice."

"Really?" said Sir Tanam. "I am most curious, my lord. How do you plan to do that?"

Mitor laughed. "Did you not see the great army surrounding my castle, Old Crow? Are you blind? My armies shall crush Lord Richard's and send him fleeing back to Swordgrim."

"Indeed?" said Sir Tanam. "Truly, my lord, your army seems formidable. So formidable, in fact, that I rode right through them. No one noticed my presence until my men and I knocked at your gates. Indeed, my lord, I fear for Lord Richard if he must face men such as yours."

"Wars are not always won through swords," said Sir Albron.

"Truly," said Sir Tanam. "Is that where the sorcery comes in, then?"

Albron smiled. "One more warning, sir. I'll not have you insult my betrothed."

"Bah!" said Mitor. "You came here for a reason, Crowley. Have done with it. I'll not have all my day wasted with your squawking."

Sir Tanam bowed. "As you say, my lord. Your army is clearly superior. You'll soon have the chance to prove it. Lord Richard's army is three days march from here."

Mitor jerked. "What?"

"Impossible," said Albron.

"Quite possible," said Sir Tanam. "After Sir Mazael's most splendid rescue of his sister, I made haste for Swordgrim. Once Lord Richard had heard my news, he marched. He had already gathered his armies. With him is all the power of Swordgrim, the armsmen of his loyal vassal Lord Jonaril Mandrake and a dozen other lords...including Lord Astor Hawking of Hawk's Reach, Sir Commander." Sir Tanam bowed to Sir Commander Galan. "Perhaps you'll have the opportunity for a reunion."

Sir Commander Galan made a fist. "You mock me?"

"Not at all," said Sir Tanam. "I speak the truth. Lord Richard is three days from here with twenty-five thousand men. You really didn't know? Your scouts must be formidable, my lord Mitor. Truly, I fear for my lord Richard."

"Do not mock me!" snarled Mitor. "Has the Dragonslayer sent you to surrender, to submit himself to my rightful lordship?"

Amusement flickered across Crowley's battered face. "Not at all. Lord Richard wishes for this to end without bloodshed. Consequently, he is giving you one final chance, Lord Mitor. Disband your armies and travel to Swordgrim with your court and family. You will face his judgment for your acts. He will be merciful. These are his terms."

"What acts are those?" said Mazael.

Sir Tanam scratched at his nose again. "Ah...well, treason, to start, rebellion, murder, inciting banditry...oh, and sorcery and idolatry. Let's not forget those. Lord Richard has no quarrel with you, Sir Mazael. You acted out of ignorance when you freed Lady Rachel. No doubt you'd have sided with Lord Richard had you known the truth."

"I will not fight against my sister," said Mazael. "These stories of a San-keth cult are the worst sort of slander."

"Perhaps," said Sir Tanam. "I've heard stranger things, but not many. You do know, Sir Mazael, that if you side with Lord Richard, you'll become the new lord of Castle Cravenlock once he is victorious?"

"Treason!" bellowed Lord Marcus Trand. He shoved his way to Mitor's side. "My liege lord, I knew he plotted against you from the start. Let me..."

"Silence!" said Mitor. "Speak not another word, Old Crow, or else you and my brother will die inch by inch."

"It is folly, you know," said Simonian. "Lord Mitor is the rightful liege lord of the Grim Marches. The gods will surely favor him and grant him victory. Stand with him now, while you still can, Sir Tanam." He smiled. "It is not yet too late."

Sir Tanam laughed. "Whatever gods you pray to favor Lord Mitor, I've no doubt. But I'm quite sure the gods of heaven favor Lord Richard."

Mitor quivered with rage. "A moment, Old Crow. My advisors and I need to discuss my answer for Richard Mandragon's follies."

Sir Tanam bowed. "By all means. Do hurry, though. You only have a few days left." Crowley crossed the courtyard and rejoined his lancers.

"Impudent old crow," said Sir Albron. "So Lord Richard wished to send his rightful liege lord an emissary? Well, my lord, let us make an answer. Hack off the Old Crow's head and send it back. Richard Mandragon will have his answer."

"That is dishonorable in the extreme," said Sir Nathan. "Will you advise Lord Mitor to murder a guest?"

Sir Albron's malicious smile fixed on the old knight. "Honor, Sir Nathan? Where is the honor in abducting Lady Rachel?"

"Lady Rachel was neither harmed nor mistreated," said Nathan. "There is a difference between that and slaughter."

"Indeed," said Albron. "Perhaps when I'm your age I'll have gained the wisdom to understand it. Sir Tanam is a fool, my lord Mitor. He has marched with fifty men into the heart of your power. Kill him now. Let Richard Mandragon know the price of opposing you!"

Mazael scoffed. "Sir Tanam might be a fool. But if you listen to Albron, Mitor, you're a bigger fool still."

Albron's glittered like cold gems. "Why is that?"

"You dare call me a fool?" said Mitor, spinning on Mazael.

Mazael waved a hand at Sir Tanam's men. "Look at them, Mitor! Why were you so foolish as to invite them inside the castle? Look at the way those lancers are positioned! You give the order to attack and they'll ride you down before your men can react."

Mitor flushed. "They...no, they wouldn't dare...I am the liege lord...they cannot..."

Lord Marcus blanched. "Perhaps it would be better to parley."

"Bah!" said Sir Commander Galan. "Are we to fear this rabble? A Justiciar Knight could take them five-on-one."

"Fine, then!" said Mazael. "It's in your hands, Mitor. Command your armsmen to attack. Pray Sir Albron's steel will protect you. Trust in Simonian's arts to defend you. But you had best hope that you were wise in your choice of servants, or else you'll taste the Old Crow's lance."

Mitor's eyes flicked from Simonian, to Albron, and then to the Old Crow's lancers. For a moment Mazael thought that Mitor would order his men to attack. Mazael's hand clenched around Lion's hilt. He would make certain Rachel survived, at least.

"No," said Mitor. "I'll not have men say I stooped to the level of Richard the Usurper. I'll not murder men in the shadow of my castle. We shall parley with them. I intend to send Lord Richard a message."

"What message shall we send, my lord?" said Sir Albron.

"We shall tell Sir Tanam that his thieving master must disband his army. Richard shall come before me and acknowledge my liege lordship. He may then return to his northern estates, for I intend to take Swordgrim as mine once more. But he must leave his son Toraine as my hostage, to ensure his obedience."

"Lord Richard will never agree to such terms," said Sir Nathan.

Mitor scoffed. "I expect he won't! I am the liege lord of the Grim Marches! He will come to me and ask for peace, or else I shall sweep him from the face of the earth."

"With what?" said Mazael. "With the ten thousand rabble you have crouching outside your gates?"

Mitor's lips pulled back from his teeth. "You go too far!"

"I have not gone far enough!" said Mazael. "Think, my lord brother! This is your last chance. You can't believe that this rebellion of yours will succeed. With what will you defeat Lord Richard? Your soldiers? He has fifteen thousand more than you. Simonian's arts? Lord Richard will have brought his vassals' court wizards. With Sir Albron's leadership? Albron can't even set a decent guard. Lord Richard isn't threatening you. He's giving you one last chance to turn back from the abyss."

Mitor went deathly pale. His hands clenched into fists, the knuckles shining white through his skin, and for a moment, just a moment, despair covered Mitor's face. For the first time Mazael wondered what had driven his older brother to rebellion.

Then Mitor's face hardened. "You will regret those words, Mazael. I've tolerated you and your arrogance long enough. When I come into my liege lordship, there will be a reckoning, do not doubt it. With the Mandragons, with all the fools who supported them, and with you."

"My lord speaks justice," murmured Simonian.

"Your lord is a fool," said Mazael, disgusted.

Mitor swept away from them.

"You've reached a decision, my lord?" said Sir Tanam.

"Old Crow!" said Mitor. "You may carry this message back to your murdering lord. Tell Richard Mandragon that he is to disband his armies and dismiss my vassal lords from his service. Then he and his sons, Toraine and Lucan Mandragon, must come with all haste to Castle Cravenlock where they shall submit to my judgment." Mitor smiled. "I have not decided if I shall be merciful. Most likely not."

"I see," said Sir Tanam. "Lord Richard's not like to welcome those terms."

"I know that!" shouted Mitor. "If Richard wants peace, let him come to me and grovel for it!"

Sir Tanam sighed. "Then it looks as if I'm to wear out my poor horse riding back and forth between Lord Richard's camp and here."

"I should take your head and send it back to Mandragon," said Mitor.

Sir Tanam shrugged. "That would solve my problems, at any rate, but that would bring you quite a few more."

Lord Marcus huffed. "Who would miss an old crow?"

"I would," said Sir Tanam.

"My lord, sir knight," said Simonian. "There is no need for this squabbling. Lord Richard sent you here to parley? Then let my lord and Lord Richard parley. My lord Mitor, why not invite Lord Richard here to discuss your differences?"

"Very well," said Mitor. "You speak wisdom, Simonian." He turned to the Old Crow. "Let Lord Richard come, if he wishes to parley. Let him speak for himself!"

Sunlight glittered off Sir Tanam's battered armor. "Actually, Lord Richard anticipated such a request. He invites you to come to his camp."

Mitor laughed. "Bah! Does Mandragon think me such a fool! I will not walk into the arms of his treachery!" Mazael refrained from pointing out that Mitor had almost ordered Sir Tanam's death. "Why should I trust a lord whose vassal would abduct an innocent lady out from under my roof? I am Richard Mandragon's greatest enemy!"

Sir Tanam's smile was sardonic. "Of course."

"I have no doubt that Mandragon has his armies waiting in ambush for me, should I prove foolish enough to come to his camp," Mitor said. "Yes, yes, Mandragon knows he cannot take my host in a fair and honorable fight. He is reduced to conniving ambushes."

Sir Tanam smiled. "Indeed, my lord. I could not have said it better myself. I can see your wisdom in fearing treachery. Why not send an emissary in your name?"

"Bah!" said Mitor.

Simonian shifted. "It is a prudent suggestion, my lord. Perhaps Lord Richard can yet be made to see reason. Why should this end in bloodshed?" His rough voice took on a note of irony. "Send an emissary, my lord, someone who can negotiate in your name."

"Suppose Richard decides to commit an act of treachery anyhow?" said Mitor.

Simonian shrugged. "That is a risk the emissary shall simply have to take, I fear. But what better way to die than in the service of a wise and powerful lord?"

"Sir Nathan!" said Mitor. The old knight stepped forward.

"My lord?" said Nathan.

"You've been looking for a way to serve me," said Mitor. "This is the sort of thing that would have suited fat Othar, but the fool chose to eat himself to death rather than to serve his rightful lord." A single muscle tightened near Nathan's eyes. "I am sending you as an emissary."

Sir Tanam nodded. "A respectable choice, my lord. Sir Nathan Greatheart is famed wide and far. But Sir Nathan does not have a high title, nor vast holdings. The good Sir Nathan has not the authority to treat with Lord Richard." Sir Tanam glanced at Mazael. "Best send someone with higher rank, my lord. Someone of your own blood, perhaps."

"It is Nathan or no one," said Mitor.

"Lord Mitor," said Mazael.

Mitor turned. "What?"

"Send me," said Mazael.

Mitor laughed. "You? Why should I send you?"

"Sir Mazael's suggestion is prudent, my lord," said Simonian. "After all, what shall you lose if he is captured or killed? Nothing. And yet, he is your brother, and since you and the Lady Marcelle are childless, the heir to Castle Cravenlock." Marcelle bristled. "He has sufficient stature to satisfy Lord Richard's pride."

"I agree," said Sir Tanam. "Sir Mazael is an excellent choice. Send him. I know my lord would be most honored to receive him."

Mitor glanced at Simonian. The wizard gave a slight nod.

"Very well," said Mitor. "You may go, Mazael. I shall send fifty armsmen with you as a suitable escort." He smirked. "Sir Nathan shall go as well. Sir Tanam and Richard Mandragon seem to hold him in such high honor. Perhaps he'll help convince the Mandragons that surrender is their only option."

Sir Tanam seemed pleased. "Undoubtedly, my lord. And, I, of course, will escort Sir Mazael and company in all honor to Lord Richard's camp."

Mitor ignored this. "And take that monk!"

"Brother Silar?" said Mazael.

"Yes, him," said Mitor. "The fool has made a great nuisance of himself! Take him with you, Mazael, I command it! Richard Mandragon is such a friend to the Cirstarcians, let him take the monk."

"I would take Sir Gerald with me, as well," said Mazael, "along with Lady Romaria." He did not trust Mitor and would not leave his friend in his older brother's reach. And Mazael wanted Romaria at his side.

He did not want to endure another nightmare.

"The wild woman can ride to hell for all I care," said Mitor. "But I would much prefer Sir Gerald to remain here, as my guest, under my protection."

"As his hostage," muttered Romaria.

"Lord Malden sent Sir Gerald and myself as observers," said Mazael. "Doubtless Lord Malden would want his son to observe Lord Richard's troops?"

"Sir Gerald is my guest," said Mitor. "How would Lord Malden view it if I allowed his son to perish from Richard Mandragon's treachery?"

"Oh, poorly," said Mazael. "And just how do you think Lord Malden would view the restriction of his son's freedom?"

Mitor hesitated. Perhaps it was the hope of Lord Malden's aid that kept him defiant against Lord Richard. "Very well. Lord Malden is my friend, yes, and I shall not offend him."

Sir Tanam did a little bow from his saddle. "My lord of Cravenlock is most gracious."

"Save your flattery," said Mitor. "Mazael, prepare to depart at once. I will not have this Old Crow roosting in my castle longer that necessary."

Mazael nodded. He knew this parley was a farce, that Mitor wanted nothing more than to rid himself of his troublesome brother. Perhaps it was indeed a trap by Lord Richard. But what choice did Mazael have? Romaria had said that his dreams of blood had been triggered by hidden powers within himself, but suppose they were visions of things to come? This might be his one chance to avert those visions.

He turned to Sir Tanam. "We shall ride before noon."

Sir Tanam's grin widened. "I look forward to it."

CHAPTER 24
LORD RICHARD MARCHES

Armor glittered and flashed under the afternoon sun as they rode north. Crowley's banner flapped in the wind, while Mazael had entrusted Adalar with the Cravenlock banner, and Wesson had unfurled the Rolands' greathelm standard.

"What is that?" said Mazael.

Romaria grinned. "This?" She hefted the canvas sack hanging from her saddle.

"Yes, that," said Mazael. "It looks like a bag of rocks."

Romaria laughed and reached into the sack. "They're apples. Want one?"

"Of course," said Mazael, and she tossed one at him.

"You know, I'd never had apples before," said Romaria, taking one for herself.

"What?" said Mazael.

"They don't grow in the Great Southern Forest," said Romaria. "Not enough sun, perhaps. Are there are none south of the mountains. I'd never seen one before last month." She took a bite, swallowed. "They're quite good, really. I talked a sack out of Cramton."

Mazael gave Chariot half of his apple. "He was charmed by your beauty, no doubt."

Romaria's smile was sly. "Oh, no doubt. It's fairly common. But you're the one with the charm."

Mazael snorted. "Gods, I hope not. I prefer women."

"I had noticed. But that's not what I meant and you know it. You inspire loyalty."

Mazael snorted. "Hardly."

"Really?" said Romaria. "What about Sir Gerald? He's a son of the great Lord Malden! He needn't follow you. And Timothy and Adalar. And Sir Nathan, your old teacher, follows your orders without question."

"I don't want Castle Cravenlock, Romaria," said Mazael.

Romaria shrugged. "You might not have a choice."

"Destiny?" said Mazael. "Fate? I..."

"Don't believe in it?" said Romaria. "I thought I explained that to you. We were fated to meet."

"That's different," said Mazael. "I need you. I would have gone mad but for you. And I still could."

"And what is that? Fate, or destiny, or the will of the gods, whatever you want to call it?" said Romaria.

Mazael had no answer.

Romaria leaned towards him. "We'd best speak of this later. It looks as if Sir Tanam and Brother Silar want a word with you." The Old Crow and the monk rode up together.

"We should make Lord Richard's camp in about three and a half days," said Sir Tanam. "Longer, if any Mandragon forces demand explanations."

"You don't seem worried about any men from Castle Cravenlock," said Mazael.

Sir Tanam cackled. "Worried? Of course not! I didn't see a single one from here to Castle Cravenlock. I rode right up to the gates before anyone even saw us." He smiled. "Sir Mazael, I could march an army to Castle Cravenlock and Lord Mitor wouldn't know until we knocked him over the head."

"He's right, of course," said Silar. "Lord Mitor's defenses are limited, to say the least."

"And how would you know?" said Mazael.

Silar laughed. "Remember White Rock? Who do you think helped Sir Albert design that palisade? I know a few things about war."

Sir Tanam's eyes flicked to Lion. "That is a most fine sword, by the way."

Mazael shrugged. "Sorry I had to hit you with it."

Sir Tanam snorted. "I should be grateful you didn't hit me with the blade. It looks rather sharp."

"It has other properties, as well," said Silar.

"We'd heard of that," said Sir Tanam. "Effective against the walking dead things, right?"

Mazael stiffened. "How do you know about that?"

"One of our outrider bands slipped past Castle Cravenlock and stopped by White Rock a few days past," said Sir Tanam. "The village was buzzing with stories of your battle."

"You got a band of outriders south of Castle Cravenlock?" said Mazael.

"That surprises you? Sir Albron Eastwater is not an effective commander," observed Sir Tanam. "Do you really think he can defeat Lord Richard? I wonder, why are you siding with Mitor? If I might ask, of course. He obviously cares nothing for you. And you have everything to gain by going to Lord Richard's side. If Mitor falls, you'll be the next Lord of Castle Cravenlock."

Mazael glared at him.

"I see I've given you much to ponder," said Sir Tanam. "Worry not, Sir Mazael. Many of your questions will be answered once we reached Lord Richard's camp."

"Questions?" said Mazael. "What sort of game is your lord playing? I'm tired of games. Mitor plays one, Albron has his own, and Simonian..."

"You'll see," said Sir Tanam. He rode off, Silar following.

They passed many small villages and hamlets. Nearly all were deserted. Crowley told them that the peasants had fled north for the safety of Lord Richard's forces. The silence reminded Mazael of the stillness that would rise before storms swept down from the mountains.

They made camp near one of the abandoned river hamlets. Romaria curled up besides Mazael and went to sleep. This raised some eyebrows amongst Crowley's men, but none dared say anything.

Mazael didn't care. His sleep was dreamless and peaceful.

They next day Crowley's men veered to the northeast, setting a direct route towards Lord Richard's camp. The lands north of Castle Cravenlock's hills had been depopulated since Lord Richard's uprising, and the grass had grown thick and high. They were forced to take their horses at a walk to avoid stones and debris hidden in the grass.

Later that day, a snake in the grasses spooked Chariot. The big horse reared and threw Mazael, and he took a long gash down his forearm from a jagged rock. Mazael made a show of having Timothy tend his wound, but even as the wizard wrapped bandages about the arm, Mazael felt the itch as the skin healed itself. By the time Timothy had finished, the gash had faded to a pale pink scar, and it vanished entirely an hour later. Fortunately, no one noticed. They had accused Rachel of witchcraft and sorcery. How would the Old Crow react if he saw Mazael's flesh knit itself back together?

It troubled Mazael for the rest of the day. How powerful was the healing? Could it heal a mortal wound? Would it regenerate a severed limb? A finger of ice brushed his spine. Could he even be killed? The thought was terrifying and exhilarating.

They made camp for the second night. Again Romaria slept touching him, and again his rest was free from his father's bloodshot green gaze.

The third day of their journey was uneventful. Breezes ruffled the grasses of the Grim Marches, and Mazael saw countless blood roses. They made camp and the night passed quietly, untroubled by bandit or zuvembie.

Halfway through the fourth day, they reached Lord Richard Mandragon's camp.

Romaria smelled it first. "We're almost there."

Mazael looked at her. "How do you know?"

"I can smell it," she said.

"I can't smell anything," he said.

Romaria smiled. "You can't? I'm surprised. Twenty-five thousand men, their horses, and their pack animals smell after a while."

Gerald laughed. "Remember my brother Mandor's camp after three weeks, Mazael? He never bothered to order fresh privy trenches dug. An old woman in the village died of the stink, I heard."

Mazael grimaced. "Don't remind me."

"The most splendid lady is quite correct," said Sir Tanam. "We near Lord Richard's camp. We should arrive within the hour."

A few minutes later Lord Richard Mandragon's camp came into sight.

It was a city of tents and a sea of waving banners. Mazael saw the Mandragons' standard, the sigil of Hawk's Reach, the fiery dragon of Drake's Hall, and two dozen others. The tents themselves were lined up in neat rows, and a stake-lined ditch encircled the entire encampment.

Sir Tanam greeted the guards and rode into the camp. A thousand sounds and smells surrounded Mazael. He heard the hammering of blacksmiths, the bellow of shouted orders, the laughter of off-duty men, and the measured tread of drilling soldiers. He smelled cooking food, heated metal, sweat, blood, and the undercutting reek of the privy trenches.

A man-at-arms in chain mail and a Mandragon tabard ran up to Sir Tanam. "My lord knight, Lord Richard has been informed of your arrival. He and his captains await you and his...ah, guests in the command tent." It was less than a minute's ride to the command tent, a pyramid of green canvas atop a wooden pavilion, the Mandragon banner fluttering from a pole overhead.

"Here we are!" said Sir Tanam, sliding from his saddle. Grooms ran forward to take their horses. "Right this way, my lord knights, my lady. Lord Richard is expecting us."

A long wooden table rang the length of the tents, maps and papers covering its surface. A dozen men stood around the table. One was short and stout and wore a surcoat emblazoned with the burning dragon of the Mandrake family, undoubtedly Lord Jonaril Mandrake of Drakehall. The man standing next to him was a younger version of Sir Commander Galan Hawking, no doubt Lord Astor Hawking.

But despite the others, Mazael recognized Lord Richard the Dragonslayer and his sons at once.

Lord Richard was in his mid-forties. His red hair and beard were streaked with white, making it seem as if encircling flames crowned his head. His eyes were black and unreadable, and his crimson armor was magnificent. Mazael had never seen anything like it. The armor was a combination of hand-sized plates and gleaming chain mail. He realized the plates were scales, taken from the dragons Lord Richard had slain in his youth.

The young man besides Lord Richard wore similar armor, though his was night-black. He was fit and lean, his expression arrogant and amused without the slightest hint of fear. This must be Toraine Mandragon, the infamous Black Dragon.

Behind him stood a shorter man clad in black wizard's garb, his hooded cloak shadowing his face. This was Lord Richard's younger son Lucan Mandragon, the wizard the jongleurs called the Dragon's Shadow. Lucan's face was gaunt, his eyes hard and cold, and a mocking smirk played on his lips.

"Sir Mazael Cravenlock," said Lord Richard, his deep voice resonant. "I am pleased Sir Tanam brought you."

"Lord Richard Mandragon," said Mazael. "Now that we're certain of each other's identity, shall we begin?"

"You are refreshingly direct," said Lord Richard. "Many of my lords and knights would rather talk than act."

Mazael thought of Albron and Mitor. "I understand."

"Then let us begin," said Lord Richard. "This is my son and heir, Toraine." Toraine did not acknowledge Mazael. "This is my second son, Lucan." Lucan gave Mazael a grave nod, his dark eyes unreadable. "These are my lord captains." He introduced Lord Jonaril and Lord Astor and the others. "You've already made the acquaintance of my old crow, I understand."

Sir Tanam grinned. "Twice, actually."

"This is Sir Gerald Roland," said Mazael.

"Well met, Sir Gerald," said Lord Richard. "I did not think to see the day when I would speak peacefully to a son of Lord Malden."

Gerald bowed. "I've seen many strange things over the last

month, my lord. Why not another?" Lucan's sardonic smile widened.

"This is Sir Nathan Greatheart," said Mazael. "This is Timothy deBlanc, a wizard in my service. And this is Lady Romaria Greenshield, sent by her father Lord Athaelin to investigate these events."

"My lady," said Lord Richard. "I am pleased your father chose to involve himself. Perhaps together we can bring an end to the madness that threatens this land."

"I hope so," said Romaria.

"And this is Brother Silar of the Cirstarcians, a monk who has decided to involve himself," said Mazael.

"Brother Silar and I have met," said Lord Richard. "He advised me on the history of Castle Cravenlock before he went to assist Sir Albert Krondig against the zuvembies. Please, be seated." Mazael and his companions sat, and Lord Richard and his captains followed suit. "I assume Lord Mitor has sent a message for me?"

Mazael's mouth twisted. "Oh, yes. He commands you to disband your armies, surrender Swordgrim, travel to Castle Cravenlock, and acknowledge his liege lordship. He hasn't decided if he will show mercy."

Toraine Mandragon laughed. "Then Mitor is a bigger fool than I believed. Let us see his pride once we mount his head above his castle gate."

Lord Jonaril snorted. "A poor idea, I say. I've met the man. His head would make a terrible eyesore." Mazael remembered his dreams and tried not to shudder.

"You realize, of course," said Lord Richard, "that I have no intention of standing down. The Mandragons are the rightful liege lords of the Grim Marches. That makes Lord Mitor a rebel and a traitor."

"I realize that," said Mazael.

Lord Richard folded his hands and placed them on the table. "I also have considerable information on Lord Mitor's army. He has ten thousand men. Only six thousand are loyal. The four thousand from his own house, and two thousand more from Lords Roget and Marcus. The remaining four thousand are mercenaries of dubious reliability."

"The Justiciar Knights have gone to support Mitor's cause," said Mazael.

Lord Richard did not blink. "The Justiciar estates in the Grim Marches will only supply Lord Mitor with two thousand men. Neither Lord Alamis Castanagent of the High Plain nor Lord Malden Roland of Knightcastle can move fast enough to aid Lord Mitor. I am only three days' march from Castle Cravenlock. By the time the Justiciar Grand Master sends reinforcements, the issue will have been decided."

Toraine smiled. "If they hurry, the Justiciars will come in time to see the end of the Cravenlocks."

"I see why my sister didn't want to marry you," said Mazael. Toraine bristled, but Lord Richard stilled him with a glance.

"I also possess a great deal of information on the formation of Lord Mitor's forces," said Lord Richard.

"From the Old Crow, no doubt," said Mazael.

"Sir Tanam's scouting work has been of great benefit to me," said Lord Richard. "But the vast bulk of my knowledge has come from my many spies within the mercenary encampments. This fool Albron Eastwater is a tenth of the battle commander you are, my good Sir Nathan. Mitor's army is a farce."

"It is sloppy, my lord," said Sir Nathan. "Sir Albron will learn some bitter lessons."

"Should he survive them," said Toraine.

"Ten thousand men against twenty-five thousand are poor odds in any circumstance," said Lord Richard. "And when those ten thousand are poorly led, ill-disciplined, and improperly arrayed, the outcome is all but certain."

"I know all this," said Mazael. "I came here for a parley, not for a recitation of facts I already know."

"The parley has yet to begin," said Lord Richard. "I merely state what I will do. Tomorrow, I will march. I will fall on Castle Cravenlock and I will smash Mitor's armies to shreds. Once the castle has fallen, I will hang Sir Albron Eastwater, my traitorous vassals Marcus Trand and Roget Hunterson, this foreign necromancer Simonian of Briault, and Lord Mitor and Lady Marcelle. I offered Lord Adalon and his sons mercy fifteen years ago. I will not have it thrown back in my face. Lord Adalon was wise enough to know that. It seems Lord Mitor is not."

Mazael shoved back from the table and stood. "And what of Lady Rachel Cravenlock?"

"Her fate has yet to be decided," said Lord Richard. "I would prefer to spare her life."

Mazael laughed at him. "You call this a parley? This is a bill of execution."

"Lord Mitor's fate and the fate of his allies has been sealed," said Lord Richard. "I have no desire to parley with them. You, however, are a different matter."

"What?" said Mazael.

"Have you not yet realized it?" said Lord Richard. "I sent my old crow to Castle Cravenlock in hopes that Lord Mitor would send you as his emissary. Sir Tanam was instructed to work towards that end."

Mazael sat back down. "Is that it? You want me to join you, and in return for my undying loyalty, I'll become the next lord of Castle Cravenlock once Mitor hangs?"

Lord Richard did not blink. "Yes."

"No," said Mazael. "I'll not..."

"Not what?" said Lord Richard. "Betray your brother? Sir Mazael, did it not occur to you that Lord Mitor has already betrayed you? He did not send you here to parley a peace. He sent you here in hopes that I would capture you or kill you. He is afraid of you. Lord Mitor and Lady Marcelle have proven incapable of producing children. You are his lawful heir, whether he likes it or not. Most men in your position would have killed Lord Mitor and taken his place by now."

Mazael remembered what Lord Adalon had said in the nightmares. "No. I'll not do it. Do you think I'll betray my brother and my sister for the damned castle? Mitor can keep it. I'll have nothing to do with you."

"I did not expect you to," said Lord Richard. "And why not? Your brother has lied to you at every turn."

"What do you mean?" said Mazael.

"Have you ever wondered why I sent Sir Tanam to abduct Lady Rachel?" said Lord Richard.

"A hostage," said Mazael.

"Lord Mitor would not have cared what I did with Lady Rachel," said Lord Richard. "I sent my old crow to seize Lady Rachel because of the sorcery she practiced. She could have provided me with valuable information on the San-keth cult at Castle Cravenlock."

"No," said Mazael, slamming his fist down onto the table. Lord Jonaril arched a bushy eyebrow. "I listened to this slander once at White Rock. I will not listen to it again. I have seen the zuvembies. I know they're real. But I have not seen San-keth, nor fools worshipping snakes. I will not listen to this."

"Then you shut your ears to the truth," said Lord Richard.

"The San-keth cult has been in Castle Cravenlock for at least thirty years," said Lucan. His voice resembled the rustling of dead leaves. "I'm fairly certain Lady Arissa was involved."

Mazael snorted. "I lived at Castle Cravenlock for nine years! I would have noticed."

"Most of the cult's activity centered at Swordgrim in Lady Arissa's time," said Lord Richard. "We found some of their scrolls once I had defeated Lord Adalon's host and retaken Swordgrim." His dark gaze settled on Mazael. "How do you think I gathered the men to face Lord Adalon? To regain my family's place, yes. But the lords of the Grim Marches liked the worship of the snake god no more than I."

"This is nonsense," said Mazael.

Lord Richard continued as if Mazael had not spoken. "I killed all the snake-worshippers I could find. Undoubtedly some survived and restarted the cult at Castle Cravenlock."

"Slander," said Sir Nathan.

"It is not," said Lord Richard. "I considered offering Toraine in marriage to Lady Rachel for a number of years. When I decided to make the offer, the rumors of San-keth worship had already begun. At first I discounted them. But the peasants near Castle Cravenlock began disappearing. Then reports of the zuvembies filtered in. And then Lord Mitor showed signs of rebellion. I sent Sir Tanam to make the offer anyway, and to investigate. Sir Tanam?"

The Old Crow cleared his throat. "That was about six, seven months ago, as I recollect. I found the castle and town in sorry shape. I hadn't yet heard that Sir Albron had replaced Nathan Greatheart as armsmaster." He laughed. "Never seen a sorrier lot of troops, and I've seen quite a few sorry soldiers in my day. And the town was worse. Armsmen ran the place like it was their private kingdom. There was this one fellow, Brogan, had the temperament of a whelping bear and all the wits of a stone."

"I met him," said Mazael. "Briefly."

"Castle was worse," said Sir Tanam. "The servants were scared to death, just the same as the peasants. It only took a bit to figure out why. They were scared of the cult. Seems a large number of the castle residents had taken up the worship of the snake god. Lord Mitor and Lady Marcelle had, as well as Sir Albron Eastwater. Perhaps Sir Commander Galan Hawking as well." Lord Astor sighed. "And there was that Simonian villain as well. I've spent a few years on the other side of the mountains and visited Briault for a few weeks. The peasants there still whisper about this necromancer Simonian. Thoroughly unpleasant fellow. Tales have him down to the tee. So, with the zuvembies, the peasants' stories, and Simonian of Briault as Lord Mitor's guest, a blind man could have seen what was going on. I'd seen the San-keth cult during the war with Lord Adalon, and now I was seeing it again."

Sir Nathan closed eyes.

"Sir Tanam returned to Swordgrim with his news," said Lord Richard. "I was most displeased. I did not throw down one Cravenlock lord and the accompanying San-keth cult only to find myself confronted with another. I sent word to the Cirstarcian monastery west of Castle Cravenlock. They sent Brother Silar and other monks to assist my cause."

Mazael raised an eyebrow. "That so?"

Silar grinned. "My order has been here for centuries. We

remember the old tales. And we remember the dark magic and necromancy that a serpent-cult brings."

"I had no other recourse but war," said Lord Richard. "I called my vassals and gathered my armies. I also commanded my son to investigate using his skills."

Lucan's lips twisted. "It was fairly obvious. Dark magic hangs about Castle Cravenlock like a stink. Even a wizard of mediocre skills like Master Othar could have detected it."

Mazael shifted in his seat. "You knew him?"

Lucan smiled, and for an instant the bitterness vanished from his face. "Of course! I apprenticed under him, once I had finished my training at Alborg. He was no magister, certainly. But a finer master I could not have found elsewhere." Bit by bit the sardonic mask cast returned to his features. "I contacted Othar through the use of a magical sending. He already shared many of my lord father's suspicions. We soon had a regular correspondence. He believed that there was a San-keth temple hidden within Castle Cravenlock. Master Othar planned to investigate that temple, if possible." His empty eyes fixed on Mazael. "I have not heard from him since."

Mazael remembered Othar's last words to him. "Master Othar is dead."

Lucan's face could have been carved from stone. "How?"

"Necromancy of some sort," said Mazael.

Lucan snorted. "And do you need any more proof to confirm this 'slander', my lord knight? Or shall I beat you over the head with it?"

"Lucan," said Lord Richard, and the Dragon's Shadow fell silent.

"I sent Sir Tanam to capture Lady Rachel," said Lord Richard. "I am almost certain she was involved in the San-keth cult."

"No," said Mazael. "No."

"It does not matter. Were she innocent, she would have been safer at Swordgrim than at Castle Cravenlock. Were she guilty, as I believe she is, then she would have proven a valuable source of information. It was at this point, of course, that you intersected with events." Lord Richard leaned back in his chair. "Now, do you see why you must join me? There is no other choice. You will get the castle and the lordship once Lord Mitor is dead. But what of that? The cult of the serpent people is an abomination. Their necromancy and dark worship pollute the land. The Cirstarcians and Deepforest Keep see this. So would the Justiciars, if they did not hate me for reclaiming the lands stolen from my family." The Dragonslayer made a fist. "When I rose against your father, my goal was to exterminate the San-keth cult root and branch. That your father was inadvertently allied to the cult through Lady Arissa was an unfortunate circumstance. And I will do the same once more. I will destroy this new cult and wipe it from the memory of man. And you will either stand with me or against me."

Mazael thought of his mother and her hateful spite. Mazael could imagine her in a serpent cult. But Rachel? He could not imagine Rachel in a San-keth cult...but he had not seen Rachel for fifteen years. And he thought of Simonian, the way the wizard's murky eyes stared.

"I don't know," said Mazael.

"There is no middle ground," said Lord Richard. "Will you stand by and let the cult spread across the Grim Marches like a plague? It is a disease and I will stamp it out. If you stand with Lord Mitor, I shall crush you."

"What proof is there?" said Mazael. "This is all supposition. What proof do you have?"

"What further proof do you need?" said Lord Richard. "If you wish to blind yourself to the truth, that is your folly. I am offering you a chance to escape your brother's fate."

Mazael's palm smacked against the table. "You don't have any proof."

"The zuvembies." Lord Richard ticked off the points on his fingers. "The disappearing peasants. Lord Mitor's timely rebellion. I have all the proof I need, indeed, all the proof that any reasonable man would require."

"Reasonable man?" said Toraine. "A reasonable man, Sir Mazael, you are not. You shall never see the truth. Father, I say have off with his head and have done with it."

"Silence," said Lord Richard. "And why, Sir Mazael, do you persist in blinding yourself?"

"I blind myself to nothing," said Mazael. "My sister could never have been involved in this. Never. Not her."

A dead quiet answered his pronouncement.

"Then you leave me no choice," said Lord Richard. Mazael's hand shot to Lion's hilt. "I'll not attack you here. Return to Castle Cravenlock and share in your brother's..."

"Wait!" said Timothy. "My lord, please, wait." All eyes fell on the wizard, who swallowed and tugged his beard.

"What?" said Lord Richard.

"Sir Mazael, you trusted Master Othar's judgment, correct?" said Timothy.

"Absolutely," said Mazael.

"Do you remember the morning after Master Othar's funeral?" said Timothy. "When I told you of Master Othar's journal?" Mazael nodded. "It was warded and sealed. I could not read it."

Lucan smiled. "Not surprising. The old man was clever enough to protect his investigations. I designed the ward for him myself."

"Then you would know how to release it," said Timothy. "My lord knight, you trusted Master Othar's judgment in life. Trust it now that he is gone. I propose that we return to Castle Cravenlock and unseal Master Othar's journal. You say there is no proof? Master Othar would have found proof, one way or the other." The young wizard struggled for words. "The fate of so many lie in your decision. My lord knight, look at what Master Othar had to say before you make a choice."

Lord Richard looked to his wizard son. "Can you teach Sir Mazael's wizard the spell to open the journal?"

Lucan clenched a hand. "Certainly, my father. He has the badge for dispelling. The spell to open the ward sealing the journal is no more than a specific variant."

Lord Richard turned to Timothy. "And are you willing to learn the spell?"

Timothy bowed beneath the Dragonslayer's black gaze. "Yes, my lord."

"And you, Sir Mazael?" said Lord Richard. "What of you? You seem so certain of your brother's innocence. If the words of Master Othar indicate otherwise, if they show that Lord Mitor has invited the necromancer Simonian and the San-keth cult to his court, will you stand with me?"

Mazael could believe Mitor would sell his soul to the San-keth. But he could never believe it of Rachel. "I will do it. I shall return to Castle Cravenlock and read Master Othar's journal. And I will prove that you are wrong."

"Perhaps you shall, sir knight," said Lord Richard. "Perhaps you shall discover that Simonian of Briault has tricked and betrayed your simpleminded yet innocent brother and his misguided wife. Perhaps you shall then rid his court of the blight, saving myself and my vassals the trouble of killing him. We can all then go home." He paused. "But I know better. You shall discover the truth. You are in for some very hard lessons."

Mazael did not flinch from Lord Richard's stare. "One of us is."

Toraine was aghast. "You can't be serious, father. You invite this Cravenlock into the heart of our camp, tell him all our plans, extend to him your mercy, and then let him go? This is madness! He shall tell his brother everything he has seen here. It shall be our undoing..."

"I have no intention of letting Sir Mazael undo us," said Lord Richard, a hint of anger creeping into his iron tones. "Either way, he shall work to our advantage. Either he shall kill Simonian, or he shall discover the truth of his family and return to us. Our position shall be strengthened." He waved his hand. "And Lord Mitor cannot stop us. Leave and do not return until you have composed yourself."

Toraine stalked towards the tent flap. Lucan smirked at him, and for a moment Mazael thought Toraine would kill his younger brother. Then the elder Mandragon son stormed out into the camp.

"Please forgive my son," said Lord Richard. "He is often passionate."

"I know all about family troubles, my lord," said Mazael.

"Indeed," said Lord Richard. "The evening draws nigh, Sir Mazael. I invite you and your companions to dine with my family and lord captains tonight."

Mazael was surprised. "I doubt they'll approve."

"Why not?" said Lord Astor, chuckling. "Lord Richard tells us what we are allowed to approve."

"After all, we have established that you are not my enemy," said Lord Richard. "Whatever choice you make, my hand shall be strengthened. Will you not eat?"

"Then I shall be honored," said Mazael. They rose.

"Ah, not you," said Lucan to Timothy. "I do believe you have a spell to learn."

CHAPTER 25
THE MONK'S FIRST BROTHER

"What do you think?" said Mazael.

"I do not know," said Sir Nathan.

Mazael and Romaria sat with Sir Nathan amongst the supplies of Lord Richard's camp. Night had fallen, and it was quiet here. The light from a thousand bonfires lit the camp, and guards marched back and forth on their rounds.

"A serpent cult," said Sir Nathan. "I would never have believed it. I heard the stories, of course, but I had always believed them to be nothing but stories. Dust and lies."

"Three months ago, I believed zuvembies to be stories," said Mazael.

"As did I," said Nathan. "I do not know, Mazael. I simply do not. I did not know Lady Arissa well. I spent most my time in the field against Mandragon forces. But what little I saw was not favorable."

Mazael smiled. "I saw more of her. None of it was favorable."

"But could she have renounced all Amathavian gods, all that was right, and turned to the god of serpents?" said Nathan. "I do not know if I can believe it."

Mazael could.

But Rachel...no, not Rachel.

"And a cult now," said Sir Nathan, "my heart tells me that such a thing cannot be. But my head tells me that I cannot know for certain. I have not spent much time in Castle Cravenlock over the last fifteen years. After Leah died and Lord Mitor dismissed me, I spent most my time at my keep. I doubt I have spent more than one day in ten at Castle Cravenlock. Lord Mitor holds so many secrets. And with this business of the zuvembies and Othar's death..."

"We'll find out," said Mazael. "We'll know the truth, one way or another."

"I hope so," said Sir Nathan, standing. "I shall retire. I am not so young and it has been a long day."

"Sleep well," said Mazael.

Mazael listened to the sound of feasting rising from Lord Richard's command tent. Mazael had little appetite and left early, but Lord Richard had taken no offense. Mazael suspected that the feast had been given for Gerald's benefit anyway.

"A good man," said Romaria, watching Sir Nathan leave.

"Aye," said Mazael. "I only wish we had a hundred more of him."

"Talk to Lucan Mandragon," said Romaria. "He could conjure up a few."

"Gods," said Mazael. "Certainly not. I've seen enough magic to last me a dozen lifetimes. Master Othar was a good man, but I cannot see how he could devote his life to spells."

"Spells and swords," said Romaria. "Some are used for good, some for evil." She looked at Mazael with calm blue eyes. "And how are you feeling?"

Mazael flexed the fingers of his sword hand. "Well enough, I suppose. There's been times...I wanted to kill Lord Richard when we spoke. But beyond that, I suppose I'm fine."

"And no nightmares, of course," said Romaria.

"No nightmares," said Mazael.

Romaria laughed. "I wonder what Lord Richard and his lord captains shall say when I go to your tent for the night."

"They'll say nothing," said Mazael. "It's not as if we actually do anything."

"And does that disappoint you?" said Romaria.

Mazael snorted. "What do you think?" He cupped Romaria's chin and kissed her. "But...I don't..." He scowled. "I'm pulled to you. The damned dreams. The magic in the sword. I nearly went insane and killed you and my brother. And then the healing. What is happening to me?"

"Perhaps I can shed some light on the matter."

Mazael shot to his feet, Lion lancing from its scabbard. Brother Silar approached, a lantern dangled from his grip.

The monk looked amused. "Do you greet all your visitors with a sword?"

"Do you surprise all those you would like to visit?" spat back Mazael, ramming his sword back into its scabbard.

Silar sighed and sat down atop a barrel. "You were having an interesting conversation."

"What did you hear?" said Mazael, his hand inching toward Lion's hilt.

"Mazael," said Romaria.

Silar chuckled. "I did not hear anything that I have not deduced for myself."

"You speak dangerously," said Mazael.

Silar set his lantern down and raised his hands. "I'm certain I do. But I do not want any fight. With Lady Romaria to help you, you'd certainly win." He cocked his head. "And whatever wounds I managed to inflict would vanish quite shortly."

"I've had enough games," said Mazael. "Tell me what you want."

"Very well," said Silar. "I said before that you possess some sort of power. That was not entirely true. I am quite certain what sort of power you possess."

"And what sort of power is that?" said Mazael.

"You're Demonsouled," said Silar.

Mazael had Lion out of its scabbard and against the monk's neck so fast that he didn't register the movement. Romaria came to her feet, her hand closing around Mazael's arm. A flicker of fear flashed across Silar's face and vanished. For a burning moment Mazael wanted to slash open Silar's throat, but Romaria's touch quenched the dark fire.

"You must not get many visitors," said Silar.

"What did you say?" said Mazael.

"Demonsouled," said Silar.

"Are you saying Lord Adalon was not my father?" said Mazael.

Silar shrugged. "It's entirely possible. Lady Arissa was a remarkable woman, and not in a complimentary sense. We suspect she worshipped Sepharivaim, the serpent-god, do we not? No doubt she would have flung herself at a demon."

Mazael's hand twitched on Lion's hilt, but he could not disagree.

Silar shrugged. "Besides, a demon soul doesn't require a Demonsouled parent. The taint can lie dormant for centuries, passing from generation to generation. It can appear for no reason at all. Would you mind putting that sword down? It's terribly uncomfortable."

Mazael lowered Lion. "And how do you know all this about me? More supposition?"

Silar rubbed his thick neck. "Hardly. It's obvious, if you know where to look. Your speed, Sir Mazael, is nothing mortal. Nor are your reflexes. Are you even aware of how well you fight?" He glanced at Mazael's arm. "And that cut...I've seen enough wounds to know a deep slash from a scratch. Timothy's good at his tasks, no doubt. But I've yet to see the physician skilled enough to make a deep gash disappear in two days."

"So?" said Mazael. "That doesn't make me Demonsouled. Perhaps I'm fast. Perhaps I'm very good with a sword. And perhaps I had a simple scratch."

"Perhaps," agreed Silar. "But I know what to look for."

"From what?" said Mazael, gesturing with Lion. "The books? Tomes penned by men a thousand years dead? I could write a book claiming that horses fly, but that doesn't make it fact."

"True," said Silar. His smile was distant, his hawkish face lost in a memory. "But I've seen it with my own eyes."

"Oh?" said Mazael. "So, you've seen a Demonsouled with your own eyes, have you?"

"Yes," said Silar.

Mazael laughed. "Were you drunk at the time?"

Silar shook his head. "No. I was eight years old at the time. My brother was eleven."

"Your brother?" said Romaria.

Silar blinked. "I was born in a small village on the northern edge of the Grim Marches. We were very poor. It's hard to grow anything in that soil. It didn't matter, though. We were happy. At least, I think we were." Silar flexed the fingers of one hand. "I was always in awe of my brother. He was the fastest and strongest boy in the village. No one could keep up with him. And he was an archer. The way he could use a bow and an arrow would amaze even you, Lady Romaria. I saw him take down a hunting cat at a hundred yards."

Silar shook his head. "But he was always passionate. Volatile. He could go from smiling to raging in a heartbeat. And his temper was like a storm. One day he fell into a crevice hidden in the grasses. The men pulled him out. Both his legs had been broken and one arm. We expected that he would die." Silar stared at Mazael. "Two days later he was up and about as if nothing had happened."

Mazael's hand clenched.

"After that, he began to change," said Silar. "I was only a child, but even I could see it. He flew into a rage at the slightest provocations. He almost beat an old man to death over a piece of bread. We were all afraid of him. Then a wizard came to our village, a man named Strabus. He worked with the Cirstarcians, and hunted Demonsouled and Sanketh across the kingdom. Across the world, for all I know. He warned my parents of the danger, but my father and the other men drove Strabus out of our village. That night my brother killed my parents."

Mazael heard the blood rushing through his ears. He remembered how close he had come to killing Romaria.

"I'm sorry," said Romaria.

"He wasn't my brother, not anymore," said Silar. "The demon soul within had warped him. He looked like a creature out of the pits. He would have killed me. But Strabus returned. He came too late to save my father and mother, but he used his magic to destroy what my brother had become." Silar rubbed at his chin. "After that, no one in the village would take me in. Strabus took me to the Cirstarcian monastery near Castle Cravenlock. That has been my home ever since."

"So, is that it, then?" said Mazael. He shoved Lion back into its scabbard. "Am I to become some sort of monster?"

"You might," said Silar.

"You told me the Cirstarcian monks fight dark magic," said Mazael. "Are you here to kill me?"

"No," said Silar. "I became a monk of the Cirstarcine Order to combat the darkness. I have seen it firsthand. But I loved my brother. The demon power destroyed him, not Strabus. If you are Demonsouled, and I'm certain you are, I would rather see you resist the darkness."

"What do you mean?" said Mazael. "Demonsouled are monsters."

"Some become monsters," said Silar. "Demonsouled are born with the darkness hidden in their souls. For some, it never manifests. They live, marry, have children, and die without ever knowing what they are. But for others, the darkness surfaces, usually as they reach young manhood or womanhood. They then must face themselves and try to conquer the dark halves of their souls. Men of evil mind usually embrace the power and the transformations it brings. Others find themselves overwhelmed and changed into monsters. But some can fight against the darkness and master it."

"Have you ever seen it happen?" said Mazael. "A man conquer the demon half of his soul?"

"No," said Silar.

Mazael grimaced. "And have you read about it in these books of yours?"

"Some," said Silar, "so far back it seems like legend."

Mazael laughed. "You offer me such reassurances."

"I offer you help," said Silar.

"Why?" said Mazael.

"For the memory of my brother," said Silar. He paused. "And for the safety of the people of the Grim Marches. Perhaps even the kingdom."

"What do you mean?" said Mazael.

"You are strong," said Silar. "I think the fighting prowess is only the tip of what you can do. There are other stories in the histories I have read, of Demonsouled who became bloody conquerors and carved huge empires on a foundation of death and misery. If you succumb, I don't think you'll become some a ravening beast. I think you'll become a tyrant king unlike any seen in history."

Mazael did not want to believe him, but his words rang true. Even now, Mazael saw a half-dozen ways he could kill Silar. A half-dozen ways he could kill Romaria. Battle had always seemed a glorious, vibrant experience, the only time when he felt fully alive.

He was Demonsouled.

His hand trembled towards Lion. "Perhaps I should simply kill myself."

"No!" said Romaria, clamping both her hands around his.

"The lady is right," said Silar. "Despair will accomplish nothing."

"Accomplish?" said Mazael. "How can I accomplish anything if my very soul is my enemy?"

"Much," said Silar. "You might have darkness in your soul. But there are other evils already loose in the Grim Marches. The zuvembies. You may not believe there is a San-keth cult at Castle Cravenlock, but there have been other cults in the past. And Simonian of Briault. If the tales are even half-true, then that one is worse than most Demonsouled. You can overcome them all. The gods sent you back to the Grim Marches for a reason, I believe."

"Silar is right," said Romaria. "I told you about destiny. Perhaps it is your fate to end the plague that is Simonian and his zuvembies."

"Fate?" said Mazael. "Fated to what? Kill my family and my friends in a bloodbath? Become some sort of grotesque monster? Or shall I become the tyrant that Silar fears?"

"You haven't done any of those things," said Romaria.

"Only with your help," said Mazael. "You pulled me out of madness. But I almost killed you first. Suppose I had killed you? What would have happened then? I can't. If I do have demon magic in my soul, I can't overcome it by myself."

"Whoever said you have to overcome it alone?" said Silar.

"What do you mean?" said Mazael.

"My brother tried to conquer his soul himself, I think," said Silar. "My parents and the other villagers refused to see what was happening. Strabus didn't come until it was too late. You cannot face the demon half of your soul alone. Lady Romaria will stand with you. She's said so herself. I will help you, if I can." His fingers wrapped about the holy symbol hanging from his belt. "And the gods will help you, if you'll let them."

"The gods?" said Mazael. "I've never cared much for the gods. Why would they help me now?"

Silar held up his holy symbol, the three interlocking rings of Amatheon gleaming in the camp's torchlight. "Why would they not help you? We are all their children, after all." He grinned at Romaria. "Even those of us who pray to different gods. And you, Sir Mazael, are special. You are a descendant of the Great Demon who came to earth and fathered the Demonsouled."

"Hardly special, I would say," said Mazael.

"The Great Demon was divine once," said Silar. "Fallen, but still a god. Why would the gods turn away from helping you? You are both one of their own and one of their children." He unhooked the holy symbol from his belt and pressed it into Mazael's fingers. "Take this."

"Why?" said Mazael, the steel symbol cool and heavy in his hand.

"Perhaps it will help you," said Silar.

"How?" said Mazael. "It's a piece of steel. If I want steel to help me, I'll use a sword."

"Keep it as a reminder, then," said Silar, "that the gods will help you."

Mazael didn't believe him.

But he slipped the symbol's chain around his neck anyway.

CHAPTER 26
NIGHT STALKING

Castle Cravenlock rose above them, the twilight sky outlining its battlements and towers.

"Shall we stop here for the night?" said Gerald. "We can continue on in the morning."

"No," said Mazael. "Let's keep going. We'll find it easier to do what we must if Mitor doesn't know that we're here." He grimaced. "Besides, we're too close to the camp. If we sleep here, we're liable to be spotted in the night."

Gerald looked towards the camp beneath the castle's walls. "Agreed."

"Ride through the camp," said Mazael. "If we go through town, some the armsmen might see us."

"Besides, those mercenaries will never notice us," said Romaria.

Mazael snorted. "They didn't notice the Old Crow. They'll certainly ignore us."

No sentries stood at the edge of the haphazard conglomeration of tents. Mazael had left his escort of Cravenlock lancers at Lord Richard's camp, and he and his companions passed unnoticed through the ramshackle camp. Most of the mercenaries were drunk, and paid them no heed. Mazael soon worked his way around the camp and climbed the road that led to the castle.

"Gods," said Mazael, reining up before the gates.

"What?" said Gerald.

"Look," said Mazael. "The damned gates are open. There are no guards. No men at the gate, no crossbowmen at the ramparts. Had Sir Tanam come tonight, he could have rode in, killed Mitor, and won the war for Lord Richard with one blow."

The fury was plain in Sir Nathan's voice. "Lord Mitor must bring Sir Albron to task. This is unacceptable."

"This is the work of a fool," said Mazael. They rode through the barbican, into the deserted courtyard. "Let's stable the horses and get to Othar's tower. The sooner I have firm answers to this business, the better."

Othar's tower stood in the corner of the curtain wall, a thick stone cylinder of battlements and arrow slits. It had been the home of the court wizards of the Cravenlocks for centuries. But Simonian had not deigned to take possession, and so Othar had kept his quarters there.

He pushed the door open. It was too dark to see, but Timothy muttered something. Glowing light surrounded his hand, illuminating a staircase that climbed into the murk.

"Gerald, Sir Nathan, Adalar and Wesson," said Mazael. "Stay down here and watch the entrance. Send Adalar up if someone comes. Silar, Timothy, and Romaria, come with me."

Master Othar had kept his study and workroom in the tower's top chamber. Mazael remembered the time he had spent there as a boy, reading from the old wizard's large collection of books. It looked much as he recalled. Bookshelves lined the walls of the circular room, laden with books and scrolls, and jars, glass tubing, and other strange devices burdened a long table.

Timothy walked to Othar's desk. A heavy leather-bound book rested on the corner, its copper bindings shimmering with a faint blue glow.

"The journal," said Mazael.

Timothy nodded, took a step back from the desk, and closed his eyes. He muttered a low chant, the fingers of his right hand moving with sharp gesture. There was a flash of blue light, and the shimmer vanished from the book.

"There," said Timothy, wiping sweat from his brow. "The ward has been dispelled."

Mazael opened the journal and began to read. The first entries were from several years ago, written in Othar's strong, clear handwriting. He flipped past them, seeking the more recent entries.

What he read sent a finger of ice down his spine.

The journal described Othar's suspicions over dark magic, the San-keth, and a collaboration between Simonian and Sir Albron. He read about the appearance of the zuvembies and Mitor's seeming indifference, about Othar's growing belief in the existence of a San-keth cult temple within Castle Cravenlock's walls.

About dark things...

"Sir Mazael?"

Mazael looked up from the pages. He had lost track of time.

"What does it say?" said Romaria. "You're as white as a ghost."

Mazael forced moisture into his dry mouth. "Master Othar was certain. He read the histories and the stories of San-keth cults that thrived at Castle Cravenlock in the past. He became convinced that there was a secret temple in catacombs underneath the castle, hidden for centuries. Master Othar believed he had found the entrance to the temple. He planned to investigate, and that was the final entry."

"Secret catacombs?" said Silar. "Do you mean the castle's crypt?"

"No," said Mazael. He paged through the journal and put his finger over the words. "No. He said that these catacombs predated the castle. They were here before the first Cravenlock even built a the keep." His voice shook with anger. "He said that it was an ancient temple. Master Othar thought that this temple had survived here, hidden, for centuries."

"That matches the histories of my order," said Silar. "A San-keth cult raised this castle. The house of Cravenlock was founded when the youngest son of the cult's high priest slew his father and turned to the Amathavian gods."

Mazael slammed the book shut. "If this is true, then I grew up here, with this...this temple under me all the time...gods in heaven." He closed his eyes. "Gods in heaven. Master Othar never put down a last entry. We don't know if he was right."

"What are you going to do?" said Romaria.

"The only thing I can," said Mazael. "I will go and look. Master Othar believed the temple's entrance was within the lord's chambers in the keep. He described the means to open the door." He relaxed his fist. "I have to look. I have to know. If it's true, if it's true then..."

"Then we will look," said Romaria.

Mazael managed to nod.

He took Othar's journal under his arm, and they left the study. Sir Nathan, Sir Gerald, and the squires awaited them at the bottom of the tower. Mazael told them what he had found.

"Gods," said Gerald. Wesson muttered something and spat through his fingers to ward off evil.

A hard look came into Sir Nathan's eyes. "There can be little doubt, then. There is a serpent cult in Castle Cravenlock. All that remains to be seen is if Lord Mitor has betrayed the laws of gods and men by joining it." Mazael realized that he might not have to kill Mitor himself.

"It would be wise to leave at once," said Timothy. "Lord Mitor does not know that we are here. We must warn Lord Richard of what awaits him."

"No," said Mazael. "Lord Richard already knows. He tried to warn me. I didn't believe him. And Mitor has to be involved in this. Sir Albron and Simonian are his closest allies. How could I not have seen it? Am I blind?"

"Mitor and Rachel are you brother and sister," said Romaria. "Even if you hated Mitor, you would still find it hard to believe something so dark about him."

His hands clenched and unclenched. "I have to see it for myself. I have to know."

"Then we'll have to do it quietly," said Gerald.

"I have a great deal of experience in getting into places quietly," said Romaria.

Silar grinned. "Really? So do I. How splendid."

"Interesting activity, for a monk," said Romaria.

Silar shrugged. "It is surprising what you learn if you live long enough."

"Gerald," said Mazael. "Timothy is right, though. Lord Richard knows the truth, but he still needs warning. I want you to take the squires and head back to Lord Richard's camp. Tell him of what we found and give him this journal."

And it would keep Gerald and the squires out of Mitor's clutches. Mitor's, and Simonian's.

"I'd rather face this nest of evil with you," said Gerald.

"My place is by your side, Sir Mazael," said Adalar.

"Be that as it may," said Mazael. "You and Wesson are still boys. I'll not have you perish in a pit of snakes. And you wanted to stop a war, Gerald? What do you think will happen if you die here? Your father will blame Lord Richard."

Gerald did not look happy, but he took the journal. "The gods be with you, Mazael. With luck, I'll see you shortly."

"I hope so," said Mazael.

Mazael watched them hurry to the stables. "The rest of you can make for Lord Richard's camp, if you like. This is my error. You don't have to come."

Romaria laughed. "I think not. You need me, Mazael, whether you like to admit it or no."

"Lord Mitor is my liege lord," said Sir Nathan. "I would know if he has betrayed his oath by turning to evil."

"I'm sworn to you," said Timothy. "Where you go, I'll follow."

"The Cirstarcian monks are sworn to face this darkness wherever it rises," said Silar.

Mazael was grateful for their presence. "Let's go."

219

They crossed the courtyard for the doors of the central keep, and still they saw no armsmen. Mazael pushed the doors open and strode inside. They passed through the anteroom and the vaulted great hall, both chambers deserted and quiet.

"Where is everyone?" said Sir Nathan. "Supper should just have finished."

Mazael crossed to the lord's entrance behind the chairs on the dais, to the stairs that led to the lord's chambers. As a boy, Mazael had hidden in this stairwell with Rachel, playing and listening to their father's court. He wondered if Lord Adalon had known of Lady Arissa's wickedness. For the first time, Mazael's disgust for his father's weakness mingled with pity.

He wrapped his hand around Lion's hilt and kicked open the door to Mitor's quarters. Beyond the door lay large sitting room with a carpeted floor and a half-dozen chairs, while the lord's private entrance to the chapel stood to his right. Mazael listened for Mitor or Marcelle to call the guards.

But the rooms were empty.

"This way," said Mazael. "The entrance is in the bedroom."

They passed through a carpeted library and a small dining room and entered Mitor's bedroom. A huge canopied bed dominated the chamber. Mazael wondered how often Marcelle and Mitor shared it. A gaping granite fireplace covered one wall, carved with reliefs depicting Cravenlock knights vanquishing Mandragon armsmen.

"Here," said Mazael.

He knelt before the fireplace, running his fingers along the floor. One of the granite tiles was higher than the others. He grimaced, flexed his fingers, and pulled out the tile, revealing a small niche.

A snake stared up at him.

It was a bas-relief of green marble, rubies glittering in its eyes. Just as the diagram in Master Othar's journal had described.

"Gods," said Nathan.

Mazael reached into the hole, put his fingers on the snake's crimson eyes, and pushed. He heard a deep click, and the floor trembled. With a dull groan, the back of the fireplace slid into the wall and revealed a winding staircase. A warm breeze blew out of the stairwell. It carried the stink of blood and the oily smell of snake.

"Gods indeed," said Mazael. "Light, Timothy."

Timothy surrounded his hand with shimmering light, and they took the stairs. The steps twisted down, past the castle's foundations, past the dungeons, and deep into the hill's bedrock. The walls began gleamed with dampness.

Torchlight glimmered ahead, and the stairs ended in a long,

straight passageway, wide and high with a vaulted ceiling. Walls, ceiling, and floor were built of red granite that gleamed like blood. Guttering torches burned in rusted iron scones, revealing the bas-reliefs covering the walls.

Mazael swept his gaze down the corridor. He knew the story of the San-keth race, how they and their god had allied with the Great Demon. After the Great Demon had been slain, the true gods had stripped the serpent people of their limbs and forced them to crawl in the dust in penance for their crimes.

The walls told the same story from a different angle. Mazael could not read the strange script, but the bas-reliefs were clear. They showed the San-keth tortured by the capering and gleeful Amathavian gods. Later carvings detailed the punishment the humans and Elderborn would undergo when the serpent god rose in glory. Mazael was suddenly glad that he had sent the squires away. They were too young for such horrors.

The worst part was the utter lack of dust. There were no cobwebs. The walls and floor gleamed as if freshly polished. The torches had been recently lit.

The corridor ended in a massive set of black double doors carved with mating serpents. Mazael saw flickering red and green light from beneath the door. The scent of blood grew thicker.

"You'd best dismiss your spell, wizard," said Silar. "If there are any San-keth priests about, they might have the skill to detect your magic." Timothy extinguished his light.

"Gods have mercy," said Sir Nathan. "This place has been here for all these years. I never knew. I am a fool."

"No," said Silar. "The only fools are the ones who come to worship here." He pointed. "Behind those doors will be the temple proper, if my order's descriptions are correct. Do you see those smaller doors in the walls, there and there? Those should lead to side chambers for storage, libraries, and the keeping of sacrificial slaves."

Mazael jerked his head towards one of the smaller doors, taking care to keep his footfalls silent, and the others followed suit. He felt as if the leering serpents carved into the walls watched him with their crimson eyes, and he drew his sword.

A jolt of power went up his arm. Lion's razor edges glimmered with blue light.

"There are creatures of dark magic nearby," said Silar. "We had best take care."

"Undoubtedly," said Mazael. He heard soft voices through the door. He listened for a moment, and held up four fingers. Romaria and Nathan nodded, while Timothy pulled a lump of crystal from his coat.

Mazael gripped the handle, pushed, and leapt through the door.

He crashed into a small guardroom. Four men wearing the tabards of Cravenlock armsmen lounged about a round table, guarding a door on the far wall. Mazael recognized them from the gang that had tried to hang Cramton and his family.

The armsmen gaped up at him for a moment.

"Ah, hell, it's him!" said one, scrabbling for his sword.

Mazael took the armsman's head with a single swing. As the other guards lurched to their feet, Timothy held his crystal high. It flared with white light, and the armsmen shrieked and held their hands over their eyes. Mazael wheeled and killed another, while Romaria's bastard sword plunged into a man's chest. The final armsman ran for the closed door. Silar vaulted over the table, his arms wrapping about the man's neck. There was a cracking sound, and the armsman slumped to the floor.

"Nice trick," said Romaria.

Silar stepped over the body. "One hardly needs weapons to kill." He looked at Mazael. "There's your proof. This temple has been in use for quite some time. And these armsmen are Mitor's. They would not be down here without his knowledge. Look at your sword. There are creatures of dark power here we are not equipped to face. Let us leave at once and make for Lord Richard's camp."

Mazael heard chanting through the closed door, warm air seeping through the cracks in the wood. "There's a ceremony going on in there."

"Most likely that's where everyone is," said Silar.

"Including Rachel," said Mazael.

"Yes," said Silar. "Now we must leave at once!"

"I have to know," said Mazael. He reached for the door.

CHAPTER 27
THE TEMPLE

The door opened into a scene from hell.

Mazael stepped onto a balcony encircling a cavernous hall that resembled the interior of the great cathedral he had seen years ago in Barellion. That cathedral had been decorated with carvings of gods and saints. But here, statues and carvings of limbed serpents killing humans adorned this temple, this pit. A stone altar rested atop a dais at the end of the temple, overlooked by an enormous stone statue of a giant snake. It was an image of the serpent god Sepharivaim, worshipped by the San-keth people and by human apostates. The air was heavy with the scent of smoke, strange incense, and blood. A dull, droning chant in bastardized Tristafellin rose from the floor. Mazael ignored Silar's hiss of warning and stepped to the edge of the balcony.

A great mass of people knelt before the altar. There were servants from the castle, Cravenlock armsmen, and men wearing the finer garb of knights.

"Mitor," said Mazael.

Mitor knelt at the front of the crowd, his forehead resting against the crimson stone floor, Marcelle besides him. Lord Marcus Trand and Lord Roget Hunterson knelt behind Mitor like a pair of mongrel hounds crouching behind their master.

"Rachel's not here," said Mazael.

"I'm happy for you," said Silar. "Let's go."

"This is a dangerous place. We should leave. Now," said Romaria.

"Brother Silar is right," said Nathan. "We must..."

The reverberating crash of a great gong drowned out his words, its clang echoing through the temple. The kneeling men and women began wail in ecstasy and terror. A huge drum thundered, its vibrations thrumming through the stone.

"Simonian," whispered Romaria.

Mazael saw the necromancer at the far end of the temple hall, cloaked in black robes, watching the worshippers with amused contempt.

"Right," said Mazael. "Let's get..." He froze.

Sir Albron Eastwater marched into sight, clad only in a loincloth around his waist. The kneeling men and women parted for him. Rachel walked on Albron's arm, clad only in a shift of translucent black gauze. Golden bracelets wrought in the shape of serpents glittered on her wrists and ankles, and crimson runes marked the pale length of her arms and legs. A diadem shaped like twisting silver serpents supporting a great golden cobra with glittering ruby eyes rested upon her brow.

"She's one of them," said Mazael. Strange that he felt no pain, no rage.

Only...surprise.

"Gods," said Sir Nathan. "Look!"

Albron's body began to shimmer, his flesh rippling as if dissolving into mist.

"An illusion!" said Timothy, his voice an excited whisper. "That was the spell I sensed about him. An illusion, to hide his true form!"

The illusion dissolved to reveal a moldering skeleton, sparks of green fire glimmering in its joints. It was the same green fire Mazael had seen in the empty eyes of the zuvembies. A huge emerald-scaled snake was coiled around the skeleton's spine, its tail dangling through the hip bone to brush against the floor. The snake's head reared up in its place, its black-slit yellow eyes roved over the kneeling worshippers.

Rachel's arm remained hooked about the animated skeleton. Mazael wanted to scream.

"A San-keth serpent priest," said Silar. "Sir Albron's true identity."

"Why is it riding that skeleton?" said Romaria.

"The gods stripped the San-keth of their limbs," said Silar, "so the serpent priests use their dark arts to transform human skeletons into undead carriers, of a sort. The priest can control the limbs through its necromancy." Silar swallowed. "Sir Mazael, the markings on Lady Rachel's arms..."

"What about them?" said Mazael. He did not recognize his own voice.

Silar met his gaze. "It means..."

"Hail!" Mitor stood, his arms spread. "Hail to Most High Priest Skhath of Karag Tormeth. Hail to Rachel Cravenlock, his chosen, on whom he shall father children in the name of our great lord

Sepharivaim!"

"Children?" said Mazael.

"They're called calibah...changelings," said Silar. "They're half-human, half-San-keth. They..."

"She lied to me," said Mazael. "She said...she told me..."

"I know," said Romaria.

"Lord Richard was right," said Mazael. "They were all right. How could I not have seen it?" Fury rose to the forefront of his churning thoughts. "She lied, the wretched scheming..."

Skhath's voice was a sibilant, grating hiss, nothing like the illusionary Albron Eastwater's smooth voice. "The time is nigh. Soon our armies shall sweep Lord Richard and his impotent gods from this land. Soon the glory of our lord Sepharivaim shall shine over the lands of Dracaryl. The blood of our sacrifices shall turn the rivers red." Rachel knelt before him, the thin fabric of her shift stretched tight against her body. "Soon shall Mitor Cravenlock, faithful servant of the true god, reign as king over the Grim Marches, over all lands. And soon shall the worship of Sepharivaim and his glory fill the world!"

A roar of glee rose from the worshippers.

"Like hell it will," said Mazael. "Let's get out of here. I'll..."

"Most High Priest!" Simonian's voice rang over the temple, and the necromancer pointed at the balcony. "Intruders disturb these sacred rites!"

A dead silence fell over the hall. Mitor gaped at Mazael. Rachel saw Mazael and blanched, color flooding into her cheeks.

"What? Him!" said Skhath. "Kill them!"

The mob lurched to their feet and broke into a run. Rachel backed behind the altar, while Simonian and Skhath began casting spells.

"Damn!" said Mazael. "Run!"

"Not yet," said Romaria. She raised her bow and began shooting.

Her first arrow raked into Mitor's side. Mitor shrieked, blood dripping down his robes. Her second arrow hummed towards Skhath, only to lodge in the skeleton's rib cage, but the San-keth cleric flinched and ceased his spell. Her third arrow lanced towards Simonian's head.

Purple fire flared from Simonian's body and consumed the arrow an instant before it would have plunged into his flesh. The purple flames flashed, and a line of fire blasted towards Romaria. She ducked, and the line of flame carved a deep gash into the stone wall. Lion flared in Mazael's fist, the lines of blue light growing into sapphire flame.

"Now we run!" said Romaria.

They sprinted towards the guardroom as Simonian finished his spell. Orbs of green fire flashed from his fingertips. Mazael ducked, but the green spheres shot over his head and veered to the right.

"What were those lights?" said Mazael. He sprinted through the guardroom.

"I don't know," said Timothy. "I've never seen such a spell!"

"Nor I," said Silar.

Mazael raced into the great vaulted corridor. The green flames whirled and danced above them, and then vanished into the carved walls.

"Perhaps his dark art failed," said Sir Nathan.

Hidden doors in the walls slid upon with a rumble, and out stepped ten gaunt figures armored in gleaming black breastplates, chain mail, and helms. Lion blazed in Mazael's fist, brighter than it had during the battle with the zuvembies. The creatures that had stepped out of the walls were not alive. Their flesh clung to their bones like dry leather, their empty eyes bright with necromancer's fire. Each carried a curving scimitar and a round shield, and the undead things moved with fluid, unearthly grace.

"Gods have mercy," said Sir Nathan.

Silar stepped to the side. "This is great necromancy. These creatures are monstrosities out of legend." The creatures moved into a semicircle, scimitars waving.

"I don't care if they're the gatekeepers to hell itself," said Mazael. The battle rage rose in his mind, and he welcomed it. "I mean to walk out of here. The gods pity whoever stands in my way!"

Mazael spun, the flat of his sword banged against Romaria and Nathan's blades, sheathing their weapons in azure flames. He came out of his spin, took two running steps, and brought Lion down in a blazing arc for a creature's head. The sword exploded through the creature's helm and sank into its skull. The green light in its eyes flickered and died, and the creature collapsed in a heap of bones and black armor.

The other creatures came at Mazael in a rush, and he parried their attacks. Romaria and Nathan fought beside him, their blades rising and falling.

Timothy stepped forward, breathing hard. His hands flew through a series of rapid gestures, red sparks flaring between his fingers. He flung the sparks at a pair of the creatures. They shuddered, sparks dancing up their withered limbs, and bones and armor flew in all directions.

Mazael attacked a pair of the dead things, Lion crashing against shield and scimitar, blue flames reflecting in polished black armor. The creatures were deadly quick, their scimitars stabbing like the fangs of serpents. But they seemed so slow to Mazael, so very slow. His two-handed swing cut one in half with a blazing flash. The surviving creature came at him, scimitar raised high. Romaria's sword rammed into its back, and blue fire drowned out the green. The creature crumpled to the marble floor, and Romaria's cool eyes met Mazael's.

Some of his rage throttled back and he nodded.

Mazael and Romaria spun through the press of monstrosities side-by-side. Romaria's bastard sword crashed against black shields and Lion clanged against flashing scimitars. Romaria's attack played out, and she stepped back. One of the creatures lunged for her and met Lion's point instead. Blue flame blasted through the creature, flinging it to the ground.

Mazael parried the attacks of another creature. He realized the creatures were skillful, but could not handle more than one opponent at once. Mazael retreated, drawing the creature after him. It came at him, scimitar twirling, and never saw Romaria step up and plunge in her sword into its back.

Mazael risked a glance around. Only three dead things still stood. Sir Nathan and Silar each fought one, while Timothy's face contorted as he fought to work another spell. Mazael ran towards them.

He hacked at the creature Silar faced and took its hand off at the wrist. The creature twitched, and Silar's hands lanced forward and tore the dead thing's head from its crumbling shoulders.

Sir Nathan pivoted, his heavy greatsword coming up over his head. His sword sheared through a dead thing's chest, flames sputtering and dancing on the steel. The creature thrashed as its rotted form burned away. Silar's hands darted out, clamping about the wrist of the sole surviving creature, and tore its arm away. The creature flailed, and Mazael and Romaria hacked it to pieces.

Silence fell over the corridor.

"Well fought," said Sir Nathan.

Silar grinned. "Simonian's magic might have power, but the magic of old Tristafel is stronger still."

"Care to test that?"

Mazael turned, Lion's power burning up his arm.

Simonian stood before the twisting stairs to Mitor's rooms. His black robes cloaked him like wings of darkness, and his murky eyes danced with glee as they swept over the fallen creatures. "Impressive. Impressive indeed! I did not think even you would have the power to overthrow the warriors of the dead, Sir Mazael."

Mazael lifted Lion, the sword's glow bathing the corridor in blue-white light. "I mean to leave this pit. Stand aside, necromancer, or you're next."

Simonian laughed. "I'm afraid I can't let you do that, not after what your half-breed friend did to poor Mitor."

Mazael stepped forward. "Why do you care? You asked me to kill Mitor. Get out of my way."

"Just why would you want to leave?" said Simonian. "If the most lovely Lady Romaria has slain Mitor, then you are Lord of Castle Cravenlock. You could overthrow the Mandragons. You could make yourself king. King of the world, perhaps. What's to stop you?"

"I don't want to become Lord of Castle Cravenlock," said Mazael.

"Then why not turn around and make them pay for what they have done?" said Simonian. "Make Skhath pay. And Rachel, dear, sweet Lady Rachel, so innocent and kind, who would never betray you..."

"Shut up," said Mazael.

"They are in disarray," said Simonian. "The snake-kissing rabble wail to their slithering god for aid. Why not go back and finish it? I will help you, I will lend my arts to your cause. Together we will make Skhath pay for his sins. And together, we shall make Rachel pay for her treachery!"

"I..." said Mazael. He wanted to make that wretched serpent Skhath pay. "I...can't...I want..." He wanted to make Rachel pay.

The rage burned through him in a black storm.

"You raised the zuvembies," said Romaria. She pointed her burning sword at Simonian. "Your necromancy killed Master Othar. Why should he listen to you?"

"You are a liar and a deceiver," said Sir Nathan.

Mazael's mind cleared. "They're right. You're in my way. Last warning. Move."

Simonian sighed. "If it must come to this..." His hands snapped up and began moving in a spell.

Mazael sprinted for the necromancer, Romaria and Sir Nathan a half-step behind. Simonian thrust his hand forward, green light glimmering at his fingertips, and Mazael lunged. Lion's blazing point slid past the wizard's hand and plunged into his chest, meeting no resistance at all. Mazael staggered, recovering his balance, while Simonian vanished in a scattering of smoke.

"He's gone," said Nathan.

"An illusion!" said Romaria. "He was never there at all."

Mazael heard Simonian's voice. The necromancer stood by the temple doors, and Mazael raced for him.

But it was too late. Simonian spread his arms wide. Green light exploded from his fingertips, stabbing into Mazael's eyes and sending lines of pain into his head. He heard Romaria scream, heard Sir Nathan shout a challenge.

Mazael roared and managed to take another staggering step before everything fell into darkness.

CHAPTER 28
RACHEL'S TRUE LOVE

The air smelled of blood and rot.

Mazael flickered in and out of consciousness. He realized that he sat on a cold stone floor, his back pressed against a rough wall. Steel cuffs pinned his arms to the wall, and a heavy chain bound his ankles. Incoherent images flickered across his thoughts. He saw Romaria, her eyes clear and her face smiling. He saw Sir Nathan and Master Othar. He saw his father. He saw Simonian. He saw Rachel with golden serpents wrapped around her wrists, crimson sigils scribed on her arms...

The rage made his mind swim back into focus.

Thin streams of torchlight leaked through in the narrow window, illuminating the straw-packed floor and the rusted chains. He groaned and leaned his head against the cold stone of the wall.

His weapons and armor were gone, of course.

Mazael jerked against the chains. What had happened to Romaria and the others? Were they locked away in other cells? Or had they been killed?

A wave of guilt surged through him. How could he have been so stupid? The evidence had been right before his eyes. Yet he had insisted Rachel would never do such a thing. He had said and thought that over and over again. And now he would pay the price for it. At least he had sent Gerald and the squires away.

"Out there!" yelled Mazael. "Can anyone hear me?"

A shadow appeared in the small windows. "Keep quiet!"

"Where are the others who were with me?" said Mazael. "What happened to them? Answer..."

The door banged open. A pair of Cravenlock armsmen stormed inside. Both had the sigil of a twisting serpent tattooed upon their foreheads.

"I said keep quiet," said one guard.

"Where are they?" said Mazael. "Tell..."

The guard's cudgel crashed into Mazael's chin, smashing his head against the wall.

"Keep your mouth shut, else I'll shut it for you," said the guard.

"I'll take that stick and shove it up..." said Mazael.

They rained blows upon his head and torso. Mazael fought to keep his eyes open, fury howling through him. For a moment he thought he could tear the chains from the wall. Then a cudgel impacted his head with a loud crack, and everything went dark.

Mazael awoke some time later. His head felt as if it had swollen to twice its normal size, and his breath whistled through new gaps in his teeth. His left eye would not open, and a stabbing pain filled his chest. Broken ribs, no doubt.

"I'll kill them," he rasped. "By all the gods, I'll kill them all, Rachel and Skhath and Simonian..."

But he couldn't. Skhath would kill him as soon as possible.

How could he have been so foolish? He had trusted Rachel. And now he would die for it.

"Rachel". Blood fell from his smashed lips. "I'll kill her, at least."

"Why do you suffer this to continue?"

Mazael's head jerked up. Red eyes stared at him from the darkness of his cell.

"Who?" he said.

A shape took form in the darkness, and Simonian of Briault stepped out of the shadows and into the feeble light.

"You," said Mazael.

"Indeed," said Simonian. "I see your perceptions haven't suffered."

"How did you get in here?" said Mazael.

"Through the shadows," said Simonian.

"Magic?" said Mazael.

"Of course," said Simonian. "My arts give me mastery over many things." He lifted one hand, sparks of green light dancing around his fingertips. "Shadows are the least of what I command. Illusions and the powers of the mind are mine. Even the dead respond to my call, as you have seen. But compared to power over men, these things are little more than the deceptions of a street magician." He closed his fist, the lights vanishing. "I can bend nations to my will and make them dance to my song. What is that, I ask you, if not true power?"

Mazael lifted his head to meet the wizard's gaze. "Monstrous. As are you."

"Monstrous?" said Simonian. "There's a fine word. Who calls me monstrous? Sir Nathan? That dried old stick? He lived in the castle for years and never knew of the San-keth. Blind, that's what I'd call him, or monstrously stupid. Does young Timothy deBlanc call me monstrous? That stripling wields the simplest of simple magic. He can neither attain nor understand the powers I wield. And Romaria Greenshield calls me a monster?" He laughed. "Has she even told you what will happen to her?"

"She told me that she only has half a human soul," said Mazael. His head did not hurt so much. "She told me of the disease."

"Disease?" Simonian laughed. "She doesn't even know the entire truth, does she? Oh, our fair Lady Romaria possess two halves of a soul. One half Elderborn and one half human. One half is infused with the magic of the earth and the other is the mundane piddling soul of a human. That's why her touch shields your dreams, incidentally - together you have one complete human soul. But that will do her no good, in the end." He rocked his hand back and forth like a scale. "The conflict between the two halves of her soul shall destroy her. Either her human half shall win and she'll waste away, or the magic in her Elderborn half will conquer, transforming her into a mindless, bloodthirsty beast. I rather imagine she'll be less attractive to you then. If you wish to bed her, do it soon."

"Either kill me or leave me in peace," Mazael spat. "Don't waste my time with this nonsense."

"Nonsense?" said Simonian. "How little you know." He traced a finger through the blood drying on Mazael's chest. "Those guards came close to killing you. Yet you seem rather well for a man who was on death's door just a moment ago. Why, it's as if your wounds are stitching themselves together before my very eyes." His murky eyes filled with amusement. "Why do you suppose that is?"

"Leave me in peace," said Mazael.

"And I saw the way you controlled the magic in that wretched Tristafellin blade," said Simonian. "The last men who had the power to control such magic lived millennia ago. Yet here you are, a simple knight-errant with no training in the magical arts. Stronger and faster than any other man. Tell me, why do you suppose that is?"

"Leave!" said Mazael, his voice stronger.

"I'll tell you," said Simonian. "You're Demonsouled, Mazael." He smiled. "Like me."

It was a moment before Mazael could speak. "What?"

"We are both Demonsouled, you and I. We share the same

heritage," said Simonian. "We are descendants of a long-dead god. The demon magic resides in our souls. I have embraced it and mastered it. With it I can wield magic far beyond the skill of any mortal. I did so long before you were born. And look at you, my kinsman. Your wounds heal as I speak. You can control other magic with your will. You can move faster and are stronger than any lesser man. All this, and you have barely tapped the tiniest part of what is possible! You have the potential to become one of the greatest Demonsouled who have ever existed." He laughed. "If I am monstrous, as you claim, what does that make you? A saint?"

"No," said Mazael. The pain in his chest had lessened. "No. No! It is madness and insanity. I will not give in to it!"

"Madness?" said Simonian. "It is power. Power to make yourself over as you will, to do as you wish, to make others do as you command. Why would you refuse such a thing? Because that fool Othar and that wretch Nathan told you? What do they know?"

"They were better men than you," said Mazael.

"Is that so?" said Simonian. "Tell me, do they know of your true nature? I thought not. What would they say if they found out the truth? Master Othar was such a vigilant defender of this castle. So vigilant he walked into the protective spells warding this place, and didn't notice as the magical fingers wrapped about his heart and squeezed. How would he have reacted if he had known his fine young student had a demon's soul? And old Sir Nathan, that paragon of honor and loyalty. Do you think Sir Nathan would smile and pat you on the shoulder? Or would he take his greatsword and plunge through your gut?"

"I don't want to hear this," said Mazael. "Sir Nathan was right. You are a liar. I won't listen to you."

"Liar?" said Simonian. "You wound me. I don't want to lie to you. I want to save you."

Mazael laughed. "Save me? You knock me out, leave me hanging in these chains, and you want to save me? You are a liar."

Simonian sneered. "And you deny the truth! I want to teach you to save yourself. Who knows of your true self? The half-breed Romaria? The monk Silar? Is that all? Romaria keeps your secret because of her own dichotomy, and Silar's vision is darkened by the memory of his brother. But what of the others? What of Sir Nathan and Sir Gerald? Knights are sworn to slay demons and protect the innocent." His mouth twisted in a mirthful grin. "What of the Cirstarcian monks? They kill Demonsouled and San-keth without mercy. Their full wrath would fall on this place, if they knew all its secrets. What of young Timothy deBlanc's masters, the bloated magisters of Alborg? They ban all dark magic, save those practiced by themselves. What do you think they will do to you, if given the chance? And the great and noble Lord Richard Mandragon, slayer of dragons. Will he allow a Demonsouled in his realm? All the powers of this world are arrayed against you. How do you think you can survive?"

"Shut up!" said Mazael.

"And Most High Priest Skhath and his betrothed Lady Rachel Cravenlock," said Simonian. "How Skhath would love to kill you! He thinks to transform the Grim Marches into a San-keth theocracy with himself as High Priest and Mitor as King." Simonian laughed. "King! Mitor? Bah! He couldn't rule a latrine. But you could rule so much more than the Grim Marches."

"What do you mean?" said Mazael.

"Let me teach you," said Simonian. "I can show you. I can tell you how to unlock the powers within you." He made a fist. "The healing, the speed, the battle instincts, they are nothing before what you could do, what you could become." He shook the chains binding Mazael's wrists. "You could tear those chains like paper. You could shatter that door as if it were made of glass. And then you could kill them all. Mitor and his cronies, Skhath and his whore Rachel, all of them. What could stop you?"

Mazael could not speak, remembering Silar's warnings.

"And I would help you," said Simonian. "Who could stand against us? There is nothing we cannot do. We could tear down this castle, if we chose. We could kill Lord Richard and reign over the Grim Marches. And then what? The impotent old king and the magisters? Mastaria and the Knights Dominiar? The world? What is to stop us?"

"The gods," said Mazael, thinking of Romaria. "Fate."

"The gods?" said Simonian. He snarled. "The gods care nothing for anything but themselves. Fate? I make my own fate. I can teach you to do the same."

"I don't want anything from you," said Mazael.

"You would come to regret those words," said Simonian. "Fortunately, I will not give you the chance."

"You can't force me to do anything," said Mazael.

"Quite true," said Simonian. "But I can help you to make the right choice." He grinned. "Your friends are alive, you know."

"What?" said Mazael.

"My spell was fashioned to stun," said Simonian. "They're all well and safe, sharing cells near yours. They're alive. For now."

"You bastard!" said Mazael. "If..."

Simonian continued. "I would strongly advise you to accept my offer. If you don't, why, I fear one of your friends will have a fatal encounter with my spells. Romaria, I think. And another one, and another, and another, until they're all dead, unless you embrace the demon magic in your soul." He smiled widened. "And after they're dead, I'll find Sir Gerald Roland and those squires. Such fine young men. I think I'll let you watch as I kill Adalar. Or perhaps I'll keep Sir Nathan alive to the last, and have you both watch as the boy chokes out his last. Wouldn't that be thrilling? You already have the blood of so many enemies on that Tristafellin sword of yours. Why not add the blood of a few friends?"

"You bastard," said Mazael. "You murdering bastard!"

Simonian titled his head to the side. "Ah. You have some visitors coming. I'll let you speak with them in privacy. Think over what I have said once they are done. You'll soon learn the wisdom of what I have to offer." Simonian gave a small bow and stepped back into the shadows. His robes blurred with the darkness, and then the wizard was gone.

Mazael's teeth ground as he fought to suppress his fury. A part of him wanted burst free from the chains and kill them all. The thought sickened him. Yet what choice did he have? Simonian was going to kill them. He was going to kill Romaria.

"Gods," whispered Mazael. "Amatheon and Amater and Joraviar. Help me, if you care. Don't let me become like him. And save them from him. Please." He hung his head. "Please."

Mazael sat in the darkness for a long time, his body tingling and shuddering as his Demonsouled nature did its healing work. His chest and face itched as the cuts and bruises faded. He felt a deep crawling as his cracked rib pulled itself together. His swollen eye leaked blood, and then he could see through it once more. Stabs of agony in his jaw as new teeth rose from his gums. He wondered what the armsmen would say when they saw him recovered from the beating. He could not help but laugh at the thought. It kept him from crying.

A rattle in the lock jerked Mazael out of his daze. The door opened, spilling brilliant torchlight into the darkened cell. Mazael squinted against the glare.

"Leave us," said a harsh voice. The smell of dusty bone mingled with the dry stench of a serpent's scales. "My future consort and I wish to speak with Sir Mazael alone."

"As you wish, Most High Priest," said one of the armsmen.

Skhath stepped into the cell, green fire flashing about the joints of his animated skeleton. The San-keth's coils shifted against the skeleton's spine, his black-slit yellow eyes fixed on Mazael. Rachel stood at his side, dressed in a black gown.

"I should kill you," said Skhath.

"Do it, then," said Mazael. "Slither off that skeleton and we'll see who's stronger."

Skhath made a strange hissing sound, and his mouth yawned open to reveal a pair of glistening ivory fangs. "I ought to. Great Sepharivaim has given his people this gift. We can kill with a single kiss."

"Great Sepharivaim?" said Mazael. "The same great Sepharivaim who gave his people arms and legs? Oh, wait, I had forgotten. Without that magicked skeleton, you'd crawl in the dust like the worm you are."

"It was the human and Elderborn gods," said Skhath. "They stole our limbs from us for daring to challenge their tyranny. And we shall regain what was taken from us one day. We shall take all the world when Sepharivaim rises in glory."

"That," said Mazael, "is the worst tale I've ever heard. Try telling it in the town tavern. You might get a crust of bread."

"You ask for death," said Skhath.

"Why not have Rachel do it?" spat Mazael. "She's willing to let you crawl into her and father monsters in her womb. She should be more than willing to kill me."

"Mazael," said Rachel, her voice anguished. "Don't."

"Don't what?" said Mazael. "Tell you the truth? Perhaps you're right. Why should I? You didn't bother to tell me."

"You don't understand," said Rachel. "You couldn't. How could I have told you?" She knelt besides him. "It's not so bad. What have the Amathavian gods ever done for us? They let Lord Richard overthrow Father. He wasted away and died from failure. If he had listened to Mother, none of it would have happened. She knew the true way, the way of Sepharivaim. He rewards his followers." She took one of his hands. "Why is this such a bad thing? Skhath came after Father died and told Mitor of the true way. Why don't you join us? Mitor can't have children. He can't even lie with a woman anymore, his health is so bad. With the power of Sepharivaim behind us, Mitor and Skhath will conquer the Grim Marches. Mitor will become king and Skhath High Priest. When Mitor dies, you'll be the new king of the Grim Marches." She smiled. "Join us, Mazael. You can be a king! We..."

Mazael spat in her face.

She flinched away.

"You're worse devils than Simonian!" Mazael said. "You are all serpents, you and him and Skhath! Why should I believe any of you? Go to hell, all of you, to whatever pit Skhath and his crawling god came from!" Rachel turned away from him, crying.

"Foolish human," said Skhath. "Do you not see that there is no other way?"

"Simonian said much the same thing," said Mazael. "I didn't

believe him, either."

Skhath hissed. "Simonian was here? The necromancer plays dangerous games. He is not a true believer. Still, he has his uses. I shall have to kill him one day." Skhath made that strange sound, his fangs bared. Mazael realized that it was a laugh. "It's odd. He even suggested the idea to me."

"The idea?" said Mazael.

"There has always been a temple beneath this castle," said Skhath. "It has lain abandoned for centuries. The Lady Arissa dabbled in the true way for a time, amongst other things, but she lacked the strength for her ambitions. The archpriests of Karag Tormeth sent me here to reopen the temple beneath Castle Cravenlock. I arrived, disguised as a human knight, during Lord Richard's uprising. As I watched the fighting, a most wondrous idea came to me. My people prefer to work out of the shadows, using humans as our puppets. But this human Dragonslayer led a force scarce half the size of his foe's and defeated it through superior battle tactics. Why could I not do the same?" Skhath's skeletal fists clenched. "I will do what no other follower of the true way has done. I will raise a nation to the glory of Sepharivaim. I shall purge the Grim Marches of the Amathavians and their gods. The rivers shall darken with their blood. The power of Sepharivaim shall rise over the Grim Marches."

"Grand plans, from a thing that has no arms or legs of its own," said Mazael.

"Enjoy your tongue, while you can," said Skhath. "I shall relieve you of it soon enough. I would have killed you once Simonian had taken you, but Rachel pleaded for your life. Since she will birth changelings to slay the enemies of great Sepharivaim, I will heed her words. I shall give you one day to decide. Either embrace mighty Sepharivaim and swear to serve his servants the San-keth, or else I shall put you and all your companions to death." His fork-tipped tongue flicked at the air. "Your bodies shall be raised as carriers in the service of Sepharivaim's priests. Your body would serve me nicely. Think upon what I have said. The day of the San-keth rises over the Grim Marches. Stand with me and rise with me, or stand with Lord Richard Mandragon and be swept away." Skhath made the laughing sound. "It is your choice. Come, Rachel. Let us leave this wretch to decide his fate."

Skhath swept out of the cell. Rachel looked at Mazael, still crying. She turned her back and followed the San-keth priest into the hall. The door slammed shut after them, blocking out the light.

It was hopeless. Lord Richard would not march for another three days. Simonian and Skhath would kill Mazael's companions tomorrow.

There was no way out of this stinking dungeon.

But there was one way, wasn't there? The demon magic within his soul. All that power, waiting for him to touch it. To make him strong and powerful.

To make him like Simonian...

"No," whispered Mazael. He shook his head. "No."

But was there any other way? Romaria would die if he did not act. Yet he knew the awful power of the demon power. He could have killed every man in Castle Cravenlock the morning of Master Othar's funeral.

"Gods help me," Mazael said. "If you're there, help me."

Simonian's words echoed in his head over and over again. Mazael felt as if his heart had transformed into an orb of pulsing fire, his blood into burning metal. He tried to push out the fire in his mind. He would not succumb!

But it was of no use.

He could not stop thinking of Rachel, and thinking about her poured oil upon the fire of his rage. Why should he not claim the demon magic within him? He could snap these chains, break through the door, and free his friends. He could smash Skhath's skeleton and choke the wretched serpent to death. He could rip Simonian's lying tongue from his bearded head. And he could tear Rachel's black heart from her chest.

Yes...

There was a thump outside the door, followed by a low conversation. Keys jingled, and the door swung open.

"Sir Mazael?"

Mazael's fury drained away and left a slight sick feeling.

He stared in astonishment. Bethy stood in the doorway, keys dangling from her first. Behind her stood fat Cramton, beads of sweat sliding down his forehead. The two armsmen lay at their feet.

"Sir Mazael!" said Bethy. "You must wake up!"

"I'm awake," said Mazael. "What's going on?"

"There's no time," said Bethy. She hurried into the cell and began opening the locks that held his chains. "Can you walk? We heard the guards beating you."

"I'm fine," said Mazael.

"You're certain, now?" said Bethy. The shackles on his ankles fell away. "It sounded bad."

Mazael forced a grin. "They didn't do a good job. What's going on?"

"We're getting out of here," said Bethy. "We've heard the rumors, me and Cramton. We know the Dragonslayer lord and all his men are coming. We're getting out of here, before the Dragonslayer comes."

"Yes," said Cramton. "It's not safe. Lord Mitor and the other snake-worshippers take a different child from the countryside every day now for their sacrifices."

"We didn't take the oaths," said Bethy. She went to work on the shackles binding his arms. "Not like the others did. That's why Brogan and his men burned down the Three Swords. They kissed the snake, but we didn't. I tried to warn you, Sir Mazael, that day in the kitchen..."

"But we didn't dare tell you the whole truth!" wailed Cramton. "Lord Mitor and the snake priest would've known, I say. They always know what they shouldn't."

"Dark arts, I tell you," said Bethy. "We were afraid."

"That's fine," said Mazael. He got to his feet in one motion, ignoring Bethy's outstretched hand and astonished stare. "You found your nerve now."

"We heard you were to be sacrificed to the snake god tomorrow," said Bethy. "We couldn't let that happen. You helped us."

"I'm grateful," said Mazael. He stepped out into the corridor.

"Take us with you," said Bethy. "The others from the inn took the oath and kissed the snake. Even Cramton's family. They were scared. Me and old Cramton are the only ones left who haven't. We can show you the way out. Please, please, take us with you. I don't want to give my soul to the snake god."

"Nor do I," said Cramton. "I'm afraid of snakes, I fear."

Mazael nodded. "Did you kill the guards?"

Bethy gave him a wicked grin. "No! We just brought them some ale, that's all. Must work up a thirst, standing down here all day. Of course, we mixed it with some sleeping draught.."

Mazael laughed. "Let's get the others, and get out of this hellhole. Lord Richard is expecting me."

Bethy unlocked Sir Nathan's cell, and the old knight blinked with astonishment. "Mazael? How..."

"No time for talk!" said Bethy. "Pardons, my lord knight, but they kept your weapons and armor in the storeroom at the end of the hall."

"Of course. I'd best get our weapons," said Nathan. "Cramton, with me."

"We know a tunnel that leads right to the courtyard from here," said Bethy. She undid another lock. "It opens up near the stables. I guess one of those snake priests dug it for a quick escape."

She pushed open the door. After a moment, Romaria staggered out, blinking at the light.

"You're all right," Romaria said. She stared into Mazael's face. "Are you..."

"I'm fine," Mazael lied.

"No, you're not," said Romaria.

Timothy and Silar emerged from their cells. Sir Nathan and Cramton returned, bundles of armor and weapons in hand. Romaria took her bastard sword and bow from Cramton. Mazael took his chain hauberk, helm, breastplate, and leather gauntlets from Nathan. After he secured the armor, he reached for Lion.

As his hand closed about the hilt, a jolt of pain shot up his arm, and the blade glimmered with blue flames.

As if he were a creature of dark magic.

"What is it?" said Romaria.

Mazael stared at the sword. "Nothing." He buckled his sword belt about his waist and drew the blade. The metal glimmered in the torchlight, but the flames did not reappear.

"Is everyone ready?" said Cramton.

"They'd best be," said Bethy, "cause we're going." She pointed. "That way goes back to the black temple, the way we came. Let's go this way instead. We know the way up to the courtyard."

She snatched a torch from the wall and set off down the corridor, Mazael and the others following with weapons drawn. Bethy stopped and put her ear to the cold stone wall. She nodded and pressed a jutting piece of masonry. A part of the wall slid back, revealing a corridor that spiraled up into the rock.

"This goes up to the courtyard," said Bethy. "The other way keeps going down, past the snake temple. It opens up between two boulders at the base of the hill near the west wall."

"Why do we not take that way?" said Timothy. "Surely, it would be easier to escape if we fled the castle!"

"Explain to me how we are to outrun Mitor's troops without horses," said Mazael.

"Ah," said Timothy.

They climbed up the steps, and the stairs ended in a large room that looked as if it had served as a barracks long ago. Splintered remnants of furniture filled the corners, along with some dusty bones. A massive iron-bound door rested in a narrow alcove. The dark oak planks looked long stiffened to the hardness of granite.

"Here," said Bethy. "There's another stair behind that door. It opens up in the wall behind the stables."

"How did you find all this?" said Sir Nathan. "I had never dreamed there were such extensive catacombs beneath the castle."

"Lord Mitor and the snake-kissers went down here when you and Sir Mazael weren't at the castle," said Bethy. "They all go to the temple and never anywhere else. I don't think they even know what's all down here."

She pulled a key of corroded black iron from a pocket in her dress and thrust it into the lock. "Turn, damn you." She jiggled the key. "Turn..."

The key shattered in Bethy's hand and clattered to the floor.

"Oh, dear," said Cramton.

"Oh, gods," said Bethy. She stuck a finger in the lock. "It's jammed. There's no other way up to the courtyard."

"We could still go through the door at the base of the hill," said Timothy.

"Not likely," said Sir Nathan. "That door will open right into the mercenary camp. Without horses, we'd never make it through them."

"We may have to go through the temple and Mitor's living quarters," said Romaria. "We got in that way, after all."

Mazael shook his head. "No. If there's a ceremony in the temple, they'll spot us there. And if there's not, someone will see us in the castle, certainly in Mitor's chambers." He lifted Lion. "We'll have to cut through the door."

"But it's half a foot thick and hard as iron!" said Bethy. "Your swords would chip away before you put a dent in it."

Mazael swore. "Timothy, do you have any magic that might work?"

"Perhaps," said Timothy. "But Simonian or the San-keth priest might sense such a spell."

"Then we'll go through the temple," said Mazael. They would certainly perish, but perhaps he would have the chance to kill Rachel first.

"Wait," said Silar. "There may be another way. A moment, please."

The lean monk stepped towards the door and closed his eyes. His spread his arms, palms flat, and lifted them above his head. His breathing became rhythmic, his lips moving through a whispered chant.

"What is he doing?" said Sir Nathan.

"This is no time to be praying!" said Timothy.

"On the contrary!" said Cramton.

Silar's hands clenched into fists, his chant rising in volume. "For my flesh is iron, for my flesh is stone, for the gods are might, and my fists are their vessel, for my flesh is iron, for my flesh is stone, for the gods are might..." His body swayed with the rhythm of his chant, and his eyes snapped open. "And my fists are their vessel!" His fists blurred. The door shuddered with his first blow. It splintered on his second. Iron-shod wood bent inward on the third.

The fourth shattered the door in a spray of wooden splinters and twisted iron shards.

"Gods in heaven, man!" said Sir Nathan. "How in their name did you do that?"

Silar took a deep breath and unclenched his fists. "Twenty years of discipline and meditation, and you can do that, too. Come along, now. We haven't the time to loiter." Mazael shook his head and followed Bethy through the door.

The stairs ended in a circular room with a sandy floor, the ceiling a maze of beams and planks. Mazael supposed they were in the foundations of a tower.

"Here," said Bethy. "The trigger is right here."

She pushed a stone, and a portion of the wall slid aside. Feeble rays of morning sunlight glinted into the dark chamber. Mazael saw at the hindquarters of a gray horse, and the smell of manure and straw washed over him.

"The stables," said Bethy.

Mazael stepped past her and through the opened doorway. He saw Chariot and the other horses, the big stallion snorting and pawing the ground in irritation. No one had disturbed their mounts, thankfully.

"This way," said Mazael. "Timothy, steal some horses for Bethy and Cramton." The wizard nodded, straw rustling beneath his boots. "Hurry. The castle will awake soon."

"Those that aren't sleeping off last night's festivities, at any rate," said Silar.

"I can't ride a horse!" said Bethy. "I don't know how."

"Sir Nathan, she'll ride with you," said Mazael.

The courtyard was dark and empty, and a few guards paced on the walls. Four men stood guard at the barbican gate. At least the portcullis was up.

"Mitor's learned something from our entry, I see," said Nathan.

"We can ride down the men at the gate," said Silar. "But do you see the two crossbowmen on the barbican rampart?"

"My lord knight," said Timothy. "My sleep enchantment. It is a simple spell, and weak enough to avoid Simonian's notice."

"Can you get both?" said Mazael.

Timothy grimaced. "No."

"It's only sixty yards. I'll the get the other," said Romaria. She strung her bow.

Timothy raised his right hand and began to chant, yellowish light flaring at his fingertips. Mazael saw one of the crossbowmen fall. The other man turned as Romaria's bow twanged. The armsman shuddered, a arrow sprouting from his throat, and collapsed behind the battlements.

"Go," said Mazael.

They rode out across the courtyard. The guards at the barbican paid no notice until Mazael was twenty paces away.

One of the armsmen stepped forward, a bored expression on his face. "Most High Priest Skhath has ordered no patrols for this..."

Mazael spurred Chariot, and the guard just had time to scream before Lion opened his throat. Romaria slew another, her blade splitting his head down the middle. One guard gripped his halberd with both hands and tried to charge her from behind. Mazael batted aside the thrust and Chariot kicked out, stunning the armsman. The sole survivor turned and tried to run for the keep. As he ran past Silar's horse, the monk's palm shot out. The armsman's head snapped back, and he joined his companions on the ground.

"We'd best make haste," said Sir Nathan.

They galloped through the barbican gates, past the town, and north to Lord Richard's waiting armies.

CHAPTER 29
WRATH OF THE DRAGONSLAYER

"There," said Romaria. "I see them."

"How?" said Mazael, blinking in the midday son. "It's only been a day and a half."

"Lord Richard must have marched when he heard Sir Gerald's news," said Nathan.

"I would have," said Silar.

Richard Mandragon's army spread across the horizon, followed by a column of dust. Mazael saw a sea of fluttering banners, heard the distant boom of marching drums.

"Horsemen," said Sir Nathan.

A dozen riders galloped towards them, led by a horseman in magnificent black dragon's scale armor. The hilt of a sword rose over his armored shoulder, and the black dragon of Lord Richard marked his crimson shield. The armored rider reined up before Mazael, pulling off his helm.

"So!" said Toraine Mandragon. "It appears you've survived the treachery of your family after all. We are relieved. You didn't happen to kill Lord Mitor on your way out, did you?"

"No," said Mazael. "The opportunity never arrived."

"A pity," said Toraine. "I would have killed him. Then Castle Cravenlock would have had a new lord, and a new name, for that matter."

"Undoubtedly," Mazael said. "I don't care."

Toraine's dark eyes flashed. "My father has commanded that you are to be brought to him at once. This way, if you please."

"You're too kind," said Mazael. "Lead on." Toraine scowled, and his riders settled in an armored wedge around Mazael and his companions.

They rode through Lord Richard's army, past rank after rank of pikemen and company after company of archers. But the core of the army was the knights, the heavy horse. Mazael counted six thousand in all, armored in heavy plate and armed with war lances, battle axes, and hammers. The knights alone could tear through Mitor's hodgepodge mass of armsmen and mercenaries.

Mazael found himself looking forward to the battle.

Lord Richard and his captains rode with the lancers, the Mandragon banner flying overhead. The Dragonslayer sat atop a great black stallion, his red armor brilliant in the sunlight. The Old Crow rode close to his master's side, along with stout Lord Jonaril and slender young Lord Astor rode with him. Gerald rode at Lord Richard's right hand, Adalar and Wesson trailing behind him.

Lucan rode some distance behind them, a shadow in his black cloak.

Gerald's eyes widened. "Sir Mazael! You're alive!"

"No thanks to myself," said Mazael. "The monk and Timothy were right. We should have turned back."

Lord Richard's eyes fixed on Mazael, and then turned toward his followers. They moved off, along with Mazael's companions, leaving him alone with Lord Richard.

"Sir Mazael," said Lord Richard. "Did you find what you sought?"

"Yes," Mazael said. "I found. I saw. All of it."

"So," said Lord Richard. "You have seen the truth. Your decision?"

"You were right," said Mazael. "Mitor and Sir Albron and their followers are all monsters. I'll follow you."

"Excellent," said Lord Richard. "You have made the right choice."

"There are two things you must know," said Mazael. "Sir Albron isn't a knight. He isn't even human. He's a San-keth priest disguised beneath a spell of illusion."

Lord Richard nodded. "We anticipated as much. My vassals have brought their court wizards. And my son's arts are capable." Disapproval showed in his eyes for a moment.

"You'll need them," said Mazael. "There's something else. Simonian isn't human. Not fully, at least."

"Another San-keth priest?" said the Dragonslayer. "We are prepared for such."

"No," said Mazael. "He's Demonsouled."

Lord Richard fell silent. "How did you gain this knowledge?"

"He told me," said Mazael.

"Does Brother Silar know?" said Lord Richard.

"He knows quite a bit," said Mazael.

"Then we shall leave the matter for his consideration," said Lord Richard. "The Cirstarcians have experience dealing with both San-keth and Demonsouled. Brother Silar wishes to assist? Then let him."

Mazael nodded.

"My captains and I will have a council of war when me make camp," said Lord Richard. "Speak no more of this until then. My men already whisper rumors."

Mazael nodded. Lord Richard made a small gesture, and his captains returned to his side. Mazael steered Chariot past them to rejoin his companions. Sir Nathan was telling Gerald what they had found under the castle.

"Gods!" Gerald said. "Such vileness! I never would have thought. Well, it certainly explains the decrepit state of the chapel, if all the inhabitants of the castle pray to the god of snakes." He shook his head. "Gods, Mazael. I always took your stories of your brother with a grain of salt. It seems I should have believed them and worse. I feel sorry for your sister, though. She seemed a sweet child."

"Child?" said Mazael. "She's older than you."

"She seemed so lost, though," said Gerald.

"Lost?" said Mazael. "She knows right where she is. She is a liar and a murderess, and I will bring her to justice myself!" Gerald flinched from the iron in Mazael's tone.

They left him alone after that, and he rode in silence.

The army marched until Lord Richard gave the command to halt at sunset. The ordered tent city Mazael had seen a week earlier rose out of the plains. Tents were pitched, trenches dug, and stakes placed. The smells of cooking food, oiled metal, and excrement rose into the night.

Mazael threaded his way through the bustling camp to Lord Richard's command tent. It rose from the center of the camp, banners flying from their standards. The Roland standard of silver greathelm on a blue field flew at equal height with the Mandragon banner. Gerald's work, Mazael supposed. Beneath the banners of Roland and Mandragon flew the Cravenlock standard of three crossed swords on black. Since Mitor had probably not joined Lord Richard, Mazael supposed the Dragonslayer had something else in mind.

He ducked under the heavy canvas flap and into the tent. Several long tables had been laid out, one covered by maps, the other by food. Lord Richard's vassals and captains stood talking.

"Sir Mazael!" said Sir Tanam, appearing with a pair of wooden cups. "Here, take this. You look as if you need a drink."

Mazael drained the cup in one pull. "That, and many more."

The Old Crow laughed. "Ha! Never get drunk the night before a battle, I say. The night after, however, is quite a different matter."

Mazael grunted and handed his cup back to the Old Crow.

"Mazael!" It was Gerald, his armor gleaming with new polish. Poor Wesson looked exhausted. "Where have you been?"

"Thinking," said Mazael.

Gerald laughed. "You used to warn me against worrying too much."

"A lot can change in a month," said Mazael.

Gerald's expression sobered. "That is true. And a lot more will change tonight, I fear." He paused. "Lord Richard has news for you. I fear you may not like it, thought it is necessary."

Mazael frowned. "What news?"

"Let us begin," said Lord Richard, his voice cutting like a knife through the babble. His vassals and captains took their seats. Mazael sat down besides Romaria, and she reached out and squeezed his hand. A cloaked man sat across from Mazael, and pulled back his hood to reveal a lean, angular face with gold-slashed silver hair and deep purple eyes. It was Sil Tarithyn, the ardmorgan of the Tribe of the Wolf. A gasp of surprise went up from the Dragonslayer's captains, but the Elderborn's unblinking eyes fixed on Mazael.

"We have a guest and an ally come to our cause," said Lord Richard. "Ardmorgan Sil Tarithyn of the Tribe of the Wolf."

"A wood demon," said Toraine. "What can they do for us?"

Lucan laughed. "That wood demon, my brother, could put an arrow through your eye at a hundred paces. Even with that fine dragon helm of yours." Toraine sneered, but fell silent.

"The lands of the Elderborn have been afflicted by the zuvembies, just as ours have been," said Lord Richard. "Sil Tarithyn and his warriors have ventured from their woods to destroy the creatures. Their foes are our foes. Shall we turn away aid when it is offered?" Toraine glared but did not answer.

"And we have a second ally come to our cause," said Lord Richard. "Sir Mazael has made the decision to join with us against his rebellious and apostate brother."

Toraine smiled. "A wise choice. Why should all the Cravenlocks die?"

"Lord Mitor is a rebel," said Lord Richard. "He has turned against his rightful liege lord and his rightful gods. Hence, he has forfeited his lands and titles. Sir Mazael is now Lord Mazael of Castle Cravenlock...if he chooses to take the title. If not, it shall pass to my son Lucan." A rumble of discontent passed through the assembled lords.

It was not something Mazael wanted. For the rest of his life, men would say he had murdered his older brother to take Castle Cravenlock. Yet he had no other choice. Mitor and Rachel deserved death for their crimes, and Simonian had to be stopped. Silar's warning repeated in Mazael's mind. Suppose the demon magic overwhelmed him? Would he become the tyrant the monk had feared, something worse than Simonian?

He had to take the risk. He had no other choice.

"I accept," said Mazael.

"Excellent," said Lord Richard. "I hope Lord Mazael will do much to insure peace once our battle is won. Now, Lord Mazael, we would consider it a favor if you described what you saw at Castle Cravenlock."

Mazael told Lord Richard's assembled vassals and captains what he had seen, of Othar's journal, of the temple beneath the castle, the true natures of Sir Albron Eastwater and Simonian of Briault. He did not mention his own nature.

Toraine laughed. "My, my, saved by a tavern wench! Hardly the sort of thing that goes into a song of the heroic."

"And how would you know?" said Lucan. Lord Richard silenced his sons with a dark look.

"So," said Lord Jonaril, reaching for a goblet. "We had always suspected Mitor of allying with dark powers. It appears his crimes are worse than even I suspected." He smiled. "The fool has sealed his own fate. No one, not even Lord Malden Roland or Lord Alamis Castanagent, will fault us from eradicating this perversion from the face of the earth."

"Indeed," said Gerald. "My father has his...ah, disagreements, with Lord Richard, but he would not deny Lord Mitor's crimes."

A gleam came into Lord Jonaril's eyes. "And there are, of course, the matters of Lord Roget and Lord Marcus and Sir Commander Galan Hawking. A pity they chose to ally with Mitor. Sir...ah, pardon, Lord Mazael shall receive the Cravenlock lands, certainly. But as for the others, their lands are forfeit without a doubt, and shall have to go to more deserving, loyal men. And the Justiciar lands will revert to Lord Richard, of course."

Lord Astor sighed. "It is a shame. My brother is proud and brave, but he did have a penchant for allying with lost causes. Though I'd never have thought him capable of forsaking the gods."

"Perhaps he did not, my lord," said Sir Nathan. "We did not see him the temple, nor did he seem aware of its existence. Revenge against you and Lord Richard were his motives."

Sir Tanam laughed. "Heresy or treason." He chopped his hand

down. "Either one gets the axe."

"Might I remind you, my lords, that the battle is still to be fought?" said Lord Richard. "Matters of spoils, lands, and titles shall wait until after our victory. We must know the order and rank of our enemy. Sir Tanam?"

The Old Crow cleared his throat. "I have done extensive scouting around Castle Cravenlock. Lord Mitor has, at most, four thousand armsmen. Rather less since Lord Mazael has been there, I imagine. Mostly foot, with a thousand horse. The Cravenlock forces have declined since Sir Albron took over. Snakes can't ride horses, I suppose. Lords Roget and Marcus together have another two thousand. The Justiciar forces are the most formidable...fifteen hundred sergeant foot soldiers and five hundred heavy lancers. To top off this motley crew, Mitor has brought in the mercenary scum of every city from Knightport to Forgotten Sea. Most, if not all, these men are encamped at the base of the castle's hill." He looked at Mazael. "Am I right?"

Mazael nodded. "Mitor keeps about four or five hundred men in the castle proper."

Toraine laughed. "Hardly an army. More of an unwashed mob, I say. We shall cut through them like a scythe through wheat."

"Take heed, young one," said Sil Tarithyn. "You speak true. The men are nothing. The dark powers that the traitor lord serves in his pit beneath the earth are the true foe."

Toraine smiled. "Flesh or dark power, a blade will end them all."

"Regardless of whatever sorcery Mitor serves, his men are still flesh and blood, vulnerable to blade and bow," said Lord Richard. "We shall split our heavy lancers and place them on the right and left wings. The heavy foot and archers shall make up the center. My son shall command the right." Mazael did not need ask which son. "Sir Tanam shall take the left. I shall command the center. The rest of you shall remain with your individual forces, under the command of either myself, Sir Tanam, or Toraine."

Lord Jonaril frowned. "What is our battle plan?"

"The heavy horse will attack first, striking from either side," said Lord Richard. "The more disciplined enemy soldiers, the Justiciar knights and perhaps the Cravenlock armsmen, shall no doubt respond first. Neither Lord Mitor nor his vassals are capable commanders. Their men are undisciplined, and the mercenaries are no better. Sir Tanam and Toraine shall engage while I bring up the infantry and the archers. By that time, the enemy will have mobilized against our lancers."

"Making them unprepared for archers and infantry," said Mazael.

Lord Richard nodded. He turned to Sil Tarithyn. "My lord

ardmorgan, I do not believe your warriors are suited for such a battle. I ask you to take your men and use them as you best see fit, striking from the flanks as opportunity dictates."

"No," said Sil Tarithyn.

"You refuse my father's command?" said Toraine.

"The Elderborn are a free people, boy," said Sil Tarithyn. "We are not your Dragonslayer lord's servants. We did not come north to slay innocent men. Innocent those men are, for many of them do not know the darkness they serve. The Tribe of the Wolf came north to destroy the zuvembies, and to bring their maker to justice."

"What of the garrison in the castle?" said Lucan, face shadowed in his heavy cowl. "Surely they know of the serpent temple and its black rites. Otherwise Mitor would not keep them close. Would it not be justice to slay them as well?"

"You speak wisely," said Sil Tarithyn. "If the we must face those soldiers to reach the necromancer and the priests of the serpent god, then face them we shall."

"Then we would be pleased to have you join us in laying siege Castle Cravenlock, once Mitor's host has been crushed," said Lord Richard.

"Why not have them attack the castle during the battle?" said Sir Tanam.

"Your thoughts, my old crow?" said Lord Richard.

"Now, while I've no doubt my lord Lucan and our other wizards are more than capable of deflecting any dark magic Simonian and the serpent blokes could conjure at us," said the Old Crow, "I, for one, would rather not test them. After all, I'd rather not end my days as an old crow in truth. Feathers wouldn't suit me." A chorus of snickers rose up from the lords. "A formal battle wouldn't suit my lord ardmorgan and his fighters. But scaling the walls and creeping up on the castle garrison and Simonian...that, I think, would work quite well for them. What have you to say for that, my lord ardmorgan?"

"Our battle is with the perversions in Castle Cravenlock," said Sil Tarithyn. "They must be made to face justice."

"I do believe that is a yes," said Sir Tanam. He grinned. "We'll strike Mitor's great lumbering mass of troops, while my lord ardmorgan and his fighters distract Simonian and the garrison."

"We must have assistance," said Sil Tarithyn. "Simonian is master of dark arts. The priests of the betrayer god can call upon great necromancy. We have no druids among us. We need one of arcane skills to fight besides us."

"I'll go," said Lucan.

"You?" said Lord Richard.

"You're no warrior," said Toraine.

Lucan sneered. "Oh, no, I'm not, brother. I'll leave that distinction for you. But our lord ardmorgan here didn't ask for warriors. He asked for wizards. And in that, I believe, I fill the bill admirably, more than any other man on the Grim Marches."

"I may require your assistance," said Lord Richard.

Lucan snorted. "For what, might I ask? You brought me along to combat whatever dark power you might find in Castle Cravenlock. And I know all about dark powers, don't I?"

Lord Richard regarded his son in silence, his face a mask. "Very well. You may go. Try to prove of use."

Lucan's smile was mocking. "Oh, I shall certainly try."

"And I shall go, as well," said Mazael.

Lord Richard folded his hands. "You would serve best in my host."

"How?" said Mazael. "One among thousands?"

"We have all heard of your exploits in the Mastarian war," said Lord Richard. "There are many commands that could use your skill."

"Your men, not mine," said Mazael. "And this is my fight. My brother and my sister lied to me. They betrayed me. And I will have justice for it. And we all know full well that if I take the title as Lord of Castle Cravenlock, I will be branded a murderer for all time, regardless of what Mitor's crimes were. If I am to be named a murderer, so be it. I shall do it with my own hands."

Lord Jonaril frowned. "You plan to kill your own sister?"

"She's a liar and a betrayer," said Mazael.

"Aye," said the stout lord. "But she is just a woman! Women are frail. She was undoubtedly led down the wrong path by her brother."

"A path she walked of her own will," said Mazael.

"In a castle full of apostates, how could you blame her?" said Lord Jonaril. "Mitor and his allies, now that is a different matter. No one will blame you, my lord, for putting them to the sword. Indeed, all men of right virtue would congratulate you. But spare the woman, I ask."

"Why?" said Mazael. "So she can marry one of your sons in case I die?"

Lord Jonaril coughed.

"Regardless of his motives, Lord Jonaril is right," said Gerald.

"No," said Mazael.

"Mitor and his followers are evil, I don't doubt it. But Lady Rachel seemed only confused," said Gerald.

"No," said Mazael. "I will not spare her."

Sir Nathan cleared his throat. "Rachel was an innocent child. I do not know what she has become. But were I in your place, Mazael, I would spare her."

"It does not matter," said Lord Richard. "As Lord of Castle Cravenlock, justice is Lord Mazael's to administer. Lord Mitor Cravenlock, Lady Marcelle Cravenlock, Lord Marcus Trand, Lord Roget Hunterson, Simonian of Briault, and 'Sir Albron' shall all die at my command. What happens to Lady Rachel is Lord Mazael's concern, not mine." Lord Jonaril grumbled assent but did not look pleased, and nor did Gerald.

"Then it is settled," said Lord Richard. "Tomorrow, we shall march. The next sunrise, we shall strike. I shall send Sil Tarithyn and his men, along with Lord Mazael, ahead to scale the castle's walls and strike from the rear."

"We needn't even scale the walls," said Mazael. "Bethy showed me a passage that leads into the castle. With her help, I should have little difficulty getting inside."

"Excellent," said Lord Richard.

"And I shall come, as well," said Sir Nathan. "Lord Mitor has betrayed me. And Lord Mazael is my new liege. I am bound to follow him."

"I came to rid the land of the zuvembies and whatever hand had raised them," said Romaria. "I shall see this through to the end."

"As shall I," said Gerald. "It is my duty to put an end to this conflict, to keep my father and his lands from war." He smiled. "And I've followed Sir Mazael for the last ten years. Why should I not do the same for Lord Mazael?"

"We Cirstarcian monks are sworn to rid the land of Demonsouled and San-keth," said Silar. "It is my sacred duty to come."

Mazael looked at them. "I am glad for your aid."

"Well," said Lucan, his smile sardonic. "Isn't this a merry little band?"

"Then it is settled," said Lord Richard. "Tomorrow, we shall march. And then we shall do battle."

CHAPTER 30
DREAMS OF BLOOD

Cold wind lashed at his face.

Mazael walked alongside a churning river of blood, a spray of fine droplets coating its banks with a gleaming crimson coat.

The wind howled, bringing the sound of screaming voices to his ears. Mazael's eyes followed the road to the looming bleak towers of Castle Cravenlock. The screams pleased him. They belonged to him. He would tear them from the grasp of others and make them his own. Mazael strode towards Castle Cravenlock, intending to claim it.

Something thumped against his leg, and his glance down. Lion hung from his belt in its usual place, but a strange symbol dangling from a length of chain besides it. He reached for it, but the symbol burned his fingers. He hissed and nearly threw it to the ground, but the pain faded, and he held the symbol before his eyes. It was made of three interlocking steel rings joined together in a triangular shape. Something about the symbol made him feel ill.

The screams rose from the castle, but now they filled him with revulsion.

"So torn. But it will be resolved soon."

Lord Adalon stood on the bank of the crimson river, its splashing waves splattering his robe with blood. He held his staff in both hands, the silver raven at its top gleaming.

"How you fight with yourself!" said Lord Adalon. Red light gleamed in the depths of his green eyes. "But that is what you do. Fight. Battle. And in the end, conquer."

Mazael looked at his father, fighting a sudden sense of terrible dread.

"But why do you fight yourself?" said Lord Adalon. "The rage, the fury...the power, are they truly your enemies? You resist them. Yet they can make you over, make you greater, if you just give into them."

Mazael stared at Lord Adalon's gaunt face, his red-shot green eyes, and his twisted and yellowed teeth. "Who are you?"

Lord Adalon laughed. "You know, do you not? I am your father."

"No," said Mazael. "No. My father has been dead for ten years. He wouldn't have come back. He didn't have the courage."

"Such small faith," said Lord Adalon. "Think of me as your guide, then."

"Guide?" said Mazael. "To what?"

"To your fate," said Lord Adalon. "To your destiny."

"You sound like Romaria," said Mazael. Who was Romaria? He could not remember.

Lord Adalon laughed. "I think not. She would keep you as a sheep, docile and plodding, just as all the other cattle that wander the world. But I can show you a better way, my son. You're growing stronger, aren't you? More of your nature has come to the surface. You couldn't question me here otherwise. The time soon comes when you will have to make a choice."

"Choice?" said Mazael. "Between what?"

Lord Adalon beckoned with a bony hand. "I shall show you. Come."

Mazael backed away, his hand clutching the metal symbol, as if it could protect him from this creature that called itself his father. "No. You're a liar."

Lord Adalon's eyes flashed with crimson fire. "I, a liar? I, who have labored to show you the truth of who you are, what you are? I, who am so much older than you, so much wiser, so much stronger? I, who could crush you like a gnat?" His eyes burned red, icy winds whipping over the plain.

"What are you?" said Mazael.

Lord Adalon blinked, and the decay vanished from his features, his eyes becoming green and bloodshot once more. "I am disappointed. I see you still believe those lies the fat wizard and the old knight wove into you. Very well. Let me show what awaits you. You shall soon have an opportunity that few mortals ever have. You shall have the chance to make yourself over, to become something more than mortal."

"I don't want it," said Mazael. "I've never wanted it."

Lord Adalon laughed. "Have you? You've always wanted power, my son, whether you will admit it or not. You reveled in the power of killing. You enjoyed it. And now the Dragonslayer has made you Lord of Castle Cravenlock. More power."

"No," said Mazael. "I took it because I had to..."

"Because you wanted to!" said Lord Adalon. "More power in your fist. So much more lies before you. All you have to do is reach out and take it! But if you refuse, this is what lies before you!"

He raised his staff high and rammed its butt into the earth. The world spun around Mazael, and everything disappeared in a blazing red glow.

He felt a railing of nicked wood beneath his hand. He stood on the balcony of Castle Cravenlock's decrepit chapel, the only light coming from a pair of lanterns on the altar.

"I've been here before," said Mazael. He struggled to remember. "You've taken me here before."

"Most perceptive," said Lord Adalon. He kicked aside a piece of a rotted pew. "Dust, ashes, and decay. Is this what you choose for yourself? Death, in the end? You have the power to become a demigod among the witless sheep that are men. Why do you refuse?"

The symbol fell from Mazael's fingers, swinging on its chain and bouncing against his leg. "Because...is it not power. It is corruption."

"Corruption?" said Lord Adalon. "You don't really think that, do you? You know better."

"No," said Mazael. "I..."

Lord Adalon smiled. "Let's take a look, shall we? Let us see what will happen if you reject this 'corruption'".

He clenched his fist, and the red glow shining through the chapel's stained glass-windows brightened, bathing everything in crimson radiance.

Lord Adalon lowered his fist. "Let's meet some old friends."

Mazael heard a footstep.

Rachel stepped out of the shadows, clad in a long black robe with embroidered serpents twisting up the slaves. A golden crown of snakes rested on her head, and crimson runes marked her forehead and cheeks. Her eyes were yellow and slit with vertical black pupils.

"Mazael," she whispered. Twin fangs protruded from her lips, dripping with greenish fluid. "Come here."

Mazael's hand shot to his sword hilt and banged against his hip. His sword was gone. Rachel laughed and lunged for him.

"Isn't that a shame?" said Lord Adalon. "She's going to kill you. A pity you surrendered your power. You could have destroyed her so easily, otherwise."

A drop of venom trickled down Rachel's chin.

Lord Adalon leaned against the railing. "You may want to duck."

Mazael heard a snarl behind his shoulder, and dodged just as a dagger slashed through the air. Mitor lurched towards him, lips pulled back from his teeth in a snarl of hatred. A dagger trembled in his hand, the razor edges gleaming in the crimson light.

"Isn't he miserable, my boy?" said Lord Adalon. "Why don't you tear him apart? He's weak and slow. Oh, yes, that's right. You don't want the power. But what you refuse, others will take."

Rachel hissed and lunged, venom falling in a hissing rain to the floor. Mitor stabbed at him, the dagger's edges cutting air. Mazael groped for his sword, his dagger...but they were not there.

"Isn't it remarkable how much they hate you?" said Lord Adalon. "And for what? Their pathetic little scraps of power?" He waved his hand at the domed ceiling. "This old heap of a castle? What would they give, I wonder, to have the sort *of power you so freely reject? They will kill you to defend their wretched lives. What would they do to take what you have?"*

Mazael tried to dodge, but Mitor's dagger plunged into his shoulder. He screamed and fell to one knee. Mitor howled with glee. his arm pumping, stabbing Mazael in the back again and again.

"Poor Mazael," said Rachel. "You should have listened."

Her teeth plunged into his forearm.

The pain exploded through his veins, the agony forcing him to his feet. He smelled smoke rising from the poisoned wounds as his arm shriveled. Rachel laughed, a mixture of his blood and her venom smeared across her lips. Mazael tried to move, but could not.

"Poor brother," Rachel cooed. She kissed him on the cheek, and the poison sizzled into his beard and burned through his skin. "You should have listened to me."

Mitor plunged his dagger into Mazael's chest. The force of the blow sent him tumbling over the railing. He screamed, their laughter filling his ears.

He hit the chapel floor, and everything went black.

He regained consciousness some time later.

Mazael got to his knees before the altar. The pain was gone. The fang marks had vanished from his arm, and the burns from his face.

He stood and looked at his belt. His sword was still gone.

"I suppose that must have hurt."

Lord Adalon stepped out from beneath the balcony's shadows, his dark robes whispering against the dusty stone floor.

"How am I still alive?" said Mazael.

"An excellent question," said Lord Adalon. "All events cast shadows. Think of what you just saw as a shadow of what will happen, if you refuse the power that is your birthright."

"No," said Mazael. "That won't happen. It..."

"Oh, yes, of course, that's right," said Lord Adalon. "Mitor might be vermin, but Rachel, sweet, innocent, Rachel would never do such a thing. Oh, but she already has, hasn't she? Did she not pray to that slithering worm that the San-keth worship? Did she not lie to you? And did she not leave you to die in that dark pit beneath Castle Cravenlock?"

Mazael felt the muscles in his jaw trembling.

"And if not them, then others," said Lord Adalon. "That is the very nature of life. The quest for power. Whoever does not possess it requires it, and whoever does needs more. Even the gods themselves are no different. They grasp and clutch for the sparks of might." He smiled and made a fist "So, these are your choices. Seize the power that is your destiny and right! Or lie down and die, and let others tear it

from your corpse. And it is a choice you must soon make."

Mitor walked out of the shadows, a poisoned dagger clutched in his fist. Rachel stood next to him, her body draped in the clinging folds of her black robes. Her reptilian eyes watched Mazael, the fangs jutting over her lips.

"And so the choice comes," said Lord Adalon. "Will you give in to those weaker than you? Will you let them kill you? Or shall you take what is yours and destroy all who stand against you?"

Lord Adalon pulled a sheathed sword from his robes. The scabbard was dark wood inlaid with golden runes. The sword's crosspiece and hilt were covered in crimson gold, the pommel fashioned in the shape of a roaring demon's head. Looking at it made the hair on Mazael's neck and arms stand up. The sword was both hideous.

The sword was beautiful.

"What is that?" said Mazael.

"It is yours," said Lord Adalon. He held the sword out hilt-first. "Your power is that of the Destroyer."

Mitor snarled and Rachel hissed, advancing towards Mazael.

"If you want to take it, of course," said Lord Adalon, his voice mournful. "After all, if you don't, then Mitor and Rachel will kill you. If not them, then others." He smiled. "But at least you will have done the right thing, eh?"

Mazael remembered the pain of Rachel's venom, the agony as Mitor's dagger pumped into his back. But the helplessness had been worst of all. He snarled, clamped his hand around the sword's hilt, and tore it free from the scabbard.

He caught a glimpse of the sword's long red blade, the edges bright and sharp. Then the sword burst into howling crimson flame, and a jolt of power exploded up Mazael's arm. Strength flowed through him like a molten river. Murderous fury filled his heart, and he embraced it, feeling it scour away the weakness in his limbs.

Rachel and Mitor flinched, and Mazael laughed at them.

Mitor howled, a dagger grasped in both hands, and charged. Mazael danced around Mitor's attack and slashed. The burning blade cut through Mitor's wrists like an axe through butter. Mitor wailed, crimson flames chewing at the charred stumps of his hands. Mazael stepped behind Mitor and carved off his legs at the knee. Mitor flailed and collapsed to the floor, twitching and writhing. Mazael tucked a boot under Mitor's gut, flipped him over, and stabbed down. Lord Adalon laughed.

Mazael turned from the ruined corpse and faced Rachel. Her fangs had vanished, and her eyes were now human and very wide. "Mazael...Mazael...oh, please, don't, Mazael..." She backed away from him, her feet tangling in the hem of her robes.

Mazael stepped over Mitor's corpse and raised the burning sword high. "Why don't you run?" The fear on her face was exhilarating.

Rachel tried to flee for the stairs, but she was too slow. Mazael planted his hand between her shoulder blades and shoved. Rachel went sprawling across the *floor, crying for him to stop. Her pleas only acted as fuel to the fire burning his mind. He kicked her onto her stomach, and raised his burning sword. He heard his father laughing.*

And for the first time, Mazael laughed with him.

"Stop!"

A woman stood before the altar, tall and lean, a bastard sword slung over her back. There was something in her blue eyes that tugged at Mazael. The corona of fire surrounding the sword of the Destroyer flickered.

Lord Adalon's mocking smile twisted into a grimace. "You!"

Mazael's sword point wavered. "Who are you?"

"You know," said the woman. "You tell me."

The sword's fires sputtered. "I know...you...you're..."

"Kill her!" shrieked Lord Adalon. "Kill them both. They're liars! Don't you remember the pain? Do you want them to do that to you again?"

Mazael trembled, the sword's flames roaring, and Rachel sobbed.

"He's the liar and you know it," said the woman. Her blue eyes stared into him. "He'll have you destroy yourself. He'll make you into a monster, if you let him. Don't listen to him."

"They'll kill me if I don't!" said Mazael.

"Mitor and Rachel?" said the woman, taking another step towards him. "But they don't even know you're Demonsouled. Do you really think there are hordes of enemies waiting to descend on you?" She pointed at Mazael's father. "Or is he the enemy, spinning his lies around you like a spider's webs?"

"She is the liar, my son!" said Lord Adalon. His eyes blazed red, matching the fires of Mazael's sword. "She will claim the power of your soul, if..."

"I don't even have a full soul," said the woman. Her dark hair shifted as she glared at Lord Adalon, revealing the tip of a pointed ear. "And I care for Mazael. I will take nothing from him. But what of you? You'll take everything from him, his mind, his spirit, his soul, and in the end, his life..."

"Care..." whispered Mazael.

He flung the sword aside. It struck the floor and shattered, the crimson flames winking out.

"Romaria," said Mazael. "Your name is Romaria."

"Stay away from her!" said Lord Adalon. "She'll..."

"You go to hell!" roared Mazael. "You'd have had me kill her! I don't give a damn if you're right or not, but I'll not listen to your words any longer!"

Lord Adalon screamed. His mouth stretched into a yawning black pit lined with jagged teeth, crimson flames bursting from the dark length of his staff. The floor trembled, thunder booming overhead. Cracks spread across the floor, burning light shining up from their depths...

Mazael shuddered and came awake.

He felt cool night air washing over his sweat-soaked clothes. He sat against a barrel on the outskirts of Lord Richard's camp. He remembered going there to sit and to think a while. Instead, he had drifted off to sleep. And the thing in his dreams had found him, almost made him kill Rachel. Mazael lurched to his knees, doubled over, and vomited. It felt as if hammers pounded the inside of his head, matching the writhing cramps in his gut.

After some time, the pains subsided. He fell back against the barrel, panting for breath.

"Here."

Romaria stood over him, a wineskin in her hands. He took the skin, unstopped it, and took a long pull. It helped to steady the pains in his stomach.

"Don't drink too much of it," said Romaria.

Mazael snorted. "A hangover would be an improvement." He took another drink and handed it back to her. "Thank you. That helped. I had another..."

"Dream?" said Romaria. "Yes, I know. I was in it, after all."

"What?" said Mazael. "How? It was just...just..."

"Just a dream?" said Romaria. "They're more than just dreams, we both know that. After the meal was finished, I came looking for you, because I knew your dreams would come." She smiled. "You help me sleep. I've never been able to sleep well."

"How did you know?" said Mazael.

"I found you here. You were thrashing and muttering in your sleep," said Romaria. "Then I felt...pressure in my head, so I sat down besides you and found myself in your dream." She shook her head. "You were almost lost. I didn't recognize you. You looked like some terrible god of war..."

"Or the tyrant kings Silar told us about," said Mazael.

Romaria nodded. "Yes."

"Gods," said Mazael.

"Who was that, in your dream?" said Romaria. "It couldn't have been your father. From what I've heard of Lord Adalon, he was nothing like that."

"No," said Mazael. "He wasn't."

"Perhaps it was something wearing his face, as Skhath wore the face of Sir Albron Eastwater," said Romaria.

"Perhaps it was myself," said Mazael, "a reflection of what I really am. Perhaps it was my Demonsouled nature, talking to me."

"No," said Romaria.

"You know better," said Mazael. "I almost killed you, both in the waking world and in dreams." Despair churned at him. "I..."

"No!" said Romaria. She seized his hands. "Listen to me. That thing in your dreams, whatever it was, is not you."

Mazael's laugh was dark. "You're certain of that, now? You saw what I did. You saw the Destroyer's sword." He remembered that sword's sheer strength, the power running up his arm and armoring him.

"But you haven't done any of those things!" said Romaria. "You haven't killed Mitor. You haven't killed Rachel. That creature in your dreams is a liar and a trickster. It's a devil come to tempt you. But when that madness has overtaken you, you've always managed to pull back from the edge."

"Because of you," said Mazael. "I'd have become the thing in my dreams long ago, if it weren't for you."

"I think there's a way you can stop it permanently," said Romaria.

"How?" said Mazael. "Anything."

"Don't kill Mitor and Rachel," said Romaria.

"I have to," said Mazael. "Mitor is a wretch and a traitor. And Rachel lied to me and betrayed me. She would have killed us. If anyone deserves to die it his her!" Anger rose in his voice, and Mazael fought back his rage. "It has to be done."

"Why?" said Romaria. "The thing in your dreams wants you to kill them. Why should you listen to it? You know it's a liar and a deceiver. It wears the face of a dead man, Mazael!"

Mazael wished he had never returned to the Grim Marches. But would the demon magic within him have risen to the surface anyway? If it had, he would not have had Romaria to help him fight it. He looked at her, and despite everything, was glad he had come here and had met her.

"Help me," said Mazael. "I don't have the strength. If it weren't for you, I would have fallen long ago." His fingers tightened around hers. "I need you."

"And I you," said Romaria.

"How?" said Mazael. "You're not Demonsouled, as am I."

"I don't know," said Romaria. "I just do." She leaned forward and kissed him.

"Stay with me, when this is done," said Mazael when they pulled apart.

Romaria smiled. "As what? Can you truly see me as Lady of Castle Cravenlock?"

"You'd make a damn sight better than Marcelle," said Mazael.

Romaria laughed. "For that matter, can you see me as Lord of Castle Cravenlock?"

"Oh, yes," said Romaria. "I can see you as a king."

"And you as my queen?" said Mazael.

Romaria laughed. "Or myself as queen and you as my lord

consort."

"I don't think I would mind that at all," said Mazael.

"I'll stay with you and help you, however I can." She reached down and picked up the holy symbol hanging from his belt. "But I'm not the only one who can help you."

A retort formed on Mazael's lips. Then he remembered how Bethy and Cramton had come to his aid after his prayer. He lifted the symbol, remembering how it had burned him in the dream. It had burned him when he set out to kill his siblings.

He let the symbol fall back against his belt. "I don't know what to do. Rachel and Mitor deserve death, and I want to give it to them. I don't know if can. Or if I should, rather."

"You shouldn't," said Romaria. "Give them over to Lord Richard. Let him decide what is to be done with them."

Mazael closed his eyes. She was right, but the rage in his chest still burned. "I don't know what will happen."

"No one does," said Romaria.

"Perhaps you're right," said Mazael. "Perhaps I should let Lord Richard decide their fate." He felt his face harden. "But Simonian and Skhath...I'll kill them, if I can. Skhath's a thing, not a man. And Simonian..."

"On this you're right," said Romaria. "I came north to kill Simonian, remember? We've both seen the monsters his necromancy raises from the earth. He has respect for neither the living or the dead, the earth or the gods." Her voice dropped. "If anything, think of Simonian. If you kill your brother and your sister, you may become like him."

Mazael remembered the wizard's muddy eyes, his tangled iron-gray beard, the dark smirk that often played across his face. He pictured the expression on his own features. It was not a pleasant thought.

"Gods forbid," said Mazael. "Him and the thing in my dreams, whatever it is." He clutched the holy symbol in his fist. "Gods forbid." He licked his lips and dropped his hands into his lap to hide their trembling. "Please, whatever happens, stay with me."

"I will," said Romaria, "but only if you stay with me."

Mazael pulled her close and kissed her. "That is the one thing I can   guarantee."

CHAPTER 31
THE FACE BENEATH

They reined up a mile south of Castle Cravenlock, the watch fires atop the castle's towers throwing back the night.

"Gods in heaven," said Lucan. "What an ugly castle. We ought to raze it with the San-keth inside."

Mazael looked at the dark-cloaked wizard. "Beautiful, no. Strong, yes. We're going to try to take this heap so your father doesn't lose five thousand men storming it."

"And Simonian and the priest of the traitor god must be made to face justice," said Sil Tarithyn.

"I see they've taken greater precautions since our last visit," said Sir Nathan. "The watch fires are new, and I there are extra guards on the walls."

Romaria laughed. "Hardly surprising. We did practically walk out of their temple."

"And now we're walking back in," said Timothy. "I rather wish the irony were lost on me."

"I do believe this is when my lord ardmorgan and I part from your company, Sir Mazael," said Lucan.

Sil Tarithyn and his warriors would scale the castle walls with Lucan Mandragon. They would then sweep through the castle and kill as many of the armsmen and snake worshippers as they could find. Mazael had every confidence that Sil Tarithyn's Elderborn warriors would more than match Mitor's disorganized and undisciplined men. Lucan would assist the Elderborn, but save his magical strength for a battle with Simonian or Skhath.

Mazael and his companions would use the secret entrance Bethy described. With luck, the majority of the soldiers would have been drawn off by Sil Tarithyn's attack. Mazael hoped to take Skhath and Simonian unawares - even with Lucan's aid, he did not think they could defeat the San-keth cleric and the Demonsouled wizard without the aid of surprise. For safety's sake, Mazael had left the squires with Lord Richard.

Mazael nodded. "Good luck to you, Lucan, my lord ardmorgan."

Lucan smirked. "Don't worry for me, Lord Mazael. I make my own luck."

"The Mother of our People shall bless our efforts this day," said Sil Tarithyn. He adjusted the string on his great black bow. "We fight against great evil. If it is her will that any of us shall fall, then we shall depart gladly, knowing we have helped rid the earth of an abomination."

"And good luck to you too," said Mazael. Sil Tarithyn, Lucan, and the Elderborn warriors moved towards the castle like silent wolves. "Gerald, the tabards."

Gerald produced black tabards marked with the three crossed silver swords of Castle Cravenlock, and Mazael and his companions donned them. With luck, they could pass as another band of Cravenlock armsmen. Mazael doubted the lax soldiers would spare them more than a perfunctory glance.

The reek of the camp grew stronger as they drew closer. They rode through the hodgepodge tangle of tents, stables, heaps of supplies, and flapping banners. Lord Richard would tear through this rabble like a hot poker. A drunken man in a Cravenlock tabard, bereft of his trousers, chased after a giggling woman, and both ran past without sparing Mazael another glance.

The ground grew steeper and rockier as they approached the base of the castle's hill, and Mazael reined up.

"Here," said Mazael. "Bethy said the door would be here, between those two boulders." A worn path let to a wide gap between two lichen-spotted boulders.

"You there! Halt!"

Mazael turned, reaching into his cloak for Lion's hilt. Three men in Cravenlock tabards and chain mail hurried up the hill.

"This section of the camp is forbidden to common soldiers," said an armsman. Mazael saw the green lines of a serpent tattoo on his forehead. "Only those who have taken sacred oaths of fealty to Lord Mitor are allowed here."

"Sacred oaths?" said Mazael. "You mean those who have knelt and kissed that filthy slime-crawling worm?"

"Blasphemy!" snarled the soldiers.

An armsman peered forward. "I know you! Sir Mazael! Take..."

Mazael rammed Lion through the armsman's face. Another soldier turned to attack, and Gerald's longsword plunged into his neck. The survivor ran, and made it three steps before Romaria's arrow lanced into his back and sent him tumbling down the slope.

"We should conceal the bodies," said Gerald.

Mazael shook his head. "No time. Besides, I'll wager that it isn't uncommon for some of these thugs to wind up dead in the morning."

They dismounted, secured the horses, and hurried up the path. Concealed between the boulders stood a flat plane of weathered rock, its surface pitted by wind and rain and moss. Mazael knelt and brushed away a pile of pebbles and dust, revealing a smooth lump of red granite, out of place among the gray rock, just as Bethy had described. He clenched a fist and pressed it into the stone, pushing the stone into the earth. There was a click, and the weathered rock face slid aside to reveal a dark opening. Timothy stepped into the passage, muttered a spell, and lifted his fist, the glow from his fingers illuminating at tunnel leading into the temple complex. After the others had entered, Mazael pressed a stone in the wall, and the door slid shut behind them.

"Let's pay Simonian and Skhath a visit, shall we?" said Mazael. They stripped off their Cravenlock tabards and dropped them by the door. Mazael drew Lion, the sword's edges beginning to glow.

Creatures of dark magic were nearby.

The passageway sloped upwards, the walls and floor caked with the dust of ages. Romaria ranged ahead, scouting, and returned in a few moments.

"This corridor opens into the dungeon that held us," said Romaria. "There's a guardroom with about six armsmen. I think two more are guarding the cells."

"We can take them," said Mazael.

"It sounds like there's a ceremony going on the temple," said Romaria. "I could hear the chanting. And the cells are full. Every one of them has at least one prisoner, some more than one."

"Mitor makes new friends so quickly," said Mazael. "Did you happen to see who was in there?"

Romaria shook her head. "I didn't want to get that close."

"I doubt they'll be fond of Mitor," said Silar. "We may have found some potential allies."

"Well," said Mazael. "Let's find out."

He followed Romaria into the familiar dungeon corridor, torch-cast shadows dancing on the walls. A guard looked up, and Mazael recognized one of the armsmen who had guarded his cell. The soldier just had time to gasp before Lion ripped across his throat. Another guard stood at the far end of the corridor, and shouted out an alarm. The door behind him burst open, and a half-dozen armsmen raced out.

Mazael dropped into a crouch as he heard the creak of Romaria's bow. An arrow flew over his head and flung the lead soldier to the ground. The next man tried to rush him, and Mazael blocked, sidestepped, and killed the armsman with a single quick trust. The survivors came at him in a single confused rush. Mazael backpedaled, snapping Lion back and forth as he parried and blocked.

Timothy shouted a spell and flung out his hand. Golden lights flashed around an armsman, and the man yawned, blinked, and slumped to the ground. With a cry of alarm the remaining soldiers threw down their weapons and ran. Romaria's bow twanged, flinging another man to the floor. Silar leapt forward, wrapped his arms around an armsman's throat, and smashed the man's head into the wall with a hideous crack. Sir Nathan and Sir Gerald shoved forward, their swords raised.

The fight was over a few heartbeats later.

"Is everyone all right?" said Mazael.

"For now," said Sir Nathan.

"I say, I say!" came a voice from a cell. "What is going on? Who is out there? Damn you! Mitor!"

Mazael frowned. "I recognize that voice. Find the keys."

Romaria found them in the guardroom, and Mazael opened the cell door and found himself face-to-face with Sir Commander Galan Hawking.

"Sir Mazael?" said Galan. "Mitor said he had killed you."

Mazael snorted. "You ought to know better than to trust Mitor by now."

Galan swore. "Gods, yes. To think I had been led like a sheep by that fat fool..."

"How did you wind up down here?" said Mazael.

"One of my knights saw Mitor's soldiers take a group of children captive from the town," said Galan. "They reported to me, we followed the armsmen, and discovered this pit of evil beneath the castle." His eyes had a brittle, frantic light. "Such vileness. The Knights Justiciar are sworn to destroy such creatures." He laughed, his voice hysterical. "I'd never dreamed San-keth were more than children's fables. I suppose I'll see a Demonsouled quite shortly."

"You have. Simonian," said Mazael.

Galan coughed. "Not surprising. That wizard is a foul one. Why didn't I see it? How could I have been so blind to all this?" He raked his trembling fingers through his hair. "Gods above, gods above, oh merciful gods..."

Mazael grabbed the Justiciar by the shoulders and shook him. "Stop babbling. How many of your men are down here?"

"Eight others, my preceptors," said Hawking. He grimaced. "Simonian put us to sleep with sorcery. When we awoke, we were here. Mitor told my forces that I had departed for Swordor to beseech the Grand Master to bring the Justiciar armies to our cause." He spat on the floor. "Gods be praised that I did not. To think that I had allied myself with Mitor and that serpent priest...a creature of such vileness..."

"You know better now," said Mazael. "A tribe of the Elderborn and the Dragon's Shadow are attacking the castle as we speak. Lord Richard's army is a few hours away. He will smash through Mitor's men and those mercenaries. If you want to undo some of the damage you've done, get to your men and get them clear. Or, better yet, have them fight alongside Lord Richard's men."

"Lord Richard!" said Sir Commander Galan. "Gods! I cannot decide who I hate more, him or Lord Mitor. A usurper versus a heretic, eh? What a choice! And wood elves? What good will come from consorting with those forest demons?" He grimaced. "I suppose we cannot pick and choose our allies. I shall command my men fight alongside the usurping Dragonslayer, since I have no other choice."

Mazael smirked. "How heartening. The passage is that way. Go, now. I doubt you have much time."

"I shall send two of my preceptors," said Hawking. His eyes bright and feverish with guilt. "I will stay and fight besides you, Sir Mazael...rather, Lord Mazael. One way or the other, we shall make you Lord of Castle Cravenlock once this night is over."

"Their armor and weapons are likely in the guardroom, same as ours were," said Romaria.

"Very well," said Mazael. "Hurry up and arm yourselves. We haven't much time."

Romaria opened the other cell doors, and the Justiciar preceptors stumbled. Hawking commanded two of them to return to their camp and prepare the knights and sergeants for battle.

Hawking pointed at a door on the opposite wall of the guardroom. "That door opens into some storerooms. Beyond that is the blasphemous temple."

"I know," said Mazael. "One of the castle servants got us out the cells. She knew all these rooms."

"Then let us go," said Sir Commander Galan.

Mazael kicked down the door, stepping into a high vaulted corridor. Polished red granite gleamed like fire, and closed doors rested in niches. A knot of Cravenlock armsmen stood some distance down the corridor. Besides them stood a skeletal figure with a serpent wrapped around its spine. For a moment Mazael thought it was Skhath, but this San-keth was smaller, its scales not so bright. Lion burst into hot blue flame, and the armsmen turned and flinched.

"Kill them!" screeched the San-keth priest. The armsmen raised their weapons and charged, while the priests began hissing a spell.

Mazael ran at them, Romaria raising her bow. Sir Commander Galan howled and charged, his preceptors a half-step behind. The San-keth's black-slit eyes fixed on Mazael, and its carrier lifted a skeletal hand.

Timothy stepped forward and shouted a word. Multicolored sparks flared up the San-keth's enchanted skeleton, and the creature reeled, its incantation dissolving into an angry hiss. Mazael stabbed at it, and the undead carrier disintegrated into a heap of smoking bones. The San-keth reared out of the wreckage, fangs bared, and Mazael took its head off.

The battle was over quickly, with the Cravenlock armsmen overwhelmed and slain. The hall ended in a double set of black doors. Chanting rose from behind the doors, yet Mazael heard screams and bellowed commands echoing from other chambers.

"It seems as if Sil Tarithyn and the Dragon's Shadow have made their presence known," said Mazael. The massive doors were locked and barred. "Timothy, if you please!"

The young wizard nodded and began another incantation. He pointed at the doors, and Mazael heard the bar shatter and fall to the floor. The doors swung open with a slow groan, and Timothy grunted and wiped sweat from his forehead.

Mazael stepped through the doors and into the temple, his boots clicking against the blood-red marble floor, the walls and pillars with their ghastly carvings rising around him. The huge statue of the serpent god loomed over the altar. A fresh corpse lay atop the altar, blood running down its sides, and a ring of people knelt before the dais, Mitor, Marcelle, Rachel, and Lord Roget and Lord Marcus among them. Skhath stood before the kneeling supplicants, a golden chalice in his skeletal hands.

"Drink you now of this blood, offered up to great Sepharivaim," said Skhath.

"Skhath!" roared Mazael, lifting Lion.

The San-keth reared back and hissed. "You! Kill him! I command..."

The doors on the other wall of the temple burst open, and a pair of screaming armsmen burst through. "Lord Mitor! Lord Mitor! We're under attack..." The man's scream ended in a wet gurgle as an Elderborn arrow sank into his chest.

"Stop them!" howled Mitor. "Kill Mazael, kill him now!"

"Mitor!" roared Sir Commander Galan. "Face me, you sniveling liar!"

Everything exploded into chaos. The Cravenlock armsmen in the temple drew their weapons. Skhath threw the chalice to the ground and reached for Rachel. Lord Roget Hunterson fell to his knees, clutching his chest, while Lord Marcus Trand sprinted for the doors. Skhath grabbed Rachel and pulled her up. Arrows hissed through the open doors.

Mazael charged, Romaria a half-step behind him. An armsman brandished a mace and sprang at Mazael. Mazael parried the mace, Lion ringing from the force of the blow, and Romaria took off the man's head with a powerful two-handed cut.

They fought their way through the press side-by-side. Galan Hawking howled with fury, striking left and right. Sir Nathan bellowed commands, taking command of the Justiciars as Galan raged. Mazael saw Skhath, Mitor, Marcelle, and Rachel running for a shadowed staircase under the balcony. He growled and launched a backhand that gutted a Cravenlock soldier.

"We've got to catch them!" said Mazael. Romaria gave him a worried glance, and nodded.

A soldier came at Mazael armed with a war axe and a heavy shield. Mazael beat aside his attack and went on the offensive, Lion flashing and spinning in a storm of blue flame. The man's axe clipped Mazael's shoulder, but he twisted and stabbed, Lion's point plunging into the man's heart.

He already felt the wound on his shoulder healing itself as the armsman fell.

Then they were in the clear. Mazael saw Elderborn running along the balcony, sending arrows lancing down. The air rang with screams and crashing steel. Mazael and Romaria jumped past a pair of dying men and ran for the staircase.

The staircase was as twisted as a serpent and as narrow as a needle's eye. Mazael heard Mitor's labored breath above him, and the grinding of stone against stone. Then the stairs ended in a closed stone door with no sign of a handle. Another one of the castle's hidden doors, no doubt. He had to find the trigger.

Rachel was on the other side of that door.

"Look for a hidden key or switch," Mazael said. Romaria nodded and began searching.

"Damn you!" Mazael hear Mitor's voice through cracks in the stone wall. "Damn you!"

"Silence!" said Skhath. "Simonian, you miserable traitor! I shall sink my fangs into your lying..."

"Come now," came Simonian's amused voice. "We both know you can do no such thing. If you wish to escape, simply take horses and flee through the gate."

"Save us!" said Marcelle. "Save us, save us!"

"We cannot leave through the gate! The courtyard is thick with the Elderborn." Skhath's voice rose to a sibilant snarl. "You must use your arts to take us from this place. It is our only hope!"

"Your only hope," said Simonian, and he laughed. "You have brought this on yourself. Did you really think you could conquer the Grim Marches with Mitor as your patsy?" His laughter redoubled. "You poor fool. It's rather amusing. You and Mitor both wanted to conquer the Grim Marches. Now Lord Richard, or Lord Mazael, most likely, will kill you both. A fine joke."

"Kill Mazael, at least!" screamed Mitor. "Damn you, wizard, I bought your services! Kill him!"

"Why should I do that?" said Simonian. "I have no argument with Lord Mazael."

"Don't call him that!" said Mitor. "I am Lord of Castle Cravenlock, I am liege lord of the Grim Marches..."

"Lord Mazael is more than you," said Simonian. "More than any of you crawling mortals."

"It doesn't have to be like this!" said Rachel. Her was voice so soft Mazael could barely hear it. "Mazael isn't the monster you think he is. He could show mercy yet, if we surrender. Skhath, please, there's still a way to end..."

"Do not touch me!" said Skhath. Mazael heard a crackle of a spell and Rachel's scream.

"I will kill you for this betrayal, you faithless infidel," said Skhath. "I shall do that, at least."

Simonian roared with laughter. "How do you propose to do that? Think, Skhath! Do you know what the ultimate irony is? You have failed in your purpose, but in doing so, have fulfilled mine perfectly..."

"Got it!" said Romaria. She pressed her fingers into a crack between two stones.

The stone door slid aside with a groan, opening below the balcony in the castle's chapel. Dozens of candles on the altar threw back the darkness, revealing windows that had been painted over with scenes from the San-keth temple. Simonian stood atop the altar, cloaked in his dark robes, while Skhath, Mitor, and Marcelle stared up at the necromancer. A leather weapons belt hung from Skhath's shoulder, holding a sheathed longsword and a pair of daggers.

Rachel lay sprawled at the foot of the dais, eyes closed.

"Ah!" said Simonian. "It's seems I won't have to kill you after all. Lord Mazael will do that for me." Simonian made a spinning gesture with his hand and faded from sight. Skhath hissed and lunged for the necromancer, but his skeletal fingers raked only empty air.

"He's still there," said Romaria. "It's an illusion. He's made himself invisible."

"Mazael Cravenlock," said Skhath. "You have made a ruin of everything! By the true god, I should have killed you!"

"Probably," said Mazael.

Mitor's cowered behind the serpent priest. "Kill him, Skhath, oh, please, kill him now." Mitor was haggard, his face sallow with terror. Mazael felt a moment of pity, but contempt soon replaced it. Mitor had brought this disaster on himself.

"It needn't come to this, Sir Mazael," said Skhath. "Lord of Castle Cravenlock? Bah! You'll be the Dragonslayer's slave, just as Lord Adalon and Mitor were. But I can change that. With the power of Karag Tormeth and great Sepharivaim behind you, you could become liege lord of the Grim Marches, even king..."

"Shut up," said Mazael, striding through the rows of pews.

"It doesn't seem as if slithering Sepharivaim's power did Lady Arissa much good," said Romaria. "Nor did it do Mitor any good. Do you think Mazael is that stupid?"

"You want to kill me? You still have the chance." Mazael lifted Lion. "Try." He slapped the flat of his blade against Romaria's sword, the blue flames spreading to her weapon.

Romaria swung her heavy sword in a loop. "Shall we see if a half-breed wild woman is a match for a full-blooded serpent?"

Skhath shoved Mitor and Marcelle in front of him. "You think I shall fall as easily as Simonian's zuvembies or Mitor's idiot soldiers? I shall not. I have the power of Sepharivaim behind me, humans. It is time you learned to fear his strength!"

Skhath snatched the daggers from his weapons belt, the dark blades gleaming with poison. Mazael raised his sword in guard to block any thrown daggers. Mitor and Marcelle were both screaming, begging.

Then the serpent priest stepped forward and slammed the daggers into the Lord and Lady of Castle Cravenlock.

Mazael froze in astonishment. Mitor fell to his knees, his eyes fixed on Mazael. Blood gushed from his mouth, and he collapsed to the floor in a heap. Marcelle managed to stand for a moment longer, blood trickling down her face, then she collapsed atop her husband. Blood dripped from their mouths and ears in a gathering dark pool.

"Why did you do that?" said Romaria. She looked as stunned as Mazael.

Skhath laughed and Lion burned white-hot.

The blood oozed over Mitor's face and transformed it into a gruesome mask, his clothes sizzling and smoking as the black blood touched them. Their blood flowed over their Mitor and Marcelle's bodies like a coat of paint, filling the chapel with a hideous stench. Mazael could not take his eyes from the ghastly sight.

"Mazael! He's casting a spell!" said Romaria.

Mazael's eyes snapped up as Skhath's dead hands flickered in a spell. Green light danced up his arms. "Fool! See the wrath of Sepharivaim!"

Black blood covered Mitor and Marcelle's naked bodies from head to foot.

Then the corpses moved.

"Simonian prided himself on his necromancy," said Skhath. "I do not need his help! He has nothing to match the wrath of Sepharivaim."

The two corpses stood, the black blood making them look like animated shadows. They moved with a sliding, deadly grace, a far cry above the shuffling zuvembies, or even the armored warriors Mazael had fought in the temple corridor.

"Kill them both," said Skhath. "Kill the unbelievers!"

The creatures lunged at Mazael, fingers hooked into claws. Skhath reached over his skeleton's shoulder and drew the sword.

Mazael leapt back as Mitor's animated corpse clawed at him, leaving a trail of black bloodstains on the floor. He worked his sword in intricate circles, the monstrosity flinching away from the fire in his sword. He saw Romaria struggling against Marcelle's corpse.

Skhath strode towards him, sword grasped in skeletal hand. "When I faced you before, I had to hold back, lest you discover my true nature." The serpent's hissing laughter echoed. "Now I need not."

His spellbound skeleton moved with grace and power. Mazael knew that if he could get his sword through Skhath's defense the magical fires would rip apart the skeleton. But the serpent priest moved too fast. Mitor's corpse grabbed for Mazael, the thing's fingers brushing his shoulder, and a deathly chill sank into his left arm. Skhath's silvery sword bit through Mazael's armor and skidded off a rib. Mazael grunted and staggered back to a guard stance, feeling his blood stick to the inside of his tunic. He heard Romaria's rapid breathing and muttered curses as she struggled.

"I shall make you confess the glory of Sepharivaim before I take your life!" howled Skhath. His sword went high, then low, and angled in a stab for Mazael's chest. Mazael beat aside the thrust and slashed, and Skhath rolled his wrists and caught the blow. Mazael tensed his legs and shoved. Skhath's undead skeleton was lighter than Mazael, and the serpent priest reeled back. Mazael lunged forward for the kill, but Mitor's blood-soaked corpse interposed itself. Bloody fingers raked across Mazael's cuirass, the chill sinking deep into his chest. The cold in his chest slowed him just long enough for Skhath to tear a gash down his leg. Mazael realized he could not face both Skath and the animated corpse by himself.

Romaria had been driven to the other side of the chapel, near the barred doors that opened into the courtyard. She wielded her bastard sword with both hands, the blue flame of her blade bathing her face in an azure glow. Marcelle's corpse had been slashed and torn in a dozen places, yet it still pressed forward.

Mazael attacked at Mitor's corpse in a flurry of slashes. The thing retreated from his attack, and he scored a minor hit on its shoulder. The black blood shriveled away, revealing a patch of white flesh, a keening wail escaping Mitor's mouth. But Mazael didn't dare press the attack with Skhath's sword darting and stabbing. The tip of the serpent priest's blade nicked off Mazael's helm. The blow staggered him, and he barely parried a strike that would have driven through his heart.

Skhath's hissing laughter filled Mazael's ears.

Mazael grimaced and took Lion in both hands as Skhath and Mitor's corpse drove him towards the wall. Once they had him against the wall, he couldn't evade their blows, and they stood between him and Romaria.

Mazael growled. Some of the battle-rage welled up in his mind. He welcomed it.

He parried Skhath's next slash and shoved hard. Skhath stumbled, skeletal feet clacking against the floor. Mazael wheeled left just as Mitor reached for him, twisting his sword, and Mitor's hand clamped around Lion's blade instead. There was a brilliant blue flash, and the undead thing wailed. It fell back, most of its left arm gone, the stump a sizzling mass of burned flesh.

Mazael sprinted past Mitor's wailing corpse, Lion clenched in both fists. Skhath seized his sword and rose to one knee, but Mazael was past him in a second. He heard the Mitor-thing in pursuit. Mazael ignored them. He had one chance to do this right.

Romaria and Marcelle's corpse moved in an intricate dance. Romaria's eyes fixed on Mazael's for a moment, and then she backed away from the dead thing, letting it drive her towards the wall. Mazael heard Skhath and Mitor's corpse behind him.

He sprang at Marcelle's corpse. It started to turn, but too late. Mazael brought Lion down in a huge two-handed cut, the blade slashing through Marcelle's shoulder and into her chest. Blue fire blazed, black blood shriveling. The creature shrieked, its voice a knife against Mazael's ears. Romaria drove her sword into Marcelle's ruined chest. There was another flash of blue fire, brighter than before. Mazael caught a brief glimpse of Marcelle, the black blood burned away, thrashing like a landed fish on their blades. Then her body withered into black, stinking ash.

Mazael spun in time to catch Skhath's enraged thrust. The serpent priest went on the offensive, swinging his gleaming sword in mighty two-handed blows. Romaria launched a looping swing, and Skhath hopped back, the bones of his carrier clacking.

"Kill him!" hissed Skhath.

Mitor's corpse lurched forward, and Mazael slashed Lion across the corpse's chest. Romaria took off its right arm with another chop. It wailed and stumbled back, the black blood crumbling from Mitor's pale body. Mazael saw Mitor's face, the bloodshot green eyes dead and staring, and stabbed Lion into Mitor's chest. Blue fire burst through the dead thing, and Mitor's corpse shuddered and disintegrated into a spray of ashes.

Skhath backed away from them, sword raised in guard. His head swiveled back and forth as he looked for some means of escape.

"No tricks left, snake?" said Romaria. "Seems the might of Sepharivaim wasn't so great."

"Blasphemer," said Skhath, his voice a dry whisper. He ran forward, sword raised high.

Mazael moved to parry, but Skhath's coils suddenly unwound from the skeleton's spine. The serpent, hurled forward by its carrier's momentum, flew like an arrow for Mazael's face. Skhath's jaws yawned wide, revealing gleaming white fangs. Mazael tried to change his parry in time.

Romaria's sword tore a long gash on Skhath's scaled flank. The force of her blow knocked the San-keth aside, and the serpent struck the ground, writhing and hissing. Mazael lashed out and struck the headless skeleton, smashing it with a single blow.

Skhath slithered towards the altar, leaving a trail of fresh blood. Mazael overtook the writhing serpent and brought his foot down, pinning Skhath behind the head. Skhath hissed and cursed, spitting venom, but his jaws could not reach Mazael's leg.

"Stop this! Stop this!" said Skhath. "You dare not touch a servant of Sepharivaim, you dare not, he will avenge, Sepharivaim, save me, protect me..."

Mazael's sword came down and ended the creature's frantic prayers. He kicked the staring head aside in disgust. The long scaled body stopped its thrashing and lay very still. The chapel fell silent.

Rachel still lay at the base of the altar. Her clothes were shredded and torn, her skin marked with bruises and cuts. Mazael looked at his sister and felt such a peculiar mixture of pity and rage that he thought his head would explode. Rachel had helped bring about all the darkness that had befallen the Grim Marches. She deserved to die just as much as Mitor had. Yet Rachel had been a prisoner here for the last fifteen years. And Mitor had paid enough for both of them.

Romaria touched his arm. "Don't. There's been enough death already."

"It's not finished yet," said Mazael. "Is he still here?"

Romaria nodded. She pulled a silver coin from her belt and made it dance across her fingers as she cast a spell. There was a flash, and Simonian appeared atop the altar, his invisibility dispelled.

His murky eyes shone with amusement.

"Well," said Simonian. "That was impressive. Mightier men than you have fallen to the wrath of Sepharivaim."

"Who are you?" said Romaria.

"I am who I am, dear lady," said Simonian.

"No," said Romaria. "I recognize the spell upon you now. It's the same sort of spell Skhath always wore when he masqueraded as Sir Albron Eastwater. Who are you? Another San-keth priest?"

"No," said Mazael. "What are you?"

Simonian laughed. "Perceptive, is she not? Well...why not? This beard itches terribly. And it is the end of things...why should you now not know the truth?"

Simonian's face began to shimmer and ripple, the features morphing and changing like sculptor's putty. His features flowed into those of Lord Adalon Cravenlock, the grinning Lord Adalon Mazael had seen in his dreams. The faces of a dozen men appeared, vanished, appeared again. Then the illusion vanished, revealing a lean, hawk-nosed face with a trimmed beard and cold gray eyes.

It was Mattias Comorian, the jongleur he had met at Eastwater inn weeks ago.

"Is...is that his true form?" said Mazael.

"No," said Romaria. "There's still an illusion there."

Mattias laughed. "This is what I looked like as a mortal man, many years ago." The jongleur's smoother voice had replaced Simonian's rough tones. "If you were to gaze upon me in all my glory...the sight would rather destroy your minds."

"You were here all along!" said Mazael. "You were at the inn. You were Simonian. And you were the thing in my dreams, weren't you?" His mind spun at the realiziation, filling with dread. "What manner of creature are you?"

"Why, the same as you," said the thing standing atop the altar.

"What is your name? Who are you, really?" said Romaria. "Answer!"

The creature laughed. "Names? What is a name? I've had so many in my life. Call me Mattias. It's my favorite. But in Briault I am known as Simonian the Necromancer. In Ritoria, mothers used to call me Old Man Ghoul. They still warn their children, lest I snatch them away. The Travish peasants still whisper tales of Margath the Terrible." He smiled, as if recalling a fond memory. "There was Cristiphar Barragon, who convinced the last Maendrag High Lord to lead Dracaryl to its downfall. I was Marugot the Warlock, who advised King Julius Roland to wage war to the ruin of his land. Sir Trakis of Richtofar, who counseled the Patriarch of Cristafel to lead his holy war into Travia and turn the rivers red with blood." He laughed. "Ah, names, names, so many names I have worn! I've lost count. The Elderborn call me *sar'diskhar*, the Hand of Chaos. But the High Elderborn name is closest to the truth, closest to what they called me in the palaces of Tristafel long ago...*altamane'malevagr*...the Old Demon."

Mazael remembered all the tales he had heard in his life, all the times peasants had cursed and muttered the words "Old Demon." Fear and rage coursed through him in equal measure.

But also a sensation of strange rightness. As if for the first time he had met someone who truly was like himself.

"But you needn't call me any of those names," said Mattias, the Old Demon, spreading his arms wide. "There is only one thing you can call me."

"What?" said Mazael.

"Father," said Mattias.

Mazael looked at Mattias's cold gray eyes.

The eyes were mirror images of his own.

"No," said Mazael. "That...that cannot be."

"Oh, but it is," said Mattias, grinning. "Don't you see? How many Cravenlocks have gray eyes? Look at your miserable mother. How she despised her husband, how she lusted for power!" He leered. "She would have done anything for someone who could bring her power. Look at your wretched, dead brother and your foolish sister. You are beyond them. You see, they were Lord Adalon's children, but you are my son. You are more than simply Demonsouled! Most of our so-called kindred have but the barest thread of my father's magic in their souls. But I am his son, the son of a god, and you are my son!"

"Don't listen to him, Mazael," said Romaria.

"How...how can this be?" said Mazael. His hands shook so badly he could barely hold his sword. "I..."

Mattias smiled. "Don't you see, my son? Our father, the Great

Demon, died long ago. We are his heirs, his descendants. The world belongs to us. Come with me, Mazael, and I will teach you. I will show you all you can accomplish with the power in your soul. I will show you how to transcend death, to live beyond the mortal fools who crawl across this world like cattle. I will show you how to rule them, to make them dance to your will."

"You don't have the right," said Romaria. "The Great Demon didn't have the right."

The Old Demon laughed. "My dear lady, I have the right to do whatever I wish. And so does Mazael. You, and those like you, belong to us."

"No," said Romaria. "Don't listen to him. You've heard what he's done. You've seen the vileness he has wrought here."

"I know," said Mazael. "I know." Romaria was right. Yet he felt the power within. Mattias's words had coaxed it out of the dark corners of his soul. It was sweeter than anything he'd known.

He wanted it so badly.

"Don't listen to him," said Romaria. "You don't have to. I'm here with you."

Mattias snorted. "How cloying. Do you obey her will in all matters? You are more than her and can become greater still. I offer you the power of the gods, and you heed a half-breed mortal?"

"You're a liar," said Mazael.

A glimmer of red fire flashed in Mattias's eyes. "Am I?"

"Yes," said Romaria. "He's seen the evil you've raised. He's seen what the demon power does. I swore an oath, when I left Deepforest Keep, to bring an end to your evil."

Mattias flexed his fingers. "Try."

Romaria obliged, her bow coming up with blinding speed. Mazael ran towards the altar, Lion blazing like a torch.

The Old Demon was faster.

His hand shot forward, a rune etched in lines of fire burning on his palm. It exploded in a flash of red-orange light. Romaria's bow burst into flames, and the force knocked Mazael over and sent him tumbling down the dais steps, Lion flying from his hand. Romaria shrieked in agony, and a bolt of pain shot through Mazael's chest.

Some time later, he had the strength to look up.

Romaria lay sprawled across the dais steps near Rachel. Charred ribs jutted from the ruin of her chest, wisps of smoke rising from her clothes.. Mazael came to one knee and reached for her. She was dead.

For a long time he stared at her.

"You bastard," said Mazael at last. The fury broiled up, and he welcomed it. "You murdering bastard!"

Mattias raised his eyebrows. "Bastard? That's cruel. She tried to kill me. Do I not have a right to defend myself?"

"You killed her!" said Mazael.

"She wanted to keep you from your destiny," said Mattias. "She wanted to hold you back." He smiled. "Besides, I didn't kill Romaria." He pointed. "She did."

Mazael looked at Rachel. "What?"

"Lord Richard drove out the San-keth," said Mattias. "Who do you think invited them back? She did. Who do you think convinced Mitor to allow it? Who do you think pulled Lord Marcus and Lord Roget into the worship of Sepharivaim? And who allowed Skhath to mate with her..."

"Be quiet!" said Mazael. But the anger surged beneath his mind like a river of molten iron.

"She did," hissed Mattias. A grin spread across his face like a sore. "It is her fault! Kill her! Do justice. Take the power, if for no other reason than that. You think you will become evil? Bah! Take up your power and do justice, Lord of Castle Cravenlock. Rachel Cravenlock is responsible for all that has befallen. She is responsible for Romaria's death. Kill her. Avenge all the evil that has fallen on these lands!"

Mazael stood and drew a dagger. Rachel lay at his feet, her breath fluttering in her chest. He saw the runes marking her arms and the emerald serpent scribed on her forehead. Romaria was dead because of her. The Grim Marches were at war because of her. This woman, this whore deserved death for what she had done. The rage spread through his veins like molten metal. His hand clenched around the dagger's hilt...

Something struck his boot, and he looked down. A charred apple lay against his foot. It had rolled from Romaria's burnt cloak.

A rush of memories surged through Mazael. He remembered meeting Rachel for the first time, remembered how she had always agreed with him. She had not been a strong child, nor had she grown into a strong woman. He remembered when Lord Adalon had sent him away. While he had fought, drunk, and whored his way across the kingdom, Rachel had been left here alone with Skhath and Mitor and worse creatures. She had done terrible things.

But Mazael had almost done terrible things, too.

He tossed the dagger aside. "No."

Mattias blinked. "No?"

"I can forgive Rachel for what she's done," said Mazael. "But she didn't kill Romaria. You did."

"She betrayed you!" said Mattias. "She lied to you..."

"And so did you," said Mazael. "Don't talk to me of lies, not when you weave them yourself." A cold certainty rose in his mind. "You've been here from the beginning, haven't you? You said so yourself. Skhath had fulfilled your purpose, you told him."

Mattias's cold gray eyes glittered. "You could not possibly understand my purpose. Skhath? Skhath was a fool! He thought he could carve an empire for himself. Mitor wanted power. I offered him the tiniest crumbs of it, and he followed me like a braying donkey after a carrot. And your mother wanted power so badly she would have done anything for me." He grinned. "And she did. Don't you see, Mazael, my son? It has all been for you."

"What do you mean?" said Mazael.

"I came to the Grim Marches to father you. I made you what you are. It was my seed that put the power into your soul," said Mattias. A glimmer of red light shone in his eyes, and his mouth seemed like a pit into nothingness. "Don't you see? Everything I have done has made you stronger, made you greater. Who do you think told Lady Arissa to make Lord Adalon send you away? Why do you think I made fools such as Skhath and Mitor dance to my tune? You have it in you to become greater than any mortal, greater than any Demonsouled that has ever lived! My designs called out your power, forced you to confront it, and now you can embrace it."

"My entire life has been nothing more than your lie?" yelled Mazael.

"Yes," hissed Mattias. He spread his arms, looming on the altar like a dark god. "Look at what I have done for you. Who can stand against you? Think of what you can become! Lord of the Grim Marches? King? Master of the world? Ten thousand years from now men will still speak the name of Mazael the Destroyer with fear and reverence! I will only offer once more. Embrace your destiny and take what is yours!" Power and strength seemed to roll off the Old Demon like smoke, and fear struck Mazael to the heart.

Mazael looked at Romaria, at Rachel, at the burned apple. His hand clenched around Silar's holy symbol.

He looked into his father's cold, burning eyes. "No. No! You murdered Othar and Romaria, and the gods know how many others, and for what? Nothing. I will not give in to the madness you gave me. No. I deny you."

Mattias reeled in disbelief. "No? No!" He threw back his head and laughed, cords standing out in his neck. "I knew your will was strong. You are the first of my children who ever resisted the call."

The hair on the back of Mazael's neck stood up. "There are others?"

Mattias grinned, revealing teeth that had become yellow and

twisted. "Many others. You have merely hastened your fate, you know." His hands came up to his shoulders and grasped the hood of his robes. "I never lose. My children serve me for a time. But in the end, they always rebel."

"And then you kill them?" said Mazael. Lion was too far away for him to reach.

"Oh, no," said Mattias. "You're going to have a very rare honor, my son. You're going to see my true face, without the illusion." He pulled his hood up, masking his face in shadows. "And I never kill my children."

He threw back the hood.

Mattias's skin had become gray and rotten. His face was gaunt and angular, a demon's face. Curved black horns rose from his brow and curled down his cheeks. Burning red eyes glared out from beneath matted, greasy hair. His teeth had become twisted fangs, his mouth a bottomless black pit.

"I DEVOUR THEM!" roared the Old Demon, his voice thundering with the fury of the abyss.

He leapt from the altar, his black robes billowing like a pair of wings.

Mattias's mouth yawned impossibly wide, opening like the gates of hell. Mazael could not reach Lion. All he had was Silar's holy symbol. He could still save himself. If he submitted to Mattias, submitted to the Old Demon . . .

"Gods help me," Mazael said, throwing up his fist.

Something jerked in his fist, and Mattias howled. Silar's holy symbol trembled, a rime of white light flashing across the steel, and the Old Demon took a step back.

"Help me," whispered Mazael. He fought his terror and stepped forward, the light from the three interlocked rings flashing.

"What is this?" hissed Mattias.

"Get out of here," said Mazael. "Leave the Grim Marches and never return. I can't possibly kill you. You're stronger than I. But this is my castle now. You made it that way. And I command you to leave. Now." A curious feeling of calm swept over him. The symbol pulsed with power. He could not defeat Mattias by himself. But perhaps he was not alone.

"You dare!" hissed Mattias. "No one commands me!" He leapt, claws extended for Mazael's throat.

Mazael thrust the holy symbol at the Old Demon's face. The metal exploded with white radiance, and the light filled the chapel, driving back the shadows. Mattias howled in pain, his clawed hands raised to cover his eyes.

"Go," said Mazael. "Go and never return."

Mattias staggered back. "You...ah, Mazael, I must compliment you. No one has ever had the strength to stop me. Ah, you are greater than my power, I see that now. I...will go." He turned, slumped in his dark robes.

Mazael's hand lowered. "You will?"

Mattias shuddered. "Yes." He whirled. "With your soul in my hand!"

The Old Demon moved with inhuman speed. Mazael yelled and lifted the holy symbol, and Mattias's clawed hand closed around Mazael's. His father's skin felt cold and dead. The white light from the symbol flickered as Mattias pushed Mazael back. The Old Demon's lips writhed in a ghastly grin.

"You are mine," hissed Mattias.

"Go," said Mazael. Mattias snarled, his black tongue scraping against his teeth. "Go!" Something shifted in Mazael. An iron, determined fury flowed from the symbol and filled him.

Mattias flinched.

"Go! In the name of Amatheon and Amater and Joraviar and all the gods of heaven, I command you, BE GONE!"

The words boomed like thunder, ripping from Mazael's throat with awesome force. The symbol exploded with white fire, flinging Mattias to the floor. The defaced windows of the chapel shattered, and glass shards rained to the floor, the barred doors exploding open. Rachel sighed, the runes and serpent mark vanishing from her skin. Mattias slammed into the altar, cringing from the blazing fire.

"BE GONE!" said Mazael. The floor trembled with the sound of his words. The terrible might of the Old Demon seemed insignificant before the thundering fire. "GO AND NEVER RETURN!"

Mattias howled and fled for the door. His black robes billowed behind him, becoming longer and darker, taking the shape of dark wings. With a final cry he leapt through the ruined doors and took to the air. The black, winged thing flew away to the east, vanishing into the pale pink sky. The fire from the symbol pulsed in one final burst, and faded away.

Mazael sank to his knees, too weary and too overcome by grief and wonder to stand. Outside, the sounds of fighting faded as dawn broke.

CHAPTER 32
LORD MARCUS TRAND'S LAST STAND

The battle lasted less than an hour.

The armies camped outside Castle Cravenlock remained oblivious to Sil Tarithyn's attack, the death of Lord Mitor, and Lord Richard's approaching force. Even when Lord Marcus appeared, shouting incoherent warnings of impending doom, the mercenaries remained at ease.

Then Lord Richard's army struck.

Sir Tanam and Toraine's wings of heavy horse cut through the camp like a scythe through wheat. Lord Marcus tried to rally his men from Roseblood Keep, and came under attack from Sir Commander Galan Hawking's Justiciars for his trouble. The mercenary camp disintegrated, and Cravenlock armsmen fled in every direction. Lord Marcus tried to flee and Sir Tanam put a lance through his chest. Then Lord Richard struck with his footmen and archers. The mercenaries were slaughtered and driven off, the Cravenlock armsmen broken, and Lord Marcus and Lord Roget's men were killed.

Lord Mitor's rebellion had come to a sudden and ignominious end.

CHAPTER 33
THE LORD OF CASTLE CRAVENLOCK

"My lord?"

Mazael turned, saw Adalar standing in the door. "Yes?

"Lord Richard has ridden up from the camp. He would like to speak with you on the ramparts," said Adalar.

"Very well," said Mazael. "Tell him I'll be there shortly."

He snatched up his cloak and tossed it around his shoulders. The weather had turned unseasonably cold in the last week. It was a blessing. The colder air had kept the bodies from rotting until they had all been burned. Plague would have been the last thing the ravaged lands of Castle Cravenlock needed.

Mazael swept down the spiraling stairs of the King's Tower, passing the spot where he had walked into Romaria. He had ordered her body interred in the castle's crypt and sent a message through Sil Tarithyn to Lord Athaelin in Deepforest Keep. He doubted he would receive a response.

It had made him feel better, if only for a moment.

In the courtyard, Sir Nathan and Sir Gerald drilled the surviving Cravenlock armsmen. Nathan had sorted through them, keeping those he had deemed trustworthy, and sending away the rest. All told, Castle Cravenlock had lost half of its armsmen.

Master Cramton stood on the steps to the keep and bellowed orders. Mazael had made him the castle's seneschal, and the former innkeeper had risen to the task, mobilizing the castle's host of demoralized and frightened servants. Battle damage was repaired, corpses removed, and food provided for the many guests and soldiers. Bethy was now mistress of the kitchens. Mazael had not eaten so well since he had left Knightcastle.

He spotted Lord Richard on the northern wall, his crimson armor gleaming in the morning sunlight. His son Toraine stood at his side, a dark reflection in black armor, while Lucan remained apart, wrapped in his dark cloak. The rumors said Toraine had acquitted himself well in the battle, but they also said Lucan had called up hellfire and lightning, and used them to slaughter San-keth worshippers by the dozen.

Mazael climbed the stairs up to the rampart.

"Ah," said Lord Richard. "Lord Mazael. Please, join us."

"I believe I already have," said Mazael.

"Indeed," said Lord Richard. "Toraine, Lucan, leave. Lord Mazael and I have matters to discuss."

Toraine grumbled and walked away. Lucan left without a word.

"My sons vex me, at times," Lord Richard said. "Sometimes I fear to leave Swordgrim and the Grim Marches in Toraine's hands when I die." He looked out over the plains and the wreckage of battle.

"They don't seem very fond of each other," said Mazael.

Lord Richard almost smiled. "I have done much in my life, but perhaps my sons are my greatest failure. I should not have left them entirely to their mother's care. She was a fool."

Mazael thought of Lady Arissa and nodded.

"But the past is gone. To dwell upon it is folly," said Lord Richard. "It is the future that must concern us now." He paused. "I understand you have made Sir Gerald Roland your armsmaster."

"That's right," said Mazael.

"Explain," said Lord Richard.

Mazael shrugged. "Sir Nathan wouldn't take the job. Claims he's too old. I shouted at him until I turned hoarse, but he wouldn't listen."

"Sir Nathan is a capable man, but he is old," said Lord Richard. "He is right to insist that a younger man take up his duties. And your young Sir Gerald seems most skillful, from what I have observed. Yet there are certainly many qualified knights for the duty. Why have you picked a Roland?"

Mazael laughed. "Are you afraid that I'm going to ally with Lord Malden against you?"

"It is a possibility," said Lord Richard.

"No," said Mazael, "it is not. I am tired of war. I've chosen Sir Gerald for three reasons. First, as I have said, I will not continue my idiot brother's war against you. Second, because of this, Lord Malden will not take up arms against you either. For all his flaws, Lord Malden loves his sons. So long as Gerald is my armsmaster, and I am not at war with you, he will not rise. Third, I plan to give my sister in marriage to Gerald."

Lord Richard raised an eyebrow. "Indeed?"

"Gerald always took pity on Rachel, even when I favored executing her," said Mazael. "And he is more compassionate than I. They will go well together, I believe."

"Perhaps," said Lord Richard. He looked out over the Marches. "I have a favor to ask of you."

"Take Lucan as my court wizard?" said Mazael.

Lord Richard did not look surprised. "My sons despise one another. For their sake, and for the sake of the land, they must be kept apart. Now, I know you planned to take Timothy deBlanc, as your court wizard..."

"I can have two," said Mazael. "They seem to work together well enough. And Timothy has his hands full examining and destroying the items found in the San-keth temple. Lucan's aid would be welcome."

"I am most pleased with your progress in this," said Lord Richard. "Twice now I have faced an uprising of a San-keth cult in Castle Cravenlock. I have no desire to do so a third time. Had I known there was such an extensive temple complex hidden here, I would have razed the castle and killed all the Cravenlocks."

"I'm rather glad you didn't," said Mazael.

"My others vassals grow restless," said Lord Richard. "I shall depart for Swordgrim by noon. I am certain your hands are capable of attending to matters here. Do not fail me in this."

"I shall not," said Mazael. Lord Richard nodded and left.

Mazael watched him go. He felt tired and sad, but not angry. The maddening rage had not surfaced since Mitor's death and the Old Demon's defeat. The healing was still there, as were the speed and strength, but Mazael suspected that they had become part of him forever. He remembered what Silar had told him of Demonsouled who had conquered their darker half. Perhaps he had done so, but at cost of Romaria's life. Were it not for her, he would have become as monstrous as Mattias.

"Thank you, Romaria," whispered Mazael. His fingers brushed the holy symbol dangling from his belt. "And thank you."

Grief hung on him for a moment as he thought of Othar and Romaria. He even felt sadness for his brother and his poor, cuckolded father. He sighed and clenched his fist. As Lord Richard had said, the past was gone.

He had work to do.

Mazael left the ramparts and walked back into his castle.

THE END

Thank you for reading DEMONSOULED. Turn the page for a sample chapter from Soul of Tyrants, the next book in the DEMONSOULED series. To receive immediate notification of new releases, sign up for my newsletter at this web address:

http://www.jonathanmoeller.com/newsletter.html

SOUL OF TYRANTS BONUS CHAPTER
CHAPTER 1: WOLVES AMONG SHEEP

Lord Mazael Cravenlock left the camp and watched the sun rise over the Grim Marches, as he did every morning. The dawn seemed to paint the winter-brown plains the color of blood.

Mazael scowled, his bearded jaw clenching.

The blood might prove real, soon enough.

"My lord?"

A stern-faced boy of about fifteen years stepped to Mazael's side, carrying a pile of armor.

Mazael nodded. "Adalar. I am ready."

Adalar Greatheart grunted. "Hold out your arms, my lord."

Mazael complied. The dawn's bloody rays slanted into the camp, throwing long black shadows. Squires hastened back and forth, bearing arms and armor, polishing shields and sharpening swords. Bacon sizzled over the campfires, and horses neighed and grunted.

Despite his rise to the lordship of Castle Cravenlock, Mazael still wore the battered armor from his days as a wandering, landless knight; a mail shirt, scarred steel cuirass, leather gauntlets, and a helmet. A black surcoat with the House of Cravenlock's three crossed swords was his sole mark of rank.

Around his waist went a worn leather belt with a battered scabbard. In the scabbard rested a magnificent longsword with a golden pommel shaped like a lion's head.

"Send Sir Gerald to me," said Mazael, "and get yourself something to eat before we set out."

"My lord," said Adalar.

"And I mean it," said Mazael, pointing. "Eat something. The

other squires can manage themselves long enough for you to eat."

Adalar flashed a rare grin. The boy was sterner than his father, sometimes. "My lord."

Mazael shook his head, crossed his arms, and watched the camp. He had forty knights and their attendant squires with him. More than enough for what he had in mind.

Or so he hoped.

Armor clanked, and Mazael looked over his shoulder. A young, gold-haired man in polished plate and a fine blue surcoat emblazoned with a stylized greathelm walked towards Mazael, followed by a dour, pimpled squire of about thirteen.

"Gerald," said Mazael to his armsmaster. "Are we ready?"

"Soon enough," said Gerald. He scratched a mustache trimmed with razor precision. "We'll be ready to ride soon. Mayhap these ruffians will see reason."

Mazael snorted. "And maybe we'll all sit down for a feast afterwards."

Gerald shrugged. "It does seem unlikely. Wesson! Fetch some breakfast, please."

The pimpled squire grunted and hastened to the cook fires.

"No, it'll come down to steel," said Mazael. "We've dealt with these bands before. Lord Richard killed most of Mitor's damned mercenaries, but the survivors have failed to appreciate the lesson."

"Slow fellows," said Gerald. "A pity your brother didn't think to hire smarter mercenaries."

"Mitor never thought of anything," said Mazael, scowling at the mention of his dead brother, the previous Lord of Castle Cravenlock. "And if he had hired smarter mercenaries, he might still be alive."

"No loss, that," said Gerald. Wesson returned, bearing some bread and bacon. "Perhaps we can talk some sense into this band."

"Not likely."

Gerald shook his head. "You always take such a bleak view," he said, around a mouthful of bacon.

"And I'm usually right," said Mazael. He raised his voice. "Break camp and mount up! Move! I want to be at White Rock before midday!"

The squires began rolling up tents and rounding up the horses. Mazael took a piece of Gerald's bacon and watched the camp vanish. Soon the toiling squires loaded the pack animals, the knights mounted their horses, and they were ready.

A thin knight with a pinched face and a scraggly mustache rode towards Mazael. In his left hand he carried a tall lance crowned with the black-and-silver Cravenlock banner.

"Sir Aulus?" said Mazael.

"My lord," said Sir Aulus Hirdan, his deep voice incongruous against his wasted appearance. "We are ready."

"Good," said Mazael. Adalar returned, leading a large, ill-tempered destrier. The horse looked like it wanted to bite someone. Mazael stepped to the beast's side, running his hand along its neck. The big horse stamped and snorted, throwing its mane.

"Well, Chariot," said Mazael to his war horse. "Once again. You'll kill someone before the day's done."

Chariot almost looked pleased.

Mazael sprang up into the saddle. The squires mounted their palfreys, leading the pack horses, and rode to the side of their knights.

"We ought to say a prayer before we ride out," said Gerald.

"Steel will settle this, not the gods," said Mazael.

"The gods watch over all mortal affairs," said Gerald

"Aye," said Mazael, closing his eyes. He knew that very well, knew it far better than Gerald. "Ride out!"

They rode away to the south.

###

A few hours later they came to the village of White Rock, near the silent, looming trees of the Great Southern Forest. The village itself huddled within a stout palisade of sharpened logs. White Rock had survived Lord Richard Mandragon's conquest of the Grim Marches, Lord Mitor's failed rebellion, and a small army of corpses animated by necromantic arts.

Compared to that, a band of sixty ragged mercenaries seemed a small threat. And Mazael was determined that no harm would befall White Rock. The village had sworn him loyalty, and Mazael had promised protection.

He drew his knights in a line facing both White Rock and the mercenary camp. White Rock had proven inhospitable to the mercenaries, to judge from the arrow-ridden corpses near the palisade's gate.

"Rabble," said Mazael. He rarely became angry, not since Romaria's death, but faint flicker of anger burned in his chest. These scum dared to prey upon his lands, his people?

"Perhaps they'll be wise enough to stand down," said Gerald, reining in at Mazael's side.

Mazael snorted. "Perhaps. Aulus!"

Sir Aulus spurred his horse forward, the Cravenlock banner flapping, his right hand raised in parley. The ragged mercenaries turned and faced him, muttering with interest.

"Hear ye all!" Aulus called, his stentorian voice booming over the plains. "Mazael, Lord of Castle Cravenlock, commands you to lay down your arms and depart peacefully from his lands at once. Amnesty shall be offered to those who surrender!"

A chorus of jeers and ragged laughs went up. The largest of the mercenaries, a hulking brute in rusty mail, whirled and dropped his trousers.

"Disgraceful," said Gerald. Aulus turned and galloped back to Mazael's line.

"I told you," said Mazael. He reached down and drew his longsword. Lion's blade gleamed like blue ice in the dull winter sunlight.

"They've no respect for you," said Gerald, shaking his head.

"Of course not," said Mazael. "I'm Mitor's younger brother. Mitor was fat and weak and stupid. Why should I be any different?"

Of course, Mazael was only Mitor's half-brother. But Gerald didn't know that, and neither did the mercenaries.

If they had known Mazael's true father, they might have regarded him differently.

With outright terror, most likely.

Gerald grinned, drawing his own blade. "Shall we teach them otherwise?"

"I suppose so," said Mazael.

In his younger days, he had felt a raging joy at the prospect of battle, a ferocious and delighted bloodlust. Since Romaria had died, he had felt nothing of the sort. Now he felt only disgust and a vague weariness. This was necessary, and nothing more.

But if he had to fight, he would fight well.

He adjusted his helm, pointed Lion at the mercenaries, and kicked Chariot to a gallop. The big horse snorted and rumbled forward. A half-second later Mazael's knights surged after him, swords and lances gleaming.

The mercenaries gaped at them for a moment, then lunged for their weapons in a scrambled panic. They managed to form into a ragged line, but too late to stop the knights. Mazael beat aside a spear, reversed Lion, and took off a mercenary's head in a sweeping backhand. Chariot ran down another, pummeling the man to bloody pulp.

The knights tore through the line of mercenaries. Nearly half had been cut down, without loss to Mazael's men, while the rest fled in all directions.

"Reform!" yelled Mazael, wheeling Chariot around. "Another charge!"

"Stand, lads!" roared the big mercenary in the rusty mail shirt, brandishing a ridged mace. "Stand and fight, if you don't want to die!"

Some of the mercenaries kept running. Others turned, gripped their weapons, and set themselves. Mazael guided Chariot towards the mercenary leader, raising Lion for an overhand slash.

The mercenary snarled and flung his mace at the last minute, jumping out of Chariot's path. The mace's head crashed into Mazael's breastplate with a shriek of tortured metal. Mazael hissed in pain, heard something crack within his chest. He reeled in the saddle, Lion dangling from his grasp. The mercenary yanked a dagger free and sprang, howling, and Mazael thrust out. The mercenary impaled himself and died twitching.

Mazael kicked the dying man free and found that the battle had ended. Most of the mercenaries lay dead and dying, the brown grasses stained with red blood. The few survivors stood in a ring of scowling knights. Mazael grunted in pain and trotted Chariot towards the ring. He knew the pain well; he had broken ribs more than once.

The pain lessened as he rode, an odd tingling spreading through his chest.

"Mazael!" Gerald rode towards him, blood dripping from the length of his longsword. "Are you well? I saw that mace hit you..."

"I'll be fine," said Mazael.

"Perhaps you should..."

"I said I'll be fine," said Mazael, trying not to growl. "Any losses?"

"None," said Gerald. Wesson rode up and set to work cleaning Gerald's sword. "I think you were the only one wounded."

"Embarrassing," said Mazael. He jerked his head at the captured mercenaries. "How many prisoners?"

"Seven," said Gerald. Adalar joined them, cast a concerned look at Mazael.

"Seven," repeated Mazael. "Good enough. Question them."

"Why?" said Gerald.

"We've taken a half-dozen of these mercenary bands in the last three months," said Mazael. "Mercenaries love easy plunder, not armed opposition. They should have fled long ago." He took a long, painful breath. "I think someone's hiring them."

Gerald looked stunned. "Who would do such a thing?"

"I don't know," said Mazael. "Not all my vassals were pleased to see me replace Mitor." He shrugged. "Lord Richard, maybe. Or Toraine Mandragon. Or perhaps even your father."

"My father would not do something so underhanded!" said Gerald.

Mazael shrugged again. "Perhaps not. But I doubt he was pleased to hear of me becoming Lord of Castle Cravenlock. Sir Aulus!" Mazael's herald rode over. "Question them. If I am pleased with their answers, they might yet leave the Grim Marches alive." He considered this for a moment. "Possibly."

Aulus nodded and went about his work.

Mazael sat in the saddle and waited.

A fierce itching filled his chest, as if the broken rib was knitting itself back together.

###

"Sir Roger Gravesend," said Gerald, disgusted.

The surviving mercenaries trudged away, relieved of their weapons, armor, coin, and cloaks.

"I should have known," said Mazael, shaking his head. "He was not happy when Mitor was killed."

"And rumor held that he followed the San-keth way," said Gerald. "Is he at Castle Cravenlock?"

"As it happens, yes," said Mazael, turning Chariot around. "Perhaps we'll have a long talk with him."

"How is your chest?" said Gerald.

Mazael frowned. "What?"

Gerald pointed. "That mace. It looked like a fierce blow."

"That?" said Mazael. He had forgotten. "It's fine. The armor turned the worst of it."

Gerald gave the dent in Mazael's breastplate a dubious look.

Mazael forced a smile. "I'm well. Enough talk. Let's go home."

Gerald nodded. "I would enjoy spending a night under a proper roof." He rode for the squires and knights, herding them into the line.

Mazael sighed in relief. Gerald had not noticed. It would take weeks for a normal man to recover from a badly broken rib.

Mazael's injury had healed in a matter of minutes.

No one knew the truth. Romaria had known, but she was dead at the hands of the Old Demon.

Mazael was Demonsouled, the Old Demon's son, and the blood of the Great Demon flowed through his veins.

To continue reading SOUL OF TYRANTS, visit this link:
http://www.jonathanmoeller.com/souloftyrants.html

ABOUT THE AUTHOR

Standing over six feet tall, Jonathan Moeller has the piercing blue eyes of a Conan of Cimmeria, the bronze-colored hair a Visigothic warrior-king, and the stern visage of a captain of men, none of which are useful in his career as a computer repairman, alas. He has written the DEMONSOULED series of sword-and-sorcery novels, the TOWER OF ENDLESS WORLDS urban fantasy series, THE GHOSTS series about assassin and spy Caina Amalas, the COMPUTER BEGINNER'S GUIDE sequence of computer books, and numerous other works.
Visit his website at:
http://www.jonathanmoeller.com